From *Angels Watching Over Me*

Leah had been raised to be on her own. Her mother's many marriages, their frequent moves and different schools had taught her to be independent. But she saw quite clearly that for the Amish, individuality was not a virtue. It was a curse. She stood. "Well, it looks like we've come full circle, Ethan. You were right after all—the English and the Amish can't mingle."

He stood too. "But we can care about one another," he said carefully. "We can always care."

From *Lifted Up by Angels*

"I guess I have a lot to learn about you Amish," Leah said, taking a cup of punch from Ethan.

"Things are not always what they seem, Leah. Everyone here is free to try the things of the world. But we are still accountable to our families and traditions."

"So I'm learning." She wondered what was going on inside Ethan, where he fit in this strange no-man's-land of Amish tradition and English worldliness. She felt a kinship with him. They were both searching for a place where they belonged.

From *Until Angels Close My Eyes*

The revelations about her father, mother and grandmother haunted her. How could she have never known the truth? Why hadn't anyone told her until now?

"You should have been the one to tell me," Leah said to her mother, knowing she sounded hurt. "Why am I always the last to know about everything in this family?"

"It isn't a conspiracy, Leah. I was going to tell you about your father. I just never knew how."

Lurlene McDaniel

The Angels Trilogy

BANTAM BOOKS

NEW YORK • TORONTO • LONDON • SYDNEY • AUCKLAND

RL 4.7, AGES 012 AND UP

THE ANGELS TRILOGY

A Bantam Book / October 2002

This edition contains the complete and unabridged texts of the original editions. They have been completely reset for this volume. This omnibus was originally published in separate volumes under the titles:

Angels Watching Over Me copyright © 1996 by Lurlene McDaniel
Lifted Up by Angels copyright © 1997 by Lurlene McDaniel
Until Angels Close My Eyes copyright © 1998 by Lurlene McDaniel
This 2002 edition published by Bantam Books
Cover art copyright © 2002 by Kamil Vojnar

ISBN 0-553-57098-6

Visit us on the Web! www.randomhouse.com/teens
Educators and librarians, for a variety of teaching tools, visit us at
www.randomhouse.com/teachers

Published simultaneously in the United States and Canada

Bantam Books is an imprint of Random House Children's Books, a division of Random House, Inc. BANTAM BOOKS and the rooster colophon are registered trademarks of Random House, Inc. Bantam Books, 1540 Broadway, New York, New York 10036.

PRINTED IN THE UNITED STATES OF AMERICA
OPM   10 9 8 7 6 5 4 3 2 1

CONTENTS

Angels Watching Over Me

This book is dedicated to the memory of
Emily Anne Thomas, a loyal reader
and a precious child of God.

Are not all angels ministering spirits
sent to serve those who will
inherit salvation?

(Hebrews 1:14, New International Version)

ONE

"Well, I can't believe a broken finger can land you in the hospital, Leah. Are you telling me everything? Are you sure those doctors know what they're doing? I expected Indiana to be a little more progressive. Even if we are living in the boondocks."

Leah Lewis-Hall gripped the phone receiver. Her mother sounded as if she were next door instead of halfway around the world in Japan on her honeymoon. Leah took a deep breath, not wanting to scream at her mother. But she didn't want to let her know how scared she was either. *I'm sixteen and perfectly capable of handling the unexpected on my own,* she told herself. After all, nothing about her and her mother's lives together had ever approached what was expected all these years.

Patiently Leah explained, "I saw the doctor Neil said to call in case of an emergency. He did some X rays and blood work and told me my finger was broken. Then he told me I should come to the hospital and be checked out more thoroughly. So I did."

"How did you break your finger?"

"I don't know. After I took you and Neil to the airport, it just started hurting. I didn't bang it or anything. But it hurt so bad I couldn't even sleep last night." She didn't add that sleeping alone in the old farmhouse Neil was renovating for the three of them to live in wasn't exactly restful. "Maybe the doctor thought I should be in the hospital because the two of you are so far away."

"I want to talk to a doctor. Is one around?"

"Not right now. Neil's doctor said to call him at his office and he'd discuss it with you." Leah hated acting as go-between. What other girl her age had to check herself into the hospital alone?

Neil Dutton got on the phone. "What's going on, sugar?"

Leah wanted to shout, *I'm not your sugar and you aren't my father!* Instead she explained the situation all over again.

Neil said, "Dr. Howser's a good man, and if he thinks you're better off in the hospital, then you are. Don't you worry, I'll call him and get the whole story and call you back later tonight. It's six A.M. here," he mused, "so that makes it—what? About four in the afternoon over there?"

"That's right." In Japan it was also a day later.

"I know we're a long way off, but if you want us to come home, we can be there in less than twenty-four hours."

Although being in the hospital frightened her, Leah certainly didn't want to interrupt her mother's new life. And she was positive that wasn't what her mother wanted either. Also, she vaguely remembered that Neil, a retired auto executive, had an important meeting scheduled with some Japanese businessmen on behalf of his former company. She said, "Please put my mother back on."

"Is that what you want us to do?" Roberta Dutton sounded cautious. "I mean, if you *want* us to come home—"

"No way," Leah interrupted quickly. "It's your honeymoon and I'm not a baby."

"Well, maybe we shouldn't act too hastily." Leah could almost hear the relief in her mother's voice. "I mean, wait until Neil talks to the doctor. Then we can decide what to do." She paused. "Japan's wonderful. I've already bought you some gorgeous things for Christmas, Leah. Why, I'll bet no girl in that new high school of yours will have anything as nice. I'm talking designer labels, no imitations." Her mother giggled. "Neil is positively pampering me."

Leah hated her mother's helpless-little-girl routine.

Leah knew firsthand just how strong and *un*helpless her mother could be when it suited her.

"I'm sure I'll like whatever you've picked out," Leah said dutifully. It was Thursday, and Christmas was only nine days away. Since she was in the hospital, Leah was missing a few days of school, but so what? She really didn't have any friends at the high school yet. Maybe she *was* better off in the hospital.

Rural Indiana was a far cry from Dallas. Leah hated the cold weather, the dreary gray skies, the farm-country high school, the whole bucolic scene. She missed her friends and the sophistication of Dallas. So far, everybody she'd met seemed hopelessly hick and uncool. At least the hospital was in Indianapolis, a decent-sized city. Maybe she could persuade her mother to send her to a city high school starting in January. She could commute to the farm on weekends.

"So," her mother said, "it's settled. We'll talk to the doctor and call you later."

"Sure," Leah said listlessly. "No use rushing back until we know something more."

"That's my girl," Roberta said with a soothing lilt. "You were always so mature for your age, Leah. I know you can handle a few days in the hospital without me. While you're there, you get anything you want. Neil said he'd pay for it. Besides, I'm convinced that the doctor is overreacting. You're going to be perfectly fine, dear. Perfectly fine."

Leah hung up and scrunched down under the covers, hot tears brimming in her eyes.

A woman knocked on the door, and Leah quickly swiped her hand across her eyes. "Come in."

"Hi, I'm Molly Thasher, your day nurse. Just call me Molly. I'm here to take temp and blood pressure. It's routine."

Molly's smile was so genuinely pleasant that Leah felt her spirits lift. "You don't look like a nurse," she told the thirty-something woman, whose long light-brown hair was clipped back by a gold barrette. She wore taupe slacks and a cranberry-colored long-sleeved shirt. A colorful Christmas pin on her shoulder twinkled with tiny lights.

"We try to dress real casual on the pedi floor. It's less scary for the younger kids."

"The pedi floor?"

"Pediatrics. You're in the adolescent area, but we're so crowded right now we may have to stack new patients in the hallway. I can't remember the pedi floor ever being this full." She slipped the blood pressure cuff around Leah's arm.

"Will I get a roommate?"

"You might. Each room can accommodate two

patients, but it is possible to get a private room. Would you mind sharing?"

Leah thought about it and decided it didn't matter. Maybe she'd feel less isolated if she had a roommate. "Only if he's really cute," she told Molly.

The nurse laughed. " 'Fraid not. Your roomie would definitely be female." Molly picked up Leah's left hand. Leah's forefinger had been strapped to a curved metal splint with gauze and tape.

Leah was embarrassed because her injury looked so insignificant. "My doctor isn't sure what's wrong with me."

Molly grinned. "Well, at least you're mobile. You should explore the place. We've got a nice game and rec room. Plenty of free snacks too, so long as you're not on a restricted diet. In fact, we're putting up a Christmas tree Saturday night; why don't you come help decorate it?"

Leah couldn't think of anything she'd like to do less. "I'll think about it," she said.

"So where are you from?" Molly pumped up the blood pressure cuff, and Leah felt it tighten around her arm.

Leah started to say "Dallas," but realized that Texas wasn't home anymore. "From Knightstown. My mother just remarried and the guy, Neil, bought this big farm and is fixing it up for us."

"Sounds exciting. That's pretty farm country."

It isn't to me, Leah thought, but she didn't say it. "Neil's always wanted to be a farmer. His first wife died a couple of years ago. He met Mom in Dallas three months ago and they just got married and went to Japan for their honeymoon." She wasn't sure why she was babbling on and on to Molly about things the woman probably couldn't care less about.

"My father was a career navy man, and he was once stationed in Japan," Molly said. "The country sounded so exotic to me, so romantic. Boy, did I ever want to go over and visit him."

"Didn't you get to?"

"No, he was back home in a year and then he got out of the service. He and my mother are retired now, and they have a condo here in Indy."

Leah had never known her father and never would. He'd left her and her mother when Leah was barely three, and he'd died when Leah was ten. In fact, aside from her mother, Leah didn't have any family. The only grandparent she'd ever known had been her father's mother, Grandma Hall, who had died from liver cancer when Leah was ten. And since Grandma Hall and Leah's mother didn't get along, it had been difficult for Leah to be a part of her grandmother's life.

Molly folded the blood pressure cuff. "I've lived all my life in Indiana, but I've always wanted to travel the world."

"Why don't you?" Leah couldn't imagine being stuck in one place all her life. Maybe because she and her mother had always moved around so much.

"Oh, I'm married, I have two kids, and we're settled. Maybe my husband and I will travel when we both retire."

It all sounded deathly boring to Leah. Molly started to leave. "Will you be back?" Leah asked, not wanting to be left alone.

"My shift ends soon, but the night shift is a great bunch of nurses. You'll like them." Molly paused at the doorway. "I'll see you tomorrow."

Leah offered a smile, but when she was alone she lay in the bed feeling sorry for herself. Sick of moping around, she decided to do some exploring. She climbed out of bed and felt her leg buckle as pain shot through her kneecap.

TWO

Leah grimaced and leaned against the bed, waiting for the throbbing to subside. *Now what's wrong?* The pain had an eerily familiar quality. Was her knee broken too? She took a deep breath and counted to ten. Gingerly she put weight on her leg, and thankfully her knee didn't give. She rubbed it. The knee was sore, but the sharp pain had gone away.

"Probably twisted it getting out of bed," she mumbled. She found her robe and went out into the hall.

The ward was a cheerful-looking place, with a spotless expanse of patterned linoleum that looked as if it belonged in a kitchen, not a hospital. The doors of the rooms were different bright colors, with animals painted across them and along the walls. A small sign on the wall marked one of the doorways as Toddler Ward #1.

Farther down the hall, another door was painted to look like the open mouth of a rabbit. Its sign read Baby Ward.

Leah soon discovered that the entire floor was constructed like a giant wheel, with spokelike halls leading to patient wards and rooms. At the hub of the wheel stood the nurses' station, a large circular desk where the nurses congregated, keeping track of charts and monitoring individual patients with computer screens and banks of machines. The younger and sicker patients were closest to the hub.

The long corridor walls were painted with scenes from fairy tales. There were two waiting rooms on the floor for parents and relatives. And in a spacious rec room Leah discovered a gathering of younger kids watching a *Snow White* video on a giant-screen TV. The rec room also had neon-colored plastic climbing toys, and the carpet was patterned with games such as hopscotch and tic-tac-toe.

Leah tried the three doors at the end of the room and discovered video games, a snack bar and kitchen, and a library. The snack bar's counter held bowls of fresh fruit, graham crackers and granola bars, and containers of fruit juices in bowls of ice. Vending machines lined one wall, and several tables stood in the center of the room. A young mother, patiently feeding a gaunt little boy, nodded at Leah. The boy had no hair and was attached to an IV line that led to a pole beside the table.

Leah shuddered. The little boy reminded her of Grandma Hall. Leah could remember visiting her sick grandmother in the hospital as though it were yesterday. Just like the little boy, her grandmother had been attached to an IV line and had been bald from chemotherapy treatments. At the time, her grandmother's wasted body had terrified Leah, who loved her grandmother dearly in spite of her mother's hostility.

Leah grabbed an apple from a bowl and retreated to the library, where she sorted through teen magazines in an attempt to forget the painful memories. She flopped onto a comfortable love seat and began to read. The magazines were filled with ideas for Christmas gifts and holiday fashions and only gave her pangs of homesickness.

All her friends, she was sure, would be going to holiday parties and on shopping expeditions and skating at the ice rink at Dallas's Galleria Mall. She was stuck in a hospital while her mother was thousands of miles away. *No use feeling sorry for yourself,* Leah insisted silently. A glance at the clock showed that it was six.

Hoping she hadn't missed the dinner cart, Leah returned to her room but stopped just outside the doorway. Another bed had been placed in the room, and on it sat a girl who looked about five years old. The girl was sobbing and clinging to a woman dressed in a peculiarly old-fashioned style of clothing. Her dark blue skirt brushed the floor. The sleeves of her blouse were long, the neck high. A filmy white cap covered the woman's long hair, which was twisted into a bun at the nape of her neck. She wore no makeup and no jewelry, and she had no wedding band.

"There, there," the woman cooed soothingly. "Do not cry so, Rebekah. You're hurting my heart with such a flood of tears. You know I must go home to nurse the baby. But Charity and Ethan will come tomorrow."

"Don't go, Mama," the girl sobbed.

Feeling like an intruder, Leah wasn't sure what to do. Just then a man stepped from behind the open closet door. He too was dressed in a strangely old-fashioned way. His suit was dark, without lapels or buttons, and he held a broad-brimmed black hat in his big, rough hands. He had a beard but no mustache, and his long hair brushed the top of his collar. "Come, Tillie, the van's waiting downstairs. We've a long way to go tonight and it's beginning to snow."

"Papa," the child wailed, reaching for him. "Don't leave me, Papa." He hugged her tightly.

For the first time, the woman noticed Leah. "We did not mean to disturb you. Rebekah's scared, but she'll quiet down after we've gone."

Leah stammered, "I-It's okay. I don't mind. You're not bothering me one bit." Fascinated, she stared at the threesome. She stepped forward and held out her hand to the girl. "I'm Leah. We're going to be roommates."

The small girl's body quivered as she struggled to stop crying. "Leah?" she repeated, staring at Leah's flowered robe and dark, shoulder-length hair. "Are you a plain person?"

The question thoroughly confused Leah. "Plain enough."

"We're Jacob and Tillie Longacre," the girl's mother explained. "We're Amish."

Visions of photos Leah had seen of horse-drawn buggies and farms in Pennsylvania flashed in her head. She knew absolutely nothing about the Amish. She managed a cautious smile. "I—um—I'm just a regular person."

"We hate to leave our Rebekah, but we can't stay this night with her. Her sister Charity and her brother Ethan will come tomorrow, but until then she must be alone," Jacob explained.

"She's so young," Rebekah's mother said, wringing her hands.

"I'm not going anywhere," Leah said, feeling a surge of sympathy for little Rebekah. She knew what it felt like to be deserted. "Can we be friends?"

The girl was quiet. She bit her lower lip, picked up a rag doll and hugged it tightly against her chest. "Will you stay in the room with me?"

"That's my bed right there," Leah said, pointing across the room.

After a few more hugs and whispers, Rebekah's

parents edged toward the door. At the doorway Tillie turned to Rebekah and said, "Remember what I've told you. The Lord's angel will watch over you until we can be with you." She smiled at Leah and said, "Thank you." And then they were gone.

For a moment Rebekah stared with wide blue eyes at the empty doorway. Slowly tears began to slide down her cheeks. Flustered, Leah reached out and awkwardly patted the tiny girl. "Would you like to watch TV?"

Rebekah shook her head.

"That's a pretty doll. What's her name?"

"Rose," Rebekah said, sniffing.

The doll was as unadorned as the child who clutched her. Rebekah wore a simple long nightdress with a high neck, and a cap like her mother's over a head of wispy golden curls. Her cheeks looked rosy, her blue eyes red and swollen from crying. Leah felt at a loss. She didn't have any siblings.

Rebekah looked up at her. "Are you an angel?"

"No way," Leah said with a smile. She sat on the edge of Rebekah's bed. "Do you know why you're in the hospital?"

Rebekah held out her arm. A bright red splotch stained the inside of her wrist and lower arm. It looked swollen. "A spider bit me. And I got sick."

Sitting close to the child, Leah could feel heat emanating from her small body, and she realized that Rebekah's cheeks were rosy because of a fever. "Did you bite him back?" she asked.

Rebekah looked startled, then giggled. "No."

Making Rebekah laugh made Leah feel better than she had all day.

Two nurses bustled into the room, and Rebekah shrank back. "We have to put in an IV," one of the nurses explained.

Terrified, Rebekah shook her head.

"I'll stay with you," Leah said quickly.

One of the nurses eyed her. "Are you her sister?"

"Her roommate."

Rebekah clutched at Leah's hand. "Don't leave, Leah."

The single plea cut like a knife through Leah's heart, and she knew there was no way she could leave Rebekah.

Leah moved closer to Rebekah and reached for her small hand. "Look at me, not them," she instructed.

Obediently Rebekah fixed her gaze on Leah. "This is nothing," Leah said, hoping she sounded more convincing than she felt. "A piece of cake."

"Cake? Can I have some cake?"

Leah remembered the snack bar. "If it's all right with the nurse, I'll get you a cookie or something as soon as they're finished."

The nurse flipped open Rebekah's chart. "No food restrictions. The dinner cart's on its way, but a cookie would be fine."

"Lie still, honey," the technician said. "This will just be a little prick."

Leah smiled reassuringly at Rebekah, who lay rigid on the bed. From the corner of her eye, Leah watched the lab technician gently slide the needle of the IV under the skin on the back of Rebekah's hand. The child trembled, but she didn't move. Leah felt queasy. She watched as a tear slid from the corner of Rebekah's eye. "You're doing great," Leah said, still clasping Rebekah's hand.

Soon the IV was in and running, the tubing taped to Rebekah's arm and safety-pinned to the bedsheet. "This medicine will make you feel better," the nurse said, patting her patient.

When they were gone Leah stood and said, "I'll get you that cookie now."

Rebekah clutched at her. "Don't go, Leah. Please don't leave me."

Leah started to explain that she'd be right back, but the look of terror in Rebekah's eyes stopped her. "I won't leave," she said softly. "I won't leave you alone tonight for a single minute."

THREE

As she tried to fall asleep that night, Leah's mind flashed to a memory of when she was six years old. She and her mother had been living in a trailer, and Don, her mother's second husband, had been gone for more than a month. Her mother had tucked bedcovers around Leah. "Don't leave, Mama," Leah had pleaded.

"I have to go to work, Leah. But all the doors will be locked and I'll be back before you get up in the morning for school."

"Don't go," Leah wailed.

"Hush! Stop that. I don't want to go, but I have to if we want to eat next week. Close your eyes and go to sleep."

Leah had lain stiff and unmoving in the dark, listening to her mother's car driving away into the night. Dogs howled. Trees rustled in the wind. Terror made her heart pound until she thought it might pop out of her chest. She was alone. Totally alone . . .

"Leah?"

The sound of Rebekah's voice snapped Leah back to the present. "What?" she asked softly.

"Will you read me a story?"

"Um . . . I don't have a book." She remembered the library, but she doubted Rebekah would let her leave the room long enough to go there.

"I have my book." Rebekah pointed to the shelf in the bedside table.

Leah turned on the bedside light and retrieved a Bible storybook. "So, which story do you want to hear?"

"Read about Mary and the angel."

Leah rarely attended church and wasn't very familiar with the Bible, but she flipped open the well-worn book and scanned the table of contents. She found the story and read about how an angel of the Lord came to a young virgin to announce that she would bear God's Son. To Leah it had always sounded sort of farfetched. She knew virgins didn't get pregnant and remain virgins. Still, the story must have soothed Rebekah, because soon the little girl was asleep.

Leah stole back to her own bed and crawled between the sheets. Her knee again felt sore, and a nagging ache in her lower back made her toss restlessly. But she must have slept because she was startled awake when someone slid a blood pressure cuff around her arm.

"I'll be gone in a minute," the night nurse whispered.

"I only have a broken finger," Leah grumbled, irritated that she was being awakened to have her arm squeezed and a thermometer thrust in her mouth. Didn't these people have anything better to do than pester patients at night?

The night nurse performed the routine procedures on Rebekah too. Once the nurse had left the room, Leah heard Rebekah whimper. She called out, "Hey, it's okay. I'm right over here. Can you see me?"

"I'm scared, Leah."

Leah thought about getting up and going over to the child, but her back was sore and a draining fatigue was sapping her strength. "Do you want me to tell you a story?"

"Can you tell me about Abraham and Isaac?"

"Um . . . I'm afraid I don't know that one. How about *Snow White*?" she offered, reminding herself to leave out the scary parts about the witch.

"Who?" Rebekah asked.

Her question surprised Leah. She thought every little girl had seen the Disney version of the fairy tale. "How about *Cinderella* or *Sleeping Beauty*?"

"Who are they?"

Now Leah was at a loss. How could Rebekah not have heard these famous stories? "Never mind. How about I tell you all about where I used to live in Texas?"

"Is that far away?"

"Sure is." Leah started her story, describing the cowboys and Indians of legends—and wished she'd paid more attention in history class. In no time Rebekah drifted off to sleep.

Leah slept too, but she woke up when she heard someone come into the room. *Not another checkup,* she thought, moaning to herself. How did they expect a person to get well when the nurses kept waking her all night long? But the nurse didn't come to her bed. She went to Rebekah's. Through sleepy eyes Leah watched the woman smooth the sheets and tuck in the blankets around the sleeping child.

Her movements were whisper-soft, and she seemed so caring, so gentle, that a peaceful feeling washed over Leah. She was suddenly glad she wasn't alone in the farmhouse. At least in the hospital she could be near other people.

The nurse stood silently beside Rebekah's bed, and Leah drifted off to sleep.

She was awakened the next morning not by nurses but by doctors making rounds. Dr. Howser said, "Good morning, Leah. How are you feeling today?"

"Tired. Nurses kept coming in and out all night long."

He smiled. "Taking vital signs is hospital routine, I'm afraid. I want you to meet a colleague of mine."

He stepped aside, and another doctor peered down at her. "I'm Dr. Thomas, an orthopedist," the man said. "I'm a bone specialist and I've been called in to consult on your case."

"What's wrong with me?" she asked the tall, slim doctor.

He smiled reassuringly. "That's what we're going to find out. I've got a telephone conference scheduled with your parents this afternoon—"

"Neil's not my father," Leah interrupted.

"Sorry," Dr. Thomas said. "Anyway, Dr. Howser got your mother's approval to run some tests on you."

"What kinds of tests?" Leah was starting to feel uneasy.

"Blood work, of course. But also a CT bone scan."

"What's that? Will it hurt?"

"It's a kind of X ray that gives us a three-dimensional look at the inside of your body, and no, it doesn't hurt."

"Why would you want to see my bones?"

"To see what you're made of," he said with a twinkle in his eye.

"Sugar and spice and everything nice," she shot back, making him laugh. She quickly added, "Dr.

Howser took an X ray of my finger yesterday. He said it was broken. What else is there to see?"

"The X ray showed that there was a small hole in the bone. The hole weakened the finger and caused it to break. I want more X rays to confirm that finding. And I want to evaluate the condition of other bones in your body."

Neither doctor looked much concerned, which made Leah feel calmer. "So does this mean I'll be stuck in the hospital?"

"At least for a few days," Dr. Thomas said. "You've been staying by yourself at home, haven't you?"

She'd been staying by herself off and on since she was six, but she rarely told anyone that. People might get the impression that her mother was neglectful. She wasn't. But she *was* busy with her own life. "I can take care of myself," Leah told the doctors. "Mom's on her honeymoon, but she'll be back before Christmas."

"And we can reach her by phone," Dr. Howser assured his colleague.

Dr. Thomas flipped open Leah's chart. "You told Dr. Howser you've been tired lately."

"Sort of. But I've been busy too. I mean, this fall we moved up here, Mom got married, and I started a new school."

"Any other aches and pains?" He wrote as he talked.

"My knee's sore. And my back too."

"Where?"

She placed a hand against the small of her back. "Right here. Down deep. I think maybe I twisted it or something."

Dr. Thomas examined her, kneading her spine and manipulating her knee. She squirmed because the areas were sore and felt bruised. Finally he said, "Someone will come up later and take you down to X ray. And we'll see you again on rounds tomorrow morning."

When they were gone Leah looked over at Rebekah, who was staring at her. "Did they wake you up with all their talking?"

"I want my mama."

Leah wanted hers too, in a way. She smiled and said, "I'm sure she'll be back today for a visit."

Rebekah's lower lip began to tremble. Leah struggled out of bed and padded across the floor to Rebekah's bedside. The child's face still looked feverish, and her arm looked redder and more swollen. The IV bag was nearly empty. Leah wondered when Rebekah's doctor would be in to see her. "How about breakfast?" she asked, hoping to distract her. "I think I hear the cart coming down the hall."

Leah stopped talking because Rebekah didn't look interested. Her small shoulders began to shake, and sobs escaped from her mouth. Instinctively Leah put her arms around the girl. "Oh, Rebekah, don't cry," she begged, feeling helpless.

She saw the nurse call button and reached for it. But suddenly a male hand clamped over hers and a strong, firm voice boomed, "What are you doing to our sister?"

FOUR

Leah spun, only to stare up into the face of a tall blond-haired boy with intense sky-blue eyes.

"Ethan!" Rebekah cried. He scooped her up, and Leah stepped aside and bumped into a girl. She appeared to be Leah's age and was dressed in a simple long-sleeved brown dress. She wore a gauzy head covering identical to the one Rebekah's mother had been wearing.

The girl smiled and held out her hand. "I'm Charity Longacre, Rebekah's sister. You must be Leah. My parents spoke of you."

Thoroughly flustered, Leah eased backward toward her side of the room. She hadn't expected anyone from Rebekah's family to show up so early. Nor had she expected to face such a good-looking guy while she wore a shapeless hospital gown. She hadn't brushed her teeth either, or combed her hair or put on a smidgen of makeup. "It's so early," she mumbled.

"We left Nappanee, where we live, at five this morning. It's a hundred and fifty miles, and we didn't know what time breakfast would be served here in the hospital. We didn't want Rebekah to have to eat alone." Charity pulled off a cape and smoothed the long, full skirt of her dress. Her brown hair was parted in the middle and twisted into a bun. She wore no makeup, not even lipstick, but her green eyes were fringed with incredibly thick lashes, and her cheeks looked rosy from the cold outside.

Leah slid between the bedcovers and tugged them up to her chin, trying not to look as ill at ease as she felt. "Breakfast is on its way," she said.

Ethan turned, then averted his gaze from Leah in the bed. She saw color rush into his face and realized he was embarrassed by her presence. "I—I'm sorry if I spoke harshly to you," he said.

Harshly? Leah thought. *What a weird word for a teenage guy to use.* "No problem. Rebekah was crying, and I was just trying to calm her down."

"Where's Mama?" Rebekah asked.

"She'll be here later," Charity said. "After breakfast and morning chores. And she'll be bringing the baby so she won't have to rush home to nurse him."

"Who's feeding my chickens?" Rebekah asked.

"Simeon," Ethan said with an impish smile. "And not very gracefully either."

Rebekah giggled. Charity smiled at Leah and explained. "Simeon's seven and Rebekah took over hen duty from him last fall. He doesn't like taking up work in the henhouse again one bit."

"You have chickens?" Leah asked. Neil's farm had no animals, but what if he wanted them someday? Would she have to feed chickens and pigs? She didn't like the idea.

"We have many animals," Charity said. "Ours is a working farm, where our whole family lives."

"How many of you are there?"

"Mama and Papa, seven of us, and Opa and Oma, our grandparents, too."

"You *all* live in the same house? And you're telling me Rebekah has *six* brothers and sisters?"

"There are three boys and four girls in our family," Charity said with pride. "Sarah's the oldest at nineteen. Ethan, seventeen"—she nodded toward her brother, who was sorting through a duffel bag with Rebekah—"me, I'm sixteen; our sister Elizabeth, she's twelve; Simeon; Rebekah; and Nathan, the baby, who's two months."

Leah had many friends in Dallas, but none had such a large family. While she sometimes wished she had a sister, she'd never wanted a whole bunch of sisters and brothers. In fact, when the kids she knew discussed large families, it was always with an air of disdain, as if too many siblings were an embarrassment. But Charity acted as if her large family were something to be proud of. "Sounds . . . large," Leah finally commented.

Charity laughed. "If the Lord wills it, most of the Amish have large families. Our house has been in our family for over seventy years, and one day it will go to Ethan because he's the oldest son. Right now we're getting ready for Christmas Day. Mama and Oma have been baking for weeks. And Papa and Opa are in the workshop late at night. I can't wait—"

"Charity!" Ethan barked. "We came to be with Rebekah, not bend the ears of her roommate."

Charity's face flushed beet red, and she dropped her gaze. "He's right. I'm sorry."

"She can talk the ears off of field corn," he said apologetically.

"I don't mind," Leah said. She thought the three of them were different and interesting. And she was lonely and wanted someone to talk to.

Just then an orderly entered, balancing breakfast trays. "Good morning." She set the trays down on utility tables in front of Leah and Rebekah.

Leah raised the cover on her plate and grimaced.

"What's wrong?" Charity asked.

"Eggs. *Ugh.* I hate eggs."

Charity studied her quizzically. "But you must eat breakfast?"

"I usually skip breakfast. Or I eat a muffin or fruit on my way to school."

"On the farm, I help Mama cook meals every day," Charity said. "We always have platters of bacon and eggs, hot biscuits, butter and honey before the men begin work in the fields."

"Well, sure," Leah said quickly. "I guess if you were going to plow the north forty you could eat that way. But most of us do other things all day. You know, like sit in school and listen to boring teachers."

"You don't like school?" Charity asked.

"It's so-so. Do you like it?"

"I no longer go to school. I completed my learning and now I help with the farm."

"You're finished with school?" Charity had sounded pleased with her achievement, but Leah was shocked. "How *can* you be?"

"Our bishop sees no purpose in school beyond eighth grade. Wisdom and understanding are much more important than knowledge and facts."

"Your *bishop* decides when you quit school?"

"I know all the important things," Charity countered. "I can calculate. I can read. I speak English and German. I have memorized many pages of Scripture. I know all that is necessary to be a wife and mother."

"A *what*?" Leah was stunned. "Don't you want to go to college?"

Ethan moved to stand beside his sister. "You cannot go babbling to outsiders, sister. The English do not understand our ways. You make us sound foolish."

Leah felt a flash of anger. "You don't have to bite her head off. I mean, we're just talking. And I'm trying to understand your ways. Which sound pretty primitive to me."

The two Amish teens stepped back, as if Leah's anger had stung them. They both looked confused, and Leah was embarrassed. But it was Rebekah's cry that diverted everyone's attention.

"Don't yell at each other," she pleaded.

Both sister and brother turned and tried to console her.

"Are you mad at Leah?" Rebekah asked. "She is my friend. Don't be mad at her."

Leah felt her anger dissipate. "No one's mad," she said. "I'm sorry, Rebekah. I didn't mean to yell."

"And we're sorry too," Ethan said. He cast a glance at Leah. "Forgive me for speaking unkindly to you."

Leah shrugged, not trusting her own emotions. Ethan might have been one of the best-looking boys she'd ever met, but he was also the most unusual. She didn't know how to react to him.

Molly, the nurse from yesterday, breezed into the room. "Time for meds." She introduced herself to Rebekah, Ethan and Charity, checked Rebekah's IV and hung a new bag of clear fluid on the IV stand, chattering as she worked.

When she got to Leah, she said, "I'm supposed to take you down to X ray." She returned with a wheelchair, and when Leah protested, saying that she could walk, Molly shook her head. "No way. Every patient rides."

Leah was glad to get out of the room for a while and escape the tension her words with Ethan had caused. "Do you know anything about the Amish?" she asked Molly.

"A little. There's a large community of them up in Nappanee, along with a tourist attraction called Amish Acres. The Acres lets you take a peek at Amish life as it was a hundred years ago—which, incidentally, is about the same as it is today. These people live very simply. And they're not only exceptional farmers, they're also outstanding craftsmen, especially in carpentry work."

"Well, I think they're weird," Leah declared. "And I do mean *weird*."

"Not weird . . . just different. They call themselves plain people because they don't believe in adornments of any kind. They separate themselves from the rest of us, whom they call English—the out-worlders."

Leah recalled Ethan calling her "English" and "an outsider" back in the room. "They're plain, all right. Did you know that Charity doesn't even go to school because some bishop thinks she should just get married and have babies? Is that backward or what? I'll bet they treat women like slaves."

"You're wrong. The Old Order Amish have built their lifestyle on the values of love, forgiveness and peace. They're such pacifists that Congress has exempted Amish men from military service. Mostly they just want to be left alone."

Leah shook her head. "Doesn't sound like much fun to me. What's wrong with civilization?"

"Plenty, to their way of thinking. They believe the outside world will contaminate their culture and change them and their ways. They avoid such contamination at all costs."

"But if that's so, then everything in this place is a contaminant." It unsettled Leah to think of herself that way.

Molly stopped the wheelchair in front of a door marked "Radiation Lab." "Well, fortunately they aren't against modern medicine. Good thing too. Rebekah is one very sick little girl."

FIVE

Molly's statement sobered Leah. "She is? All she told me was that a spider bit her."

"Yes, a brown recluse spider. That can be bad enough, but now a strep or staph infection has set in and is moving up her arm from the site of the bite. Her doctor's got her on a powerful IV antibiotic. That's why she's in the hospital."

Leah was worried about Rebekah. And she felt protective of the child, although there was no need for that with Ethan around.

A technician stepped up to Leah. "You ready?"

She started, having forgotten for a moment why she was there. "I'm ready," she said.

"I'll come back for you," said Molly as she left the room.

The technician wheeled Leah into a small lab. "First

thing we do is inject a little radioactive fluid into you," he said. "Your bones absorb it and then show up nice and clear on the film."

After the injection Leah had to kill time in a tiny waiting room that had been decorated for Christmas. Candy canes and glass balls were strung on a tinsel garland hanging along one wall, and a tiny artificial tree with blinking lights sat on a TV set. A lopsided angel perched atop the tree. One of her wings was bent. Leah felt a wave of self-pity sweep through her. She'd just as soon skip Christmas this year. The holiday was all tinsel and glitz and had no meaning.

The technician returned and led her into a room with a table and an enormous machine with a flat, glasslike plate. "This is the camera," he explained. "You climb up on the table, lie flat and be still. The camera will move along your body and photograph your skeleton one part at a time. This will give your doctor a look at your entire bone structure."

"What's my doctor looking for, anyway?"

The technician shrugged. "You'll have to ask him. All I do is take the pictures." He settled her on the table and left the room. Soon his voice came through a speaker. "All ready?"

"Let's do it."

The huge camera moved with a mechanical clunking

down her body. After a short time the technician announced, "All done."

Leah returned to the wheelchair and waited for Molly. It seemed as if she sat there forever. Just when she'd decided to wheel herself back up to her floor, Molly hurried into the room, visibly upset. "Leah, I'm so sorry! I didn't mean to leave you stranded down here, but we've had a minor disaster on the floor."

"What kind? Flood? Tornado? Fire? Is everyone okay?"

"Nothing like that. Someone stole the Christmas tree for the pedi floor."

"Stole it?"

"It's a big artificial tree, a really good one. We take it down every year and put it in the same storage room. But this year when we went to haul it out, it was missing."

"Sort of like the Grinch stealing Christmas."

"Worse. If I ever find out who did it . . ."

"So what're you going to do about a tree?"

"Well, we're taking up a collection to buy a new one so we won't have to postpone tomorrow night's decorating party."

"I could put in a few dollars," Leah said, thinking of Rebekah. She wondered if Amish children had ever heard of Santa Claus.

Molly patted her shoulder. "Patients shouldn't have to help bankroll a Christmas tree. But thanks for the offer."

When Leah returned to her room, Charity was sitting in a chair beside Rebekah's bed, knitting. Ethan wasn't there. Rebekah was sleeping, so Charity pulled the curtain that separated Rebekah's and Leah's beds and took a chair over to Leah's side of the room. "Would you like to sit and talk?" she asked.

"Where's the watchdog?" Leah asked.

Charity giggled. "You mean Ethan? He's exploring. Neither of us has ever been to a hospital before."

"Hospitals are pretty boring. Especially when you feel fine." Leah filled Charity in about what was going on with her medically. "Basically, they aren't telling me anything."

"They will tell your parents, won't they?"

"My mother," Leah corrected. "Neil's not my father."

"Doesn't your real father know you're in the hospital?"

"No. He died when I was ten."

Charity looked startled. "Oh—I'm so sorry, Leah. You've never even known your own father?"

Her words stung, but Leah quickly realized that Charity was only curious. From the viewpoint of Charity's supertight family, a family with no father might seem as strange as a two-headed dog. "He took off when I was three. My name, Lewis-Hall, is the last name of both my parents put together."

"My mother took my father's name," Charity said. "I thought every woman took her husband's name."

"Lots of people hyphenate last names. And some women don't change their names at all. If I took a new last name every time my mother remarried, my name would be a foot long."

"How many times has she married?"

"Neil is number five." Charity looked so shocked, Leah felt compelled to explain. "But she's done better every time. You know, some women work for a living, some marry." All at once she felt foolish under Charity's incredulous stare. "Well, don't Amish women ever remarry?" she asked.

"Only if they are widowed."

"You don't believe in divorce?"

"Under some circumstances it is allowed, but marriage is a holy union. It is a covenant, like the one God made with his people. It should not be broken."

Leah rolled her eyes indulgently. "Not anymore. Don't you know what's going on in today's world?"

"No. And I'm not sure I want to know."

Charity's naïveté was beginning to get on Leah's nerves. "Well, here's a news flash: People don't stay in bad marriages anymore."

"People think we are strange because we choose to be the way we are," Charity said softly. "But what's normal about taking many spouses and not having a family home?"

Leah stiffened. "Different strokes for different folks."

Charity studied her with her clear green eyes until Leah began to feel squirmy. She decided to change the subject. "Um—so, how's Rebekah?"

Charity's brow puckered. "Not so good."

Leah sat up straighter. "She's not improving?"

"It's slow. But many people are praying for her—" She stopped abruptly.

"It's all right. You don't have to watch every word you say around me. I had friends back in Dallas who prayed."

"But you don't?"

"I just never got into religion." Now Leah felt self-conscious about her lack of sophistication in a world that Charity knew intimately. "Maybe we shouldn't talk about this stuff. I—I like you and I don't want to say anything more to hurt your feelings."

Charity's face broke into a generous smile. "I like you, too, Leah Lewis-Hall. I have never had an outsider friend."

An outsider. That's what Leah had been all her life. She and her mother had moved so often, she'd never felt as if she belonged anywhere. And despite the defiant confidence she showed Charity, she was embarrassed by her mother's five marriages. Why couldn't her mother just get it right so that they could live like regular people?

Leah asked, "So is your mother coming later today?"

"She can't. I haven't told Rebekah yet because it will

upset her. Baby Nathan is sick with a fever, and Mama must stay with him. Papa is coming tomorrow—Saturday. Until then Ethan and I will have to substitute for our parents."

"Maybe you could call your mother later tonight and let Rebekah talk to her."

"We have no phone."

"You're kidding!"

"None of the Amish where we live have phones."

"But how did your mother let you know about the baby?"

"She went into town and used the phone. We are not opposed to using phones, we just do not believe in owning them."

This made no sense to Leah. "But if you use phones, why not have one in your house?"

Charity smiled patiently and, leaning forward, said, "We have no electricity, no cars, no modern things. Life on our farms is as it was a hundred years ago. The Bible says that Christians should separate themselves from the world, that we should be "in the world, but not *of* the world.' We 'hold fast to that which is good.' For us, faith is lived out in our community. We marry our own kind, birth our own kind, bury our own kind.

"We believe that God created all things and that he sustains all creation. We believe that man is sinful and that only the blood of Jesus can redeem us from our sins.

We expect to die and go to heaven and glorify God forever. We are not like you, Leah. But also, we are not backward, or stupid, or foolish. We are Amish. And I am not ashamed."

Leah listened dumbstruck. Charity was so certain of what she believed that she could speak about it without stumbling over words. And without apology. Leah knew she should respond but she didn't know how. The sudden buzz of the phone rescued her. Quickly she rose to answer it before it could ring again and wake Rebekah.

"Hello?"

"Leah, darling! Neil spoke with your doctors just an hour ago. Can we talk?"

SIX

"I'm stuck in the hospital, remember?" Leah replied. "What else is there to do but talk?" She held her hand over the mouthpiece and told Charity, "It's my mother."

Charity waved and slipped behind Rebekah's curtain.

From faraway Japan, her mother's voice said, "Don't act sulky, Leah. You're being cared for."

But not by you, Leah thought. "So what did the doctor tell you?" she asked.

"Not a darn thing! Honestly, I hope they know what they're doing at that place. You'd think they could tell us something by now."

Leah was disappointed. "They still don't know what's wrong with me?"

"Evidently, according to Dr. Thomas," her mother said, then quoted, "you're 'manifesting symptoms that are consistent with any number of health problems.' As if that's supposed to pacify me. At any rate, they've scheduled more tests starting Monday morning, and once they can evaluate the results, they *might* be able to diagnose you. There's no excuse for dragging this thing out."

"I don't want to spend Christmas in the hospital."

"I'm sure you won't have to. But until I get some sort of definitive word from your doctor, I'm not cutting my honeymoon short. That seemed okay with you the last time we talked."

"Sure, it's fine." Leah forced herself not to sound disappointed.

"But don't you worry. We're flying into Indianapolis December twenty-third, just like we planned. We'll come straight to the hospital and spring you. Then it's home to the farm for Christmas Eve and Christmas Day. We'll put up a tree and put out all our presents. Why, I'm even planning to cook a turkey with all the trimmings."

"But what if they still don't know what's wrong with me?"

"Then we'll find another doctor after Christmas. But I'm sure that won't be necessary. Now, is there anything else we need to discuss?"

Leah could think of a hundred things. She wanted to say "I'm scared" but couldn't get the words out. She wanted to say "I love you."

"Um, Mom, I—"

"Whoops! Sorry, dear, I've got to run. Someone's at the door. I'll call you before Monday. *Ciao.*"

Leah held the receiver for a long time, listening to the dial tone that only moments before had been the voice of her mother. With tears welling in her eyes, she hung up.

She decided to take a belated morning shower and put on her makeup, hoping it would make her feel better. She was just adding the finishing touches—not easy with her broken finger—when Molly came in to take blood pressures and temps. By now Rebekah was awake, but she lay in the bed listlessly. She looked feverish. Charity tried to soothe her while Molly worked.

"Did you find the missing tree?" Leah asked, coming out of the bathroom as she spritzed on an expensive perfume.

"Still missing," Molly said.

Leah told Charity what had happened.

"Stealing is wrong," Charity said, sighing. "This outsider world of yours is not a very nice place, Leah."

Was she asking Leah to defend the world at large? "There are good people too," Leah said. "Aren't there, Molly?"

"A few saints. An angel or two."

"Where's the angel?" Rebekah asked.

"The angels are watching over you, little sister. You just can't see them," said Charity, smoothing Rebekah's damp forehead.

"Can you see any angels, Leah?" Rebekah asked.

"Not really." Believing in angels was a little like believing in fairies and elves, Leah thought. Interesting mythology, but not scientifically valid.

Molly said, "I think *you're* an angel, Rebekah. Now, why don't you close your eyes and let this good medicine do its work." She adjusted the drip on Rebekah's IV.

Rebekah sighed. Molly turned to Leah. "You look pretty. Got a date?"

Leah ran her fingers through her thick hair. "Actually, I think I missed my date with the lunch tray. I'm starved."

"My fault," Molly said. "I didn't get you back up here in time. But don't worry, there's plenty to eat in the rec room. Pizza, sandwiches, fresh fruit—go help yourself."

"Do you want me to bring you something?" Leah asked Charity.

"No, thank you. We ate already." Charity smiled at Leah.

The rec room was more crowded than before. The giant-screen TV was now showing *The Little Mermaid* for a group of engrossed kids, as toddlers climbed on the plastic play equipment. Some of the children were hooked to IV lines that hung from poles standing next to them. Some were bald from chemotherapy treatments.

Some had broken limbs in casts. A candy striper aide sat in a corner, overseeing the group and running interference when two toddlers had a confrontation.

Leah ventured into the kitchen and stopped short. Ethan stood in front of a vending machine, contemplating the selections.

"You have to put money in. You can't just wish the stuff out," Leah said, hoping to make him smile.

Startled, he jumped back. "You surprised me." His cheeks reddened, and he dropped his gaze. He didn't offer her the hoped-for smile.

"Sorry," she said irritably. Why did he always look away from her? Did his religion forbid him to look her in the eye? "Do you want me to help?" she asked.

"I—I have no money for the machine."

"I have quarters." She reached into the pocket of her robe. "Here. Let me treat you. What would you like?"

"I cannot take—"

"Of course you can," she interrupted. "Buying you a candy bar doesn't make us engaged, does it?" She popped in two quarters. "What's your favorite?"

"I don't know. I've never had one before."

"Are you joking?"

"Is this funny to you?"

"Only strange," she said, more hesitant now, her annoyance subsiding. "I'll pick for you." She punched a button, and a Milky Way bar dropped down the chute. She picked it up and handed it to him. "This is one of my favorites. Try it."

Hesitantly he took it from her, careful not to touch her hand. "Thank you."

She tried to make eye contact, but Ethan kept his gaze on the candy bar. Again her anger flared. She spun and stalked over to the counter and a platter holding a stack of wrapped sandwiches. She grabbed one, took a fruit drink, and dropped into a nearby chair, pointedly ignoring Ethan. The guy might be good-looking, but he was a jerk as far as she was concerned.

From the corner of her eye she saw that Ethan hadn't left the room. He just stood by the door, shifting from foot to foot. His shirt was white broadcloth. His pants were the same wide-legged style as his father's. He wore heavy, dark boots. There was nothing fashionable about him. He was nothing like any of the boys she'd known back in Dallas. She tried hard not to look at him. Still he didn't move.

She couldn't stand it anymore. "What!" she cried. "What do you want? Is the candy bar poison or something?"

He shook his head, his gaze riveted to the floor.

"Then what's wrong, Ethan? Is there something wrong with me? Is there a particular reason why you won't look at me or talk to me?"

"No." He came closer until he was standing over her, staring straight down into her eyes.

His gaze was so intense that Leah felt as if it might burn her. She swallowed hard. Her hands trembled, and her heart began to race. "What is it? Do you dislike me?" Her voice quivered with false bravado.

"Dislike you?" He looked as if she'd slapped him. "I do not dislike you, Leah Lewis-Hall. I think that you are the most beautiful girl I have ever set my eyes upon."

SEVEN

"You do?" Leah stared at him. "You actually think I'm pretty?"

"It is impossible for me not to think so. You *are* beautiful."

She felt herself blush. No guy had ever been so forthright with her. In her experience, most guys liked to play head games with girls. They liked to come on strong, then back away if a girl showed any interest. She grew wary. Maybe Ethan was the same way. "I'll bet you've told lots of girls they're pretty," she said tentatively.

He shook his head. "I have only taken Martha Dewberry home but once in my buggy."

"You've lost me, Ethan. What's a buggy ride got to do with feeding girls a line?" Leah pushed out a nearby chair with her foot, inviting Ethan to sit.

He sat. "What is this 'feeding a line'?"

"Giving somebody a compliment in order to get something you want from her." She wondered if she was going to have to explain every idiom in the English language to him.

"You mean *lie?*" He recoiled. "I do not lie, Leah. If I tell you you are beautiful, it is because it is so."

She couldn't help smiling. "Well, thank you for thinking so. I would have never guessed you felt that way. You acted as if you wanted to avoid me. That can hurt a person's feelings, you know."

"Have I hurt your feelings?"

"I'm getting over it."

A smile slowly inched across Ethan's face. "Good. I do not want to hurt your feelings."

She measured him quietly. Ethan's hands were large and raw; he must work hard. His face was lean, with the hint of a beard in places. His hair curled against his collar and flopped appealingly across his forehead. She wanted to touch it, but she didn't dare. She asked, "Are you going to tell me about Martha Dewberry and your buggy ride together?"

He regarded Leah seriously. "It is our custom that when a man is interested in a woman, he takes her home from church or community gatherings in a buggy. It is his way of telling others that he has special feelings for this person."

Despite herself, Leah felt a tiny flare of jealousy.

"Where I come from, if a guy likes a girl, he asks her out on a date and he picks her up in his car. Or his parents' car."

"We have no cars."

"That's what your sister told me. But you don't mind riding in them."

"Public transportation is fine for long trips, but for each one of us to own a car would be prideful. And it would break apart our community."

Every family Leah knew owned a car. Sometimes two or three cars. Neil had given her mother a car for a wedding gift, and Leah had used it to drive herself to the hospital. But she could see how vehicles separated people. She thought of people driving on the expressways, each locked alone inside a car, cut off from fellow travelers. "So, are you a good buggy driver?"

He grinned. "Passable."

"And do you like this Martha Dewberry? Is she your girlfriend?"

His brow puckered while his gaze lingered over Leah's face. "She is Amish."

And I'm not. She heard the unspoken message in his comment. Suddenly she wanted to turn the talk away from their differences. She liked Ethan. But nothing could ever come of their friendship; they were from two very different worlds. She moved forward. "I'll bet you've never played a video game, have you?"

He shook his head. "I have not ever seen one."

She grabbed his hand. "Come on. Let me show you how."

She led him into the semidarkened video game room. Several kids clustered around machines, but she saw a vacant one back in a corner and took Ethan toward it. "Sit," she directed. She positioned herself across the table from him. "I've played this one before back in Texas. It's got levels of difficulty, so we can start slow, until you get the hang of it." She paused, suddenly stricken by a thought. "It wouldn't be against your religion, would it?"

His features glowed by the pale purple light emanating from the game. "Play is not forbidden. We play many games. I can see no harm in trying this one."

It didn't take him long to catch on. Ethan's hand flew on the trackball, spinning and turning it. Leah threw up her hands in defeat as he soared over the million-point mark. "Are you sure you've never played a video game before? If I didn't know better, I'd bet you'd suckered me."

His face was lit with a heart-stopping grin of genuine pleasure. "What do you mean—'suckered'?"

"You know, *pretended* not to know how to play."

"I told you, Leah, I do not lie." His eyes twinkled. "It is an exciting game. I like it."

"You have to admit that modern conveniences aren't all bad."

He leveled his incredibly blue eyes on her. "They have their pleasures."

A tingling sensation prickled up her arms. "Too bad you need electricity to play it."

He laughed. "Electricity is not the only need. Time is necessary too. With so much to do on the farm, who would have time for video games?"

"It seems to me that work is all you have time for."

"Work is a good teacher. It gives us Amish a sense of meaning and purpose."

"Does it give *you* meaning?"

He pondered her question, and she hoped he could tell that she was genuinely interested in his perspective.

"Work helps me understand that my life is but one small part of God's greater order," he said. "The seasons come. They go. Harvest comes, and with it, God supplies our needs. But if we did nothing but *wish* for a good harvest, if we did no work to produce a good crop, then that would be foolish. And worse, it would presume on God's benevolence."

Presented that way, his point of view made perfect sense to Leah. "Don't you ever get curious about the rest of the world, though?"

She could tell she'd hit a nerve. For all of his confidence about his lifestyle, there was yearning too. And by the way he played the video game, she guessed, there was intense competitiveness. "I cannot tell you otherwise, Leah. Yes, I do wonder what certain things would be like among you English. Since I've been here in this hospital, I have seen many people who care and who help others. Like Amish ways.

"But I have also seen your newspapers and your television programs since I've been here. They tell terrible stories about your world. People kill others to steal their cars—even when they have cars of their own." He shook his head. "This is not a world where I want to live."

Leah couldn't deny that horrible things went on in the world every day. "All right, I agree. The world's not a perfect place. But why not try to change it instead of hiding from it?"

He shook his head. "The elders tell us that it is far more likely that the English will change our ways than that we will change theirs."

"Do you always do what the elders say?" Both he and Charity quoted rules and words of others. Did they ever think for themselves?

"*Gelassenheit*," he said. "That's German for patience and resignation. It means obedience to the Amish community. It is not something we *do*. It is something we *are*."

Leah had been raised to be on her own. Her mother's many marriages, their frequent moves and different schools had taught her to be independent. But she saw quite clearly that for the Amish, individuality was not a virtue. It was a curse. She stood. "Well, it looks like we've come full circle, Ethan. You were right after all— the English and the Amish can't mingle."

He stood too. "But we can care about one another," he said carefully. "We can always care."

She knew he meant *care* in a brotherly way. But after spending time with him, she didn't want to be just another sister to him. She wanted to be a girl who mattered to him the way Martha Dewberry mattered. Except that Leah wasn't Amish. And she never would be.

That evening, Leah overheard Ethan tell his sisters that he was returning home on a shuttle bus. Rebekah reacted immediately, asking him not to leave her and Charity. Leah reacted too, but quietly, deep inside herself. She knew she was going to miss him.

"Papa needs me to work, but I will be back," Ethan said.

"When?"

"Tomorrow evening. By suppertime."

Leah's heartbeat accelerated. *Good. He's coming back.* When he left the room, he passed the table where she sat, trailed his fingers across the surface and softly brushed her arm. She met his gaze and felt a rush of yearning. She wanted to stand up and throw her arms around him. Instead, she sat perfectly still.

She was preparing to go to bed when Dr. Thomas

came into the room. Leah was surprised to see him there so late on a Friday night. "I got tied up in the emergency room with a leg fracture; that's why I'm so late making rounds," he explained.

"I'm not going anywhere." She felt apprehensive. "So, do you know anything about what's wrong with me yet?"

He shuffled her chart, laden with X rays and papers. "I know that I want to do a biopsy on your knee first thing Monday morning."

EIGHT

"Why do you have to do a biopsy?" Leah asked Dr. Thomas.

"A biopsy is nothing more than a diagnostic tool—"

Leah cut him off. "I *know* what a biopsy is! That's how the doctors discovered that my grandmother had cancer." She gasped. "Do you think I have cancer? Is that why you want to do a biopsy?"

"Now, calm down. There are some cancers that have a hereditary factor, but that doesn't necessarily mean you have cancer. I don't want to make a false diagnosis, and since we don't know what's wrong with you yet, I want to do this test. I'll put you under an anesthetic, take out a tiny sample of bone tissue from your knee, and send it to the lab for evaluation. Your knee might be sore for a day or two, but that's all."

Leah felt afraid. "Do whatever you have to."

The doctor patted her arm. "You'll be okay, Leah. We'll take good care of you. I'll see you Monday morning." He smiled reassuringly as he left.

Leah pulled the bedcovers up to her chin and closed her eyes. She didn't want Charity or Rebekah to see the tears that were about to roll down her cheeks as, for the first time since entering the hospital, she surrendered completely to memories of her grandmother.

Grandma Hall had tried to stay involved in Leah's life even after Leah's father had abandoned them. It wasn't easy. For reasons Leah still didn't understand, her mother had tried to keep Leah away from her grandmother. Her mother didn't want Grandma Hall to see Leah at all. But Grandma Hall found ways to keep in touch. She sent Leah letters, even when they lived in the same city, and whenever she could, she stopped by Leah's school during recess to visit.

Leah remembered her grandmother as cheerful and smiling. She carried hankies that smelled like roses, and she loved to wear red. Most importantly, she was Leah's only tie to her father—the father her mother wouldn't allow her to mention. The father Leah longed for, instead of the steady stream of men who had dated her mother.

Leah's grandmother had told her stories about her father when he was a little boy and showed her photos of him as a child, as a soldier in Vietnam, as a new father proudly holding baby Leah. And when she'd ask, "Why did my daddy go away?" Grandma Hall would say, "He just had to go, honey. But he always loved you. And he still does."

When Leah was ten, Grandma Hall had gotten sick, and Leah's mother had relented slightly about allowing Leah to visit her. Although feelings between the two were strained, Leah's mother had often brought Leah to the hospital. "Hi, darling," her grandmother would say, and she would stroke Leah's hair tenderly.

Leah had hated the hospital. Her grandmother looked awful, gaunt and pale, with IVs stuck into bulging blue veins. Leah hated the way the place smelled and feared the equipment, tubes, and syringes, as well as the nurses who shuffled in and out, dispensing medicine but bringing her beloved grandmother no relief. Secretly Leah hoped one day to walk in and see her father visiting his mother. But it had never happened.

Grandma Hall lived three months from the time she was diagnosed. She might have survived longer, except that one day when Leah and her mother went to visit, Grandma Hall was sobbing uncontrollably. "He's dead, Roberta. My boy's dead. I got a letter from some hospital out in Oregon. They found him unconscious in an alley."

That was when Leah knew her father was gone forever. And after that, Grandma Hall went downhill quickly. She died, a shadow of herself, hooked to machines, in pain, alone in the hospital.

And now, Leah thought, *here I am, all alone, in a hospital.* Grandma Hall, if she had been here, would have held Leah's hand and told her not to worry, that she'd protect her. But Grandma Hall was dead. That left Leah's mother—and tender loving care had never been one of her strong suits.

Leah wiped her eyes with the edge of her bedsheet and rolled over. Charity was preparing for bed on a rollaway cot that had been brought into the room. "How's Rebekah?" Leah asked.

"Her fever's down." Charity was wearing a long nightdress of cotton flannel, and her light brown hair hung down her back in a long braid. "And the swelling on her arm has gone down too. I have prayed for these things to happen. And I have asked God to let her go home in time for Christmas. It wouldn't be the same without all of us together."

"Are you trying to tell me you believe your prayers made her well, and not the medicine she's been taking?"

"Of course the medicine helped her. But prayer is strong medicine too. Sometimes it is all we have when nothing else works."

"You know, I want Rebekah to get well, but I'm going to miss the two of you when you leave." And Ethan too, she thought.

"What did your doctor tell you?" Charity asked. Leah explained about the biopsy. "I will say extra prayers for you that this biopsy gives your doctor the answer he is looking for," said Charity.

They told one another "Good night," and Leah switched off the light over her bed. Dim light from the hallway leaked under the bottom of the door, and the wall switches glowed in the dark. As her eyes adjusted, Leah could see Charity kneeling beside her bed, her hands folded and her head bowed. The simplicity of the pose brought a lump to Leah's throat. She wondered if there really was a God after all. Then she thought of her beloved Grandma Hall, dying in the hospital. Leah was touched by Charity's taking the time to pray on her behalf. But nothing had helped her grandma when she was sick: not prayers; not doctors; and not all the love Leah held in her heart for her. What could possibly help Leah?

Leah was awakened by a night nurse for vitals, but long after the nurse had left the room, she remained awake. She kept thinking about Ethan and how attracted she was to him, in spite of his simple and unsophisticated ways. Maybe that was what attracted her. He was singleminded and focused, confident of what he believed, positive of the direction his life would take.

Leah couldn't say any of those things about herself. She meandered through school, doing just enough work to get by. She'd vaguely thought about college, but only because it seemed like the thing to do, not because there was anything particular she wanted to study or learn. Yet she didn't want to be like her mother either, drifting from place to place, marrying and remarrying, always searching for something more or better or just different.

Leah sighed. All this thinking wasn't helping her go back to sleep. She turned over. With a start, she saw a woman standing beside Rebekah's bed. *When did she come into the room?* Leah peered through the gloom and recognized her as the nurse who'd come in the night before. The woman leaned over Charity's cot and smoothed her covers. Then she went to Rebekah's bed and took the child's small hand in hers. Leah heard Rebekah giggle quietly, then begin animatedly whispering with the nurse.

Watching the scene, Leah realized this nurse really had a way with children. And Molly had certainly done a lot to make Leah feel cared for and comfortable. *Nursing.* Maybe that would be something she'd like doing. Leah toyed with the notion, turned it over in her mind, and discovered that she liked it.

Leah continued to watch the night nurse and Rebekah whispering, and slowly a calming peace stole over her. Her eyelids grew heavy, and as the silence of the night closed around her, she fell fast asleep.

"I'm hungry." Rebekah's voice woke Leah and Charity.

Leah rubbed the sleep from her eyes and saw the little girl sitting up in bed with her doll in her lap. Morning sunlight flooded the room. "Are you okay, Rebekah?" she asked.

"Yes, but I am hungry."

Charity got out of bed and scurried to Rebekah's bedside. She felt her forehead with the back of her hand. "I think her fever is gone." She flashed Leah a smile. "It seems she is well."

"That's a relief!"

Molly walked through the doorway. "What's a relief?"

"We think Rebekah's much better," Leah said.

"I'm hungry," Rebekah repeated.

"That's a good sign," Molly said with a grin. "The breakfast trays are on their way, so let's get a temp before you eat." She slid a digital thermometer under Rebekah's tongue. While she was waiting for the readout, she asked Leah, "Did you sleep well?"

"Except for when the nurses came for vitals in the middle of the night. I didn't think I'd ever get back to sleep. Then another nurse came in, and watching her and Rebekah must have made me sleepy, because the next thing I knew it was morning."

"What other nurse?"

"Gabriella," Rebekah said around the thermometer. "She's my friend. She comes in and talks to me."

"Gabriella? She must be brand new."

"She's nice," said Rebekah.

"Well, it must be nice to have that much free time." Molly removed the thermometer when it beeped. "But that's the difference between the day and night shifts. Maybe I'll switch and not have so much work to do."

"Who'll I talk to all day?" Leah kidded.

Molly chuckled, turned to Charity and said, "Good news. Your sister's temperature is normal."

Charity clapped. "Wonderful! When can she go home?"

"Not until her doctor says she can. Infections can be ornery. We want to be sure it's truly gone before we release her."

Leah thought of how lonely it would be without company in the room. "Are you leaving me, Rebekah?"

Rebekah's face puckered. "Oh, Leah, you are my best-ever friend. I'll come visit you. Won't we, Charity?"

Everyone laughed, but Leah knew that once the two girls were gone, they wouldn't be back. Leah doubted that Charity's parents would allow her to make the trip again when there was no reason other than a social call.

Later that morning, after Leah had showered, washed her hair, and put on makeup, she went to the library on the pediatric floor and checked out some books about nursing. She was reading at the table in her room when Ethan came in, smiling.

Rebekah squealed with delight. Ethan beamed at his sisters, then cast a sparkling blue-eyed glance at Leah. "I told you I would return. And guess what? I have brought you all a big surprise."

NINE

"A surprise? What is it? Tell me, Ethan." Rebekah was bubbling over with excitement.

"Papa is downstairs with it."

"I want to see Papa!"

"You will in just a little bit. After he takes care of delivering the surprise."

"Am I included in your surprise?" Leah asked, smiling.

"Yes," Ethan said, turning his clear blue eyes on her.

"What is it?"

His sisters were asking the same question, but he didn't take his gaze off Leah's face as he answered, "It is a Christmas tree to take the place of the one that was stolen. Papa and I cut it early this morning from the woods."

"*Our* woods?" Charity asked, sounding astonished.

"Yes."

"A *Christmas* tree?"

"Yes."

Leah hadn't a clue why Charity was so surprised, nor did she really care. She only knew that gazing into Ethan's eyes was making her heart pound and her pulse race.

Molly hurried into the room. "The front desk says there's a man with a Christmas tree down in the lobby. He says his name is Longacre and he wants to bring it up to the rec room."

Ethan turned. "Our papa. I told him of the theft and he said he would like to bring a tree for the children. We cut it, and a trucker from town helped us get it here."

"We—all of us nurses—are so grateful, Ethan. Yes, have him bring it up in the freight elevator. I'll call a custodian to help."

Ethan left, and Leah and Molly followed him. "It's pretty nice of them to bring the floor a tree, but why is it such a big deal?" Leah asked.

"The Amish don't celebrate Christmas the way we do," Molly said. "They never decorate Christmas trees, and they never focus on exchanging lots of Christmas presents."

"Then why are they doing this?"

Molly shrugged. "You'll have to ask Ethan."

In the rec room, everyone was waiting for the tree delivery. Before long, a handcart carrying the giant evergreen burst through the doorway. Guided by the custodian and steadied by Ethan and his father, the tree was enormous, so tall that it scraped the ceiling. Ice clung to a few of its branches.

"It's wonderful!" Molly cried. She and a group of nurses had gathered at the door to watch.

"Where do you want it?" the custodian asked.

Nurses scurried to make a place for it in a corner of the room. Leah watched Ethan help set the tree in a bucket of water and anchor it down. She couldn't take her eyes off him. His forearms bulged with exertion, and his shirt stretched taut across his back. In minutes the tree stood securely, its pungent pine scent filling the room.

"It did not seem so large in the woods," Ethan's father said.

"It's perfect. Thank you so much, Mr. Longacre. The kids will love it," Leah heard Molly say. "I hope we have enough decorations for it. We'll go ahead with the decorating party after all." She turned to one of the nurses. "Call the cafeteria. Tell them what's going on and see if they can't rustle up some cookies, or some kind of Christmas goodies."

The crowd began to break up.

"Now, I am going to see my daughters," Jacob told his son. Charity had remained in the room with Rebekah.

"I will come shortly, Papa," Ethan said.

When they were alone, Leah walked over to him. "This was very nice of you. But Molly said the Amish don't make a big fuss over Christmas."

"Christmas is important to us, Leah. It is the day Christ was born."

"But it's different for you than it is for us. Why did you bring the tree?"

"It is true that our ways are not your ways, but Christmas is special for us. In our house we exchange gifts. Not all Amish do, but we do. It is a day of feasting and visiting and being with our family."

"But we're not in your family. We're 'English.' "

"I told Papa of all the children who can't go home for Christmas Day. I told him how much the Christmas tree means to them."

"So this is just an act of Christian charity?" Leah wasn't sure how she felt about that.

"It is a kindness, yes. But it is also a way of bringing you a little of my farm and home. The woods are very beautiful and the trees have stood there many years. I wish you could see them."

Leah had already begun to grasp Ethan's deep love for the earth and living things. She understood that giving up the tree had not been done lightly. "I wish I could see them too." She bent several needles of the tree and released more of the heavy pine aroma. "But I guess this is the only way I'll ever go there."

He didn't say anything, and she felt her heart sink a little. Their worlds were far apart, and there was nothing she could do to bridge the gap. He was Amish. She was English.

"Did you hear that Rebekah's fever broke this morning?"

"It did? That's wonderful. I will go see her right away." Halfway to the door he asked, "Are you coming with me?"

"Not now. I'll let all of you visit together for a while."

"But it's your room too."

But not my family, she thought. "Go on. I'll come later." Suddenly she panicked at the thought of his leaving without her seeing him again. "Will you stay for the party tonight?"

"Papa wants to go right home. There are chores to do, work that can't wait. And tomorrow is Sunday, the Sabbath. That is a day for rest and for church and family. Charity and I will both leave . . ." He let his sentence trail off. "But this is probably not interesting to you. Forgive me."

Everything about him was interesting to her. "I—I'll miss all of you when you leave for good."

"And I shall miss you, Leah."

The sound of her name on his lips made her heart flutter. "But you'll be back on Monday?"

"Is this important to you?"

She told him about her biopsy. "I—I think it would be easier if I knew someone was going to be with me when I woke up from the anesthesia. It's no big deal. Just a nice thing to know."

A wry smile turned up the corners of Ethan's mouth. "I think, Leah Lewis-Hall, that you are not so brave as you sometimes pretend."

Leah squared her chin. "I'm used to being alone. I just thought . . . forget it. I don't want you to put yourself out or anything."

"Put myself out?"

"It means—"

"I know what it means. I cannot understand how you would think that it would be a bother to me to be here when you wake up from your surgery. You are not a bother, Leah. You are special."

The way he said the word *special*, the way he was looking at her, made her want to throw herself into his arms. "That's nice of you to say."

"I did not say it to be nice. I said it because it is true."

"And you don't lie."

He grinned. "You know me well."

She returned a smile. "You'd better go visit with Rebekah before your father comes looking for you."

"Don't stay away too long," he said as he left the room.

She stood for a long time, looking at the space where he had stood, wishing with all her heart that things could be different. That this Christmas she could ask for and receive the gift of Ethan in her life long after the holiday was over.

Leah killed as much time as she could before returning to her room. At the door, she paused and peered inside to see Ethan, his sister and their father clustered around Rebekah's bed. The little girl was sitting up and chattering excitedly. Charity saw Leah in the doorway and hurried over and took her arm.

"Guess what, Leah. Papa has given his permission for Ethan and me to stay for the party tonight. Isn't that wonderful?"

TEN

The party was set to start at six-thirty. Charity took Rebekah to the rec room in a wheelchair. Leah helped guide the child's IV pole alongside; although Rebekah's fever had broken, her doctor had not authorized her being taken off the antibiotic.

The rec room swarmed with kids who were decorating the tree from boxes of ornaments piled on the floor. Two orderlies, an intern, and Ethan were patiently stringing lights around the tree, while Molly supervised and nurses helped the children.

"I thought your shift was through for the day," Leah said, to Molly.

"It is, but I couldn't leave everyone to party without me. I called my husband and told him I'd be late tonight." She clamped her hands over her ears. "Loud in here, isn't it?"

"All good parties are loud." Leah noticed Rebekah and Charity standing to one side, staring wide-eyed at the activity. With their odd clothing, they did look a little out of place.

"Ethan's gotten into the swing of things, hasn't he?" Molly asked.

Leah watched him scurrying up a ladder with a handful of lights, which he proceeded to loop carefully around the tree. Even though his clothing was as dated as his sisters', he somehow looked less out of place. "I'm glad their father let Ethan and Charity stay," Leah told Molly.

"When are they leaving?"

"Ethan said they were catching a nine o'clock van."

"The party should be over by then."

"Do you think Rebekah will go home soon?"

"Sure, as long as she continues to improve. Hospital stays are expensive. Doctors try to get patients out of here quickly."

Leah realized that since she wouldn't be released until her mother and Neil came to get her on Thursday, she'd have been a patient for more than a week. Her hospitalization was going to cost Neil a bundle. She wondered if he would resent her for spending so much of his money when he wasn't even her father.

"Of course, most people have insurance," Molly said. "But the Amish don't."

"They don't have *any* insurance?"

Molly shook her head. "They believe in taking care of their own. Rebekah's bills will be paid in full by the Amish community."

Leah remembered the times she and her mother had had no one to fall back on. Leah's mother had never wanted to accept charity, especially not from Grandma Hall. They had had to apply for food stamps once, and when she was old enough to understand the meaning of taking public assistance, she had felt ashamed about it and hadn't wanted anyone at school to know. "I'm glad the Amish take care of each other," she said. "It must be nice."

"You're going to miss them when they go, aren't you?"

Leah gave Molly a self-conscious glance. "The room will be lonely without someone to talk to. And after they leave, I'll never see them again." Just saying it gave Leah a jolt.

"You could still visit them sometime. Maybe this summer."

Leah wondered what life was like on an Amish farm in the summer. Ethan and Charity must work all day. And at night, there'd be no TV or even electricity by which to read a book. She sighed. "I don't think so. Sometimes I wonder why we even met. It seems so pointless."

"Sometimes things happen for a purpose we can't

see until much later. Sometimes we never know why," Molly said. "Whoops!" she interrupted herself. "Someone needs my help." She darted off to untangle a small boy who had managed to wrap himself in a garland of tinsel.

Leah went over to Charity and Rebekah. "So what do you think of all this Christmas stuff, Rebekah?"

"She's confused," Charity admitted. "As am I. Why do you decorate trees?"

"To celebrate, I guess."

"Celebrate what?"

Leah fumbled for words. "It's just what people do this time of the year. They decorate for the holidays, give presents and eat turkey dinners and do family stuff."

"Just like us!" Rebekah exclaimed.

Charity glanced around at the frenzied activity in the room and shook her head. "Not like us at all."

"Listen, why don't we slip into the library where it's quieter," Leah suggested. "We'll come out when it's time for cookies and Christmas music. I think one of the doctors is dressing up as Santa Claus."

"Who?" Rebekah asked.

"I'll explain later." Leah hustled her into the library, with Charity following close behind. The room looked friendly and smelled like books. The closed door kept out most of the noise.

"Look, Charity," Rebekah said, holding up a colorful picture book from a nearby table. "What's this about?"

Leah watched Charity leaf through pages filled with photos of paintings of beautiful angels. "Angels?" she asked Leah with astonishment. "Is this what you English think angels look like?"

Leah stiffened at the words *you English*. She studied the renderings of golden-haired beings wearing long, flowing robes and expressions of rapture. "I guess so."

"Why are they wearing these bird wings?"

"Because angels can fly." Leah paused, suddenly unsure. "Can't they?"

"Angels are spirits. They come and go as they please," Charity said. "Only the cherubim and seraphim have wings."

Leah stared hard at the book. She'd always seen angels drawn as attractive people wearing wings. "They don't look like this?"

"A cherub is a fearsome creature with four sides and four faces that look like a man, a lion, an eagle and a bull. The cherubim's wings cover their hands, and when their wings beat the air, it sounds like thunder. They flash fire as bright as lightning."

Leah listened, openmouthed. What Charity had described sounded more like a monster. "You're kidding. How do you know this?"

"It's written in Holy Scripture, in the Book of Ezekiel."

"*All* angels look like this?"

"No. . . . Isaiah says the seraphim have six wings and they fly through the Temple of God, singing 'Holy, holy, holy.' "

"But aren't there other kinds of angels? You know, regular angels?"

Rebekah giggled. "You're funny, Leah."

Charity smiled too. "There is Michael, the Archangel, the guardian of Israel. And he leads armies of angels in battle against the fallen angels of Lucifer."

"You mean they go to war against each other?" Leah had imagined that angels hung around old churches and looked pretty.

"Lucifer once led a great rebellion against God, and for his disloyalty he and all his angels were thrown out of heaven. Now Lucifer roams the earth seeking men's souls, leading people away from God, deceiving us and causing us great trouble."

Leah was astounded. "All this is in the Bible? I had no idea." She thumbed through the angel book again, trying to imagine this strange spirit world.

"You know, angels can assume human form if they wish. Perhaps that is why they have been drawn this way." Charity touched one of the pictures. "Angels are strong and powerful. They are immortal, but they do not have souls as we do. They do God's bidding, but they serve people too."

"Serve? Like how?"

"In the Psalms it says that God commands his angels to guard us in everything we do. And in the Book of Hebrews it says that we are to be charitable to strangers because we do not know when we might be entertaining angels."

Charity's knowledge about angels astounded Leah. And it intrigued her to think such possibilities existed. "So now I have to be nice to *everybody*?"

Charity giggled. "You sound as if kindness is a chore."

Leah blushed. "Well, there are people I know who *aren't* angels for sure. But you really believe angels exist, don't you?"

"Of course."

"Even though we can't see them?"

"We can see them if they allow us to, but even if we do meet one, we do not always know it. They can seem most ordinary."

"But why would one appear to a person?"

"Sometimes to help us if we are in trouble. Sometimes to fight off evil."

"Why don't they always come to people's rescue?" Leah wondered where the angels had been when her grandmother had been in such terrible pain and had lain dying.

"Sending an angel is God's choice."

Leah could tell by the expressions on the faces of the Amish girls that they believed everything they were saying. Personally, she thought the whole discussion was bizarre. To her, God seemed arbitrary and angels better imagined as the sweet-faced, winged creatures she saw in the books, rather than the frightening creatures Charity had first described.

The library door opened, and Molly poked her head inside. "Come on, you three. We're about to put the angel on top of the tree."

Out in the rec room, Leah stood against the wall with Charity, Rebekah and Ethan, but her mind was elsewhere. Charity's voice, her words and deep convictions, were impossible to forget.

An intern had climbed the ladder with the angel and was placing it on the topmost branch of the tree. The decorative angel was robed in a red-and-white velvet gown. Its hair was golden, and its wings of wire were overlaid with white gauze. The intern scrambled down the ladder and folded it hastily. Across the room someone flicked off the overhead lights.

"Are we ready?" Molly called.

A chorus of children's voices called, "Yes!"

Molly threw a switch, and hundreds of lights blazed

to life on the tree. The onlookers clapped and cheered—
all except for Leah and the three Amish beside her. In the
beautiful glow of the Christmas lights, their faces looked
troubled. Leah allowed her gaze to linger on the angel,
which was bathed in pale yellow light from the bulbs on
nearby branches.

She was positive that the others in the room thought
the angel ornament was beautiful, perfect. But to Leah,
the angel now looked waxy and fake. It was just a doll,
bearing little resemblance to the heavenly creature it was
supposed to represent.

ELEVEN

Leah didn't sleep well that night. She tossed and turned, remembering the party and her Amish friends' reactions to it. Rebekah had been frightened of the man dressed as Santa Claus and had taken the gift he offered only after Leah had taken it first and pressed it into her hand.

"May I have it?" Rebekah had asked Ethan, who had looked uncertain about the whole thing.

"I'm not sure you should take something from a stranger," he said.

"It's all right," Leah told them. "It won't be much. Probably a plastic toy or some candy."

Ethan nodded, and Rebekah carefully pulled off the paper, her movements slow and deliberate—so different from the other kids, who were ripping paper and ribbon to shreds to get to their gifts. Inside hers was a plastic doll. "I like Rose better," Rebekah said solemnly, handing the doll to Leah.

"You can keep it," Leah said. "It's a present."

Rebekah shook her head. "No, thank you. She is not right for a plain person."

Later, Leah had asked Charity, "What could be so awful about taking a plastic doll?"

"We do not believe in collecting material things. Rebekah has a doll. Why does she need two?"

Eating cookies and cake and drinking punch were much more to their liking. They all loved sweets, and Ethan ventured a grin of approval when he bit into a powdery white butter cookie decorated like a snowman.

Charity whispered, "Oma makes wonderful gingerbread, but I like this very much. Maybe even better."

A nurse stepped forward with a guitar and invited the audience to join her in singing Christmas songs, including "Frosty, the Snowman," "Rudolph, the Red-Nosed Reindeer" and "Jingle Bells."

The Amish listened, and Leah tried to imagine what it must be like to hear these songs for the first time. When the nurse began to lead the group in singing carols, Leah glanced at Charity to see if she knew the words. Charity knew them well, and even Ethan and Rebekah sang along. Leah sang too, even though for her, the carols were simply a tradition of the season. For the Amish, singing the words had religious meaning.

When "Silent Night" was played, Charity sang softly in German. As the beautiful music played, Leah felt a lump rise in her throat, in spite of herself. The shimmering tree, the music and children's voices gave her goose bumps. When her gaze fell on the Christmas angel atop the tree, she deliberately glanced away.

After the party, Leah and Rebekah returned to their room and said goodbye to Charity and Ethan. This time Rebekah didn't cry at being left, but Leah felt pangs of regret. She caught Ethan's gaze, and their eyes held. For an instant she thought he might give her a farewell hug. But he didn't. She felt disappointment, although she hadn't really expected him to do something like that.

"Good night, Leah," he said softly.

"But you will come back?"

"On Monday."

"My biopsy—"

"I will be here when you wake up from your surgery."

"Do you promise?"

He touched her cheek. "Yes, I promise."

Long after they were gone and Rebekah slept, Leah lay awake, listening to the night sounds of the hospital. She wished she could sleep away the night and the whole next day. She wanted the biopsy to be over. She wanted Ethan to return.

She sighed and threw back the bedcovers. Perhaps a walk to the rec room would make her feel sleepy, or at least help pass the time.

The rec room was deserted. The aroma of the Christmas tree filled the room, and although its lights had been turned off, it still looked magnificent.

She stood in front of it, fingering the fragrant pine needles and remembering other trees and other Christmases. The tree comforted her. She imagined the woods it had come from. The tree too had been snatched from all that was familiar and thrust into a world that was completely foreign.

Behind her she heard the door open, and she turned to see a nurse silhouetted in the doorway. Leah squinted, then recognized her. "You're Gabriella," she said. "Rebekah talks about you. I've seen you in our room at night."

Gabriella's auburn hair was short with long fringy bangs, and her eyes were dark brown. "She is a precious child, but I've been looking for you."

"I'll bet you're doing bed checks and found mine empty. Sorry about that, but I couldn't sleep." Leah expected a lecture about being out of bed in the middle of the night.

"I knew where to find you."

"There's noplace else to go," Leah said with a heavy sigh.

"Where would you go if you could go anywhere?"

Leah paused, struck by the question. *Where would I go?* "I'm not sure."

"You're not unhappy here, are you?"

Leah thought about Rebekah, Charity and Ethan. "I'm not unhappy," she said.

"Come," Gabriella said, taking her hand. "You should go back to bed."

Obediently Leah followed her out of the rec room and down the hall. "What's bothering you? Why can't you sleep?" Gabriella asked.

"I—I think I'm worried about Monday," Leah confessed. Until that moment, she hadn't consciously been thinking about the biopsy at all.

Gabriella stopped, rested her hands on Leah's shoulders and looked deeply into her eyes. "Don't be afraid, Leah. Everything will work out for the best."

"But how do you know?"

"Things happen for a purpose. Even if we don't understand them."

Leah sighed. "You sound like Molly."

"Molly likes you very much."

"I like her too," Leah said. "She's nice. And she really cares about people."

"You remind her of someone."

"Who?"

"That's for Molly to tell you."

Curious, Leah started to question Gabriella, but the nurse took her hand and led her back to her room. Together they checked on Rebekah, who was sound asleep. The child's skin was cool, and Leah realized that Rebekah really was getting well.

Gabriella smoothed Leah's bedcovers and, reluctantly, Leah crawled between the sheets. "I'm still not sleepy," Leah insisted.

"Do you want me to stay with you until you fall asleep?"

Leah started to say *I'm no baby,* but stopped. "My grandma Hall is the only other person who's ever done that for me. But that was a long time ago."

Gabriella took her hand. "Then it's my turn now."

Leah found the woman's touch comforting, and soon a feeling of serenity and contentment stole over her. Her eyelids grew heavy. "Gabriella, why are the Amish so different?"

"It is their belief and their custom to be different."

The answer didn't satisfy Leah. "I like them, but I don't understand why they live the way they do."

"Sometimes simplicity is a good thing. It keeps people focused on what's important."

Leah yawned, and her thoughts turned again to her

upcoming surgery. "Things will be all right with the biopsy, won't they?"

"God never puts more on a person than the person can bear."

Leah fell asleep and dreamed of Amish buggies, of men who looked like Ethan, and of huge pieces of medical equipment towering over her like birds of prey, intent on devouring her.

"Will you read to me from my book?"

Rebekah's question pulled Leah from her deep sleep. Sunlight spilled through the window, and her breakfast tray sat on her bedside table, the plate still covered by a stainless steel dome. She'd slept so soundly, she hadn't even heard it being delivered. She shook her head to clear it and struggled to a sitting position. "What time is it?"

Rebekah stood beside Leah's bed, her eyes level with the mattress. The IV line had been removed from the girl's hand, and a Band-Aid covered the place where the needle had been. Rebekah shrugged.

Still groggy, Leah smiled. "That late, huh? I'd better get moving."

"You were sleeping so long."

"Yeah. I guess I stayed up too late. Why didn't you wake me?"

"Because Gabriella said not to."

"You talked to Gabriella?"

Rebekah nodded and offered a bright smile. "She told me goodbye. She said I'd be going home tomorrow."

Leah felt jolted. Gabriella wouldn't have told Rebekah that unless it was true. *Going home.* And away from the world Leah was a part of.

TWELVE

Leah mumbled, "Well, I guess after you leave, Gabriella and Molly will be my only friends."

Rebekah looked stricken. "You will be lonely."

Leah tousled the child's hair. "Don't worry about it. My mom will be here Thursday." She got out of bed. "Let me freshen up and then I'll read to you."

Leah quickly showered and was putting on her makeup when Rebekah appeared in the bathroom doorway, shyly looking in. "May I watch?"

"Sure."

Rebekah had already dressed. She fluffed the skirt of her dress and settled on the edge of the tub, where she studied Leah intently with saucer-wide eyes. "Why do you put paint on your face?"

Leah glanced down at her. "To look pretty."

"But you already look pretty."

"Well, thanks, but without mascara, my eyes disappear."

"They do?" The child sat up straighter, squinting to examine Leah's eyes more closely.

Bemused, Leah said, "I guess that doesn't make sense to you. Let's just say I put on makeup because it's my custom, like wearing that cap on your head is yours."

Rebekah seemed to accept this explanation, but when Leah turned the blow-dryer on her shoulder-length, precision-cut hair, Rebekah asked, "Why do you cut your hair off? The Bible says hair is a woman's glory."

"What does that mean?"

"I don't know."

Leah laughed. "I like my hair this way, and I think it looks best on me. I guess it's hard for us to understand each other's ways sometimes."

Rebekah nodded and changed the subject. "My sister Sarah got married in November. She married Israel Kramandam."

"That's nice. Did they go on a honeymoon?"

"What's a honeymoon?"

Leah realized that if the Amish didn't believe in mingling with the world, it was doubtful they would indulge in this particular custom. "A kind of vacation two people take when they get married," she explained.

Rebekah giggled. "Who would do their work? Who would feed the cows?"

"Sorry—I forgot about those cows. So, what do an Amish couple do when they get married?"

"They go around visiting people on other farms. They get to sleep over and get presents." Rebekah's face looked animated. "Then in the spring, they move into their own house. I liked Sarah's wedding. Everybody came."

"Who's everybody?"

"All the plain people. Mama said three hundred were coming and for Papa to fetch enough chairs because no one was going to say that Tillie Longacre didn't know how to put on a wedding feast," Rebekah said in an imitation of her mother's voice. "Mama and Oma cooked and cooked for weeks. I helped."

"Wow, that's a lot of people." Leah thought about her own mother's weddings. The last three ceremonies had been attended only by Leah and one or two of her mother's friends. "Was your sister's dress pretty?"

Rebekah's brow knitted as she considered the question. "All our dresses are plain."

"Didn't she wear a fancy wedding gown?"

Rebekah shrugged. "It was white. But not fancy."

"Were there flowers?"

Rebekah shook her head. Neil and Leah's mother's wedding had been small, but Leah's mother had worn an expensive dress of pale blue silk and carried an exquisite cascade of orchids and roses, and the ring Neil

had slipped onto her finger had been huge and glitter-
ing. "I personally think your plain way is better," she said.

Leah's approval obviously pleased Rebekah. "When I grow up and get married, will you come to my wedding?"

"Could I come? I mean, since I'm not Amish?"

Rebekah pondered the question. "I'll ask Ethan. He knows everything."

The mention of Ethan made Leah's pulse quicken. "Well, you have to grow up first," she told Rebekah. "And by then, who knows where I'll be?" Rebekah looked as if she didn't understand, and Leah realized that for a girl whose family had lived in the same place for generations, the concept of moving from state to state, city to city, rented apartment to rented house wouldn't make any sense at all.

"Come on," Leah said, taking Rebekah's hand. "Let's go read your book, and I'll let you show me some more stories about angels. That way I'll be able to recognize one if I see it."

Rebekah giggled. "You can't see them, Leah."

Leah feigned exasperation. "Just my luck. So how am I supposed to believe in something I can't see?"

Still clinging to Leah's hand, Rebekah tilted her head upward. "Because you see them with your heart, not your eyes."

Leah nodded, saying nothing but wishing she had the same simple faith.

Leah found Sunday afternoon unbearably boring. She didn't want to watch TV, especially since Rebekah wasn't used to it. The rec room was too noisy and the video game room was full of kids waiting to play. Even the library offered no refuge. She was standing in the kitchen, ready to throw herself on the floor in frustration, when Molly walked in. "Rescue me!" Leah cried, grabbing the nurse by the shoulders.

"Bored, are we?" Molly asked with a laugh.

"Watching paint dry would be more exciting."

Molly glanced at her watch. "I'm filling in for a friend who's sick, but I don't have to sign on for another thirty minutes. Why don't you throw on some street clothes and I'll take you downstairs to the main cafeteria. Maybe the change of scenery will do you good."

Leah practically set a speed record dressing in jeans and a sweatshirt. She must have lost some weight—a quick check in the mirror revealed that her jeans looked baggy. But except for the plastic ID bracelet on her wrist, she didn't look like a patient at all.

"You know," she told Molly during the ride down in the elevator, "I'm going to be pretty miffed if they can't find anything wrong with me after I've wasted almost a whole week in the hospital."

"Is your knee still sore?"

"Yes." Leah rotated the kneecap and winced. "And my back too. Maybe it's arthritis from waiting around this place for so long."

Molly chuckled. "I don't think so. By tomorrow night you'll have a diagnosis. Hang in there."

They entered the cafeteria, a spacious, carpeted room with banks of floor-to-ceiling windows. Outside, the weather looked raw and blustery, with flurries of snow swirling wildly. Leah shivered, missing the sun-drenched Texas weather.

"This place makes the best cake. They call it Chocolate Decadence and believe me, it *is*!" Molly said. "Want to try a piece?"

"Is that a trick question? You bet I do!"

Molly went to the dessert area of the food bar and returned with a plate of triple-layer chocolate cake studded with white chocolate chunks, slathered with chocolate icing and drizzled with dark chocolate syrup. She also carried an extra plate and two forks. The cake tasted so good, Leah savored each rich bite with a sigh.

"Feel better?" Molly asked.

"Much." Leah laid down her fork. "If I forget to tell you later, thanks for being so nice to me."

"You're easy to be nice to, Leah."

"You really make me feel like a person instead of a

medical dilemma. The doctors make me feel like I'm some sort of puzzle to be solved."

"Doctors get so focused on a patient's symptoms and medical data that they sometimes lose sight of the human element. I guess that's where nurses come in. And I'm glad you feel that I'm your friend. For me, that's an important part of nursing."

Leah took another bite of cake. "I was thinking the other day about what it might be like to be a nurse. I mean, everyone has to do something for a job. Do you think I would make a good nurse?"

"It's hard work," Molly said. "And getting harder. I plan to go back to school in the summer just to learn more about certain diseases. Nursing isn't for the faint-hearted, Leah."

"And maybe I'm not smart enough."

"If it was just memorizing medical information, anyone could go into nursing, but in order to be a good nurse, you must genuinely want to take care of sick people. I've been on different rotations all over this hospital, and I'm telling you, some people are real pills. They're demanding and cranky and you have to keep reminding yourself that they aren't purposely trying to make your life miserable."

Leah laughed. "Is that why you stick to the pedi floor? Because you're bigger and can make the kids do what you want?"

"How'd you guess?" Molly's eyes twinkled; then her face softened. "Actually, I'm on the pedi floor because I really like the kids and hate seeing them suffer. And"— she took a breath—"because of Emily."

"Who's Emily?"

"She was my sister."

"Was?"

"She died when she was just fourteen—more than twenty-five years ago. And I haven't gotten over it yet."

THIRTEEN

"Your sister died? What happened to her?" Leah saw pain etched in Molly's face.

"It was leukemia. Back then we didn't have the drugs and chemotherapy protocols we have now. Bone marrow transplants were highly experimental too. Most kids who got the disease died."

Leah shuddered and thought of Grandma Hall. "How old were you when it happened?"

"Emily was diagnosed when I was eight and she was twelve, but I remember it like it was yesterday. My parents were beside themselves. And for a while, I was jealous of all the attention Emily was getting. But once I saw how sick the chemo made her, I got over being jealous."

"I never had a sister, but sometimes I wish I did."

"Well, Emily truly was a special girl. She was smart, pretty, popular, but not the least bit stuck-up. I adored her. When she got sick, she was in the hospital for weeks at a time. We lived on a farm, and the only hospital that had a children's oncology unit was three hundred miles away. Mom had to stay with Emily, and during the week Dad worked and stayed with me while I went to school.

"On the weekends, he and I would drive the three hundred miles to visit. I resented it at first, but one time when I got there, Emily was vomiting horribly and all her hair had fallen out from the medication. It was such a shock seeing her bald, I broke down crying and ran out of the room. Emily had had beautiful, long hair, and in less than a week it was totally gone."

Leah saw the mental picture all too clearly. "How did you decide to become a nurse?"

Molly pushed her cake plate aside and leaned back in her chair. "There was a nurse on the floor, an elderly woman, who would sit with my sister for hours when my mother had to get away and get some rest. She was so patient and kind. I'll never forget her. She knew the special patients, the really sick ones, by name. She called them her little angels. Every time Emily had to return to the hospital, Mrs. Duncan was there to take care of her."

"Did your sister have to go back to the hospital often?"

"Not at first. But when she was barely fourteen, she went out of remission, and then she was there almost all the time. The week she died, I stayed out of school. My dad had a neighbor look after the farm, and we all sat by Emily's bedside, watching her die."

Molly paused, and visions of Grandma Hall on her deathbed passed through Leah's head. "It was terrible," Molly said. "But Mrs. Duncan stayed with us the whole time. And at Emily's funeral, she took the day off and drove to our place for the service. I knew then that I wanted to be like that lady. I never considered being anything but a nurse."

Molly's story had touched Leah. "I'm really sorry about your sister. And I know what it's like to lose someone you love." She told Molly briefly about her grandmother's illness and death. "I know how much Ethan and his sisters believe in God, but I wonder why God lets these things happen."

"God doesn't owe us an explanation," Molly said. "But still, there's something comforting about faith. And it's hard *not* to believe in God when you live on a farm all your life. Every winter, all life seems to die. Yet every spring, life returns. Scientific explanations aside, it always seems miraculous to me."

Leah thought about Ethan and his family. Maybe their faith sprang partly from their sense of belonging to the land.

Molly looked at her watch. "I'm late for duty."

The two of them hurried back upstairs, Leah deep in thought. Maybe after this biopsy was complete and she was back on Neil's farm, she could think about making friends at her new high school. Maybe this new life in Indiana wouldn't be so bad after all.

If only my mother can just make this marriage work.

Leah was given a pill to help her sleep that night, and early the next morning a nurse gave her a shot to relax her before her surgery. The medicine worked; she was feeling very calm when an orderly arrived and rolled her on a gurney down the hall to the elevators and the surgical floor.

Once in the O.R. area, Leah was shifted to a gurney and hooked up to an IV line. Efficient nurses busied themselves with patients waiting in a line of hospital beds for one of the four operating rooms. Even though she was feeling relaxed, Leah wished at this moment that her mother could be there.

Dr. Thomas appeared. He wore a green surgical scrub suit and a green cap over his hair. "How're we doing?" he asked.

"A little scared," Leah mumbled.

His eyes crinkled at the corners. "Well, once the anesthesiologist gets hold of you, you'll sleep through the whole thing." He patted her shoulder.

The anesthesiologist talked to her briefly, then slipped a needle into her IV line. "This is going to make you sleepy," he said.

He left, and Molly's face peered down at her. "Hi."

Leah managed a smile of gratitude. "You came to see me."

"I couldn't let you go in there without telling you good luck."

"Will you be here when I wake up?"

"No. They'll take you into recovery, and once you're fully awake, you'll be brought back to the floor. I'll see you there."

Leah reached for Molly's hand, and as the medication spread, making her feel weightless and numb, she mouthed, "Thank you." The last thing she saw was Molly's smiling face and, over Molly's shoulder, the face of Gabriella. Leah wanted to thank the other nurse for coming too, but the drug was making her so drowsy, she couldn't. Gabriella blew her a kiss, and then a curtain of darkness descended over Leah.

She regained consciousness in another room, where other patients were also awakening from operations. Nurses took her blood pressure every fifteen minutes and offered her sips of water. Her knee was sore and bandaged, and her finger had been rebandaged. Had the doctor taken a sample of that bone for the biopsy too? In no time she felt clearheaded, and an orderly took her back to the pediatric floor.

As the orderly rolled Leah's bed into place, Rebekah cried, "You're back! Oh, Leah, you're back."

Leah said, "I slept through the whole thing." Her throat was sore, and when Molly came to welcome her, she explained, "That's from the tube they put down your throat during surgery. It'll clear up in a day or two."

"Have you heard anything about what's wrong with me?" Leah asked.

"No. They'll call your mother and talk to her about it."

"Why? I'm the one going through this. My mother's halfway around the world. Don't I have any rights?"

"You have lots of rights. It'll be up to your doctor. He'll decide how much to tell you. And I know Dr. Thomas. He's pretty straightforward with his patients." Molly gestured to a vase of beautiful flowers sitting on Leah's bedside table. "These were delivered while you were having your biopsy."

"Who sent them?" Molly handed her the card. It read: *We're thinking of you. Recover quickly. Call you later. Love, Mom and Neil.* Leah was pleased, and also a little embarrassed about her outburst. She peered up at Molly. "I guess they didn't forget what was happening today."

"I guess not," Molly said with a grin. "I hear the lunch trays, so I've got to run. I'll check in with you before my shift ends."

Rebekah sidled over to Leah's bed. "Are you all right, Leah?"

Leah scooted up in the bed, putting on a cheerful expression for the child. "Just fine. See?" She pulled back the covers and showed Rebekah her bandage-wrapped knee. "The doctor took a tiny chip of my bone and sent it to the lab to be examined."

"Why?"

"To see why it's sore. To see why my finger broke for no reason."

"My oma has rheumatism," Rebekah said. "Mama fixes her some tea to make it stop hurting." Her face brightened. "Maybe she can make some tea for you."

"Maybe."

The door swung open. Expecting the lunch trays, Leah turned. But the doorway was filled with Ethan. Rebekah ran to him.

Leah's mouth went dry and her heart hammered. He had come, just as he had promised.

FOURTEEN

"Hello, Leah." Ethan scooped Rebekah up in his arms and approached Leah's bed.

"Hi." She realized that she didn't have a bit of makeup on, not even lipstick.

"Your biopsy went well?"

"I did fine, but I don't know anything yet—"

"Where's Mama?" Rebekah interrupted.

"Mama's home, fixing you a welcome-back dinner. Papa's downstairs signing you out. You're coming home."

"Gabriella already told me."

Leah's heart sank. She was glad for Rebekah, but she was going to miss all of them. "Did Charity come with you?" she asked. "I wanted to tell her goodbye."

"She is here. She dislikes the elevator and is walking the stairs."

Charity entered the room, flushed from the climb, her eyes sparkling. After hugging her sister, she asked Leah about her surgery.

"Help me, Charity," Rebekah said. She'd gone to the closet and dragged out a small duffel bag.

Minutes later Mr. Longacre arrived. Not wanting to be in the way while they packed up the child's few belongings, Leah eased out of bed and into the hall, using a pair of crutches. Her knee was sore, but she hobbled down to the rec room. It was crowded with children.

Leah let herself into the library, which was empty. She sank into a chair and stared at the floor. Her days and nights in the hospital stretched before her like a ribbon of lonesome country highway. Her mother and Neil wouldn't be arriving for three more days.

When she heard the door open, she willed the intruder to go away. She wasn't in the mood to be disturbed.

"Leah?"

She turned to see Charity. "Are you all leaving now?"

Charity nodded. "Rebekah wants to say goodbye. And so do I."

"Goodbye," Leah said. She started to say, "Tell Rebekah I'll call her," then remembered that they didn't have a phone. She sighed. "All right, I'll be back to the room in a minute."

Charity stepped forward. "I'm glad you are alone,

because I want to give you something." She thrust out a small package wrapped in brown paper and tied with twine.

"What's this?"

"A gift. For Christmas. I made it for you."

Instantly Leah felt ashamed. She'd been feeling sorry for herself and hadn't given a thought to a present for anyone. "I—I don't know what to say."

"I hope you like it."

"Can I open it now?"

"If you wish to."

Leah heard eagerness in Charity's voice. She tugged at the string and pulled away the paper. Inside lay a piece of linen cloth, and on it, etched in meticulous tiny pink and green cross-stitches, was a cascade of small blossoms surrounded by leaves. Her name, LEAH, was stitched in the center. "It's so beautiful! Thank you."

"Do you really like it? It's a covering for a pillow for your bed. I hope every time you look at it, you will think of me."

Leah didn't know how to sew, but she knew fine stitching when she saw it. The threads were even and delicate, and the image of Charity working so diligently to create the gift brought a lump to Leah's throat. "I won't forget you," she said. "You're a real friend, and your gift is wonderful."

"Plain people are not supposed to feel prideful, but I

feel much pride. Perhaps God will forgive me for this small sin," Charity confided shyly.

Leah stood and hugged her. "I'll put this on my bed as soon as I get home."

"Before we return to the room, Ethan wants to talk to you," Charity said.

Leah felt her heart almost stop. "Ethan's with you?"

"Right outside the door. I told him I would make an excuse to Papa so that he could have some time alone with you."

"Your father wouldn't approve, would he? He wouldn't want Ethan to be alone with an English girl. I don't want the two of you to get into trouble."

Charity retreated to the door and with a mischievous grin said, "Sometimes it is easier to get forgiveness than permission."

When Ethan came into the room, Leah felt her mouth go dry. He was so tall, and his serious blue-eyed gaze turned her knees to jelly. She had long since gotten over his old-fashioned way of dressing. The shapeless, unstylish dark fabric covered the gentlest person she had ever known. He walked over and stood looking down at her. "I will be leaving soon, Leah."

"Then I guess this is goodbye forever."

"You cannot say that, for no one can see into tomorrow."

She squared her jaw. "If you weren't Amish, I could

phone you. I could drive to your house and you could come to mine. I could meet you at a mall. We could go to a movie together. I could ask you to a dance at my school."

"But I *am* Amish."

Leah fought back tears as she grasped the impossibility of their situation. "Are you going to take Martha Dewberry for another ride in your buggy?" She pictured a warm summer night under countless stars. And Ethan in the moonlight with another girl. An Amish girl.

Gently he ran his fingers along the side of her face. "There is only one girl I want to take in my buggy. It is not Martha."

"Are you just saying that to make me feel better, Ethan?"

"I told you, Leah Lewis-Hall—I do not lie."

"Have you ever kissed her, Ethan? Have you kissed any girl?" Leah's voice was barely audible, and she was trembling. Her heartbeat quickened.

Mutely he shook his head.

She whispered, "Will you kiss me?" She wanted to be his first kiss. Her mother once told her that the first kiss was the one a person never forgot. She wanted Ethan to remember her for all time. "For hello and goodbye at the same time," she added.

He lifted her chin with his forefinger and very

slowly lowered his head until his mouth was only inches away. His breath smelled like cinnamon and felt warm on her skin. Gently he pressed his lips to hers, and she closed her eyes and sank into the velvet softness of it. Leah had been kissed before, but she knew that this kiss, Ethan's kiss, was the one that would matter to her for the rest of her life.

When he ended the kiss, when he stepped back, she saw that he looked shaken. She hoped he didn't feel guilty about kissing her. "I—I . . ." She fumbled for words.

He placed the tips of his fingers against her mouth. "Your lips are lovely, Leah. Worth waiting for." He took a deep breath. "My father may come looking for me. We should return to the room."

"If I leave with you," Leah said, "he'll see what has happened between us on my face. I can't hide it."

Ethan nodded. "Then you return to the room and I will go straight down to the lobby."

She cast him one last lingering look and hurried from the room as quickly as her sore knee would allow. Pausing outside the door, she fought to regain her composure.

Rebekah sprang toward her like an overeager puppy when Leah stepped into their room. "I've been waiting for you to come! I couldn't go without saying goodbye."

Rebekah flung her arms around Leah's waist. "I miss you already."

"I'll miss you, too. You were the best roommate in the whole world."

"Papa has taken Rebekah's things down to the lobby," Charity said, her gaze sweeping Leah knowingly. "The bus is leaving soon. Ethan?"

"He went straight downstairs."

Charity nodded and took Rebekah's hand. "Then we must go now."

Leah felt a wave of panic. How could she let them leave her? "Can I write you?" she asked suddenly. "Does the mailman deliver to the Amish?"

Charity broke into a smile. "Of course." She grabbed a pencil and jotted down her address. "Write me—us," she corrected. "If you wish to write to my brother, enclose it in a letter to me and I will make certain that Ethan gets it. I will be praying for you, Leah. I will pray that your tests come out well."

Leah watched the door swing shut behind Charity and Rebekah. The silence in the room made her feel depressed and anxious. It wasn't her tests that worried her. It was losing her friends that was breaking her heart. It was losing Ethan because they came from two different worlds. No amount of wishing could change things. Amish and English simply didn't mix. Leah realized that it was almost a miracle that they had gotten to meet and become friends at all.

Leah sat at the table in her room, her dinner tray in front of her, toying with the food. She heard a light knock and sat up. Her door opened and Dr. Thomas entered.

The look on his face told her that he had news he didn't want to deliver. She set down her fork. "What is it?"

He pulled a chair closer to hers. "I believe I have a diagnosis for you."

"And?"

"And based on the results of your bone scan, you have osteogenic sarcoma. Bone cancer."

FIFTEEN

Leah thought she was having a bad dream. "Bone cancer? There must be a mistake."

Dr. Thomas took her hand. She pulled away, not wanting this man to comfort her when he was shattering her world. "Osteogenic sarcoma is a disease that hits teens and people in their early twenties," he told her. "It often starts in the leg bones, the femur and tibia. It's unusual for it to be present in the kneecap or finger. A tumor has grown on the inside of your finger and weakened the bone. That's why it broke. Another tumor is growing under your kneecap."

"I don't believe it."

"I wouldn't make it up, Leah."

"So *if* it's true, what are you going to do about it?"

"We'll fight aggressively," he said. "Chemotherapy is part of the standard treatment."

She recalled the cancer patients on the pedi floor; children bald from chemo, hooked to IVs. And Grandma Hall. This couldn't happen to her. "I don't want chemo."

"Leah, your life is at stake."

"I want to talk to my mother." The words surprised her.

Dr. Thomas nodded. "I have a call in to her. When she calls back, I'll send for you. I'll put all of us on my speakerphone and we'll have a three-way conversation."

Leah's eyes stung from holding back tears. "Can I be by myself now? I have to think about what you've told me."

The doctor stood. His hand rested on her shoulder. "Leah, I know this is a blow, but you can lick it. I promise to help you every step of the way."

Long after he was gone, she sat at the table, numbly staring into space. Somewhere down the hall, someone was playing Christmas music. How could she feel joy and peace when she'd been told she had cancer?

She sighed, and a long, shuddering sob escaped. Leah clenched her fists together. *I won't cry,* she told herself. Crying would make the whole thing real. Crying would mean acceptance, and she wasn't ready for that.

Leah felt like a caged animal. She wanted to tell someone. She wanted to call a friend and talk. Except that she had no friends. Charity and Ethan were on their way home, and even when they got there, Leah couldn't call them. She could write them a letter, but by the time they got it, the news would be old. And besides, it wasn't as if they could drive back to Indianapolis to console her.

Her door opened, and Molly came hesitantly into the room. Her expression told Leah she'd heard the news. "Leah . . . honey . . . I'm so sorry."

"Maybe he's wrong," Leah said. "Doctors can be wrong, can't they?"

"They can." Molly paused, then added, "But I don't think he'd have told you what he did if he wasn't sure."

Leah drooped. "Why is this happening to me, Molly?"

"I don't know why. But I do know that you have a wonderful doctor to help you through it."

"But I don't want to go through it."

"Leah, chemo treatments aren't like they used to be." Molly seemed to know that it was the chemo, not the cancer, that was scaring Leah the most.

"But he could be wrong," Leah insisted.

Molly didn't answer. Instead she put her arms around Leah, and together they stood while the joyous strains of Christmas music danced in the air around them.

Eventually dinner trays were cleared away. For the first time since she had checked into the hospital, Leah turned on the TV set in her room—mostly to keep herself distracted.

The room was lonely. She missed Rebekah and Charity. Most of all, she missed Ethan. She flipped through the TV channels aimlessly.

A night nurse brought her a pill. Leah asked, "What's this?" She was half afraid it was some form of chemotherapy.

"A sleeping pill," the nurse said. "Dr. Thomas thought you might need it tonight."

"Do you know if Gabriella's come on duty yet?"

"Who?"

"Gabriella. I don't know her last name, but she works on this floor at night."

The nurse shrugged. "Sorry. I don't know her, but I'm rather new to the nursing staff. If I run into anyone with that name, I'll send her straight to your room."

Leah swallowed the pill and waited for it to take effect. Much later during the night, she was vaguely aware that someone had come into her room. She struggled to talk, but she was too drowsy. She felt the squeezing band of the blood pressure cuff and the cool metal of the stethoscope against the inside of her arm.

"Gabriella?" she whispered.

No answer.

Leah fell back into a deep and dreamless sleep.

"Leah, wake up!"

Someone was shaking her. "Go away."

"It's six A.M. Dr. Thomas sent me. I'm supposed to bring you to his office. Your mother's on the phone, and she wants to talk to you."

Leah struggled to throw off the grogginess from the sleeping pill. The nurse helped her up, settled her into a wheelchair and headed down the hall. Leah grabbed a carton of orange juice at the nurses' station and sipped it during the ride up in the elevator. By the time she arrived at Dr. Thomas's office on the top floor, she was fully awake.

His office was small and cramped, and he was sitting behind a desk heaped with medical books and file folders. The nurse put on the chair's brake and left. Leah heard her mother's voice through the speaker phone. "This is preposterous," she was saying. "My daughter checks into your hospital less than a week ago with a broken finger, you diddle around with all kinds of testing and then you call and tell me she has *bone cancer!*"

"Mrs. Dutton, please listen—"

"No! You listen. I want to talk to Leah. Now."

Dr. Thomas looked at Leah.

She leaned forward. "I'm here, Mom."

"Oh, darling, are you all right?"

"Not really."

"You just sit tight, baby. I'm coming home just as

soon as I can get packed up. Neil's making arrangements to get our tickets changed even as we speak."

The calendar on Dr. Thomas's desk showed that it was Tuesday, December 21. It was late Tuesday in Japan. If everything went like clockwork, the soonest her mother and Neil could be there would be the next night. "Please get me out of here," Leah said. "Please don't make me spend Christmas in this place."

"Not to worry, Leah. We'll get you out of there as soon as possible—"

"Mrs. Dutton." Dr. Thomas cut in. "Now that we know what we're dealing with, we should get Leah started on chemo immediately."

"You do *not* have my permission to do *anything* to my daughter before I get there," her mother said sharply.

"I don't recommend waiting."

"I want a second opinion," Leah's mother said stubbornly.

"All the opinions in the world won't change the diagnosis, Mrs. Dutton."

Leah swallowed. The doctor wasn't backing down, but neither was her mother. At that moment, Leah was glad her mother was so strong-willed.

"I stand by my original statement," Leah's mother said. "Don't do anything to my daughter except take care of her daily needs until I get there. Is that clear, Dr. Thomas?"

"Perfectly." The doctor didn't look pleased. "I'll let you sign off with Leah."

"Mom . . . I sure wish you were here."

"I will be soon, Leah. You just hold on until Neil and I get there. We're not going to give up without a fight. You can count on it."

SIXTEEN

Leah felt immensely relieved after the conversation with her mother. Dr. Thomas still insisted that she had bone cancer. But at least Leah didn't feel so alone anymore. Just knowing that her mother was hurrying to be with her brought her comfort.

Now all I have to do is kill time until Mom arrives.

She hobbled to the rec room, using her crutches, and discovered that it was full of kids. She could barely stand to look at the ones who were obviously on chemotherapy. Their bald heads and gaunt bodies made her queasy with dread. This might be how she would look in a few months.

Leah ended up in front of the Christmas tree. The clean pine scent blocked out the medicinal odors of the hospital. She thought back to when Ethan had strung the lights in the tree's branches.

She gazed at the elaborately dressed angel ornament and thought over the strange things Charity had told her about angels. Nothing was the way it seemed. Leah had thought angels were just pretty inventions by the creators of fairy tales. Now she half believed they might be real. She had thought that her broken finger and sore knee were no big deal, but she'd been told she had bone cancer. She had thought Ethan and his sisters were backward and strange. Now she thought of them as dear friends whom she would remember as long as she lived. Nothing was ever the way it seemed.

Carefully she broke off a small twig from the towering tree. She wanted to take it back to her room and place it under her pillow so that she could smell its aroma and imagine the snowy woods on Ethan's farm. Maybe by touching and smelling the pine needles, she could imagine herself closer to Ethan and the things that he loved.

She went to the library, picked up a copy of the Bible and returned to her room, curious to read about angels for herself. She read several stories, but she could not get a clear picture of these strange, heavenly beings. Sometimes they appeared as ordinary people. In other places they were "bright lights," striking fear and awe in people.

Molly stuck her head in the doorway. "Feel like a visitor?"

Leah smiled. "If it's you."

"It's me." Molly came inside and pulled out a chair at the table where Leah was sitting. "You reading the Bible?"

"I figured it couldn't hurt. Charity and Ethan made me curious."

Molly nodded. "Are you feeling better today?"

"As good as a person can feel after she's been told she has cancer."

"It's a bad blow, Leah."

"Yeah. Just think, when people ask what I got for Christmas, I can say, 'Bone cancer, how about you?' "

Molly made a face at Leah's black humor, then said, "Don't forget. I'll be your nurse if you stay in this hospital."

"I appreciate that." Leah remembered their conversation about the nurse who had taken care of Molly's sister. "You'll be my Mrs. Duncan, won't you?"

"Yes. Except your case will have a better outcome than Emily's and your grandmother's. All cancer isn't fatal, you know. Many people can be cured. Or at least have long periods of remission."

Leah wasn't comforted. "If I do have bone cancer and I have to have chemo, what will it be like?"

Molly took a few minutes before answering. When she spoke, her words sounded as though they were coming from a medical text. "You'll be put on a protocol of drugs that will take from nine months to a year to administer. Most of the chemo is toxic—it kills cancer cells and normal cells. Your immune system will be weakened, so you'll have to be very careful about germs. Even a common cold can land you in the hospital.

"They'll probably want to surgically insert a catheter—a plastic tube—into your chest, for administering the chemo. That way they won't have to stick you with needles for every dose. No swimming and no contact sports while you're wearing the device because you might get an infection."

Leah grimaced, hating the idea of a tube protruding from her chest. "Will I throw up?"

"Sometimes. Some of the drugs are stronger than others. You can experience everything from mild nausea to vomiting."

Hearing all of this made Leah lightheaded. "Will my hair fall out?"

"Yes. You can wear a wig until it grows back. And it *will* grow back, Leah. The hospital sponsors seminars for cancer patients to help them cope. And to help them look good and feel better about themselves throughout their treatments. You'll learn makeup tricks and get clothing tips."

"Whoopee," Leah said without enthusiasm.

Molly smiled. "Any other questions?"

"Not right now. I think I know more than I want to know."

Molly leaned forward. "I have a question for you."

"Sure, ask me anything."

"Tell me about Gabriella."

Leah was caught off guard. "What about her? I mean, she's your friend, isn't she?"

Molly shook her head. "I don't know her."

"Are you serious? She's on the night shift. I thought you knew her."

Molly's expression looked guarded. "I know everybody on every shift. There's no Gabriella on our staff."

"But I've talked to her. She came into my room at night. Actually, she visited Rebekah first, and then she started talking to me when Rebekah was leaving."

"This troubles me, Leah. I've never met the woman and there's no record of her in our personnel files."

A creepy sensation inched up Leah's spine. "That's weird."

"Very weird," Molly agreed. "Listen, you need to alert us if it happens again. Push your call button no matter what time of day or night."

Leah frowned. "But she's been really nice to me. She would sit by Rebekah's bed all night when she was scared."

"Nurses haven't got time to sit by a patient's bed all night. The night-shift staff is minimal, and there's plenty of work to do."

"But why would she do it?" Leah watched Molly's

face as she considered the question, as if deciding how much she should say.

"I don't want to frighten you."

"Too late."

Molly leaned forward. "There are some strange people in the world, and most of the time they're harmless. Some of them like to hang around hospitals. Fantasize about being nurses and doctors. Goodness knows why—there's nothing very glamorous about our jobs.

"Anyway, these people sometimes sneak into hospitals and pretend to be part of our community. Once we had a woman who haunted the neonatal ward—where the newborns are. She would sneak in and try to hold the babies. We tightened security and caught her. She went to a psychiatric hospital."

"And you think this Gabriella is some kind of a nutcase too?"

"I don't know what to think. But you and Rebekah are the only people who've seen her, and since Rebekah's gone, she may come back and visit you again."

"She already has."

"What!" Molly sat bolt upright. "When?"

"The night Rebekah left. I ran into Gabriella in the rec room. She walked me back to my room and stayed with me until I fell asleep."

Grim-faced, Molly shook her head. "I'm having security beefed up. What does she look like?"

Leah closed her eyes to get a clearer picture of Gabriella. "She's pretty. Her hair's short and reddish. I think her eyes are brown. She's about your height and size." She opened her eyes and saw Molly's worried expression. "I don't think she'd harm anybody, Molly."

"Probably not," Molly said slowly. "Still, she doesn't belong up here. I don't like the idea of anyone sneaking in at night and bothering our patients."

"Well, if she shows up again, I'll push my call button."

"Good. Now, let me go and have a talk with security." Molly stood, told Leah not to worry and left.

Leah shuddered. What a crummy day this had turned out to be! She'd learned about the horrors of chemo and about a weirdo stalking the halls at night. A weirdo only *she* could identify.

Still, try as she might, Leah couldn't picture Gabriella doing anything mean, and she didn't want her to be turned in to security. "You'd better not come and see me again, Gabriella," she muttered under her breath. Then she clicked on the TV and turned the volume up to chase away the chills she felt.

Leah spent most of the next day reading, playing video games and watching TV. She wanted to keep her mind as busy as possible. When her mind did veer to the subject of cancer, she quickly shut out the frightening thoughts and grabbed something else to do.

After dinner, as she was settling down for the night, she heard a commotion in the hallway. Moments later her door swung open and there stood her mother—her face flushed from the icy December air—wearing a long fur coat and a look of steely determination.

SEVENTEEN

Leah threw her arms around her mother, hardly believing how much she'd missed her.

"Honey, we got here as soon as we could. Neil had to move heaven and earth to change our tickets so close to the holidays, but he did it."

Neil stood behind Leah's mother, looking tired but triumphant. Snowflakes clung to his head of silver-white hair, and his blue eyes were full of concern. "How are you, Leah?"

She was surprised to find she was glad to see him too. "I'm better now that the two of you are here," she told him.

Her mother squirmed out of her coat and flopped into a chair. "We're exhausted. We flew from Japan to Los Angeles, then from L.A. to Chicago, but that's as far as we got. All air traffic was grounded in Chicago because of the weather. So Neil rented a car and we drove the last two hundred miles in a snowstorm."

"Thank you," Leah said to Neil.

"We're family," he said with a grin.

"How was Japan?" Leah felt obligated to ask. Now that the preliminary greetings were over, she felt awkward and overwhelmed.

"Japan was wonderful. We'll have lots of pictures to show you, but this isn't the time to talk about it." Roberta glanced at her husband and said, "Neil, be a dear and see if you can find us a hotel near the hospital. I need a hot bath and a good night's sleep."

"Are you hungry?" he asked.

"Order us a pizza." She turned to Leah. "I've eaten so much fish lately, I'm about to grow fins."

Neil left, and Roberta climbed up on Leah's bed and hugged her again. "It's *so* good to be back in the good old U.S.A. I thought I was too old to get homesick, but when I passed through customs in Los Angeles and that customs agent stamped my passport and said 'Welcome home,' I got all teary-eyed."

Leah allowed her mother to unwind, knowing that she'd get a chance soon enough to tell her what had happened in the hospital. She was glad of the distraction. She wasn't sure what she was going to say, or how much she wanted to tell her mother about the past week.

Her mother picked up Leah's bandaged hand. "So, this is what caused all the trouble?"

"And this." Leah tossed back the covers to expose her knee, still wrapped.

"I find it hard to believe. Honestly, you've been the picture of health all your life."

"Dr. Thomas said that this kind of cancer mostly hits teenagers."

"I still think we should get a second opinion. Neil thinks so too."

"If . . . If it's true," Leah said hesitantly, "then I want to stay in this hospital."

"Whatever for?"

"I know the nurses. I made some friends."

Her mother sighed and rubbed her temples. "We'll have to talk about it tomorrow. I'm too tired to think straight right now. But I will tell you one thing. If this Dr. Thomas doesn't impress me, you'll be out of here in the blink of an eye."

"I'm quite sure of my diagnosis, Mrs. Dutton."

Leah heard Dr. Thomas, but she kept her gaze on her mother. They were seated in his office, and her mother was regarding him warily.

"It's simply hard for me to believe, that's all," her mother said. "I mean, *cancer*."

Dr. Thomas picked up a stack of large gray envelopes. "Let me show you and Leah something."

He stood, turned and flipped a switch, and a light board attached to his wall glowed with fluorescent light. He extracted a piece of X-ray film from each envelope and snapped each one to the board. "Come closer."

Leah moved forward with her mother and saw a series of grayish white bones, from a skull all the way to bones in the feet. "Is that me?" she asked, fascinated.

"Yes. This is your skeleton, top to bottom, from your bone scan."

Leah was impressed and a bit freaked out. It was strange seeing herself without skin.

"So where's the problem?" her mother asked.

"Here," Dr. Thomas said, drawing a circle around Leah's right kneecap with a marking pen. "And here." He drew another circle around her left forefinger.

Leah squinted and saw that both areas looked dark, like small holes.

"Remember," the doctor said, "bones are dense and show up white on X-ray film. Dark space is the absence of bone."

"So?" Leah's mother asked.

"These dark areas indicate that the bone has been eaten away. This is very typical of bone cancer."

"But a few X rays can't tell the whole story," her mother argued.

"True, but based on these, I did the biopsy."

"And what did that say?"

"Here's the pathologist's report." He picked up a file and handed it to Leah's mother. "It's inconclusive, unfortunately. But based on years of treating this disease, I think Leah has osteogenic sarcoma."

As he spoke, Leah began to feel icy cold.

"You *think*?" her mother retorted. "This is just your opinion?"

Dr. Thomas sighed. "My opinion counts, Mrs. Dutton. I'm a specialist who's treated many cases of this disease."

"All right, all right. If this is true, how do you treat it?"

Leah knew the answer already.

Dr. Thomas didn't answer immediately. Instead he laced his fingers together and leaned forward. "Long-term treatment, chemotherapy."

"Long-term? What about the short term?"

"Sometimes drastic measures are needed to preserve a person's life."

Leah felt a tingling sensation all through her body. He was leading up to something horrific. She could sense it. "Like what?" she asked, her heart pounding.

"Like removal of the appendage with the tumors."

"Y-You mean, removing the tumors," she clarified.

"No. I mean amputating your leg and finger."

"No way!" Her mother exploded off her chair.
"Leah's a young woman with her whole life ahead of her.
You cannot cut off her leg! I won't let you."

Dr. Thomas shook his head sadly. "Mrs. Dutton, I
don't like telling you this either, but this *is* the only way
to maximize her recovery. After the amputations, she'll
undergo chemo. Once she goes into remission, we'll monitor her closely. The cure rate—"

Leah stopped listening. She was numb. She tried to
imagine her leg gone, her finger missing, a tube in her
chest, needles and medicine. She began to cry.

Instantly her mother was at her side. "Oh, honey,
it'll be all right."

Leah couldn't talk. It would *never* be all right.

"There are prostheses now that look very lifelike,"
Dr. Thomas was saying. "You'll go through rehabilita-
tion. We'll work with you."

"I don't want you to cut off my leg!" Leah shouted. "I
want you to leave me alone!" She pushed herself out of
the wheelchair and limped out of his office as quickly as
her aching leg allowed her to move.

EIGHTEEN

Leah lay in bed, facing the wall, refusing to eat or talk to anyone who came to see her. Not even Molly could raise her spirits. "I'm supposed to be off for a week starting tomorrow," Molly said. "But I don't want to go away and leave you like this." When Leah didn't respond, Molly squeezed her shoulder and added, "You have friends to help you through this."

Her mother paced the floor, muttering under her breath, sometimes stopping by the bed and saying, "We don't have to take his word for this, Leah. I know X-ray technicians can do sloppy work. And the pathologist's report isn't even conclusive."

Leah let her mother voice all the anger and frustration she was feeling. But she still had to face her own fear alone.

"I want to go home for Christmas," Leah said, the first words she'd spoken in hours.

"Don't you worry. There's no way I'd keep you here for the holidays."

"Then after Christmas—" Leah's voice broke.

"We're not going to think about that now."

"When are we going to think about it?"

Her mother leaned over Leah's bed and stared into her eyes. "You know, Leah, for a long time I had to do things I didn't want to do, just for the two of us to survive. I worked jobs I hated, left you with day care centers when I wanted to stay home with you. I even married men I didn't honestly love so that you and I could have a better life.

"I really love Neil and he really cares about us. He's the father you *should* have had all these years." Leah winced at the mention of her father. Her mother continued. "But that's not what I want to say. What I want to say is I'm not ready to give up this fight. Everything I have, I got because I fought for it."

Confused, Leah asked, "What are you talking about?"

"I'm going to make Dr. Thomas run that bone scan test again before we check out."

"And the biopsy?"

"We may do that again too, after the holidays, of

course. I can't explain why I have a bad feeling about that test, but I do."

The fervor in her mother's voice lit a candle of hope inside Leah. "Do you really think the tests are wrong? Grandma Hall's tests weren't wrong."

Her mother shrugged. "I don't know what to think. All I know is that I would never forgive myself if I let them cut off your leg when I have this gnawing doubt inside me." She looked away for a moment, and Leah was shocked to see tears in her mother's eyes. Her mother never cried in front of her. "I have some regrets about the way I treated you and your grandmother, Leah."

"What regrets?" Leah had not heard her mother discuss her grandmother since the day of her funeral.

"I should have been kinder to her. She truly loved you, and I kept her out of your life for far too long."

Leah felt tears brimming in her own eyes. "Why did you? I loved her too. And I only got to be with her when she was dying."

Her mother sniffed and hung her head. "I was bitter about your father leaving us. He wasn't well, you know. I mean psychologically. He couldn't handle the responsibilities of marriage and a family, so he left. I took it out on your grandmother because I couldn't get even with him. That was wrong of me. Then, once he died, my anger seemed so pointless."

Shocked by her mother's confession, Leah stared. Her mother was asking her to forgive her for her past mistakes. "Is that why you want Dr. Thomas to run the tests again? So you won't make another mistake?"

Her mother smiled ruefully, hugged Leah with startling strength, and then straightened. "I owe it to you. And I owe it to her too. Now, if you'll excuse me, I've got to corner Dr. Thomas."

Dr. Thomas agreed to redo the bone scan, as Leah's mother told her with a great deal of satisfaction. The test was scheduled for the following morning. Afterward, Leah would be checked out and sent home for Christmas. Once the holidays were over she would return to the hospital for reevaluation by a second bone specialist. Although she didn't want to spend another night in the hospital, Leah very much wanted the test run again.

Late in the afternoon, sensing that her mother was emotionally wrung out, Leah insisted that she and Neil go back to the hotel. "Come back in the morning," Leah told them. "I feel better about everything now. And I have plenty of stuff to do to keep busy."

"Are you sure? I will admit that jet lag is catching up with me."

"I'm sure," Leah said, waving them out the door.

Neil gave her a grateful look.

Once they were gone, though, Leah felt lonelier than

ever. When she heard a knock on her door an hour later, she eagerly called, "It's open!"

The door opened a crack, and Ethan's voice said, "Leah?"

Her heart almost stopped. He was the last person she had expected to see. "Yes?" Quickly she raked a hand through her tousled hair.

He entered the room, a serious, questioning look on his face. She swallowed and willed her hands to stop trembling. "How are you?" he asked.

"Not so good," she admitted. Her bravado slipped away and tears spilled down her cheeks. Quickly Ethan came to her and held her hands in his, and she sobbed against his shoulder. The fabric of his jacket felt rough on her cheek, but she felt safe and protected.

Haltingly she told him of the diagnosis, adding through her tears, "I don't want them to cut off my leg and finger. I've had them both for sixteen years. I've grown attached to them."

He peered into her swollen eyes. "Of course you are attached to them. But if they have the potential to kill you . . ." He didn't finish the sentence.

"My mother thinks the tests may be wrong. Do you think that's possible?"

"All things are possible."

She clenched her good hand in frustration. "It's not fair, Ethan! Why is God doing this to me?"

"God is not the author of illness," he said patiently.

"Don't defend God to me. If he's God, he can do anything, can't he?"

"Yes—"

"Well, then why did God let this happen to me?" she interrupted.

"We cannot always see God's purposes—"

She waved his answer away. "I don't *care* about purposes. What about my life? I don't want to wear an artificial leg. I don't want people staring at my hand and asking, 'Why's your finger missing?' People will ask, you know. They'll see me as a freak."

"Then that is their problem." Ethan's voice rose to meet the level of hers.

She didn't want pat answers. "It's *my* problem, Ethan. It always will be. How many guys are going to want to date a girl with one leg? Not everybody in the world is a tolerant, kind Amish person, you know."

He recoiled at her sarcasm. "Do you think I don't have questions for God, Leah?"

"What questions could you possibly have?"

His brow was puckered in anger, but his eyes were filled with sadness. "I do not understand why, when there are so many Amish girls, I have to care so much in my heart for an English one."

His words stopped her cold. Fresh tears welled up in her eyes. Then he was holding her face between his large, work-callused palms and kissing her cheeks, her eyelids, her mouth. She thought her heart would leap out of her chest; she thought she would suffocate from sheer delight.

Ethan kissed her, then abruptly stopped and pressed his forehead to hers. She listened to his ragged breathing. "Forgive me," he whispered.

"No," she said.

"I should not—"

She placed her fingers against his lips. "It happened. You can't take it back."

"I did not come here for this."

"Why did you come?" It suddenly occurred to her that he had no reason for being there. And the trip to visit her so close to Christmas probably wasn't approved by his family.

"I dreamed you needed me."

"You dreamed?"

His cheeks colored. "The dream was very real. I felt you were in danger, and that you needed me to be with you."

Until that moment, she hadn't realized how much she did need him. "Will you get in trouble for coming?"

He smiled. "Yes. But I do not care. I *had* to come."

"Does Charity know you're here?"

"She'll figure it out."

"I don't want you to get into trouble because of me."

"I will not leave you."

"Tomorrow, after the test, I'm going home."

"Then I'll stay until you leave."

She felt suddenly shy, awkward. She understood what he was giving her. He was disobeying his community. She should make him leave now, but she didn't have the strength. She needed him. And she wanted him. "Do you have a photo of yourself?" she asked. "I'd like to have it with me when I go home. And I'd like to have it when I come back to the hospital."

He shook his head. "The Amish do not like to be photographed. Preserving our personal image is thought to be prideful and indulgent."

She was disappointed. "But it isn't against your religion, is it?"

"Not strictly." He looked pained and anxious because he couldn't give her what she'd asked for. "I would like a picture of you, Leah."

"I have my school pictures at home. I'll mail one to you." She was glad to be able to give him something tangible of herself to hold on to.

"I will always keep it."

"So now what?" she asked.

"So now we stay together until your test tomorrow."

"Ethan, I'm glad you had the dream. I'm glad you'll be here with me all night."

He hugged her. "I knew I had to see you."

They played video games, they snacked on cookies and apples, they talked until very late. Leah didn't remember falling asleep, yet she awoke with a start and realized that she was in bed in her room. A lamp had been left on, and she peered around the room, looking for Ethan. He wasn't in the room with her. But someone was. Standing beside her bed was Gabriella.

NINETEEN

"What do you want?" Leah reached for her call button.

Gabriella looked surprised. "Leah, why are you afraid of me?"

"I—I'm not."

"Yes, you are. I can see it in your eyes. I did not come to harm you."

Leah's fingers touched the call button, but she didn't push it. "Where's Ethan?"

"He went down to the lobby. He'll be back soon."

"Did he tell you that?"

"No. But I know where he's gone."

Leah told herself to call for the night nurse, but she couldn't make herself do it. "You'd better go away before the hospital finds out you're here."

"Is that what you want?"

Suddenly angry, Leah snapped, "Listen, I know you're a fake!"

"A fake?"

"Yes. Molly found out about you visiting me and Rebekah and she's really upset about it. She says she doesn't know who you are or why you're here. But she says you don't belong here."

"Molly said that? But I know Molly well."

"Stop lying!" Leah balled her fist around the covers. "I've got enough trouble without you hanging around. I have cancer, Gabriella. The doctors want to cut off my leg and finger." Leah was shaking with emotion and glaring at the young woman.

Gabriella shook her head. "I know. I didn't come to upset you, Leah. I came to help you."

"Then leave." Leah fought to regain her composure. "You've been nice to me. I don't want to have to turn you in to hospital security."

Gabriella stepped closer to the bed. "I will not see you again, Leah. But I would like you to do me a favor before I go."

"What?"

"There's something in the library for Molly."

"What is it?"

"A gift."

"What kind of a gift?" If Molly didn't know Gabriella, why would Gabriella give her a gift?

"A very special book."

"I don't know . . ."

"She will be very glad to have it."

"How do you know?"

Gabriella smiled. "I just know."

Leah wanted to shout that she was sick of the mysterious smiles and enigmatic conversation. Instead she asked, "Will she really want this book? I don't want to upset her, and she's pretty upset already about you sneaking around the hospital pretending you're a nurse."

"I never said I was a nurse."

"But you acted like one. What else was I supposed to think?"

"I cannot help what you thought. I never pretended to be anybody except myself." Gabriella's voice was soft. She held Leah's gaze, and inexplicably all Leah's fear and anger vanished. She saw a beautiful woman with gentle brown eyes. "You have many questions," Gabriella said.

"Yes," Leah answered, her voice barely a whisper.

"It will take a lifetime to answer them." Gabriella reached out to Leah. "I have a gift for you too, Leah."

"What?" Gabriella took Leah's hands in hers and placed them on Leah's wrapped knee. Then she tenderly covered Leah's hands with her own. Warmth from their combined touches spread through her sore knee.

"Do you want to be well?"

"Of course."

"Then *believe*."

"Believe what?"

"Believe in the power and goodness of God."

"I—I believe . . ." Leah stared into Gabriella's eyes, and suddenly she *did* believe. She believed in a power higher and stronger than what could be seen or explained. She closed her eyes, and a feeling of peace enveloped her. When she opened her eyes, she was alone, still clutching her knee. All she saw was the darkened corners of her room and the lamp glowing on the table. Nothing remained of Gabriella.

Leah told Ethan everything, but he could make no sense of it either. "Perhaps you fell asleep and dreamed this," he suggested. "How does your leg feel?"

She rotated it. "I'm not sure. About the same, I guess."

"Did she frighten you?"

"A little. She's strange. And after what Molly said about—" She interrupted herself. "Ethan! Help me to the library."

"Why?"

"Gabriella said there was a book in the library that would mean a lot to Molly."

"What book?"

"I don't know, but I need to find it."

He helped her with her crutches and walked with her as she hobbled down the dimly lit hall. In the library, Leah peered around at the shelves.

"How will you know which is the right book?" Ethan said.

Leah didn't know what drew her to the right side of the room, to the third shelf, halfway over. But that was where she instinctively went. She leaned against the bookcase, handed one crutch to Ethan and gingerly tugged a small book off the shelf. The book was worn, bound in green leather, and fastened tightly with an old-fashioned clasp lock. The lock wouldn't budge. "This is it."

"How do you know?"

"I just know."

Ethan swept his hand over her hair. She looked into his eyes and forgot about the book, forgot about everything except his nearness. "You are beautiful, Leah. And I know that you will be all right."

Her heart pounded crazily. "What makes you say that?"

"Because it is Christmas." His smile almost lit the room. "And because I do not lie."

• • •

Leah was taken down to X ray first thing in the morning. She introduced her mother to Ethan as "my guardian angel," and when he looked startled, she patted his hand and said, "It's just a figure of speech."

She endured the radioactive injection, sat and talked to Ethan and her mother while it was absorbed into her bones, and lay perfectly still on the table for the scanning camera. Then she returned to her room and started to pack. She was almost finished when the X-ray department sent for her a second time.

Again she went down to X ray, where a very agitated technician said she had to repeat the procedure.

"Why again?" her mother demanded. "Can't you get it right?"

"Look, lady, I know how to do my job, but whatever her doctor's looking for didn't show up clear enough, so I have to do it again."

Leah glanced at Ethan, who shrugged and squeezed her hand.

Much later, as she was leaving the floor to go home—in a wheelchair, as all patients were required to do—Molly hurried up to her. "I'm so glad I caught you. I wanted to say goodbye and let you know I'll be here after the holidays when you come back." She saw Ethan and looked surprised.

"I came to keep her company," he explained.

Leah remembered the book and reached into her bag. "I have something for you. Actually, it's from Gabriella."

"She came to see you?" Molly looked alarmed.

"Don't be worried. She won't be back." Leah handed Molly the book. "She wanted you to have this."

Molly took it, then gasped. All the color drained from her face. "Where did she get this?"

"What is it? What's wrong?" Seeing Molly's reaction made Leah's heart skip.

"It's my sister's diary. It's been missing for all these years. We knew Emily kept it. I saw her writing in it, but after she died, we couldn't find it anywhere." Molly hugged the book to herself as tears streamed down her face.

"Gabriella told me it was in the library, and that's exactly where Ethan and I found it."

"How can that be? That library's been revamped and restocked many times over the years. Someone would have found it before now."

"I don't know how," Leah said, equally baffled. "But that's where we found it. Just like Gabriella said we would. It's locked."

"I have the key. I've kept it all these years." Molly wiped her eyes. "Oh, Leah, what a wonderful present for my parents. We're supposed to go there for Christmas dinner. I'll take it with me and we'll read it together." She looked at Leah. "Thank you. And thank this Gabriella when you see her."

"She told me that I won't see her again," Leah said. "And I believe her."

The elevator door slid open. "Let's blow this place," Leah's mother said.

In the lobby, they waited for Leah's mother to drive the car to the front door. Outside, snow was falling. Leah saw a gray van off to one side. Ethan touched Leah's cheek. "My ride to Nappanee is waiting for me. I must go."

Leah clung to his hand, not wanting him to leave her. "Ethan, I want you to know how much it mattered to me to have you come stay with me."

"I wanted to stay with you."

"I don't want you to be in trouble because of it."

"I cannot change what I have done." He squared his jaw. "You should not worry about me."

"I'll write you. Charity and Rebekah, too."

He grinned and stroked her hair. "We'll wait for your letter."

"Please tell them Merry Christmas, and that it helped knowing they were praying for me."

"So are you no longer angry with God?"

She sighed. "I guess not. I need his help, don't I?"

He bent and kissed her forehead. "Merry Christmas, English."

"Merry Christmas," she whispered. She watched him step out into the snow, his dark coat, pants and broad-brimmed hat stark against the white snow. She pressed her hand to her mouth and felt the lingering warmth of his touch. She watched him disappear into the van, and she hoped with all her heart that angels would watch over him forever.

TWENTY

January 30

Dear Charity,

Thanks for your letter. I *love* hearing from you. I'm mailing you two letters in this envelope, one for you and Rebekah, the other for Ethan. Could you please give it to him?

Since you asked for my news, I'll give it to you in detail. Where to begin? . . . I went back to the hospital right after New Year's Day and Mom, Neil and I met with Dr. Thomas and two of his colleagues. I wish you could have been there. It's hard to write down what happened, but I'll try. Dr. Thomas hung four sets of my X rays on his light board, which included a series he'd had done that very morning. The first few sets of X rays showed big dark spots where cancer had eaten away my bone. But on the newest set of X rays the spots were smaller! He explained that the X rays were showing that the cancer wasn't nearly as advanced as they originally thought. So I endured another biopsy which showed that while there were still some questionable cells, the doctors felt that after a round of chemotherapy, I'll eventually be all right. In other words, NO amputation! What a relief!

Mom went ballistic (which means crazy-angry). She shouted, "What if you'd cut off Leah's leg and then found you'd made a mistake? Then what would you say?" Dr. Thomas insisted he hadn't made a mistake. He assured us his diagnosis had been correct. He explained that sometimes X rays can look different from each other, but he did agree that he was mystified by the shrinking spots. He showed us some pretty interesting stories in a medical book about patients who go into "spontaneous remission" with absolutely no help from medical science. He admitted that there really *are* some weird unexplained healings. I mean people who were at death's door—much worse off than me—and then their sicknesses mysteriously vanished over time. That's when Dr. Thomas recommended chemo. He said it was the smart, responsible thing to do. I'm not crazy about taking it (I'll probably lose my hair and be sick), but I guess it's best not to take a chance that I'm not having a "spontaneous remission."

Neil was real quiet through the whole discussion. But right after Dr. Thomas finished with his explanations, Neil says, " 'Spontaneous remissions'—in my day we called them miracles." It made me laugh, and, of course, think of you and Rebekah. It also made everybody in the room relax a little.

Anyway Dr. Thomas agreed that there were some things science couldn't explain. Whether we call it a spontaneous remission or a miracle doesn't matter to me. All I know is that I still have my leg. And in spite of having to go through chemo, I have a good feeling about this, Charity. You might even say I have faith. Maybe your prayers for me helped after all.

Which brings me to the part Gabriella may have played in all of this. Only Rebekah and I ever saw her. But she *did* exist. Emily's diary is proof enough for me. Molly can't understand how it could have been in the library all these years and nobody ever found it. It's a real mystery, and only Gabriella knows the answer.

Speaking of books, did I mention that I got my own Bible for Christmas? I've been doing a lot of reading in it, especially about angels. I keep thinking of all the things you told me about them the night we decorated the Christmas tree, and so-o-o, I'm going to tell you something that may make you think I've gone nuts. Charity, I think that Gabriella might be an angel. That would explain so many things about her. The way she seemed to appear and disappear. The way I felt so peaceful the last night I saw her. She may even be responsible for the craziness with my X rays! I honestly can't find another way to explain the things that have happened. But you're smarter about these things, what do you think?

Anyway, I *do* know that you and Rebekah and Ethan are angels too. *Earth* angels who came into my life when I needed a miracle! Thanks for your friendship. Please keep writing and tell Rebekah that if she ever sees Gabriella again, she should throw a net over her. I have a hundred questions I want to ask her.

Leah

Lifted Up by Angels

*This book is dedicated to my friend
Mary Lou Carney—who took the notes!*

For he will command his angels concerning you
to guard you in all your ways; they will lift
you up in their hands, so that you will not
strike your foot against a stone.

(Psalm 91:11–12, New International Version)

ONE

"Leah, this makes no sense to me. Why would you want to rent an apartment in a hole in the wall like Nappanee, Indiana, when you could be sailing to Fiji on a windjammer with Neil and me for the summer?"

Not bothering to answer her mother's question, Leah Lewis-Hall dragged her suitcase into the bedroom of the sparsely furnished apartment. She was seventeen, but if she lived to be a hundred, she still wouldn't be able to explain it to her mother. She'd tried before they'd driven from Neil's sprawling, wonderful farmhouse that morning, but her mother didn't get it. How come she couldn't understand that Leah did not want to tag along with her and Neil, husband number five in her mother's life? An entire summer with them would never be her idea of fun. Not when she could be near the Longacre family, the kindest people she'd ever met: Rebekah, Charity, Ethan . . . Especially Ethan.

Leah's mother glanced disdainfully around the small room. "Good thing Neil had a friend in the real estate business up here, or I would never have let you come."

In spite of Neil's being many years older than her mother, Leah liked him. After six months of being married to her mother, Leah realized, Neil had a better understanding of her than her mother did. When Leah explained to Neil her plan and what it would mean to her, he had helped her get both a place to live and a job working at a bed-and-breakfast in Nappanee. Neil truly seemed to understand when Leah had flatly said to him, "I wanted to make my own summer vacation plans. It's been a rough year." The nine days Leah had had to spend in the hospital just before Christmas while her mother and Neil had been in Japan on their honeymoon were the toughest of her life. That was when she had been diagnosed with bone cancer.

"Dr. Thomas does want me in for another checkup at the end of June," Leah said now.

"They misdiagnosed you in the first place," her mother insisted. "You could come to the South Seas with us. You are fine now. That doctor just scared us to death."

Leah didn't know what to believe. Her early X rays and bone scans had clearly indicated that parts of her knee had been eaten away by cancer. Then, during her hospital confinement, Gabriella, a mysterious figure, had come into her life. Later X rays showed that the dark spots had shrunk even before any treatments. This had totally shocked her doctor.

"I went through six weeks of chemo for nothing then?" Leah asked her mother with a grimace.

"Insurance," her mother countered. "Besides, you did fine with chemo."

"Not much fun, though." Leah would never forget the bouts of nausea following each drug protocol. "Well, I'm here already. Neil understands, so why can't you?"

Her mother grabbed a grocery sack full of Leah's shoes and headed to the closet. "Can you cook well enough to even feed yourself?"

"I can cook. And I have Grandma's recipe box." Her deceased grandmother was another sore subject between Leah and her mother, so Leah was glad when there was no comment. "I really will be fine, Mom. Stop worrying."

"I can't believe you'd rather clean toilets than sail to Fiji," her mother grumbled.

They'd already visited the small inn where she was to work. It was a two-story frame house with an old-fashioned parlor, family-style dining room and four quaint bedrooms and bathrooms upstairs. Leah would be responsible for fresh bed linen daily, cleaning chores, and serving breakfast and lunch to guests. Her workday would begin at seven A.M. and end at three every afternoon. She'd be off on the weekends.

"You'll be a *maid*." Her mother chewed her bottom lip fretfully.

Leah rolled her eyes in exasperation.

Her mother tagged behind Leah as she went into the tiny kitchen. "Is your phone working? I sent in a deposit and told them to turn it on."

Leah picked up the receiver and held it out so that they could both hear the dial tone.

"I'll call and check on you before we drive to the airport tomorrow." Neil and her mother were to fly from Indianapolis to Los Angeles, then to Hawaii, where they would board the sailing vessel that would take them to the South Pacific island of Fiji.

"I'll be fine, Mother."

"Are you positive those Amish people will look after you? Don't you think I should meet them?"

"You read Charity's letter. She's glad I'm here for the summer. And no, you do not need to meet them." When Leah had first formed the plan to work in the area for the summer and had written Charity about it, Charity had written back to say it would be nice to see her again. Now that Leah was actually here, she hoped she'd not acted presumptuously.

"It just seems so . . . s you, that's all." Her mother b "And I can't believe you're so casua summer. Even though the diagnosis makes me anxious."

Leah sorted her mother's mismatched into a drawer, knowing she was acting more self than she felt. She reminded her mother that it was who'd taught her self-reliance and independence in th first place. "Mom, I'm going to have a good time this summer, and so are you and Neil. August will be here before we know it."

"You have the ship-to-shore phone number," her mother reminded Leah. "If you have any problems—"

"Don't worry," Leah interrupted.

"There's still time to change your mind, you know."

"I'm not changing my mind."

Her mother sighed and glanced at her watch. "Maybe we'd better buy some milk and things at the grocery store before I go."

"I can shop by myself. You'd better get on the road if you want to be home before dark." They'd driven up in separate cars, Leah's mother in the car Neil had given her for a wedding gift and Leah in the sporty red convertible he'd given to her after her last chemo session. "You deserve it," he had said, handing her the keys.

Her mother hugged Leah. "I'll miss you."

to Neil. He's

k."

mention such

r and waved

n she stood

hugged her

ets, she told

on her own.

. . . odd to go off and leave

oke into Leah's thoughts.

about living alone all

was wrong, it still

163

silverware

assured

she

Leah wasted no time going to the grocery store; instead she took out the roughly drawn map Charity had sent her and followed it to the Longacre farm. The Indiana countryside was flat, the road straight as an arrow as it passed fields of young corn plants. The late-afternoon sun felt warm on her head and shoulders, but although it was late May, the breeze still held an edge of coolness. In less than fifteen minutes, she turned off the main high- way onto a gravel road marked as the entrance to the farm. Far back on the property, she saw a rambling two- story farmhouse. Of course, no telephone poles, no wires for electricity led up to the house. The Amish kept their own ways and did not want modern conveniences.

Leah stopped shy of the well-cared-for lawn. The screen door banged open and Charity, gathering her skirt, darted off the porch. She wore a long, plain brown dress covered with a long white apron. The ties from her prayer cap flapped as she ran toward the car. "Leah, how pleased I am to see you!"

Leah scrambled from the car and embraced her friend, a lump of emotion clogging her throat. "You look wonderful!"

Charity stepped an arm's length away. "And you look beautiful. Too thin, I think."

"Left over from the chemo treatments. But I didn't lose much hair." Leah spun, and her dark hair, now shoulder length, fluffed in the breeze.

"You must tell me everything. But first, we must go out to the garden, where someone is waiting to see you."

Charity led Leah around to the back of the house, where two women and two girls were tending a large vegetable garden. Leah recognized Charity's mother, Tillie, at once. Upon seeing Leah, the child beside Tillie dropped her hoe and ran, arms outstretched to meet her.

"Rebekah!" Leah cried, catching the girl in her arms. "You've grown so big." She hadn't seen Rebekah since she'd left the hospital room they'd shared.

The six-year-old beamed a smile at her. One of her front teeth was missing, making her look even cuter than Leah remembered. "I thought you'd never get here. I've been waiting all day," Rebekah said.

"I'm here now," Leah answered with a smile.

Charity introduced her sister, twelve-year-old Elizabeth, and her grandmother, whom they called Oma. The baby, Nathan, now eight months old, lay asleep on a nearby blanket. "We shall all rest and take some lemonade," Tillie Longacre announced. "And you must join us for dinner tonight, Leah."

Holding Rebekah's hand, Leah followed the group to a wooden picnic table, where chunks of ice sparkled in a pitcher of lemonade. "Thank you. I'd like that," Leah said, feeling oddly out of place in her modern clothes. She was what the Amish called English. She was not one of the "plain people." She felt her differences keenly.

"I want you to come see my chickens," Rebekah said.

"I can't wait to see them. Actually, I don't think I've ever seen a live chicken up close and personal."

Everybody laughed.

Before her mother had married Neil and moved to his farm, Leah had lived in Dallas and attended a huge metropolitan high school. After the move, she'd experienced culture shock.

"Leah can visit your chickens later," Charity said. "Right now, I want her to walk with me to the barn."

"That's where Ethan is," Rebekah declared. "He's been looking for you all day too."

Leah saw a sidelong glance pass between Tillie and

Oma. She wondered if they approved of her visiting Ethan. But she couldn't help the tingle of excitement that skittered up her spine at the thought of seeing him again. She recalled their bittersweet goodbye the previous December in the hospital lobby.

"Come with me," Charity said, setting down her glass of lemonade.

Leah abandonded her lemonade and followed Charity across a wide field toward a large gray barn. The closer they got, the more nervous Leah grew. What had Ethan been thinking? What if he didn't think she was pretty anymore? What if he'd decided his girlfriend, Martha Dewberry, was more to his liking because she was Amish? Ethan had written to Leah, but his wording had been stilted and awkward, just as he'd been toward her in the hospital before they'd become friends. Before they'd kissed.

At the door of the barn, she smoothed her hair. "I look a mess."

"You look lovely," Charity said, stepping aside.

In the barn's dim interior, Leah saw Ethan pitching hay down from a loft. His plain white shirt was damp with perspiration, his dark trousers speckled with straw. He was hatless and his thick blond hair looked ruffled. She gazed up at him, her heart pounding crazily. He looked down suddenly. She couldn't move, could scarcely breathe.

In that instant, Leah realized that Ethan was the *real* reason she had come to Nappanee for the summer. Ethan, the Amish boy who lived in a world more different than any she had ever known. Ethan, the Amish boy she had fallen for months ago.

TWO

"Leah!" Ethan called. "I'll be right down." He descended the ladder.

Nervous, Leah looked back toward Charity for moral support, but Charity had slipped away.

"Hi," Leah said when Ethan stood in front of her.

His brow knitted. His startling blue eyes stared directly into hers. "My eyes have been hungry for the sight of you."

His quaint way of phrasing sentences had put her off when they'd first met. Now his words were like music to her. "And my eyes for you. How have you been?"

"I am fine. But it is not me we should be talking about. How have *you* been?"

"I made it through chemo and all. It really wasn't so bad."

"So the cancer in your bones is gone for good?"

Leah wasn't sure how to answer. More than any-thing, she wanted to believe it was gone. "I have to go for checkups every three months for two years. If there's no relapse, the doctors might pronounce me cured." She gave him the answer her doctor had given her mother when she had asked the same question.

"That is good. Have you seen Gabriella again?"

"No. And I don't think I will, either."

"If she was an angel from the Lord sent to heal you, it does not seem likely that she will appear to you again. There is nothing left for her to do for you."

"Everybody else thinks she was a nutcase who somehow slipped through hospital security. All I know is that before she came to see me that last time, I was facing having my leg amputated. After she touched me, my X rays started changing." Leah shrugged. "Maybe it was just a coincidence. I guess I'll never know for sure who she was."

"I am glad you will be working in Nappanee for the summer, because I will be able to see much of you," Ethan told her. "Charity told me where you will be working."

His assurance made Leah feel better. "I like the own-ers, Mr. and Mrs. Stoltz," she said. "There'll be another girl working with me, but I haven't met her yet. You and Charity will have to come visit me in town. I have a cute little apartment, not too far from the inn, and a car to get me there. No excuses for ever being late." Leah felt as if she was babbling, but she couldn't seem to stop.

"You will live by yourself?" He made it sound slightly scandalous.

"Sure I will. I can come out and pick you up if you want. Can you ride in my car with me?" She knew the Amish would use modern transportation when necessary. She wasn't sure if a visit to her apartment counted as necessary.

"I can ride with you."

"Of course, I'd like to ride in that buggy of yours sometime." Leah gave a nervous laugh. An Amish boy only asked a girl to ride in his buggy when he was interested in her romantically. It was Leah's way of asking if he still cared about her or if, since December, Martha had won him back.

He raised his hand as if to touch her cheek but drew back at the last second. "There is much I would like to do with you, Leah."

Her knees went weak. "I—I won't be in the way this summer, will I?"

"In the way?"

"You know. A bother, a pain."

"How could you be in my way? I want you near me." The sound of running feet interrupted them. "There you are!" Rebekah exclaimed. "Ethan, can Leah come back to the garden now? She's staying for supper, so you can see her later."

"You are staying?"

"Your mother invited me." He looked solemn, making her ask, "Is it all right to have dinner with your family?"

"Oh yes. Please. It is good to think about seeing you at our dinner table tonight."

"Even though I'm English?"

He grinned. "I have eaten with you before. You are very civilized."

She returned his smile. "I promise not to throw my food."

Rebekah tugged on her hand. "Come. I'll show you the chickens on the way back."

Leah tossed Ethan one last glance and followed the little girl outside. The bright sunlight made her squint. She gazed around the beautiful stretch of farmland. Far back on the property, she saw another house. "Who lives over there?" she asked, pointing.

"My sister Sarah and her husband, Israel," Rebekah said.

"I remember." During their hospital stay, Rebekah had told Leah about her sister's Amish-style wedding: very different from most weddings.

"Yes, and guess what?" Rebekah lowered her voice,

although there was no one around to overhear. "Sarah's going to have a baby." The little girl giggled. "Her stomach is fat. I saw my cat have kittens, so I know these things."

Leah suppressed a smile. "That'll make you an aunt. And your mother a grandmother. And your oma a great-grandmother."

Rebekah's eyes grew large. "I'll be an aunt?"

Leah stroked the child's head, which was covered by a black prayer cap, and remembered how she used to long for a sister when she was growing up. "Yes, you will."

After looking over the chickens in Rebekah's charge, Leah accompanied the girl to the house. They entered a spacious kitchen filled with the smells of baking bread, roasting meat, and simmering vegetables and gravies. A table, filled with mixing bowls and resembling a command center, stood in the center of the room. Cupboards reached to the ceiling along two walls, and a sink with a hand pump stood under a window. Leah saw Elizabeth toss wood into a large black cast-iron stove. The room was overly warm. Then she realized that the house had no electricity, so that meant, along with a woodstove for cooking, no air-conditioning or fans.

"Rebekah, set the table, please," Mrs. Longacre said.

"What should I do?" Leah asked when Rebekah had scurried away.

"Help me peel carrots," Charity answered.

Leah started scraping vegetables into the sink. "Ethan looks great," she told Charity quietly. "Thanks for letting us be alone together."

"He's been eager to see you."

Pleased, Leah said, "I wasn't sure. I mean, I know I'm not the ideal girl for him to bring home to Mom and Dad."

"Our family has had English here before."

"Really? Who?"

But Charity clamped her lips together, and bright spots of color appeared on her cheeks. "Forgive me. I should not have spoken of the past."

Leah knew they couldn't talk freely with Charity's mother and oma so close by, but she was puzzled. What did she mean? And why act so secretive about past dinner guests?

In an hour the meal was ready, and Mrs. Longacre stepped out on the porch and clanged a large bell. "Calling the men in from the fields," Charity explained.

When the men arrived, Charity introduced her family. "You remember Papa and Ethan. And this is my grandfather, Opa, and my brother Simeon."

Leah smiled at the Amish men without meeting Ethan's eyes. Mr. Longacre welcomed her, but his greeting seemed stiff and formal.

In the dining room a long table with straight-backed chairs took up most of the floor space. No pictures hung on the walls, no rug covered the hardwood floor. A pull-down shade was the only decoration on the window. Serving dishes, heaped with food, garnished the bare tabletop. Mrs. Longacre hung an oil lamp from a low ceiling hook over the table and lit it with a long match.

Mr. Longacre took his seat at the head of the table, and the other men sat to his right in descending order of age. Mrs. Longacre took a chair on his left, and then the girls sat, with Leah between Charity and Elizabeth. Baby Nathan's high chair was wedged between the parents. Leah tried not to fidget.

"We shall thank God," Mr. Longacre said.

The blessing was brief and spoken in both German and English. The men passed the bowls among themselves first, then to the women. *No "ladies first" rules here,* Leah thought. The meal was quiet, the only sounds being those of bowls scraping against wood and utensils striking plates. When a bowl was emptied, Charity or Elizabeth, taking turns, went to the kitchen and refilled it. Leah thought the food was good, but she was too nervous to really enjoy the meal. She sensed tension in the room and wondered if her presence was the cause of it.

"Bud threw a shoe this afternoon," Opa said at one point.

"He'll have to be taken to the blacksmith," Mr. Longacre said.

"I can take him tomorrow," Ethan said.

"You have other tasks," his father replied.

"I will take the horse," Ethan said, surprising Leah. His tone almost sounded defiant—not at all Amish.

Ethan's father gave Ethan a hard look. The grandfather said, "Let him take the horse, Jacob. It is his choice."

Mr. Longacre gave an imperceptible nod, and although Leah knew something out of the ordinary had occurred, she didn't have a clue what it was. Her stomach continued to tighten, and by the time the meal was over and the table cleared, she wanted to jump out of her skin.

When the women began cleaning up and the men retired to the barn, Leah followed Charity out into the yard. Night had fallen, and without a porch light, Leah could hardly see two feet in front of her. Charity began to fill a large pot with water from the outside pump.

Leah caught her friend's arm. "Something's wrong, isn't it? Please tell me, Charity. What have I done to offend your family?"

THREE

Charity set the pot down. "Whatever do you mean?"

"I could tell something was wrong tonight," Leah said in a rush. "Everyone hardly said a word at the dinner table."

"Oh, Leah, forgive me. I forget you are not accustomed to our ways."

"No, I'm not," Leah said, quietly. "And now I feel the differences more than ever. I'm English. Your family dislikes me. Maybe I'd better just go away."

"Do not say such a thing. My family *does* like you. You were so kind to Rebekah in the hospital. We will never forget that." Charity took Leah's hands in the dark. "Let me try to explain things to you. It is true we do not talk much at meals. For us, mealtime is not a time for idle chatter. It is a time to reflect on God's bounty and generosity to us."

"Your father and Ethan talked. And they didn't exactly sound happy, either. What's the big deal about taking a horse to get a shoe?"

Charity dropped Leah's hands. "Walk with me," she said.

Leah went with her to the edge of the yard, where the light from the kitchen windows dropped off. An old wagon wheel had been propped against a large rock and a flower bed had been planted around it. The sound of chirping crickets broke the stillness, and fireflies flickered in the darkness.

"Family is very important to us Amish," Charity said.

Family was important to Leah too. All her life she had wanted to belong to a family—a real family, not the kind her mother kept manufacturing. Her mother couldn't make any marriage work. She kept getting divorced, and she and Leah kept moving from place to place. Leah had never known her real father, and she had seen her beloved grandmother—also someone her mother didn't get along with—die of cancer. Leah still felt keenly the loss of her grandmother, her father, and the family life she'd never known. "I can see how close your family is," she said, "but I know there was something going on tonight between Ethan and your father. Is it me? Tell me the truth."

Charity didn't answer right away, and when she did speak, her words were halting, as if her thoughts were difficult to express. "Among us Amish, no man is baptized until he knows he wants to accept our ways and live according to all Amish traditions. After baptism, he becomes a church member. He marries and works. He obeys the church elders and lives simply."

Confused, Leah asked, "Why are you telling me this?"

"Because Ethan is not yet baptized."

"What does that mean?"

"It means that he still has freedom to choose what he wants to do with his life," Charity said quietly.

"What kind of freedom?" This news surprised Leah, for she had assumed that the Amish way of life was ordained from birth.

"When an Amish boy turns sixteen, he is free to experiment with worldly things. It is called *rumspringa*— 'taking a fling.' All our fathers have done so, and they give their sons much leeway. Boys are exempt from chores and even church on Sundays. They are allowed to stay out all night on weekends with other Amish teens at parties and dances. Parents don't forbid this kind of thing because the Bible teaches that forbidden fruit becomes more appealing. Amish parents hope that if they look the other way, then their boy will eventually grow tired of the pleasures of the world and come back to simple ways. Most of them do."

Leah asked, "What about you girls? Do you 'experiment' too?"

"Yes."

"Have you?"

Charity was quiet, and Leah wondered if she'd pushed her friend too far. She'd already heard more than she'd bargained for. Finally Charity said, "I have played with my hairstyle. And put on makeup and worn English clothes. I—I have allowed a boy to kiss me."

Leah almost smiled. She'd been doing these things for years. But she could see that for Charity, such actions could be daring. "I'd like to hear about your boyfriend."

"You will not tease me?"

"Why would I tease you?"

"It is—" Charity stopped, then started again. "Sometimes teasing is done among us. I do like it. Ethan does not like it, but it is the way of our community. Others think it is funny to tease. That is why we keep our feelings inside. That is why we hide the things we do from others' eyes—even from our family. Especially when it comes to having a boyfriend or girlfriend. When a boy invites a girl to ride home in his buggy from Sunday-night singing, he is careful to conceal it from his friends, because they will tease him."

The implications of Ethan's asking Martha to ride in his buggy took on new meaning to Leah. If he would risk being teased by his friends and family, then he must truly care about Martha. Leah felt jealous of an Amish girl she'd never met or even laid eyes on. "And so, is

Ethan starting to experiment? To test? Is that why your father sounded cross with him?"

"Ethan is testing, yes. But he does not tell me much. He keeps to himself, and none of us knows what he's doing. Or thinking." There was hurt in her voice.

"But Ethan is seventeen, and when we met in the hospital, he didn't seem to be experimenting." Leah had trouble accepting what Charity was telling her because it went against everything she'd come to believe about the Amish. *All-night parties? No church attendance?*

"There were reasons why Ethan chose not to begin at sixteen, but I cannot speak of them."

That bothered Leah, but she couldn't force Charity to tell her. Instead she asked, "What other things do Amish boys do when they're taking their flings?"

"Some get fancy buggies. They buy radios and CD players. Some get driver's licenses and some even own cars. More liberal Amish parents allow the cars to be parked behind their barns."

"And these parents just pretend not to see it?" Leah was amazed. "What else?"

"They wear worldly clothing. Drink alcohol. Smoke," Charity answered, sounding uncomfortable. "Other worldly vices."

Like trying out worldly girls? The light of understanding turned on in Leah's head. She could be nothing more than an experiment to Ethan. She could be just a diversion in his fling-taking. She swallowed hard. "How about drugs?" she asked, embarrassed to let Charity know what she was thinking.

"Never. Well . . . I've never heard of anyone around here trying drugs. Boys are still expected to work on the farm or to take a respectable job in town or at a factory. They still live at home, and when at home they must be part of the family."

"How long do they get to experiment?" Leah kept her tone calm. Inside, she was still reeling.

"Until they decide to be baptized. Or leave the community."

Leah saw that Amish boys were no different than other boys she'd known. She felt disappointed.

As if sensing her disillusionment, Charity said, "Amish people are not perfect, Leah. We separate ourselves from the world, but what is easier? Giving up something you've never done, or choosing to live plainly *after* you have tried the English way of life? What good is a sacrifice if it isn't truly a sacrifice?"

The screen door opened and Charity's mother called for her to come inside.

Feeling guilty for keeping Charity talking instead of doing her chores, Leah said, "I guess I should be going."

"Since tomorrow is Saturday, we have many preparations to make for Sunday," Charity explained. "We don't work on the Sabbath, so everything must be done ahead of time. Tomorrow, I will make bread and rolls for Sunday dinner."

Leah realized that Charity wasn't inviting her to join them. "I start work Monday, and I have lots to do before then," she said, knowing it wasn't the truth. She had nothing to do.

Quickly Charity glanced over her shoulder. "Why don't you come to our Sunday-night barn dance? Amish kids will be there from all over. You can meet them."

"But I'm English."

"You will be welcomed because you are with us. We will ride together in Ethan's buggy. We will have a good time."

Leah wasn't sure she should tag along. But Charity's invitation sounded sincere. "Well . . . maybe . . ."

"Come to the house Sunday around six o'clock," Charity said hurriedly. "I must go inside now."

"Tell your Mom thanks for dinner," Leah called as Charity returned to the house. She stood in the yard for a few minutes, feeling alone, and wondering if she'd done the right thing by coming to Nappanee for the summer. She couldn't stand the thought that her mother might have been right.

And now that Charity had explained about fling-taking, Leah was more confused than ever. Had all that she and Ethan shared in the hospital been part of some lifestyle experiment?

Leah went to her car. The brightness of her head-lights made her squint. She turned toward the road, look-ing back only once. In an upstairs window, she saw a curtain move. In the window, backlit by a flickering lamp, Ethan stood peering out at her. Her heart ached. She gunned the engine and the tires spit gravel as she left the old road for the highway.

A phone call from her mother and Neil to say goodbye before they took off woke Leah on Saturday morning. After hanging up, she realized she'd never gone to the grocery store and didn't have a thing in the house to eat. She showered, dressed in jeans, grabbed her car keys and headed for the closest fast-food restaurant. After eating, she drove slowly around the town that was to be her home for the next three months. Heads turned at the sight of her bright red car and made her feel self-conscious.

She saw Amish buggies in parking lots and in front of stores. They looked strange, dark and antiquated, amid all the modern cars and pickup trucks. The horses seemed unfazed by the noise of traffic. She pulled along-side a buggy at a traffic light, and the horse never gave her a glance. "Want to race?" she asked the uninterested animal.

Leah shopped for groceries, put the sacks in the backseat and headed to her apartment. Just as she pulled into an intersection, from out of nowhere, a boy wearing in-line skates zipped in front of her car. She hit the brakes hard. He threw his hands against her fender, careened backward, and landed hard on the asphalt.

Heart pounding, Leah cried out, turned off the engine and jumped from the car. "Are you all right?" She hurried to where the boy sat dazed on the ground. When she got to him, she gasped. Her car had just struck Simeon Longacre.

FOUR

"Simeon! Oh my gosh! Are you hurt?"

He reached for his broad-brimmed straw hat, which had been knocked off. "I am all right," he told her. But Leah saw that the palms of his hands were scraped and bleeding. His pant leg was torn.

Leah was shaking. "I'll take you to a doctor."

"No. I am fine. Please, do not worry about me." He struggled to his feet shakily, and she reached out to steady him.

"What are you doing out here anyway? And on skates?"

"I deliver small packages from the pharmacy on Saturdays to people who are shut-ins. Ethan brings me into town."

"Let me take you to get checked over. Please."

"No, I am fine, really. I have fallen before." He

examined his skates. "I think they are undamaged." He started to push away from Leah. She caught his elbow.

"No you don't. In the car."

"I am fine. I can manage."

"No way. Where's Ethan?"

"At the blacksmith's."

"Tell me how to get there."

As she followed Simeon's directions, Leah fought to calm herself. What if she'd run over Simeon? *That* would certainly ice it with Ethan and his family! She glanced at Ethan's kid brother. "I didn't know Amish could own skates," she said above the drone of engine.

"They are allowed," Simeon said, poking curiously at the buttons on her dashboard. "Roller skates and ice skates have always been allowed. But these are the best because they are both."

"You know, maybe you should wear a helmet. Knee pads, elbow and wrist pads might not be a bad idea either," Leah said. "It's so much safer."

"Those things are showy. Not for plain people."

Leah was amazed by Simeon's logic, but she didn't argue with him.

Leah drove to the outskirts of town, turned onto a paved country road and followed it until Simeon pointed to an old barn set back from the road. She turned into a rutted driveway that led to the barn. An unhitched black buggy stood in front. From inside, she heard the sound of metal hitting metal. She saw Ethan holding the rope halter of a large draft horse while a man hammered an iron horseshoe on an anvil. An open furnace glowed red.

Ethan looked shocked as Leah and Simeon entered the barn. "What is wrong, Simeon?"

"We ran into each other," Leah said. "Literally."

The blacksmith nodded a greeting but didn't stop his work. Leah saw that he was Amish by his beard—full on his chin but with no mustache.

Briefly Simeon told Ethan what had happened. "Are you hurt?" Ethan asked his brother.

"No. And I have other errands to run for Mr. Fowler."

Ethan looked anxious, glancing back to the black-smith. "Um—I will be finished here shortly and can give you a ride back into town."

"I can give him a ride," Leah said. "Come if you want. I'll bring you back."

"I do not want to cause a burden for you."

"I offered, didn't I?"

Persuaded, Ethan helped his brother into the back-seat and got into the front. Soon they were speeding down the road, radio blaring and wind whipping. Leah cut her eyes to Ethan, saw a look of pure exhilaration on his face and thought, *He likes cars*.

When they arrived at Simeon's place of employment,

Ethan held the seat forward as his brother climbed out of the car. "I will return for you at four o'clock in the buggy."

Simeon thanked Leah, then skated around the side of the building.

"Simeon could have been badly hurt today when he fell," Leah said, checking traffic in her rearview mirror. "When I asked him about safety gear, he said you Amish consider it fancy. Is that true?"

"Some bishops do not allow their people to use in-line skates at all. We are fortunate that ours is more liberal."

"Do you skate?"

"Yes. And you?"

"Sure. Maybe we could skate together sometime."

"I would like that, Leah."

The way he said her name made goose bumps break out on her arms. What was it about him that affected her so? Why was she attracted to him when they had so little in common? On impulse, she asked, "Would you like to see where I live? My apartment isn't far from here. What am I saying? Nothing in this town is far from here."

He laughed. "The town is small, but still too big for many Amish. Too many tourists. They are always following us, taking pictures. It is annoying."

She knew that the Amish didn't like having their

photographs taken. She wondered if Ethan still kept the one of her she'd given him in December. "I'm a tourist. Do I annoy you?"

"Oh, Leah, I am sorry. Not you. You are not annoying."

He sounded so stricken that she had to laugh. "I accept your apology."

"Yes," he said suddenly. "Yes, I would like to see where you live, very much."

She drove the couple of miles to her apartment, unlocked the door and flung it open. "Ta-da. Home."

He entered slowly, carrying the two bags of groceries she'd all but forgotten about. Many of her things were still in boxes, but the sofa was uncluttered. "Would you like something to drink?"

He nodded, setting the bags on the countertop that divided the living room from the tiny kitchen. She rummaged to find the soft drinks she'd bought. He asked, "May I look around?"

"Bathroom's that way, the bedroom beyond it. Excuse the mess." She put ice into paper cups while he explored. With a start, she remembered that her lingerie was lying all over the floor. And when Ethan returned to the kitchen area, the redness of his face told her he'd seen every filmy, lacy piece of it. She decided not to mention her unmentionables. "So, what do you think?"

"I think you are very fortunate to have such a place for your own."

"Even though it has electricity?"

"And running water too."

She smiled and handed him a cup. "I don't know how you Amish live without such stuff. I don't think I could."

"Charity tells me you will come to our barn dance tomorrow night." He changed the subject.

"Do you mind?"

"I would like it very much."

The intensity of his gaze again raised gooseflesh along her arms. "Charity says we'll ride over in your buggy."

"It is best not to take your car."

"Because I'm an outsider? That won't change whether or not I drive, you know."

"You will meet many tomorrow night who dress as you do, talk as you do, go to English schools and have many English ways. Do not concern yourself with your differences."

"But these different ones, are they still Amish?"

"Some are from less strict districts of Amish, but yes. The important thing is getting together, having a good time."

"Will your friend Martha be there?" She hated to ask, but she had to know.

"Yes," he said simply.

"I don't want people staring at me all night. They won't, will they?"

"If they do, it is only because you are so pretty."

"I'm just me," she said. "And to be serious, I'm not sure where I fit in in this world of yours."

"I do not know either. Yet you are here."

Leah stared into the cola-colored depths of her cup. Since her stay in the hospital, she had become fascinated by the Amish lifestyle. Not that she ever wanted to live without electricity and running water. But there was something appealing about the simplicity of it. "I'm looking into my future and can't see where I'm going. I graduate next year, and I don't know if I want to go on to college. My grades are so-so, but I could probably get in if I work hard next year. But that's the problem. I don't know what I want." She turned toward him on the sofa. "You're lucky in some ways. You know what you want. You know what's in store for you."

He studied her intently before saying, "You are wrong, Leah. I do not know what I want."

She blurted out, "But you're Amish. You told me you like being Amish."

"That does not mean that I don't want to try out English things."

Her heart began to hammer. "What things?"

"Things that make me hungry for what is not Amish."

Leah's chest felt tight. "What does your family think about your trying these things?"

"I have kept them a secret," he confessed reluctantly.

"But why? Charity told me that parents expect their kids to experiment."

His cheeks flushed. "I did not want to bring shame upon my father."

"When we met in December, you hadn't tried anything English. I remember the video games and the candy bars." She wanted to add *"and our kiss,"* but lacked the courage. "Why start now?"

"Things have changed since December. Please, I cannot talk about my reasons for deciding not to join in with the others until now."

Leah didn't press him. "So what things have you done?"

He reached out and stroked her face with his fingertips. His skin felt rough against her smooth, soft cheek. "I have met you."

She swallowed hard, feeling as nervous as she had when she was thirteen, the very first time she was about to be kissed. But she wasn't thirteen. And she had been kissed many times. She squared her chin, determined to tell him what she was feeling. "I don't want to be some kind of experiment, Ethan."

"I do not understand."

"I don't want to be some experience you're dying to

have. You know—smoke behind the barn, drink beer, date an English girl."

Ethan looked shocked. "I am not this way, Leah. Yes, I have tried out some of the things you've said. All these things are frowned upon by my family. But I have never been with a girl I did not choose to be with. And since I met you last December, there is no other girl that I want as much as I want you."

The thudding of her heart made her hands tremble. He was telling her things she wanted to hear, but she wasn't about to jump in headfirst. She didn't want to embarrass herself and say or do things that she might regret later. She and Ethan were as different as day and night. Their attraction for one another was real, but she couldn't hang her heart on an attraction. "This scares me, Ethan."

"I am scared too. But not enough to go away unless you tell me I must."

"I—I can't." She stared down at her hands.

"Then I would like to see you as much as I can while you are here this summer. Is this all right with you?"

It was more than all right, but the knowledge didn't make her feel carefree and lighthearted. The knowledge was heavy, weighted with an understanding: Ethan was special. If she gave him her heart, he would treasure it. And if he gave her *his* heart— She cut off her train of thought abruptly. "We have a whole summer," she said cautiously. "I'll be with you as much as you want. And when the summer's over, we'll decide where we go from here."

He raised her chin with his finger and peered into her eyes. His gaze pierced, but it held only honesty and trust. "Yes. This is what I want too." Then he brushed his lips softly over hers.

FIVE

When Leah returned from taking Ethan back to the blacksmith's, she busied herself with unpacking her remaining boxes and putting her rooms in order. Still, by Sunday evening, she was a bundle of nerves. She kept remembering their conversation. She kept seeing Ethan's face and hearing his voice. There had been times in her life when, once a guy showed an interest in her, she would drop him because the thrill had been only in the chase. It wasn't that way with Ethan. He was special to her in ways she didn't even understand.

When Leah arrived at the farm, she hugged Rebekah and then climbed into the small, enclosed black buggy with Charity and Ethan. She was careful not to sit too close to Ethan, careful to talk mostly to Charity while they were in the yard and in sight of Mrs. Longacre. Leah saw concern etched in the woman's face and figured

Tillie Longacre didn't approve of the attachment of any of her children to Leah.

Ethan clicked with his tongue and slapped the reins against the horse's rounded rump, and the buggy headed for the gravel road. "The barn dance is at the Yoder farm, a few miles from here," he explained. "It will not take long to get there."

Sandwiched between Charity and Ethan, Leah felt like an oddity. They were dressed in Amish style, plainly. She'd chosen a long denim skirt and a solid white T-shirt and had worn only blusher and pale pink lipstick, but, compared to them, she thought she looked overdone. "I've never ridden in a buggy before," she said, making conversation.

"It is not fast like your car," Ethan said.

"Slow is good sometimes."

Charity asked, "Will you take me for a ride in your car as you have my brothers?"

"Whenever you want."

"I will have to come into town with Ethan for such a ride. My papa would not approve."

Leah didn't like being cast in the role of perpetually bad influence, but she hated to tell Charity no. Glancing at Ethan, she said, "I'd like to see those woods where your father cut the Christmas tree for our hospital floor."

"I will show the woods to you."

Darkness fell and Leah watched the stars come out.

Eventually Ethan turned the buggy down a side road and Leah saw a farmhouse and a barn off in the distance, windows aglow with electric lights. "Is this an Amish farm? I see lights."

"The Yoders are not as strict as Papa," Charity said. "That is why so many like to gather here."

The barn was surrounded by buggies as well as automobiles. Music spilled from an open door. Ethan pulled back on the reins. The buggy lurched to a halt. He hopped out, tied the horse to a railing and came around to help his sister down. Then he reached up to help Leah. She stood, and the buggy swayed. "I'm not used to floors that keep moving after the vehicle stops," she said with a nervous laugh. The horse shifted, and Ethan's strong hands gripped her waist. He lifted her as effortlessly as if she'd been a doll. She stood on the ground facing him, his hands still encircling her waist, and for a moment she could scarcely catch her breath. He smelled fresh and clean, like soap. He'd left his hat on the seat, and his homespun shirt was open at the neck, making him look less Amish. *For my sake?* she wondered.

Once inside, Leah tried to ignore all the eyes that stared, the heads that turned. The gathering was large, full of kids in their early teens, dressed in a mix of plain Amish and modern clothing: jeans, denim shirts, khaki slacks and stylish T-shirts. She felt as if she'd stumbled into a stage production where everyone was in costume. The animated conversation from the different groups slowed as people checked her out. Ethan gripped her hand, and he and Charity led her over to a cluster of girls dressed Amish-style.

"This is my friend Leah," Charity explained. "You know, the one I told you about from the hospital."

The girls were polite, but curiosity burned in their eyes. In the background, conversation grew louder and someone put on a CD. Funky music blared from speakers set up in the corner of the barn.

"Come," Ethan said. "We'll get some cookies."

Leah was certain she'd never choke one down, but she went with him to a long table filled with refreshments. From the corner of her eye, she saw a group of boys at the end of the table. Several were holding beer cans. "Are they drinking beer?" she asked.

"Yes. Some of the boys sneak it in sometimes," he said, giving a disapproving look. "But it should not be here." He looked at her. "If you'd like one, I can get it for you. I know they have more outside."

"No way. I hate the taste of the stuff." Leah was surprised to see the boys drinking. "I guess I have a lot to learn about you Amish," Leah said, taking a cup of punch from him.

"Things are not always what they seem, Leah.

Everyone here is free to try the things of the world. But we are still accountable to our families and our traditions."

"So I'm learning." She wondered what was going on inside Ethan, where he fit in in this strange no-man's-land of Amish tradition and English worldliness. She felt a kinship with him. They were both searching for a place where they belonged.

Three of the boys dressed English-style drifted over to them. They stopped in a semi-circle in front of Leah and Ethan. The biggest guy, standing over six feet with hands the size of footballs, spoke to Ethan in German. Ethan answered in German in a tone that sounded sharp. Then Ethan said, "In English, Jonah. Say what you want to say in English."

Jonah acknowledged Leah with his eyes. "It is not common for English to attend our parties," he said. "Especially English that nobody knows."

She squared her chin. "I'm Leah Lewis-Hall, and I'm working and living in Nappanee this summer. I do know some people here. Not you, though. Glad to meet you." She smiled, although her insides quivered like jelly.

"And I am Jonah Dewberry. My sister Martha is over there." He pointed to a row of chairs where several girls sat looking at them. Martha wore jeans, boots, and a blue T-shirt. Her long dark hair hung loose down her back. With dismay, Leah saw that she was quite pretty.

Martha gave a little wave, and Ethan nodded at her, then turned back to Jonah. "Now that we have all met, perhaps you will move out of our way," Ethan said.

Jonah moved aside, and Ethan stepped around him, taking Leah with him. "Ethan," Jonah said, "tell me, do English girls *schnitzel* as well as Amish girls?"

Ethan's face turned bright red. "You must find this out on your own, Jonah," he replied evenly. "If you can find an English girl who will *schnitzel* you."

Jonah's face reddened. He leaned closer. "I have another question. Now that you are dating English, will you become one of us?"

"I am one of you."

"You still dress Amish. You still hold yourself apart. Separate. You are proud."

Leah knew that to call an Amish person proud was an insult, and she could see by the way Ethan stiffened that the remark had hit home. She held her breath.

Ethan turned and looked Jonah directly in the eye. "What I do is my business. Who I decide to be with is my choice. I am leaving with Leah now. Will you take Charity home for me?"

Jonah nodded. "If she will come with me."

"If you ask her, she will go."

Once outside, Leah stopped short. She was glad to be out of the barn, but she felt confused. "Wait a minute, Ethan. I don't get it. At first I thought you and Jonah would come to blows. I mean, most of the guys I know would have been swinging fists at each other by now. It's clear to me that Jonah didn't like you bringing me here. He thinks you should be with his sister."

"I do not care what he thinks." Ethan helped Leah into the buggy and untied his horse from the railing. "Jonah is Amish. I am Amish. Amish do not fight, no matter what. Not even in wars for the country. It is our way."

Leah settled onto the hard buggy seat. "But you were angry with each other."

"That is true."

"So why did you ask him to take Charity home? That doesn't seem like a nice thing to do to her."

"Jonah cares for my sister." He clicked his tongue and the horse went forward. "He would jump at the chance to be with her."

"But what does Charity want? Maybe she didn't want to go home with that—that Neanderthal!"

Ethan chuckled. "Oh, she likes Jonah Dewberry very much. He has taken her home in his buggy many times, but lately he runs with older, wilder boys. Boys who may not return to Amish ways."

Leah sighed in exasperation. The whole thing sounded like a soap opera to her. "Is Jonah her boyfriend? I mean, does *she* like this guy? He seemed very unfriendly."

Ethan slipped his arm around Leah's waist and pulled her closer to him on the buggy seat. "He is jealous because I came with the prettiest girl."

Leah accepted his compliment silently, knowing it wasn't the truth. She'd been around enough to know that the Amish kids weren't going to welcome her into their midst regardless of who had invited her to come along. It might turn out to be a long summer!

Lost in thought, Leah listened to the clopping of the horse's hooves on the roadway and watched the late-rising moon peek from behind a cloud bank. She recognized the Longacre property as the buggy turned onto it and felt a twinge of disappointment. Although the dance had been a flop, she'd hoped that their evening together might have lasted longer.

Ethan didn't drive the buggy to the place where her car was parked. Instead, he took them across a bumpy field toward a wooded area. At the edge of the tree line, he halted the buggy, hopped out and helped Leah down. "Come," he said. "I will show you a place like no other."

She followed him through the woods. A soft summer breeze stirred through scented pine needles, making a whispery, papery sound. They came into a clearing where a giant rock rested on a cushion of leaves and needles. He lifted her up and settled her on top of the boulder.

"This is my favorite place," he said. "Here, I feel

peace. Whenever I am confused or angry, this is where I come."

She turned her face heavenward. A thousand stars twinkled above her. Moonlight bleached the ground snowy white. "It's really beautiful, Ethan. This is where the Christmas tree came from, isn't it?"

"Yes." He stood gazing down at her, his face lit on one side by the silvery moon.

Leah said, "It's more like a church than some churches I've been in. I've been going to a church back home, you know." She wasn't sure why she was telling Ethan this, except that she knew his faith was important to him. "I figure I owe God something, I mean, since my bout with cancer and all." She reached for Ethan's hand and rested it on the knee where her cancer had been discovered. The warmth from his palm spread through the material of her skirt. "I'm glad you were there for me. I'm not sure how I would have made it if it hadn't been for you and Charity."

"Knowing you has been special to me, Leah." He touched her hair.

Her heart skipped a beat. "I'm sorry your friends don't approve of me."

"I do not care what my friends think."

"What did Jonah mean when he said 'schnitzel'? Is it a bad word?"

He chuckled. "It's a made-up word that some Amish

use for 'kissing.' An older Amish girl usually kisses—
schnitzels—a boy when he turns sixteen."

She felt the stirring of jealousy. Had the kiss she
and Ethan shared in the hospital truly been his first? "So
tell me, do I measure up? Do I *schnitzel* as well as an
Amish girl?"

He cupped her face in his rough, work-worn hands.
"I do not know. You are the only girl I have ever kissed."

Her body began to tingle. "It's hard to believe you
weren't kissed before."

"It is the truth." He offered no other explanation.

Leah burned with curiosity to know why not.

"But," he said, "I want very much to kiss you now."

All other thoughts fled her mind. She slid off the
rock to stand facing him. "I would like for you to kiss
me." She raised her arms to encircle his neck.

He pulled her body closer, pressing his hands
against the small of her back. He lowered his mouth to
hers, touching her lips with a velvet softness that left her
dizzy. And longing for more.

SIX

"Hi. I'm Kathy Kelly. You must be Leah." A cute girl with a tangle of brown curly hair grinned at Leah.

Leah returned the smile. "I guess we'll be working together."

The two of them stood in the hallway of the Sunshine Inn Bed and Breakfast, dressed in the shapeless uniforms that Mrs. Stoltz insisted her helpers wear. Kathy said, "This is my second summer working at the inn. I'll only be here through July Fourth weekend, though. Then I'm off to cheerleading camp. How about you? You ever do this kind of work before?"

"No. I worked in a fast-food place when I lived in Dallas."

"Dallas—wow, lucky you. I've been stuck here in Dullsville since my parents moved here when I was in seventh grade. I'm saving for college. How about you?"

"Just living here for the summer."

"You mean you *chose* to spend the summer here?"

"It's a long story." Leah certainly didn't want to go into her life history at the moment.

"You're not Amish, are you?"

Leah shook her head.

"Me either." Kathy rolled her eyes.

"What's wrong with being Amish?"

"Nothing . . . if you like being ignored. I went to school with some of them and they sure keep in their own little circles. Tight as gum stuck to your shoe."

"Do you know the Longacres? I'm kind of a friend of theirs." Leah wanted Kathy to know that she didn't want to hear her trash the Amish.

"Oh, don't get me wrong," Kathy said. "I like a lot of the Amish kids, but no matter what you do, you'll always be an outsider to them. They don't really have much use for us English."

Kathy's words felt like a splash of cold water to Leah. Was she fooling herself about Ethan? The night before, he had kissed her in the moonlight until her blood fairly sizzled and her knees went weak. And he'd told her he would see her every chance he got. Now Kathy's remarks were making her wonder.

Kathy tipped her head and puckered her mouth in thought. "Longacre . . . Let me think."

"Ethan and Charity," Leah supplied.

"I sort of remember Ethan. He was in eighth grade when I started in seventh. He was really cute. But the Amish kids hardly ever stay in school beyond eighth grade, so once they're out of middle school, we don't see much of them. You interested in Ethan?"

"Sort of," Leah said.

"Well, good luck, if you have a thing for him. Really strict Amish parents never let their kids mingle with the likes of us."

Leah felt an enormous letdown. She didn't have time to dwell on it, however, because Mrs. Stoltz dashed out of the kitchen and started issuing orders about the day's work. Soon Leah was up to her elbows in soapy water. She and Kathy changed bed linens, scrubbed bathrooms and washed windows the entire morning. Mrs. Stoltz clucked her tongue over every streak they left behind and every piece of brass that didn't sparkle. She told them that the next day they would have to work faster. When Leah went to her car, she felt ready to collapse from exhaustion.

"The first day's always the hardest," Kathy told her as they stood in the small parking lot adjoining the inn. "And Mrs. Stoltz is pretty nice once she sees that you're trying to do a good job and not goofing off."

Leah rubbed the back of her neck. "Who had time to goof off?"

Kathy laughed. "See you tomorrow. Oh. Here's my phone number if you ever want to do anything on weekends."

Leah took the piece of paper Kathy handed her and got into her car. *Weekends.* She remembered Ethan's promise to spend as much time as he could with her, but after what Kathy had said, Leah wondered if it was going to be possible. Absently she rubbed her knee. It felt sore. Fear jolted her. The soreness was in the same knee where bone cancer had been discovered. *It's nothing,* she told herself. *I just overworked it today.* She threw the car into gear and screeched out of the parking lot.

Because Charity and Ethan had no phone, Leah couldn't call. She had no way of knowing if they missed her or even thought about her. On Friday, she drove to the farm. She had hardly shut off the engine when Rebekah came racing to the car, her long skirt flapping behind her. "Leah! Come quick! I have something to show you."

Leah jogged behind the little girl all the way to the henhouse. Inside the low wooden building, the warm air smelled like chickens and chicken feed. "Wow, this place needs some air freshener," Leah joked. "What's so important?"

Rebekah took her over to a small, wooden, bowl-shaped trough. "Look." The trough was an incubator, and in it eggs were in various stages of hatching. Rebekah scooped up a fuzzy baby chick and handed it to Leah. "Are they not wonderful?"

"He's cute, all right." Leah cradled the soft yellow creature against her cheek. The downy feathers tickled. Below, the others peeped noisily. "So now you have even more chickens to look after."

"Would you like to have one for your very own?" Rebekah asked.

"How can I keep it at my apartment?"

Rebekah thought for a moment. "I will keep it here for you. I will feed it and take care of it. But it will always be yours, Leah. And you can come visit it whenever you like."

Leah's heart melted at the girl's sweet gesture. "Thank you, Rebekah. This is the nicest present anyone has ever given me."

"I told Charity you would like my present. She said she didn't think a grown-up English girl would like a chicken, but I knew you would because you're my friend. You helped me in the hospital, even when no one made you help me."

"Do you remember the hospital?"

"Oh, yes. I remember the shots and the Christmas party and the funny bed that moved up and down." Rebekah giggled. "I liked to push the buttons and make it move."

"Do you remember Gabriella? The nurse who sometimes came to visit us?"

"She was pretty," Rebekah said. "She held my hand when I was scared and when you were asleep."

Leah was glad that someone else had seen the elusive Gabriella. There were times when she wondered if she'd imagined her. "Gabriella helped me too."

"I can't wait to see her again," Rebekah said confidently.

"How do you know you will?"

"She told me so the night before I went home."

Leah figured that Charity and Ethan had not shared with Rebekah Leah's ideas about Gabriella's being an angel. If they had, Rebekah would certainly have mentioned it to Leah by now. "Well, tell her hi from me if you do see her," Leah said. "Where's Charity?"

Rebekah slipped her hand into Leah's. "Everybody's in the kitchen making jelly. We can help."

Leah hesitated. She wasn't sure she'd be wanted, but Rebekah fairly dragged her into the farmhouse kitchen. She found the women in the family hovering over pots boiling on the woodstove. Charity was washing jars in the sink and lining the clean ones up on the countertops and tables. "Leah!" Charity said. "How nice you are here."

Leah shifted from foot to foot self-consciously. Tillie and Oma smiled at her, but she thought the smiles looked stiff. "I'll just stay a minute. You look busy."

"We make jelly a couple of times during the summer. And we put up vegetables from our garden so we'll have plenty to eat during the winter," Charity explained. "Soon Rebekah, Simeon and a few of their friends will set up a roadside stand for the tourists to buy what we don't use."

"I guess I'm used to just going to the grocery store and buying what I want," Leah said. "My mother didn't cook very much when I was growing up because she worked."

Leah saw Charity's mother and Oma exchange glances. She recalled how Charity had spoken about Amish women and their devotion to home and family. "Of course, Mom had to work," Leah added defensively. "Sometimes I'd cook supper. I have my grandmother's favorite recipes. Maybe you could come over sometime and we could bake bread or something."

Charity flashed Leah a big smile. "That would be fun for me."

Charity's mother asked, "Would you like to help us make jelly now, Leah?"

"Sure," Leah said, surprised by the offer. She really wasn't looking forward to going back to her tiny apartment and spending the evening alone. "What should I do?"

Tillie led her over to a large basket of green apples.

"You can peel these. And when we're finished, you can take some jars of jelly home with you."

"Thanks," Leah told her, and set to work, grateful to be busy. Grateful to be a part of the busy household, if only for a few hours.

Leah was putting gasoline in her car later that evening when she encountered Jonah Dewberry filling up a battered green car at the pump in front of her.

"Hello, Leah," he said cordially. "Do you remember me?"

"It's Jonah, isn't it?"

He nodded. "How are you liking your stay?"

"I'm liking it fine, so far."

"I saw your car out at the Longacre farm this afternoon."

"I was visiting." She didn't fully trust Jonah and didn't want to get overly chatty with him.

"Ethan speaks well of you."

"Oh? What does he say?"

"That you are . . . different. Special." But before Leah could feel pleased, Jonah added, "For English."

She stiffened. "I can't help who I am, Jonah."

He pulled the gas nozzle from his car, put it away and screwed on his gas cap. "The elders have a saying that we are taught from the time we are small children. It is, 'If you only date an Amish girl, you can only fall in love with an Amish girl.' "

His rebuke stung. "Do you mean 'Play safe'? Do you always play safe? Don't you do things you're not supposed to do? I thought that was the whole point of taking a fling."

"My family would not approve of all that I do. But I have never brought home an English girl. It is a kind of fire that I know better than to play with. There are many Amish girls to pick from. I know one day I will want to be baptized, and marry, and have a family. Be careful, English, that you do not take my friend where it will be impossible for him to get back home."

Stunned into silence, Leah watched Jonah climb into his car and drive away.

SEVEN

Back home Leah usually slept in on Saturday mornings. But that Saturday, the ringing of her doorbell startled her awake. She grabbed her robe and stumbled to the door, peered through the peephole and saw Ethan standing on her doormat. She unlocked the door and pulled it open. "Well, hello," she said, not hiding her surprise. "I didn't expect you."

He took a step backward. "I am sorry. I have awakened you."

"It's okay. Really. Come in."

"I have come to call on you." He held his straw hat in his hand.

Leah glanced out the door, half expecting to see his buggy down in the parking lot. "How did you get here?"

"I caught a ride with a farmer headed into town."

She rubbed sleep from her eyes. "Give me a few

minutes." She hurried off to make herself more presenta-
ble, returning quickly dressed in jeans and a T-shirt, her
teeth and hair brushed. "You want a soda? I start every
day with one." She felt unnerved. She'd not seen much of
Ethan since their night in the woods in the moonlight.
Suddenly, here he was, acting as if no time had passed.

He followed her into the shoe-box-sized kitchen. "I
came too early. I waited as long as I could, but I wanted
very much to see you. I did not mean to wake you."

She glanced at the clock. It was ten A.M. "What time
do you get up?"

"Five-thirty."

She groaned. "That's indecent. I can hardly get myself to work at seven every morning."

"I would like to call on you tomorrow too," he said.

She took a gulp of soda. "But tomorrow's Sunday.
Don't you have church?"

"I have decided not to go."

The news sobered her. She knew what it meant.
"Your family might not like this decision."

"Papa is not pleased. But he knows it's my right."

"Ethan . . . Are you sure about this?" Her run-in
with Jonah came back to her. She felt guilty. Would
Ethan have made this choice at this time if it hadn't have
been for her?

"I know what I want, Leah."

Momentarily overwhelmed by emotion, she handed

him a soda and walked back to the sofa. She noticed a large bag bearing the name of a department store propped against a cushion. "Yours?" she asked.

"I bought these things last week. May I use one of your rooms?"

"Sure. Use the bathroom."

She waited on the sofa, thoughtfully sipping her soda. She looked up and stared when he emerged. His Amish clothes had been exchanged for jeans and a blue chambray shirt, his wide suspenders for a belt with a shiny silver buckle. "You look great," she told him.

He seemed pleased. "Not Amish?" He sat on the sofa with her, holding his homespun clothing rolled up in a ball on his lap.

"Less Amish."

"How can I look less so?"

She frowned. "Ethan—"

"It is what I want." His eyes, made even bluer by the hue of the shirt, were serious.

She cleared her throat. "You probably need a stylist to cut your hair."

"Ma and Oma have always cut my hair. What should it look like?"

"We can look through some magazines at guys' haircuts. There's got to be a stylist in town who can cut—"

"I cannot!" Ethan interrupted. "Not in Nappanee. It would shame me."

She thought for a moment. "Look, I have to go in for a checkup in Indianapolis at the end of the month. Maybe you could come along and get your hair cut there."

His expression turned to one of concern. "You should not have to go for this checkup alone."

"It's no big deal," Leah said, but deep down she knew it wasn't the truth. She was scared about the checkup. Often her knee throbbed at the end of the work-day. She didn't want bad news from her doctor. And she certainly didn't want to hear it by herself.

Ethan scooted closer. "My haircut is not important. Would you like me to go with you to your appointment?"

"I'll have to go during the week because of testing. What about your farmwork?"

"I wish to be with you, Leah."

"I'm supposed to get a letter telling me when to report, so I'll let you know. Thanks so much, Ethan. It's nice of you to offer." She felt greatly relieved at not having to go by herself. "I plan to see Molly—you remember her, don't you? The nurse who was so nice, whose sister's diary Gabriella helped us find?"

"I remember her."

Leah took the bundle of clothes from his lap, running her palms over the rough weave of the white shirt and black trousers. The pants had no cuffs and only buttons, no zipper because zippers were considered prideful. She wondered if Ethan could put off his Amish upbringing as easily as he had the clothing. She picked up the bag, saw several other shirts and pairs of pants and dumped the old clothes inside. "So," she said, "what would you like to do today?"

"Isn't that a VCR machine?" He pointed to the piece of equipment sitting on the shelf under her TV set.

"Sure is. Neil insisted I have one in case I had nothing to do when I wasn't working."

"Can we rent some movies? I have been with my friends and seen movies before, but now I want to see many more."

"We can go as soon as the video store opens. But first, how about breakfast? I haven't eaten, and if you've been up since five-thirty, you must be hungry."

They went to the closest fast-food restaurant, where Leah ordered a biscuit and a soda and Ethan ordered pancakes, biscuits, eggs, bacon, two cartons of milk and a container of orange juice.

"You're going to eat all that?" she asked when they were settled at a table.

"Isn't it good to eat?"

"Of course, but I'd weigh as much as your horse if I ate like that."

He laughed. "You are prettier than any horse, Leah."

She giggled. "Thanks. I think."

Leah drove with Ethan to the video store after breakfast. Together they pored over the titles. If he picked up one she thought might embarrass them both, she shook her head. Once they returned to her apartment, she made popcorn and popped a video into the machine. They sat on the floor and spent the afternoon nibbling on snacks and watching movies. Leah couldn't decide what was more interesting—watching the movies or watching Ethan watching the movies. He mostly laughed at sight gags and pratfalls, rarely at verbal humor. Sometimes he even asked her what an actor meant in a scene with dialogue. His naïveté and unworldliness amazed her, and even though he'd told her once that he'd tried English things, she began to wonder just how much he'd actually done. Still, it felt good to be with him.

When they had watched three movies in a row, afternoon had turned into evening. Ethan said, "I am hungry. Where shall we go to eat supper?"

"You've been eating all afternoon." Leah felt slightly ill from her pig-out on junk food. "How can you be hungry?"

He shrugged. "It's a mystery, but I am." A grin split his face. "Let us try another place with fast food."

She groaned, but minutes later they were driving down the road in the convertible. "You just like riding in my car," she said above the *whoosh* of the wind.

"I like everything I do with you."

"Tell me, what are your friends doing tonight?"

"The Amish like to go to The Rink. But so do the English. It's a roller rink and game room. Turn right at the next light and I will show you."

She drove into a parking lot filled with cars and Amish buggies. Several of the buggies looked less than plain. They bore tassels and reflective tape cut in fancy designs. The harnesses were studded with ornamentations. Even the horses looked fancy. "Excuse me," Leah said, "but are those Amish buggies, or did space aliens drop into this place?"

"Aliens?" Ethan's brow puckered. "Oh, Leah, you are making a joke. No, the buggies belong to Amish. Some make their buggies fancy. Their parents do not like it, but they do not forbid it. It is our way."

Our way was becoming increasingly peculiar to Leah. What she had once thought taboo for the Amish was considered all right if done at certain times in their lives. Or, at least, parents and elders looked the other way while the kids did it.

Leah heard music blaring from the skating rink. Inside, the old-fashioned wooden floor was crowded with skaters. In an adjoining room, game tables were set in rows and kids were shooting pool. A selection of video games lined one wall. People looked up as Ethan and Leah came in. Leah was given the once-over. A couple of boys had the nerve to wink at her. But if Ethan was uncomfortable, he didn't show it. He walked her over to a table where several couples were shooting pool. "Leah, do you remember my friends from the dance?"

She said she did even though she didn't—except for Jonah and his sister Martha. She remembered *them* very well.

"So, Ethan, you have decided to join us," Jonah said. He eyed Ethan up and down while rubbing chalk onto the tip of his cue.

"I have decided to be with my friends this summer," Ethan said.

"*All* of your friends?" Jonah asked.

"The ones who matter to me," Ethan said.

Leah wondered if Jonah and Ethan could ever be friends.

Martha stepped forward. "We have missed you, Ethan."

Leah felt her cheeks redden. Martha ignored her as if she weren't even standing there.

"Good," Ethan said, slipping his hand into Leah's. "Then you will not mind if my friend Leah joins us at our parties."

Without blinking, Martha said, "Leah is welcome."

But Leah didn't feel welcome. She felt like an intruder.

"Would you like to shoot a game of pool?" Jonah asked.

"No," Ethan said. "We have been watching videos all afternoon on Leah's machine. We came here to eat."

Jonah studied Leah. "Perhaps we can all come over and watch videos sometime."

"Maybe," she said evasively.

Ethan, will Charity ever come to watch videos with you?" Jonah asked.

"If she wishes."

Jonah nodded. "I will ask her."

Leah and Ethan walked over to a booth and ordered a pizza. While they were waiting, Leah said, "I can't figure out what Charity sees in him."

"He is Amish," Ethan said with a shrug.

"There are plenty of Amish guys around. Why him?"

"This you will have to ask my sister. But everybody knows that once Jonah has had his fling, he will return to Amish ways."

She had heard this from Jonah himself. "Do guys ever not return to Amish ways?"

"Yes," he said quietly. Color crept up his neck, and Leah knew there was something he wasn't telling her. But what? She wanted to ask, but she didn't. There was something neither Ethan nor Charity seemed to want to tell her. It maddened her, but she swore she wouldn't pry. If Ethan trusted her, he would tell her. She would wait. If it took all summer, she would wait for him to open his heart totally and tell her the secrets of his soul.

EIGHT

Leah's weekdays fell into a routine. She worked hard alongside Kathy, she returned to her apartment and crashed. She lived for the weekends. Leah had lived in Nappanee over a month when Ethan brought Charity to Leah's apartment. He promptly left so that the girls could visit with one another. "Leah, this is lovely!" Charity exclaimed as she walked from room to room. "So fancy."

"I'm glad you like it."

Leah had seen Charity's room, one she shared with Rebekah. It looked plain, almost austere, with no rugs or curtains. It contained only a double bed and a dresser. The bed was covered with a handmade quilt, a gift from Oma, Charity had explained. Perched on the bed was Rose, Rebekah's Amish doll, dressed in Amish clothing. The dresser held a hurricane lamp and a pitcher and basin used for washing up. There were no pictures or mirrors on the walls. The closet held six solid-colored cotton dresses for each of them. Wall hooks held long aprons and extra caps. Charity had explained that her winter dresses were packed away in a trunk, along with her winter cape. A single cross-stitch sampler of Scripture verse lay on a wooden rocker by the window.

Seeing Charity next to Leah's TV set, stereo, modern appliances and fixtures caused the gap between their lifestyles to stand out more than ever for Leah. By now, Leah was so used to Ethan's dressing English-style—for he never came to see her unless he was wearing his modern clothes—that Charity looked oddly archaic. "Sit. Have a soda," Leah said.

Charity perched on the couch and picked up the small pillow she had embroidered and given to Leah the Christmas before. "You have kept this?"

"It's one of my favorite presents." Leah took the pillow and ran her fingers over the finely stitched letters of her name. "Of course, it's nothing compared to Rebekah's chicken."

Charity laughed. "Leah, you are so funny."

"Do you want to watch TV or something?" Leah wasn't sure how eager Charity was to sample the world. She didn't want to offer her something she didn't feel comfortable doing.

"I do not think so," Charity said, eyeing the TV's

blank screen. "I thought it would be fun to bake bread and cookies. You told me you wanted to do this sometime."

"This could turn into a real adventure."

Charity took inventory of Leah's staples and made a list, and together they went to the grocery store. With Charity in her car, her prayer cap tied securely under her chin so that the wind wouldn't blow it off, Leah was again struck by their differences. She couldn't imagine not being able to drive, to go wherever she pleased, whenever she wanted.

They bought supplies, returned to the apartment and went right to work. First they started the bread. "Because it must rise," Charity explained. Leah watched Charity sprinkle yeast into warm water, and after measuring out a few cups of flour, she eventually ended up with a soft mound of dough. Once it had risen to twice its size, Charity placed the lump on a floured countertop and began to knead it. Watching Charity's quick, sure motions made Leah feel like a klutz. "Now you try it." Charity turned the project over to Leah.

Leah jabbed at the lump. "It feels icky."

"You must work harder. It is dough, not glass."

Leah pounded the lump, and flour puffed into her face and hair. Charity burst into laughter. "You look like a snowman."

Leah giggled too. She folded the dough over and

threw herself into kneading it. As she worked on the bread dough, Charity started making chocolate chip cookies. "Can I ask you something?" Leah said. "I know it's none of my business, but do you like Jonah?"

Charity stopped mixing the cookie dough. "I have ridden home from Sunday singing in his buggy many times."

"How about in his car?"

Color flooded Charity's face. "Do not tell anyone, please."

Taken aback by Charity's reaction, Leah said, "I won't. But what's the big deal? Buggy, car—it's still the same thing: You like Jonah."

"The buggy is acceptable. The car is not."

"You rode in my car."

"Cars are not approved by Papa, but it is better with you than with Jonah."

"He's never . . . you know . . . tried anything with you, has he?"

Charity turned wide, innocent eyes on Leah. "Do you mean, does he get fresh?"

"I guess that's what I mean."

"Jonah respects me. He would not shame me."

"I'm sorry. I didn't mean to embarrass you. It's just that he's acting English and you're still being Amish, so there's a gap between the two of you. I can tell he likes you, but I wondered how you felt. And I know how guys can be. I just don't want to see him take advantage of you." Leah didn't add that she didn't trust him.

"I have not had many experiences with boys, Leah, but Jonah is the boy I care for the most. We meet, but very carefully because my papa doesn't approve. Once Jonah is finished with his fling and returns to Amish life, then Papa will have no problem with our dating."

"When do you see him?"

"He comes to my house late at night when all are asleep. He shines a flashlight on my window. I make certain not to disturb Rebekah, and I go downstairs and meet with him. In the winter, we stay in the kitchen. In the summer, on the porch."

Leah stared openmouthed, unable to imagine sweet, dear Charity sneaking around behind her parents' backs. It seemed so out of character. "Then you've been seeing him for a long time?"

"Over a year."

"Wow, Charity. I never thought . . . I mean, I had no idea."

"We are special to each other. But it is a secret because we don't want to be teased, and because he is not ready yet to join the church."

"Are you telling me that he's the guy you want to marry?"

Charity squared her chin. "I am sixteen now and I

want very much to be married. I want to have my own house, like my sister Sarah. Jonah is a good choice. Once he is baptized, he will ask Papa if he can marry me."

"I had no idea things were that serious between you two." Leah vowed to be nicer to Jonah. "Is this going to happen any time soon?"

Charity laughed. "It may be years before I marry. You must promise to come to my wedding."

"I'll try." Leah thought about her own future— where she was headed and what might be in store for her. Marriage seemed a scary choice. Until now, it hadn't worked for her mother. Leah certainly didn't want five passes at it to get it right for herself.

Charity broke into Leah's thoughts. "Let the bread rise again and help me with the cookies."

The bread looked thoroughly beaten, so Leah wrestled the globby mass into a couple of bread pans and covered it with a cloth as Charity directed. They set it aside again, scooped spoonfuls of the cookie dough onto cookie sheets and set the sheets in the oven. Soon the apartment was filled with the aroma of buttery chocolate.

When it was time to bake the bread, Leah removed the cloth. "Yikes! Look how fat it's gotten. Is it safe?"

"It is perfect. You are a good baker, Leah."

Leah's only memory of baking was from when she was a small child. She and her grandmother Hall had baked and decorated Christmas cookies one rainy afternoon.

The bread was tucked into the oven and the two of them had collapsed on the sofa to chow down on cookies and milk when Ethan returned. "Smells good," he said, glancing from one to the other.

"Want one? Plate's on the counter." Leah pointed.

He stood looking at the mound of dirty bowls, utensils and cookie sheets and at the sticky, floury countertops. He stared hard at both of the girls. "It looks like an explosion has happened. Were you hurt, Leah?"

Leah stood, glanced into a mirror and gasped. Flour streaked her clothing and hair. It was even stuck to her eyelashes. Chocolate smudged her nose. Charity looked neat and clean, without a speck of flour on her skin or dress. The three of them looked at each other. They began to giggle, then to laugh. "I look like I took a flour shower," Leah managed to say, which started them laughing all over again.

Ethan grabbed a sponge. "I will help," he said. He gently lifted Leah's chin and swiped the cool, damp sponge down her cheeks, along her chin and forehead, and then softly across her lips. Her laughter quieted as she gazed up at him. His expression was intense, his touch feather soft. Light from a window across the room slanted through the curtains, casting him in bronze, his hair in gold. Her mouth went suddenly dry. Her pulse pounded in her ears. Every nerve ending in her body tingled. She was only vaguely aware when Charity slipped out of the room. "Thank you for the cleanup," Leah told him.

He dropped the sponge and cradled her face between his palms. "You are welcome, Leah," he answered. "Believe me, it is my pleasure."

She rose on her tiptoes to accept a kiss from his warm, full, honey-colored mouth.

Leah kept postcards from her mother and Neil stuck to her refrigerator with colorful magnets. One had been mailed from the Los Angeles airport, several from Hawaii. Each held detailed descriptions of their vacation. The latest one read:

> Dear Leah,
>
> I wish you could see these islands. I never dreamed there could be so many flowers growing in the wild. Why, there's a garden right outside our bungalow door. By the time you get this, we'll have been on the boat for three days. I hope I don't embarrass Neil and throw up. I've been seasick before and it's no picnic. But I'm so happy! I know your doctor's appointment is coming up soon, so I'll be checking with you about it. I hope you are well and having a

wonderful summer. I love you, Leah. I don't
think I ever told you that enough when you were
growing up. Forgive me my lapse.

Love, Mother

Added was a postscript from Neil sending his
love too.

In the same batch of mail, a letter arrived from Dr.
Thomas, her orthopedic oncologist in Indianapolis,
telling her that her appointment for testing and a
checkup had been scheduled for the following Thursday.

The next day after work, Leah drove out to the farm.
She went directly to the barn, where she thought Ethan
might be working. She found him repairing tools. "What
is it?" he asked when he saw her.

She told him about the upcoming appointment. "Did
you mean what you said about coming with me?"

"I will come."

Just then Mr. Longacre came into the barn. He
stopped short when he saw Leah talking to Ethan. "Good
day." He greeted her without smiling.

"I—I was just leaving," Leah said self-consciously.
No matter how many times she saw Ethan's father, she
never grew accustomed to him. The man was not rude to
her, but she felt his disapproval whenever she came
around. She hurried out of the barn, pausing to catch her

breath and slow her rapid heartbeat. Then she heard Ethan and his father talking in German.

She couldn't understand the words, but their exchange was loud and sounded angry. It ended with the noise of a slammed door. *My fault*, Leah told herself. She hurried to her car before anyone could catch her eavesdropping and sped away.

NINE

It rained the day Leah drove the hundred and twenty miles to Indianapolis. But she couldn't have cared less. With Ethan riding beside her, the day didn't seem one bit gloomy.

As she sped along the freeway, Ethan asked, "Are you nervous about the testing?"

"A little. I wish it was over. I hate hospitals. Don't you?"

"I'm not so sure. The only time I've been in one, I met you. This does not seem like such a bad thing to me. Without the hospital, how would we have ever known one another?"

He had a point there. "Okay, so I won't hate them so much anymore."

He watched as she passed a semitrailer. "You drive well."

"I like to drive. Honestly, if you ever want to get your license, I'll let you use my car to take the test."

"Papa would never approve."

To Leah, it seemed that there was very little Jacob Longacre approved of. "Jonah drives."

"I am not Jonah." He reached over and turned on the car radio, listening intently to several stations before settling on one that played country music.

"You rebel, but you don't really do anything too far out in left field," Leah said, shaking her head. "I don't understand you, Ethan. Why don't you go all the way? Like Jonah does?"

"I cannot," he said, turning his attention to the countryside passing outside the window.

Leah realized he was closing the subject. She warned herself not to pry. He would always be an enigma to her. In English clothes, he appeared to be a regular guy. But she knew her world was still foreign to him, and despite his testing of the English lifestyle, he was Amish at his core.

Once they arrived at the hospital, Leah went to the X-ray department, filled out paperwork, and sat with Ethan in the adjacent waiting room. She was scheduled for both bone scans and MRIs of her leg and hand. Since the original X rays had shown that cancer had eaten away bones in these places, these were the areas the doctors were most concerned with. "The doctors make me feel like I'm parts of a puzzle," she told Ethan while they waited for her name to be called. "Like these few pieces of me are all that matter. Sometimes a doctor hardly even looks at my face. He just stares at my knee and finger as if they're separated from the rest of my body."

"But your face is so pretty. How could he not stare at you?"

Ethan always said things that touched her. She gave him a smile. "Have I ever told you how much I appreciate you?"

When it was Leah's turn, she squeezed Ethan's hand, took a deep breath and followed the technician into the X-ray room. The procedures took about an hour, and when both were over, she and Ethan went to another lab, where she filled out more paperwork and waited to have her blood drawn. "This is my least favorite part," she told Ethan. "During my chemo treatments, they were always sticking needles in me and testing my blood. I think they wanted to see if the chemo was helping me or killing me."

He looked alarmed. "The chemo could have harmed you?"

Hastily she added, "It's all right. Sometimes you have to take a little poison and kill off good cells along with the bad ones. The important thing is killing off the bad guys."

He seemed to understand her point. "In farming, it is

the same. Some of the chemicals used to kill insects and blight can be harmful to healthy things. Once Rebekah's chickens got into rat poison and several died."

"I'll bet it broke her heart. I know how much she cares about those chickens."

"She never knew. When I found the dead ones, I quickly took them away, went to a neighbor's, and bought others to replace them."

Ethan's confession endeared him to Leah even more. Who else would have tried to protect his sister's sensitive heart so discreetly? "I think that was sweet and caring." To prove it, she kissed him on the cheek.

He pulled back, his eyes twinkling. "If I am to get such a reward for substituting chickens, I will tell you about every good deed I do."

"Don't push your luck."

"I probably did her no favor," he added thoughtfully.

"Why's that?"

"Death is part of the cycle of life, Leah. We learn that lesson very early on a farm. We see it in the changing of the seasons. We see it in the birthing of new calves. Only the strongest ones survive. We help all we can, but if it is too much expense, it is better to let the weak ones die."

His point of view surprised her. "You mean you allow money to decide whether or not a calf lives? That sounds kind of cruel."

"Feed is expensive, and a farm must be productive. It is the way of things."

"Good thing you don't feel that way about people."

"People are different. People have souls. Animals do not."

Leah thought about her dead father and grandmother. She still missed them and hoped their souls had found peace after death.

Once her testing was complete, Leah returned with Ethan to the floor where she'd spent so many days just before Christmas. As they rode the elevator up, Ethan asked, "Why do you want to visit this place? It is depressing you."

She wasn't sure herself. "I'll never really understand what happened to me here, Ethan. But *something* happened. I think I'm still trying to sort it all out."

"You had an extraordinary experience, that's for sure," Ethan told her. "But perhaps it is better not to think upon it too much."

Leah knew he was right, but she couldn't help herself. The days and nights she'd spent there; the fear she'd felt; the mysterious appearances by Gabriella, whom Leah had assumed was a nurse but who wasn't; finding the diary of Molly's dead sister—all came back to her in a rush. She couldn't let go of any part of the experience.

Leah and Ethan got off the elevator and went to the

nurses' station. Nobody behind the desk looked familiar. She asked one of the nurses, "Is Molly Thrasher
working today?"

"Molly's taking a patient down to the lab," the
nurse explained.

"We must have just missed her down there," Leah
told Ethan. Then she said to the nurse, "Would you
please tell her that Leah Lewis-Hall is here and that I'll
be in the rec room for the next thirty minutes?"

Leah and Ethan walked down the hallway, stopping
at the door of the room she and Rebekah had shared.
Two young patients were in the beds, each watching TV.
The room looked smaller than she remembered. She had
no desire to go inside.

In the recreation room, in the corner where the magnificent tree had stood, children's artwork was taped to
the wall. "I loved that Christmas tree your father
brought," Leah said. "It was the prettiest tree I ever
saw. When I couldn't sleep at night, I'd come down here
just to look at it. And I'd imagine the woods where it
came from."

"And now you have seen the woods with your
own eyes."

"With you," she said, the memory of that night with
him still bright.

Ethan slid his arm around her waist, and she

snuggled against his side. "This seems a good time to ask you," he said. "My friends are having a party on the Fourth of July. Will you go with me?"

"Do you think it's a good idea? They tell me I'm welcome, but sometimes I'm not so sure."

"They do not know you as well as I," Ethan said.

And they don't want to, either, Leah thought. She would always be English in their eyes. And she'd never forgotten what Kathy had told her that first day at work about the Amish sticking with their own kind. She said, "Tell me about the party."

"We will go to the county fair. After the late fireworks, there will be a camping party on the Yoder farm property. I would like to have you with me."

"Camping? You mean, like staying in tents outside all night?"

"The summer nights are warm. We will only use sleeping bags. It is something the group does every year. Even my father and his friends did it when they were growing up. I have not gone before, but this year I would like to go. But only if you will come with me."

"I'm having trouble imagining your father taking a fling," Leah said seriously.

"He is not such a stern man, Leah. But he does not bend easily. My father is an elder in the church and feels he must set an example for others."

"If you say so. Will Charity be at the campout?"

"Only if I go."

"So, in other words, if I don't go, neither of you will go." The invitation didn't seem as appealing cast in that light.

"I would not want to go if you do not come," he said. "Being with you is more important than being with my friends."

Now Leah felt she would be acting petty to care whether the others liked her or not. The important person was Ethan, and he wanted her with him. "I'd like to go," she told him. "I've never camped before, but I'd like to be with you too."

"Then it is settled. We will go to the fair on the Fourth of July, watch the fireworks, and spend the night camping with the others."

She gave him a smile that she hoped conveyed more enthusiasm than she felt.

Leah urged Ethan into the patient library that adjoined the rec room. It hadn't changed much. The books looked more dog-eared than ever, and someone had left the card catalog drawer open. She closed it and went to the shelf where she and Ethan had discovered Emily's diary.

She fingered the bindings, half expecting to see some reminder of Gabriella. There was none. Nothing at all to reflect that strange and wonderful night when the woman had come into her room, talked to her and touched her.

"For a long time, the Gabriella mystery drove me crazy," she said to Ethan, her thoughts turning away from the July Fourth party. "I read everything I could about the supernatural. About ghosts. About angels."

"I do not believe in ghosts," Ethan said. "But I do believe in angels."

"Do you believe that each of us has a special guardian angel?" she asked.

He looked thoughtful. "I am not sure about that. You ask so many questions, Leah. Do you believe in angels or not?"

"I do now," Leah answered emphatically. "Did you know that a lot of people think that when they die they will turn into angels?"

Ethan looked at her and said, "I saw it in a movie, when I first began to try English things. It was a story about a person who dies and comes back as an angel so that he can make up for bad things he did to people while he was alive." He shook his head. "I knew it was not true. People get new bodies in heaven, but they do not turn into angels. Angels are separate beings from people."

Leah continued to tell him what she'd learned in her reading. "I read about people who were miraculously healed. Or rescued. Some unexplainable things have happened to people—like what happened to me."

"Why do you need an explanation? Can't you just

accept the gift you've been given?" Ethan toyed with the ends of her hair, curling long strands around his finger.

"I guess I'll have to. But I still can't help wondering, why me?"

Just then the door opened, and they turned to see Molly.

"How are you?" Molly asked excitedly. "I sort of had a premonition that I'd be seeing you soon." She gave Leah a hug.

"I think I'm doing fine, but Dr. Thomas hasn't checked me over yet."

Molly turned toward Ethan, smiled pleasantly, then asked, "So, Leah, aren't you going to introduce me to your friend?"

TEN

Leah and Ethan exchanged glances. Ethan said, "I am Ethan Longacre."

"I—I didn't recognize you," Molly stammered. "I'm sorry." Leah realized that Molly had never seen Ethan dressed English-style before.

"It is all right," he said. "I guess I do look different to you."

"But very good," she added quickly. "How's your sister Rebekah doing?"

"She is well. Recovered from her spider bite."

"Good. She is such a sweet little girl." Molly looked at Leah. "I'm so glad you stopped by to see me. I've thought of you a hundred times since you were here. Come, sit." They pulled out chairs at the reading table, Molly on one side, Leah and Ethan on the other. "Tell me, what are you doing this summer?"

Leah told Molly about her summer job and living arrangements.

"Your own apartment," Molly said, obviously impressed. "I was twenty-two before I had my own place. Then I got married and had kids, and I may never have the place to myself again."

The three of them laughed. Leah said, "Tell us about Christmas at your parents', and about reading Emily's diary."

"It was a very special time," Molly said, folding her hands on the table. "Imagine hearing someone speak to you from the grave. That's how we all felt as we read Emily's entries. It was as if she were in the room with us, looking over our shoulders. It brought back a hundred memories . . . good memories. She was a wonderful girl who died before she should have. I've been looking into having her diary published." Molly glanced from Ethan to Leah. "I think her insights, her feelings about her cancer and what she was going through, would be a help to kids today."

Leah nodded slowly. "Probably so. I know I sure would have liked to read something by a person my age when I was told I had cancer. You feel so alone. If it hadn't been for you, and Ethan and his sisters, it would have been a whole lot harder."

"Thank you," Molly said. "Medical procedures may change over time, but human emotions don't. Being told you have a disease must be some of the hardest news in the world to hear. Especially when you're young, like Emily was. Her diary was really clear about how isolated and lonely she felt."

"Getting her diary published is a good idea," Ethan said. "I hope you have good luck."

"Thanks. And I haven't forgotten the role that strange woman Gabriella played in all this. I never have been able to figure out how she came to have my sister's diary." Molly leaned back in the chair. "Have you ever seen her again?"

"No. And neither has Rebekah, because I asked her."

"Well, unless she surfaces again, I'll never know. I guess that's not what's important anyway. The fact is, I have Emily's diary. I'll always be grateful for that."

Leah glanced at her watch. "I guess we should be going. I don't want to keep Dr. Thomas waiting."

They stood, and at the door, Leah hugged Molly goodbye. "It was sure nice seeing you again."

"You too," said the nurse. "Anytime you're here, please stop by." She looked at Ethan and said, "That goes for you too. By the way, I like you in those clothes."

Ethan's face reddened, but Leah could tell he was pleased by Molly's comment.

When they reached Dr. Thomas's office, the receptionist ushered them into an exam room. The doctor entered, shook Ethan's hand, then placed the newest set of

Leah's X rays on the light board. He said, "Your X rays look good. Any complaints?"

Leah licked her lips nervously. She told him about how her knee sometimes ached after work. He examined her knee, massaging the kneecap while studying the X rays. "I do see some inflammation."

Leah braced herself for bad news.

Dr. Thomas continued. "Such swelling is common among athletes when they strain their knees or elbows. Have you been bending a lot? Playing a sport before properly warming up?"

She told him about her job.

"That could explain it. I'll give you a cortisone injection at the site. If you keep having trouble, let me know. Take it easy for a few days and give it time to heal, all right?"

"All right." Leah didn't want a shot in her knee, but she'd been afraid it was more serious.

Dr. Thomas left and returned with a syringe. Leah gritted her teeth as he slid the needle into her knee. She saw Ethan turn his head. When the ordeal was over, she asked, "Am I cured? From the cancer, I mean."

Dr. Thomas put his hand on her shoulder. "Now, Leah, you know I can't say this soon after your treatment. You just completed chemo a few months ago."

"But you told me that the dark spots had started to shrink even before I started chemo."

"That is true," Dr. Thomas said. "And I have no medical explanation for it. But cancer is still a mystery in many ways. The more we find out about it, the more we realize we don't know." He removed the X-ray films from the light board. "My job is to keep watch over you. I want to see you again in the fall, so stop at my receptionist's desk and she'll make another appointment for you."

Leah got off the exam table. It wasn't the answer she had wanted, but for now it would have to do.

The doctor smiled. "I think your prognosis is very good, Leah. But remember, with cancer, it's one day at a time."

In the elevator, Leah sagged against the wall. "I'm glad that's over with."

"I can tell you are not happy with his words," Ethan said.

Leah felt tears of frustration building behind her eyes. "I guess I wanted him to tell me I was completely cured and he didn't ever want to see me again. I hate thinking every little ache and pain might be cancer returning."

Ethan ran his knuckles softly along her cheek. "You want to believe in a miracle, but you cannot. But that is what faith is, Leah. Believing in what we cannot see."

She sniffed hard. "You're right. I need more faith. And right this minute, I'm tired of talking about it and thinking about it."

"You were very brave when he gave you the shot,"

Ethan said. "You need a reward. I know, I will buy you supper and a present."

Leah fumbled for a tissue and dabbed at her eyes. "What kind of present?"

"Something to make you happy again. Something to make you smile for me."

They drove to a gigantic mall in one of the city's suburbs. The parking lot was crammed with cars; inside the mall, summer sales were announced by colorful signs decorated in red, white and blue. Flags sprouted out of merchandise displays. Aisles were thick with shoppers. Leah watched Ethan's reaction to the stores, crowds, and noise—a far cry from the sleepy little town of Nappanee.

They walked through the mall, stopping in front of store windows whenever something caught Ethan's eye. "Why are there so many stores selling clothes?" he asked.

"People like to buy clothes. It's fun."

He looked at her blankly. "I see that a person needs summer clothes and clothes for winter, but this is practical. In winter it is cold. In summer, hot. The same clothes will not do for both."

"People like to have clothes for lots of different things." Leah's closet was packed with clothes and she always thought she needed more. She added, "Plus, styles change. You can't wear the same old things year after year."

He made a face. "You are right. That would be horrible."

She punched him playfully.

By now they were walking through one of the better department stores. Ethan stopped short in front of a rack of swimsuits. His eyes grew large as he looked at an assortment of bikinis.

"Something wrong?" Leah asked.

"Do girls wear such things out in public?"

Leah was trying hard not to giggle at the expression on his face. "Only girls with great bodies," she said, holding one up. It was red, speckled with white stars. "Kind of patriotic, don't you think?"

He gulped. His gaze fell on the price tag. "We could feed a dairy cow for months on that much money."

Leah dangled the suit in front of her. "Well, I certainly don't want to cheat a poor cow out of her food."

Ethan's gaze flew to Leah's face. "You would not wear such a thing, would you?"

"There's nothing wrong with wearing a bikini," she said defensively. "And yes, I've worn one. I guess you've never lain on a beach and sunbathed, have you?"

"Is that why girls wear them? To get a suntan?"

Leah started to tell him that bikinis were fashion items in today's world. She also knew that tanning had never been the main reason she and her friends had worn bikinis. Boys noticed them in bikinis. She didn't want to admit that to Ethan. Feeling irritated, she hung the suit back on the rack. "I'm sorry, Ethan. I was teasing you, and I shouldn't have."

He stepped out of the main aisle and the flow of foot traffic. "You do not have to apologize," he said. "And I did not mean to sound so disapproving. But I believe that a woman's body should only be shared with her husband. She should not show it off to other men." He averted his eyes. "And I will also tell you that it bothers me to think that other boys look at your body."

"You're jealous?"

He pondered her question before answering. "No. Jealousy is wrong. It serves no good, so I am not jealous. But it *does* hurt my heart to think about sharing you with others. You are beautiful, Leah. I hope you will not wear bikinis, but I would never tell you what to do."

With his words, Leah felt her irritation dissolve. "I know we're coming from different places, Ethan. And I know it's hard for you to understand this crazy modern world. I guess I don't give much thought to it myself— maybe I should. Just please remember, I really do respect your values. And I don't want you to think badly of me just because we don't see eye to eye on something like clothes."

Ethan raised his eyes, and a smile softened his face. "Many of my friends tell me I am too old-fashioned. I am trying to 'lighten up.' "

"I'll cut you some slack then," she said, taking his hand. "And you needn't worry about me parading around in a bikini. I won't do that either. If I'm going to spend this much money, I'd rather buy something that covers a lot more territory!"

Ethan laughed hard. "Oh, Leah, you are very funny."

It was good to hear him laugh. But Leah felt troubled. No matter how much time they spent together, it still seemed as if they were worlds apart. She had thought that over time, they might grow closer in the way that each of them viewed the world and how to live in it. At the moment, she wasn't sure if that would or could ever happen.

ELEVEN

After grabbing a hamburger in the food court, Leah and Ethan returned to cruising the mall. Ethan stopped in front of a large toy store. "Let's go in here," he said.

Leah hadn't been into a toy store for years, but she found walking through the aisles with Ethan fascinating. His gaze darted everywhere, absorbing the array of toys and playthings like a sponge soaking up water. He stopped by a model train display. He bent down, examining from every angle the perfect replica of an old-fashioned steam engine, tracks, countryside and miniature town.

"Cool, isn't it?" Leah asked.

"Yes," he answered.

"It runs on electricity," she reminded him.

"Why would someone build this?"

"For a hobby, I guess. For fun."

He shook his head. "This person has too much spare time."

Leah didn't want to get into another discussion with him about what was and wasn't practical. She wandered off and started sorting through a table filled with marked-down items. She picked up a bright pink plastic egg left over from the store's Easter merchandise. When she pushed a button on the side of the egg, the top half popped open and a small, fuzzy chick popped up and made a peeping noise.

"Ethan, look." Leah took it over to him for a demonstration. "Isn't this cute? I'd like to buy this for Rebekah. Do you think she'll like it?"

"She has real chickens."

"So what? This is really cute. And girls like cute little things."

"But what is the purpose of this toy?"

"Purpose! Does everything have to have a purpose for you? Can't you—" Leah was just warming up when she realized that he was teasing her. "I should slug you," she said.

He threw up his hands in mock surrender. "I would rather have a kiss."

She stalked to the counter and bought the plastic egg.

Out in the mall again, Leah paused at a store window and pointed. "Here's a hair salon. Were you serious about getting a different haircut?"

Ethan craned his neck to peer past posters for hair products. "I see only women in there."

"The salon is unisex. For both men and women," she explained. "We could talk to a stylist. Look through some books. Then you could decide."

He licked his lips nervously. "No one will laugh at me?"

"No way. It's their business to make people happy with their haircuts."

"We could talk to one . . . ," he said hesitantly.

Leah caught his arm. "It might cost some money. I mean, more than you think it's worth."

"I have money."

"Then let's go talk to them."

An hour later, Ethan's thick blond hair had been washed, cut and dried into a sleek new style. It was still conservative, but it looked modern, not home-done, like his original cut. His expression throughout the process was one of stoic resignation. He never even closed his eyes during the shampoo portion. "Relax," the stylist told him.

But when it was over and he saw himself in the mirror, Leah saw a grin creep out around the corners of his mouth. She thought he'd never looked more handsome, but she knew flattery would only embarrass him. Once they were out in the mall, she said, "I like it. Do you?"

"Yes. But back home, I will be teased by my friends."

"If they don't have anything better to do than tease you about a haircut, then tell them to get a life."

Ethan grinned. "I will tell them."

Leah looked at her watch. "It's almost nine. I think we'd better start back."

In the car, Ethan said, "Today was fun, Leah. I liked being with you. I liked the adventure."

She thought it odd that he'd consider a visit to a hospital and a mall adventurous. Then she reconsidered. He'd probably never spent a whole day doing things that didn't revolve around his family or farmwork. The Amish probably thought that shopping without a specific purpose was frivolous. "Anytime you want another adventure, tell me," Leah said. "I liked being with you today too."

It was after midnight when they turned onto the Longacre property. "Stop the car here," Ethan said. "I will walk the rest of the way to the house."

Leah turned off the engine. "Good thinking. We don't want to wake anybody up." She asked, "You won't get in trouble, will you? With your father, I mean." She hadn't forgotten their raised voices the day she'd stopped by to tell Ethan about her doctor's appointment.

"If you are asking if Papa is angry at me for leaving today, the answer is yes."

Leah winced. "I'm sorry. I didn't mean to make him

mad at you." She played with her fingers in the dark. "I know he doesn't like me."

"That is not true. He has not forgotten your kindness to Rebekah when you were in the hospital together."

"Okay, so he tolerates me. But he doesn't like your hanging around with me."

"He has reasons," Ethan said, not bothering to deny that Leah's observation was correct.

"Such as?"

Ethan didn't answer, and the silence stretched into a long, awkward minute. "I cannot say. But it is not *you* as a person, Leah."

His refusal to tell her was infuriating. Still, she was determined not to nag him. "Look, I know you get up at five-thirty. And I've got to go to work in the morning also."

"Leah, I am not keeping a secret to make you angry, or because I do not care about you," he said, as though sensing her feelings.

"You don't owe me any explanations, Ethan. I am English and you are not. I guess in your father's mind, that's reason enough." She started the engine. "I hope you don't catch too much flak about your hair."

Ethan opened the car door and stepped out into the weak pool of light cast by the car's interior lights. "Wait," he said, before she could pull away. He reached into his shirt pocket and pulled out a small package. "This is for you. I told you I was going to buy you a present."

"When did you buy it? We were together the whole day."

"That is a secret. Open it."

She took a small box from the bag. In the box, nestled in cotton, was a porcelain lop-eared rabbit, not more than a few inches long. It glowed alabaster white in the light from the dashboard. "Oh, Ethan. It's beautiful."

"It is small. It is cute. You said girls like such things."

Leah realized that she couldn't hold a grudge against Ethan. Her annoyance with him evaporated. "You're a very thoughtful, kind person, Ethan. Thank you—not just for the present, but for going with me today. It meant a lot to me."

"You are welcome. You make me happy, Leah. Happier than anything else I have ever known."

Leah watched him walk toward the old farmhouse and back into his Amish world. She drove off, to return to hers.

The next day, Mrs. Stoltz asked Leah to go out to the Longacre farm to buy fresh vegetables for her kitchen. "They have the best in the whole area," she told Leah, "and I know you're friends with them."

Leah figured Kathy must have said something to Mrs. Stoltz about Leah's knowing the Longacres. She was happy to have an excuse to see her friends.

"I like Ethan's haircut," Charity said as she and Leah walked in the garden, picking ripe vegetables. Colorful flowers, used as natural insect repellants, grew between the orderly rows.

"Everyone noticed it then, I guess."

"Yes. It was noticed."

"Did your family approve?"

"Rebekah and I approved."

"But your parents didn't?"

"Not Papa. He told Ethan that he looked fancy."

Knowing her fears had been realized, Leah asked, "What did Ethan say?"

"He told Papa that it was his hair and that he could do with it as he liked."

"You mean they argued about it." Leah couldn't understand what was so bad about Ethan's getting his hair cut differently. He'd done nothing wrong.

"Not an argument," Charity said, answering Leah's question. "Papa does not argue. But you know when he is not pleased."

"I'll bet," Leah muttered. She couldn't accept Mr. Longacre's stern ways.

Charity lifted the stalk of a tomato plant, plucked several rosy red ripe ones, and put them in the basket she carried. "Let's not talk of Ethan's haircut," she said. "Let's talk about the carnival and campout. Ethan says that you will come with us."

"It sounds like fun." Leah hoped she sounded sincere.

"I am excited. It is something we all look forward to while we are growing up. This is my first year to be old enough to go."

"Will you go with Jonah?"

Charity had been pulling green beans from climbing vines. At the mention of Jonah, her hands grew still. "Yes. But no one knows except you."

"Don't you think kids will figure it out when they see the two of you together? Why keep it such a big secret?"

"We go as a group, not as couples," Charity said. "Jonah will be there. I will be there. That is all."

"But you and Jonah know that the two of you are really together, right?"

"That is right."

Leah couldn't fathom this logic, but she knew it was important to Charity to pretend that she and Jonah were just part of the group, nothing more. "I won't tell a soul," she said.

Charity handed the basket to Leah, gathered the corners of her apron to make a bowl, and tossed a handful of green beans into it. "I have a favor to ask of you, Leah."

"Sure. Just name it."

"I want you to help me change my appearance for the campout."

"Like how?"

"I want to dress English for that night."

Warning bells went off in Leah's head. "Why can't the other Amish girls help you?"

"I could ask some of them, but I don't want to. I want you to help me. You are real English. They are not."

"I've seen some of them dressed up, and they look pretty real to me." It wasn't that Leah didn't want to help Charity — she did. It was that she didn't want to get into any more hot water with Mr. Longacre. She was afraid he might forbid Charity and Ethan to see her anymore. Leah knew that would make her miserable.

"Also," Charity continued, "I cannot buy any different clothes. I will have to borrow them. And I have seen how many beautiful clothes you have. I was hoping you would let me borrow some for that night. Because it means so much to me to look pretty."

Leah felt boxed in. But she knew she wouldn't refuse Charity. "Sure. If that's what you want."

Charity's face broke into a bright smile. "Oh, Leah, thank you. I knew you would help me. You are a true friend."

Leah hoped she was doing the right thing. "What if your parents find out?"

"Who would tell them?"

Leah could think of several who might let it slip—not to hurt Charity, but to hurt Leah. Still, she'd already said she would help. "Have Ethan bring you by my place this weekend. We can go through my closet and try on some stuff. See what you like. And what looks good on you."

"Yes. Yes," Charity said. "And makeup too."

Leah took a deep breath. "Sure. And makeup too."

TWELVE

On Saturday, Ethan brought Charity over to Leah's apartment. When Ethan had left to do errands, Leah and Charity sorted through Leah's closet. "I left most of my stuff back home," Leah said, tossing pieces of clothing onto the bed. "And with working every day, shopping hasn't been high on my priority list."

Charity only stared wide-eyed at the heaps of tops, shorts, skirts and slacks.

"Oh, this is cute," Leah said, holding up a colorful striped T-shirt and matching shorts. "Try it on."

"I do not think I would feel comfortable in shorts," Charity said.

"What am I saying? Of course you wouldn't. How about this?" Leah held up a pair of white jeans.

"I don't know." Charity fingered the material.

"Try them on."

Charity slipped into the bathroom to change.

"You look great," Leah said when her friend emerged.

"They are tight."

"But you have a cute figure. They look good on you."

Charity viewed her backside in the full-length mirror hanging on the bedroom door. "This is not the way I wish for everyone to see my bottom."

Leah giggled. "All right. We'll try something else."

Eventually Charity settled on a long, colorful peasant skirt and a cotton top. Leah even owned a pair of sandals that matched the outfit and fit Charity. "This is perfect," Charity said after spinning in front of the mirror.

Leah leaned back on her elbows on the bed. "You look terrific."

Charity's eyes sparkled. "I did not want to wear plain jeans like so many of the other girls will wear. I want to look different. Special."

Leah jumped up. "Time for hair and makeup."

Leah sat Charity on a chair, took down her thick hair from the bun at the nape of her neck and brushed it out. "How about a French braid?" She worked quickly, then tied the end with a red ribbon. Next she artfully applied blush, powder, mascara and pink lip gloss to Charity's smooth skin.

"What do you think?" Leah stepped back and let Charity see herself.

Charity stared at her image. "I can hardly believe it's me."

"It's you, all right."

"My friends won't know me."

"I thought that was the point."

Charity turned to look at Leah. "Will you help me dress on the night of the fair?"

"Sure. Now it's time for you to help me," Leah said. "I don't have a sleeping bag. And I don't know what's expected of me on this campout."

"Ethan and I will bring you a sleeping bag. We own several. As for the party, here's what I know about it. After the fair, we will all ride over to the Yoder farm and build a campfire. Everyone will bring food to cook and share. The sleeping bags are for those who wish to sleep. But few sleep. Most stay up all night."

"What should I cook?"

"I will bring enough for both of us. My sister Sarah has told me that mostly everyone eats, talks, visits. Some will bring radios, so we will dance. In the morning, we will remake the fire and eat again. It will be wonderful fun. You will see."

Leah had attended many sleepovers before, but never a coed one. She thought it ironic that her first all-nighter with guys and girls together would be with the Amish. "You know," she said, "except for you and Ethan, I don't have any friends in your group."

Charity tapped her finger against her chin. "I did not think of that." She flashed Leah an innocent smile. "But once they get to know you, they will like you as much as I do."

Leah didn't want to burst her friend's bubble, but she didn't have any of the confidence Charity did. Charity was too caught up in her own happiness to think about Martha. Leah wasn't. Leah had no illusions that the Amish girls would welcome her with open arms. None at all.

Leah was amazed by the number of tourists who began to pour into town for the July Fourth holiday. They came to Amish Acres, a hundred-year-old Amish homestead where the Amish lifestyle was perfectly preserved. Demonstrations of spinning, weaving and quilting took place daily. There was a large restaurant specializing in simple but abundant Amish cooking, and a gift shop filled with Amish wares that attracted carloads of sight-seers. Charity's oma had several quilts on display in the shop, as well as jars of jelly and pumpkin butter. A unique round, wooden, barnlike theater on the Acres showcased plays several days a week.

The bed-and-breakfast was full, and Leah and Kathy both worked long hours. They were changing beds together one morning when Leah asked, "Is it always like this on holidays?"

"Pretty much," Kathy said. "I'm glad I'm leaving for camp next week."

Leah realized she was going to miss Kathy. Not only because she worked hard, but because Kathy was friendly and talkative. They didn't socialize outside work, but that was because Kathy had a steady boyfriend and Leah spent whatever time she could with Ethan. "How can you go off and leave me?" Leah wailed.

"Mrs. Stoltz will hire someone else, or she already has, I guess. She knew my schedule." Kathy grinned. "And don't forget, you *wanted* to spend the summer here."

"I hadn't expected to be tripping over bodies, though. Tourists are clogging the streets."

"Tourists are a fact of life."

"The Amish don't like them very much. Not that I blame them. Tourists are always in their face, trying to take their pictures when they know the Amish don't like it. Mr. Longacre posted a No Trespassing sign on his property because a carload of tourists drove up to his house one afternoon just to look the place over. They acted insulted when he didn't invite them inside. Can you imagine people being so inconsiderate and insensitive?"

Kathy fluffed two pillows and tossed one to Leah. "Don't feel too sorry for the Amish," she said. "Sure they hate the commotion tourists cause, but they like the extra income they bring in. They tolerate the tourists because it's money in their pockets."

Leah thought Kathy's assessment harsh. She'd seen the large produce stand on the side of the highway, at the edge of the Longacre property, that the Amish community had built. There the abundance of produce, fruit, eggs, jellies, breads and other goods from surrounding Amish farms was sold. The stand was almost overwhelmed with customers. Rebekah was part of the group of younger kids and teenagers who helped out there. "There's nothing wrong with taking advantage of a bad situation," Leah said defensively.

Kathy shrugged. "The one thing the Amish really have to worry about with so many tourists around is getting run over. Those buggies are so slow, and tourists are always plowing into them."

"Really?" Leah herself had gotten stuck in traffic behind a poky Amish buggy, and she remembered Simeon on his skates.

"It happens all the time. Horses and buggies are no match for cars. Someone's always getting maimed. Or worse."

Leah grimaced. "I can see why they hate tourist season."

"One good thing about being Amish, though, is that they take care of their own. Whenever a disaster happens, the whole clan rallies to help out. Farmwork gets done, animals get taken care of—I do admire them for that." Kathy shook out fresh towels for the bathroom.

"But for the most part, I think the Amish are old-fashioned and stubborn. What's the difference between riding in a car and driving one yourself?"

Leah had often thought the same thing, but she didn't want to admit it to Kathy. "Look at the time," she said suddenly. "I told Mrs. Stoltz I'd go buy fresh salad makings for the lunch crowd. I'd better get it done."

Leah drove directly to the Amish produce stand. When she pulled up, Rebekah came running over. "Leah, I've sold six dozen eggs today," the little girl said with a big grin. Her front tooth was partially grown in, making her look especially cute.

"Good for you!"

"Are you going to the fair tomorrow night to see the fireworks?" Rebekah asked.

"Yes. Are you going?" Leah thought it best not to mention that she was going with Ethan and Charity.

"Mama and Papa are taking me. Maybe we'll see you."

Leah wondered what would happen if Charity's parents ran into them. Especially with Charity dressed English. "Maybe." Leah tugged playfully on one of Rebekah's braids. "How's my chicken doing?"

"She's getting very big. I think she will lay many eggs."

"I sure hope so. I don't want a lazy chicken. Is Charity at the house?" Leah asked.

"She's working in the apple orchard with Mama and Oma today. But you can go visit her if you want."

Leah bought the produce she needed and put it in her car. She wanted to talk about the next night's plans and decided to take a chance on going up to the house, hoping Mr. Longacre wouldn't spot her. In the distance she saw Ethan working in a field of corn and started walking toward him. On foot, she figured, she'd be less noticeable than in her car.

When he saw her coming, he came over to the fence to meet her. "Leah! I have been thinking about you."

His admission pleased her. "Same here," she said. "The corn looks like it's growing. When I first came, it was barely out of the ground."

"There is a saying that it will be a good harvest if the corn is knee-high by July Fourth." Ethan mopped his forehead with a handkerchief.

"It looks fine to me."

"*You* look fine to *me.*"

"Glad you noticed."

"I always notice you, Leah."

Her heartbeat quickened. "How do you want to handle going to the fair tomorrow night? Should I drive?"

"My family will leave for the fair after lunch. Oma and Opa will also be going. No one will be at home. Come to the house before suppertime."

"What if they run into us at the fair?"

"The fair is very large, and hundreds of people will be there. It is unlikely."

"I just don't want them to think I'm a bad influence on Charity."

Ethan took her hand. "Charity has made this choice. She would do it with or without you."

"If you say so." Still, Leah didn't feel totally absolved. What they were doing was sneaky.

Ethan lifted her chin. "We will have a very good time tomorrow night. You will see. All will be well."

Leah wanted to believe him because it was so important. He wanted his friends to accept her. She wanted it too. But Jonah had essentially told her that English and Amish didn't mix. And everything she'd seen so far this summer—the tourists, their loud voices, their inconsiderate actions—told her that was the truth. Leah was English. Ethan, his family and his friends were not. She tried hard to be respectful and tolerant of their Amish customs. But nothing could change the reality of their differences. Nothing.

THIRTEEN

Leah arrived at the farm the next day in the late afternoon. She carried in a sack full of clothes for Charity, and while she helped her dress and put on makeup, Ethan loaded the car with sleeping bags, a cooler and containers of food. He was sitting in the parlor when Leah and Charity came down the stairs. He jumped to his feet.

Charity twirled in front of him. "What do you think?"

"I think you look very pretty."

Leah could see by Charity's smile that her brother's compliment mattered to her. "Then you approve?" Leah asked.

Ethan's gaze found hers. "I approve."

They drove the several miles to the county fairgrounds with the convertible's top down. The weather was typical for July—hot and sticky. At the fair, they parked in a field crammed with other cars and walked to the admission gate. After paying, Ethan said, "We are to meet the others in the carnival area." He took Leah's hand, and the three of them threaded their way through the throngs of people.

The carnival arcade consisted of games of chance and rides and even more people waiting in long lines. At the Ferris wheel, Leah saw Jonah scanning the crowd anxiously. When Jonah saw Charity, his eyes widened, and then a grin split his face. "I like what I see," he told her when the three of them were standing in front of him.

"Leah helped me," Charity said.

Jonah glanced at Leah. "Leah has only magnified what God has already created."

"Where to now?" Leah asked.

"I will win you a teddy bear," Ethan said.

They went over to a booth where a barker was urging people to try their skill at knocking over a stack of wooden bottles with a baseball. "Win the little lady a prize!" the man shouted. "Three tries for a dollar."

Ethan slapped down a dollar bill. "I will try."

The barker grinned. "Here you go, son. Dump 'em and your girl gets her pick of prizes."

Leah leaned over and whispered into Ethan's ear. "These things are rigged. You shouldn't waste your money."

"It is only a dollar," Ethan said. "And I may get

lucky." He picked up the balls and threw them in quick succession, knocking down the bottles.

Leah didn't know who was more surprised, she or the barker. The man gave Ethan a sour smile. "You did it, kid. What does the lady want?"

Leah picked out a bear, and Ethan tucked it under his arm. "How'd you do that?" she asked once they had walked away.

Ethan flashed her a sly smile. "These people think because we are Amish we are slow or dumb. I learned long ago just how to throw the ball to beat them. They are always surprised when I win."

"And who taught you how to beat them?"

He stiffened. "Someone from long ago. It is not important."

His answer mystified Leah. He was shutting her out again from something in his past. Determined not to let it bother her, she looped her arm through his. "You're just full of surprises, Ethan Longacre. And I like surprises."

His momentary moodiness vanished with a quick smile. "I like surprises too."

Jonah won Charity a stuffed toy at the next booth. Soon the four of them had their arms loaded with stuffed animals and inexpensive dolls and toys. "What are we going to do with all this stuff?" Leah asked.

"We will leave it with friends in one of the food booths," Ethan said. "The Yoders have a concession stand."

They left their prizes with the Yoders—all except for Leah's bear, which she insisted on carrying. When they returned to the carnival area, Leah recognized some of Jonah's friends standing near the roller coaster. They were talking, even flirting, with girls who weren't Amish. She wasn't sure why that bothered her, but it did. English girls—girls like her—seemed good enough to have fun with, but not good enough to date or take home to the family. Still, she was polite when introduced to the newcomers.

Within an hour, the group had ridden the roller coaster, the bumper cars and the merry-go-round. Dusk was falling by the time Leah and Ethan got on the Ferris wheel. "Soon the fireworks will start over by the lake," Ethan said as the wheel began its slow ascent.

Leah saw the grayish blue water from the high vantage point. People were already gathered along the shore in lawn chairs and on blankets. "It already looks packed."

"Don't worry. Some of our friends are there saving places."

Since Leah hadn't yet run into Martha, she wondered if Jonah's sister was one of the friends saving places.

Their seat on the Ferris wheel swung to the very top, then lurched to a stop. Far below, Leah saw a man fiddling with the machinery. "We may have to watch from up here," she said, huddling closer to Ethan. "It sure is a long way down."

"Are you frightened? I have seen you drive. How could this be scary?"

She punched his arm good-naturedly. "Swinging in an open basket fifty feet in the air with nothing but a bar across my lap doesn't bother me one bit."

He laughed. "I like this ride best of all. It lets me see the earth as birds see it. As angels see it. Sometimes I dream that I am flying above the ground, swooping and soaring. I don't like waking up from that dream."

"You've never flown in an airplane, have you?"

He shook his head, but she saw a wistful look cross his face. "I would like to do that someday."

"You ought to see the clouds from the top side. They look like big fat cotton balls. Do you think angels play in the clouds?"

"Angels go anywhere they want." He brushed her hair with his lips. "Even on Ferris wheels at county fairs."

Leah felt as if she were melting. Ethan could say the sweetest things.

After the ride, they headed toward the lake. They searched the throngs for their friends. Charity was the first to spot them. "Over there." She waved at a group of about thirty kids lounging on quilts and blankets.

Leah settled next to Ethan, mindful of the glances from the group. She was the only non-Amish person among them. From the corner of her eye, she saw Martha. Martha kept glancing at Ethan covertly, and Leah knew that if it hadn't been for her, Martha undoubtedly would have been the one with Ethan tonight. Leah shifted so that Martha was completely out of her line of vision.

With a loud pop, the first volley of fireworks lit the sky. Cascades of color and showers of gold rained down in long streamers. Using her stuffed bear as a pillow, Leah stretched out. Ethan lay beside her and together they watched the brilliant lights dance overhead. With every burst, Leah felt Ethan's hand tighten on hers. Waves of contentment washed over her. She couldn't imagine anyplace else in the world she'd rather be than under a July Fourth fireworks display with Ethan.

Ethan asked, "Do you think your mother is seeing fireworks in the South Pacific?"

"According to Mom, a person can see a million stars out there. Who needs fireworks?" Her mother had called a few days before to hear how Leah's doctor's appointment had gone. Leah had given her mother a good report, not even mentioning her sore knee. The cortisone shot had helped immensely, but her bout with cancer seemed always to be lurking on the fringes of her mind.

Ethan sighed. "Sometimes I think about traveling all over the world."

Leah understood his longing. But for her, what he

had—home and a sense of belonging—seemed more satisfactory than sailing the ocean. "Maybe someday you will," she said.

"It does not seem likely. But I wish I could."

When the fireworks show was over, the quilts were folded and the whole group joined the exodus of people headed home. The Amish kids were going to the Yoder farm for the campout. And Leah would be with them. She hoped she didn't do anything to embarrass herself. And she hoped that she and Ethan could hold on to the feelings they had for each other—regardless of all their differences.

A stream ran through the part of the farm where the campsite was set up. A large bonfire was built and blankets spread on the ground around it. Radios, portable CD players, picnic baskets and coolers were strewn around the blankets. A keg of beer sat in the sluggish stream. Leah was certain Jonah had sneaked it in. Leah noted that this night everyone had come in cars—not in buggies. And no one was dressed Amish.

She and Ethan settled on a quilt with Charity and Jonah. Jonah headed straight for the beer keg. Ethan pulled a package of hot dogs from their cooler. "Want one?"

"Sure," Leah said.

He handed her a piece of wire and stuck a hot dog on the end. They walked closer to the fire and began cooking the hot dogs. By the time they returned to the blanket, Charity had gone to talk to other friends, and Jonah had made several more trips to the keg.

Leah and Ethan sat on the blanket, scooped potato salad onto plates and began eating. Jonah came up and held out a plastic cup full of beer. "Want a drink, Ethan?"

"This is not a place for drinking, Jonah," Ethan responded. "You should not have brought this."

"You don't like my beer?" Jonah asked. His tone sounded challenging.

"No. I do not want your beer," he said evenly.

"Why do you not want to be with your friends, Ethan?" Jonah asked. He swayed slightly. "Why are you letting your girlfriend make your decisions for you?"

Leah held her breath, waiting for Ethan's reaction.

Ethan stood. "I make my own choices, Jonah. And I do not choose to drink your beer."

Leah watched Ethan stoop over and rummage through the cooler and pull out two soda cans. He popped the tabs, handed one to Leah, and sat back down. To Jonah, Ethan said, "Why don't you eat something? We have salads. We have cakes."

"I don't want anything to eat. I want to talk to you about the way you treat your friends." He cast Leah a hard look. "Ever since she came into your life, you have no time for us. For your own kind."

"You are talking crazy," Ethan said.

In the light from the bonfire, Leah saw Ethan's jaw clench.

"Do you know what I think, Ethan?" Jonah asked.

"Because you have been drinking, I do not care what you think," Ethan answered.

Jonah leaned over so that his face was inches from Ethan's. "I think you are proud. All you Longacres are proud."

Ethan started to rise to his feet. Leah grabbed his arm. "It's only words, Ethan. Ignore him. He's drunk." She knew Ethan rejected violence, but she was angry enough to hit Jonah herself. Why was he spoiling their evening?

Jonah acted as if Leah hadn't even spoken. "You are proud. Your father is proud. Eli would have drunk beer with me."

Ethan shot to his feet. The color had drained from his face, and his hands were balled into fists. "You go too far, Jonah. Do not *ever* say that name to me. You know it is forbidden to speak it."

Jonah reeled backward. He blinked. A low growl tore from his throat, and he stalked off toward the stream.

Ethan took off in the other direction. Leah went after him. She caught up with him far downstream. She wasn't sure anyone had seen what had happened between Ethan and Jonah, but no one had followed them. "Ethan!" she called.

He stopped, then turned slowly. "Leave me be, Leah."

"No," she said, moving closer. "You can't just bring me here and run away. I can figure out that Jonah doesn't like me, maybe because of his sister. I even understand. But I saw your fists. You almost hit him back there. All because he mentioned someone named Eli. What's going on? Who's Eli? You owe me an explanation."

Ethan let out a long, slow, shuddering breath. It took him a long time to answer. At last he said, "Eli is my brother."

FOURTEEN

"Your brother?" Leah wasn't sure she'd heard Ethan correctly. "You mean you have another brother besides Simeon and Nathan?"

Ethan turned away from her. "Yes."

Leah stepped in front of him, refusing to let him walk away. "Tell me about Eli." When he didn't respond, she added, "Please, tell me."

"Eli is older than me. The firstborn." Ethan's words were halting, as if it hurt his throat to speak them.

"How much older?"

"Eight years."

Leah was shocked. "Where is he?"

Ethan shrugged. "I am not sure. I think he still lives here in Indiana."

"You're not *sure*?" she repeated. "When did you last see him?"

"When I was ten."

"You haven't seen your own brother for seven years? But why?" Getting information from Ethan was like pulling teeth. Frustrated, Leah wanted him to tell her everything and get it over with. "You sound ashamed of Eli. Are you?"

"You do not understand, Leah."

"I sure don't," she said, exasperated. "You have a brother no one talks about, or even mentions—I've known you since December and I've never once heard about him—and you won't tell me why. Don't you trust me, Ethan?"

"This has nothing to do with you."

There was no moon, so Leah couldn't see his face, but she could hear the sadness in his voice. She reached out and stroked his arm. "I care about you, Ethan. I don't like to see you hurting. I've always wondered whether you—and even Charity—were keeping something from me."

"How did you know?"

"Little things that were said. Embarrassed silences when something would come up that you both didn't want to talk about. I know now that I wasn't imagining it. Was it Eli? Or is there some other secret?"

"I have no other secrets." He sounded miserable.

"But all the Amish kids know about him, don't they? At least Jonah knows."

"Some know about Eli."

"But not me. Is it because I'm English? An outsider?" Leah's frustration turned into a feeling that she'd been rejected.

"Others know about him only if they are old enough to remember him." Ethan bent so that his forehead was touching Leah's. "We do not speak of him. Rebekah doesn't even know about him."

"Rebekah doesn't know she has another brother?" Leah couldn't believe what Ethan was saying. "Are you joking?"

"She was born after Eli left. And since we never speak of him . . ." Ethan let the sentence trail off.

"But—But—Why not?" Leah sputtered. "What's he done that's so horrible? Is he a criminal or something?"

"You are not Amish, Leah."

"What's that supposed to mean? You've always known I wasn't Amish!"

"It is hard to explain our ways to you."

Leah folded her arms across her chest. "Why don't you try? I promise to act human. Okay?"

Her sarcasm was seemingly lost on Ethan. He gently took her hand and led her to a patch of grassy ground, where he settled her beside him. Leah felt angry and hurt, but she forced herself to keep her temper and to wait in the darkness for him to finally speak.

"Eli was my big brother, and I followed him around like a puppy. He was different from me. Different from all of my family."

"How was he so different?"

"He never loved the land the way Opa, Papa and I do. He didn't like our simple ways. Eli was born smart. He loved books. And learning. When I was six, he was fourteen and in the eighth grade. He went to the English middle school—as we all did. He made straight As."

Leah knew Amish kids left school after the eighth grade because, according to Charity, the Amish saw no need for advanced education. Eventually the Amish teen would take his or her place in the community and therefore had no real need for more schooling. Farming, carpentry work and rearing families were not tasks that needed degrees. Preserving the Amish way of life superseded everything else. "Didn't Eli drop out of school?" she asked.

"No. One of his teachers came out to the farm to talk to Papa. She showed Papa test scores and told him that Eli was very smart—too smart to drop out. She said it would be a sin to let such intelligence go to waste. She talked Papa into letting Eli continue his education."

"That doesn't seem so terrible," Leah said. "Your parents must have been proud of Eli."

"They were."

Instantly Leah realized what Ethan was telling her. Mr. Longacre *had* been proud of Eli. But pride was not a virtue to the Amish. "What happened?"

"Eli was allowed to go to high school. He got on the school bus and rode away each day. He came home and did homework by lamplight. He read books, and more books. As he got older and made friends among the English, he would stay in town with them. It was very hard on Papa because he expected Eli to do his chores and help on the farm. They had harsh words. Whenever Eli did come home, he brought friends Papa did not like. Finally he stopped coming home.

"It was difficult for me too," Ethan confessed. "I loved them both, and I missed Eli in the family."

Leah could well imagine the scenes. "Is that the reason you didn't run around with your friends when you first turned sixteen? You didn't want to upset your father?"

A low chuckle escaped from Ethan. "You know me well, Leah. Yes. I did not want to disappoint Papa as Eli did."

"You didn't mind quitting school, did you?"

"I am not smart like Eli. Leaving school was not hard for me. Harder for Charity, I think. But not for me."

For Leah, school had never been an option. It was someplace she had to go whether she liked it or not. And for the most part, she liked school. She couldn't imagine not going. "What happened after Eli graduated from high school?"

"It was like chocolate cake and grapefruit juice."

"Fireworks, huh?"

Ethan nodded. "Eli was offered a college scholarship. All paid up."

Leah understood what such an offer meant. "So he had to choose," she stated. "His education or his family."

"I was ten when he left home for good." Ethan's voice grew soft. "Papa wanted Eli to take over the farm. He wanted him to be baptized, and marry, and live as Amish. But Eli said that Amish ways were backward. He said that he did not want to be Amish. He and Papa had very angry words. In the end, Eli left. I still remember the day. Eli and I shared a room. That morning, he packed everything in bags and an old suitcase. He did not have much. I begged him not to go."

Leah heard a catch in Ethan's voice. She felt his pain. "But he went anyway, didn't he?"

"That day Eli said to me, 'Ethan, now you are the oldest son. Papa will not forgive me for this. I am sorry that you are caught in the middle. It will be as if I am dead. No one will speak my name or ever talk about me around here. But I cannot be Amish. I cannot.'"

Leah felt tears swimming in her own eyes as Ethan talked. She could see the scene vividly in her mind's eye. She could feel the immense weight dropped on

Ethan's shoulders the day his brother left. "I'm sorry, Ethan."

"That afternoon one of Eli's friends came for him. I stood at the window. I watched him put his things in the car. I watched the car drive away until it was a tiny speck. I've not seen my brother again."

For Leah, many things about Ethan fell into place. Out of respect for his family, Ethan had chosen not to take his fling with the others. Jonah's taunts about Ethan's refusal to run with his friends must have been doubly hard on Ethan. And then Leah had come along. And Ethan had done what nothing else had made him do—he'd dressed English, played English, dated an English girl. He'd done it for her. "Do you know if Eli graduated from college?" she asked.

"I ran into his former teacher once. She told me that she was sorry about what had happened in our family over Eli, but that she had heard that he was getting a degree in education. That he planned to become a teacher—like her. She was proud of that. It made me very sad."

Leah calculated the age difference between Eli and Ethan. "He must be twenty-five by now. If he's a teacher in Indiana, you could find him—"

Ethan sprang to his feet. "I do not want to find him. It is *verboten*—forbidden. I could not betray Papa's wishes."

Leah knew better than to argue. "It was just a thought."

"You think this is foolish, don't you?" Ethan's question floated to her in the dark.

Leah didn't answer right away because she didn't want to upset or hurt him. Nor did she want to seem unsympathetic to the Amish mind-set. Still, it did help her understand Mr. Longacre's coolness toward her. The English way of life had taken one son already.

"Ethan, I really do know what it's like to lose someone you love." Leah chose her words carefully. "I had a grandmother—my father's mother—and for some reason she and my mom never got along with each other. It had something to do with my dad and his leaving us, but I was just a little girl and didn't have a clue.

"Anyway, I loved Grandma Hall with all my heart. She used to sneak into my elementary school during recesses and visit with me on the playground. She brought me cookies and little presents. I still miss her."

"What happened to her?"

"She got sick and died. My mother did let me visit her while she was in the hospital, but it was hard seeing her that way—hooked up to machines and suffering. It scared me." She looked up at Ethan. "Like you, I was also only ten. Grandma died and I went to her funeral. I'll never forget it."

Ethan's arm went around Leah's shoulders. He pulled her close. "This is a sad story, Leah."

"Please listen to what I'm saying. My grand-mother's dead, and I'll never see her again on earth. Eli isn't dead. You can see him."

Ethan's arms loosened their hold on her. "It is not that simple. My father would not approve. And so long as I live in my father's house, I must honor and obey him. It is our way."

"Yet it's all right for you to drink and drive cars and sample wordly stuff. You just can't ever speak to your brother again." Leah knew she was testing Ethan's loyalty, but she couldn't help it. Couldn't he see how contradictory, how hypocritical, his ways sounded to her?

Ethan sighed deeply. "I knew you would not under-stand. I should not have told you."

She took his arm. "I'm glad you told me. Because I want to understand, Ethan. I want to know everything I can about you."

He held her face between the palms of his hands. "And I want to know all about you too, Leah. You are very special to me."

She felt her knees going weak with emotion. She couldn't challenge him again. His brother Eli was a closed subject. Still, Leah couldn't help wondering if her exis-tence too might someday be blotted out by Ethan's family.

The notion left her queasy. "Your secret is safe with me, Ethan," she said. But she thought, *Eli does exist. And no amount of pretending will make him disappear.*

She took Ethan's hand. "Come on. Let's go back to the party. Charity might be looking for us."

FIFTEEN

When Leah and Ethan returned to the campsite, the bonfire had died down to a pile of glowing embers. Sleeping bags stretched across blankets and quilts in clusters. Leah heard the soft whispers of conversation mixed with music from radios. She looked around for Charity. "Where do you suppose your sister is?"

"I do not know."

"I don't see Jonah either."

"They are here, I'm sure. Charity would not go off the property."

"I hope you're right. Jonah had too much to drink."

Ethan spread out two sleeping bags. "Come here, Leah. I will tuck you in."

She crawled inside the sleeping bag, and Ethan fastened the side. "I'll bet this is how a caterpillar feels in a cocoon," she said.

Ethan chuckled and wiggled into the sleeping bag next to hers. "Sleep fast. The sun will be up soon."

Leah yawned. She snuggled closer to Ethan. "My nose itches."

He kissed the tip. "Did that help?"

"Much better." She felt Ethan's warm breath against her cheek. Her sleepiness vanished and her heart began to beat faster. "I've never spent the night with a guy before!"

"I am glad I am the first," he whispered. He freed his arms from his sleeping bag and caressed her cheek.

"No fair," she told him. "I can't touch you."

"It is better this way. If you began to touch me, I would not want you to stop."

"Stopping is hard," she said. Her blood sizzled and her pulse pounded.

He nuzzled her neck. "Leah, I would not ever do anything to shame you."

She knew what he meant. He would not pressure her for more. Leah realized how easy it would be to let herself go with him. So very easy. "You are a person of honor," she said. The word sounded old-fashioned, but it was the right word to describe Ethan. He was *honorable*. He didn't know how else to be. He made Leah feel cherished.

"Good night, my Leah." Ethan's arms enveloped her, sleeping bag and all. Soon she heard his rhythmic breathing and knew he'd fallen asleep.

My Leah. She *was* his Leah. For all their differences,

for all the chasms that separated them, she belonged to Ethan. And she hadn't an earthly idea what she was going to do about it when the summer ended.

Dawn's pink fingers streaked the sky as Leah struggled to awaken. The aroma of freshly brewing coffee made her stomach growl. Beside her, Ethan's sleeping bag was empty. She sat up and rubbed her sleep-blurred eyes. She saw Ethan hunched down over a small campfire, filling two cups with coffee. She combed her hair with her fingers, wishing she had a brush.

Ethan returned and handed her a coffee cup. "If you'd rather, I will get you a soda."

"No, coffee's fine." Leah took the cup from him and warmed her hands.

They sat together on the quilt and watched the red ball of the sun rise over the dew-drenched meadow. The morning haze began to lift, and the sky turned from pink to blue. The smell of coffee mingled with the scent of sizzling bacon. Leah said, "I had no idea mornings could be so gorgeous. The sun's always up by the time I get to work. I sleep in on the weekends."

"I have always known," Ethan said. "It is my favorite part of the day." His deep love for the land shimmered in his eyes. "Now that you know, maybe you will also want to get up at five-thirty every day."

"Naw," she said, scrunching her face. He laughed.

Charity walked over and sat down with a heavy sigh. She looked haggard. "I thought the morning would never come," she said.

"Where were you all night?" Leah asked.

"I was caring for Jonah. He became very sick." She stole a glance at Ethan, who appeared uninterested.

Leah said, "He drank too much, didn't he?"

Charity nodded. "I'm sure he did not mean to."

Angry at Jonah for spoiling Charity's evening, Leah said, "You should have let him suffer by himself."

"I could not," Charity said miserably. "He had no one else."

"Maybe he'll think twice before drinking that much ever again."

"Maybe."

Ethan spoke. "Jonah is trying to prove he's a man. But this is not the way a man acts."

"Don't criticize him," Charity said testily. "He will find his way back. I know he will."

"It is best if you ride home with Leah and me—"

"We can stop by my apartment and freshen up," Leah interjected. She didn't want Ethan and Charity arguing—especially over Jonah. He wasn't worth it, to her way of thinking.

"I will change my clothes at your place." Charity looked down at the skirt Leah had loaned her. "I'm afraid this is messed up. I will clean it for you."

"It's okay. It'll wash."

"I am sorry, Leah."

Leah didn't care about the skirt. She cared about
Charity, and she hoped her friend wasn't making a mistake in caring about Jonah.

"It's all right," Leah assured Charity. "The important thing is that you're all right. Did you have any fun
at all?"

Charity's smile looked wan. "It was not what I
expected."

"Maybe next year will be better."

"Maybe." Charity stared out across the meadow.
"By next year, perhaps Jonah will have tired of his fling."

Leah hoped so. She recalled the secret of Eli, Ethan
and Charity's brother. Would Jonah forsake his Amish
upbringing as Eli had? Leah knew Jonah could break
Charity's heart.

Leah didn't even let on to Charity that she knew about
Eli. But she couldn't look at Rebekah and not think it a
shame that the child didn't know she had another
brother. As for her feelings toward Mr. Longacre, Leah
was torn. Her own father had walked out of her life when
she'd been a small child, and all her life she'd wondered
why. What had driven him off? She had no answers.

But Mr. Longacre had disowned his eldest son. Eli's
desire to go to high school and college seemed such a

small deviation from the Amish lifestyle. This sobered Leah and disturbed her greatly. If Mr. Longacre would ignore his own flesh and blood, what chance did *she* have of his ever accepting her, a stranger and English to boot? The problem with the Amish, Leah decided, was that they never made allowances for individuality.

And yet, Leah had to admit that despite its inflexibility, she was attracted to the Amish lifestyle, to the Amish sense of community and togetherness. She wondered why people couldn't have it both ways.

Once the July Fourth weekend was over, the ranks of tourists thinned considerably. Leah went back to work at the inn. Kathy was replaced by an Amish girl named Esther, who was so shy, it was more than a week before Leah heard the girl say a word. No matter how many friendly overtures Leah made, Esther couldn't be coaxed from her shell. If Leah asked her a question, Esther turned bright red, stared down at the floor, and barely mumbled an answer. Leah missed the talkative Kathy immensely.

Leah spent the weekends with Ethan. He arrived at her apartment on Saturday mornings, stayed with friends in town on Saturday nights, and spent all day Sunday with her. This meant that he was not attending Amish church services at all. She couldn't imagine that Ethan's weekend absences won her points with his parents.

She found things to keep her and Ethan busy when they were together. They watched videos, went to movies, skated at The Rink, and drove into the country-side for picnics and shopping sprees. On the first Saturday in August, he took her horseback riding.

"Is he safe?" Leah asked, looking at the big horse standing in the yard of the riding stable. "I don't think he likes me, Ethan."

Ethan shimmied up his mount as if he'd been born to ride a horse. "The owner tells me your horse is very tame. He will not harm you. I thought you once lived in Texas."

The horse turned its neck and stared at Leah as if to say, *"Are you getting on or not?"*

Leah glanced up at Ethan. "You've watched too many movies. Most Texans wisely drive cars." She took a deep breath and put her foot into the stirrup. With an effort, she hauled herself onto the horse's back, then held on to the saddle horn and reins for dear life. "Okay, I'm on."

Ethan laughed aloud. "If you could see your face."

"I'm so glad I'm entertaining you." She shifted. The horse snorted. "How do I put him in gear?"

"Give him some slack on the reins, dig your knees into his side, and he will go."

Leah did as she was told, and the horse broke into a trot. She almost lost her balance, fell forward and hugged the horse's neck. "Where's the brake on this thing?"

Ethan came up alongside and took her horse's bridle, slowing the animal to a walk. "When you want him to stop, pull back on the reins. You must show him who is boss."

"No contest. He's the boss. He's bigger." Leah's legs felt awkward spread around the horse and saddle. "Does this ever get more comfortable?"

"It is customary to feel sore at first. But once you get used to riding—"

"I'll be too old to do it."

They rode a well-defined trail that cut through the countryside, following a stream. Before long, Leah began to relax.

"I will tell you something," Ethan said, breaking the silence. "I am learning how to drive a car."

"You are? But that's good. Isn't it?" Leah realized he was further defying his father and his Amish upbringing. "Who's teaching you?"

"Jonah."

"I'm sure Jonah gets a thrill out of seeing you try more and more English things."

"You sound as if you do not approve."

"I didn't mean it that way. I think you should learn to drive if you want to. Will you ever own a car?"

"I do not think so."

"Tell me about driving. Do you like it?"

"It is hard not to go too fast. And there is much to

remember. A car has many buttons and switches. A horse is much simpler." He patted his horse's neck.

"But a horse doesn't have soft leather seats." Leah squirmed. She couldn't get comfortable in the hard saddle.

"But a car cannot put a soft nose on the back of your neck and nuzzle you."

"I thought that's what guys were for."

Ethan burst out laughing. He looked over at her, his expression growing serious. "Sometimes—more since I have known you—I feel locked up. Like I am inside a box."

She remembered what he'd said about traveling and seeing the world. "I'd feel bad if you were trying things just because of me."

"It is my right to test, remember?"

"Well, if you ever want to get away from all this, come see me. Neil owns a farm, you know, so it won't be a total change."

"What kind of farm?" Ethan sounded interested.

"Oh, not like your farm," Leah added hastily. "Neil bought this big piece of land at an auction. He has a big house on it. You see, he lived in Detroit all his life and de-cided to retire out in the wide-open spaces."

"A farm that does not grow food?" Ethan sounded amazed. "Does he have a barn for dairy cows?"

"He keeps cars in the barn."

Ethan turned and stared, as if to see if she was teasing him. "Cars? In a barn?"

"He collects antique cars." Leah felt almost apologetic. "They're worth a lot of money. And the barn's specially made to keep the cars well preserved."

"Land is the greatest thing a man can own, but I cannot imagine owning a farm that grows nothing, has no livestock, and stores cars in a good barn." Ethan shook his head.

Leah should have figured that to Ethan's frugal Amish mind, owning land merely for the pleasure of having space around you would make no sense. Worse, it made her lifestyle seem wasteful and foolish. "Collecting cars is Neil's hobby. Sort of like that train we saw at the toy store. Just bigger. Don't you Amish have any hobbies?"

"Working a farm does not leave us with much extra time, Leah. Many of us would like to be farmers, but farmland is not plentiful any longer, so we must become carpenters or have our own stores. And I do not want you thinking that I am critical of Neil. It is just that to hear of good land lying fallow is a shock to me."

"I guess I understand," Leah told him. "I've just never thought of it that way before. Mom and I have lived in apartments and trailers all our lives, so being out in the country, with all this land around me, is a real change. I didn't even like it at first. It was lonely and miles from anything that even resembled a mall."

"Do you still not like living there?"

"I'm used to it now. And being here all summer— going out to your farm and seeing how much you like the great outdoors—has made me feel better about it."

Ethan stared off into the distance, across open fields and rolling meadows. "I cannot imagine being stuck someplace where there is no land around me. Where there are only cars and noise and too many people. The land makes me feel connected to God and all that he has made."

Leah couldn't imagine not being around cars and people and some kind of city life. She had not felt the gap between herself and Ethan so keenly in weeks. She felt it now, just as she felt the discomfort of the hard saddle and the plodding horse beneath her. Their ways of life were poles apart. Could anything ever close the gap between them?

SIXTEEN

"Hi, honey. How are you doing?"

"Mom? Where are you?" Leah hugged the phone receiver to her ear.

"Hawaii," her mother said.

"You sound like you're next door."

Her mother took a breath. "Neil and I are spending more time here before we head back to the mainland. It's been a fabulous trip. Did you get my postcards?"

Leah glanced at the colorful pictures lining her refrigerator door. "Sure did. It sounds like you've been having a good time."

"Oh, have we ever! I'm sorry you missed it, Leah. How's your summer been?"

"I'm having a great time too."

"Really? I was hoping you weren't having regrets about not coming along."

"No regrets," Leah told her.

"That's good." Her mother sounded relieved. "Well, Neil's taken a hundred pictures and made a ton of tapes with the camcorder. I can't wait for you to see them."

"When will you be home?"

"In two weeks. Summer's almost over, you know. School will be starting soon."

Leah's heart lurched. Her gaze flew quickly to the calendar on her kitchen wall, and she saw that August was well under way. She'd been so caught up in her everyday life, she'd forgotten how close it was to the start of the new school year. And to going home. Somehow, it had seemed as if her life in Nappanee would go on forever. "I guess you're right."

"When do you see Dr. Thomas again?"

"Not until fall, I think. I have an appointment card around here somewhere."

"How have you been feeling?"

"I feel fine." Leah hated being reminded that her health wasn't perfect. There were days now when she never even thought about it. And then there were days when she thought about it a lot. The soreness in her knee came and went. When it came, she took pain relievers and tried not to bend too much.

"We've got back-to-school shopping to do," her mother said. "Why don't I come and help you pack up your things on the twenty-third?"

"Um—I guess that's all right. I have to tell Mrs. Stoltz exactly when I'll be leaving."

"What would you think about driving into Chicago to shop after you come home? I've heard the bargains there are fantastic."

"Sure, Mom. That'll be fine."

"Then it's settled. I'll call you when we get back to our place," her mother added cheerfully. "See you soon. And Neil says hi."

After hanging up, Leah stood holding the receiver and listening to the dial tone. Her wonderful summer was almost over, her time with Ethan almost gone. She finally hung up the phone and leaned her forehead against the wall. She couldn't imagine her days without him. "Oh, Ethan," she sighed. "What are we going to do?"

Mrs. Stoltz needed some fresh produce, so Leah drove out to the Amish stand. She looked for Rebekah among the Amish kids working, but she couldn't find her. A girl's voice said, "If you're looking for Rebekah, she left early today."

Leah turned to face Martha Dewberry. Martha was dressed in a short summer Amish dress of pale green and was holding a basket of beets. Leah said, "Oh . . . well, thanks."

"Could I help you?"

"I—um—just need some vegetables for the inn."

"I'll show you what is freshest today. I know how Mrs. Stoltz likes high quality."

Leah reminded herself that in such a small town, everybody knew everybody else. It was no surprise that Martha could pick just the right things for Mrs. Stoltz. Still, Leah disliked tagging along behind Martha while Martha chose items from the stacks of vegetables and fruits.

"There," Martha finally said, handing Leah two sacks full of food. "This should be enough."

Leah paid at the cashier and carried the sacks to her car. Martha opened the car door for her. "I guess you'll be going home soon," she said. "You're still in school, aren't you?"

"Yes, I'm leaving soon. Yes, I still have another year before I graduate."

Martha smiled, reminding Leah of a contented cat. "Then your summer here has been successful?"

"I've had a good time, if that's what you mean." Tension crept up Leah's neck. "I like it here and I've made some good friends."

"Will you come back?"

Leah squared her chin. "I might. If I'm invited."

"It is not easy being Amish for you English. One summer is not a true test of being one of us, you know."

Is that what Martha thinks? That I'm trying to be one of them? "I guess it's never good to try and be something you're not," Leah said. "But I think it's okay to sample different things in life. Isn't that what you Amish do when you take a fling?"

Martha's cheeks colored, and Leah knew that her barb had hit home. "You are right. Experimentation is not a bad thing," Martha said. "Making the *wrong* choice is the bad thing."

Tired of dancing around the subject, Leah blurted out, "Is that what you think Ethan's done? Made a bad choice by being with me all summer?"

Martha shrugged. "It is not for me to say. Ethan is a grown man. But the summer is almost over. And you will be leaving because you are English and have another life away from here. But I will remain, because this is my place. And Ethan will be here too, because this is his place. I offer you no bad feelings, Leah. It is the way things are."

Leah turned away. Anger bubbled inside her. But she could not dispute anything that Martha had said. She had heard that patience was a virtue, and in this case, it was. Martha had patiently waited on the sidelines all summer, knowing full well that autumn would come, and with it, Leah's departure.

Partly because Martha had made her angry, partly because she just wanted to see her friends, Leah drove up to the farmhouse. She struggled to calm herself. She didn't want any of them to know she was upset. There was nothing anyone could do. As Martha had said, "It is the way things are."

Leah parked her car, opened the door and felt a wet, stinging smack against her leg. Startled, she looked down to see water soaking the leg of her jeans. She looked up to see Simeon gaping at her from the corner of the house, a water balloon poised in one hand. "Leah," he called. "I'm sorry. I was trying to hit Rebekah."

Rebekah darted from behind Leah and the old wagon wheel by the flowers, a water balloon balanced in each hand. Her sleeves were rolled up, she was barefoot, and the front of her pale yellow dress was soaked. "Oh, Leah. Are you all right?" the little girl asked, wide-eyed.

"I'm fine. I was planning on taking a shower later anyway, and now you've saved me the trouble. What's going on?"

"We're having a water fight," Rebekah said with a toothy grin.

"Does your mother know?"

"Oh yes. It is fun."

Leah took one of the balloons from Rebekah and juggled it lightly in one hand. "Fun, you say?" Without warning, she spun, heaved the balloon and hit Simeon squarely in the chest. She grabbed Rebekah and yelled, "Run!"

The two of them dashed like rabbits toward the barn, Rebekah shrieking and Leah laughing. Simeon followed in hot pursuit. At the barn, Leah rounded the corner and crouched. "Where're more balloons?" she asked breathlessly.

Giggling, Rebekah handed her the one she still carried. "This is all I have."

"You don't have more? Uh-oh. I think we're in big trouble."

"Follow me," Rebekah said. "We'll hide."

They crawled on all fours inside the barn. At the far end, Leah saw Ethan, busy heaving forkfuls of hay into stalls. He didn't see them. "Shhh," Leah said. "He might tell Simeon where we are." They scurried into an empty stall and peeked through the slats.

Simeon raced into the barn, his water balloon held high. He skidded to a stop. "Where are they?"

"Who?" Ethan asked, looking up.

"Leah and Rebekah. They're in here."

"I do not think so."

"Help me look."

Leah watched as Simeon and Ethan made their way slowly toward them. Rebekah's eyes danced and she clapped her hand over her mouth. Leah clutched the balloon and held her breath. Just as the two brothers passed their hiding place, she sprang to her feet and tossed the balloon. But Simeon, seeing it coming, dropped and rolled out of harm's way. The balloon landed with a splat on the side of Ethan's face.

"Oops," Leah said as Ethan whipped around. "Sorry about that." She offered an innocent smile and a shrug.

Simeon held his fire, and Rebekah looked up expectantly at Ethan. Ethan looked so comical standing in front of her dripping wet that Leah started laughing.

"Do you think this is funny?" Ethan asked with mischief in his eyes.

"Hysterical," Leah managed between laughs.

"I have one balloon left," Simeon said, offering his prize to his brother.

"One balloon is not enough." Lightning fast, Ethan caught Leah's arms.

She squealed as he heaved her over his shoulder like a sack of grain. "Put me down!"

"I will," Ethan said, striding purposefully out of the barn.

"Hold your breath!" Rebekah yelled. "You're in for a dunking!"

From her upside-down vantage point, all Leah saw was the ground. Then Ethan stopped, and the view of the ground gave way to one of the animal-watering trough. "Don't you dare, Ethan Longacre!" she wailed. But to no avail. Leah screeched as Ethan plopped her into the water. She came up sputtering and splashing. She grabbed at Ethan's shirtfront as Rebekah shoved him from behind. He lost his balance and fell smack on top of Leah.

They both yelped and floundered, sending water every which way.

Rebekah and Simeon came over to see and also landed in the wooden trough. All four of them sloshed around like floppy fish. Struggling to get out, Leah slipped and went down in the mud. Ethan came over the side next and slid beside her, stomach first. Leah burst out laughing again. Ethan flipped a wad of mud at her. She retaliated, and soon they were tossing handfuls of mud at each other.

By the time Leah finally wiggled away, she was coated with gooey mud and Martha's words were all but forgotten. "I should murder you."

"We Amish are nonviolent, remember?"

Leah was laughing and shaking mud off her hands and arms. "I'm a mess. Mrs. Stoltz will never send me out to buy vegetables again."

"You're a pretty mess," Ethan said, dipping into the water and wiping her cheek.

Rebekah leaped out of the trough. "Come, Leah. Let's go clean up. We'll use the pump by the house."

Ethan helped Leah to her feet. "Should I?" she asked. "I don't want to get you all in trouble with your parents."

"Charity and Mama have gone into town, and Papa is working with Opa in a field far away from the house. Come and clean up," Ethan urged her.

At the house, Rebekah told Elizabeth and Oma about the water fight, while Leah finished washing up at the kitchen sink what she hadn't cleaned off at the outside pump.

"Do you want to change into clean clothes?" Oma asked Leah.

"This is fine. Really," she added when the older woman looked skeptical. Leah didn't want to be a bother. "I can stop by my apartment on my way back to the inn. I've been away too long as it is. Mrs. Stoltz is expecting me to bring fresh vegetables in time for supper. Thanks anyway."

"As you wish," Oma said. Her face was thin, worn by years of hard work. Her eyes were the palest blue. She looked at Leah with kindness. "My grandchildren like you very much, Leah. And I have always found them to be very good judges of character."

Surprised by Oma's words, Leah offered a shy smile. "That's nice of you to say."

"You are welcome, Leah," Oma answered.

With sunlight streaming through the kitchen window and bathing her face in gentle light, Oma didn't seem stern or formidable to Leah. In some ways, she looked like Leah's grandmother, caring and compassionate. Leah felt a lump of longing in her throat. "I have to go," she said.

Leah hurried outside and down the porch steps. Rebekah and Ethan were waiting for her by her car.

Rebekah took Leah's hand. "You're fun, Leah."

"You're fun too."

"I love you," Rebekah added, hugging Leah.

Leah's eyes filled with moisture. "I love you back," she told the child.

In another two weeks, Leah's mother would be coming, and Leah would be leaving Nappanee, possibly for good. With time closing in on her, she decided that she wanted to see Charity and Rebekah more often. The following Friday after work, she screwed up her courage and drove back out to the farm—this time, to stay for a long visit. She didn't care how much Mr. Longacre scowled at her. She wasn't going to be intimidated.

Leah drove down the road talking to herself and building up her courage. In the distance, flashes of blue light caught her eye. She squinted. In the shimmering heat from the asphalt, a mass of cars and people took shape. Red lights flickered among the blue. The activity seemed to be close to the produce stand. Leah's heart leaped into her throat. She pushed down on the accelerator. The car sped forward. Leah saw police cars everywhere. And ambulances. And emergency medical technicians in uniforms. Something had happened. Something terrible.

SEVENTEEN

Leah had to park on the shoulder of the road, yards away from the roadside disaster, because of the crowd. She leaped from the car and started running, stopping only when a police officer forced her to. "Can't go closer, miss," he warned.

"But they're my friends." She strained to see around him and the knot of people. Half the produce stand was fractured. Splintered wood and smashed vegetables and fruit lay scattered on the ground. The scene was one of total devastation. Leah felt sick. "What happened?"

"You'll have to step back, miss," the officer said firmly, not bothering to answer her question. "We've got injured people here."

"Please, let me through," Leah pleaded.

The officer turned to continue directing people away.

Frantically, Leah grabbed a bystander. "Do you know what happened?"

A plump, middle-aged man wore a grim expression. "Some guy lost control of his pickup truck, swerved and plowed into the stand. My wife and I were standing on the other side or we would have been wiped out too."

"Did it just happen?"

"Maybe twenty minutes ago. They think he was drinking, or maybe had a heart attack at the wheel. He never slowed down, just smashed into them."

Leah craned her neck and saw a blue truck with an out-of-state license plate, nosedown in a ditch in the field behind the stand. The split-rail fence had been snapped like toothpicks, and rows of corn had been flattened. With a start, Leah realized that the truck was on Longacre property. She pushed her way through the on-lookers and edged around to the back of the area. A group of Amish kids, many sobbing and holding on to one another, were huddled on makeshift seats of card-board cartons and plastic baskets. Some were holding towels to their faces, arms and legs. Police officers and rescue workers were trying their best to comfort them.

Anxiously Leah scanned the group for familiar faces. *Rebekah. Where's Rebekah?* Leah tried to get closer, but another officer stopped her. "Sorry, miss. You'll have to stand back."

"I know these people. They're my friends."

"We have injuries. I can't let you in there."

"Who got hurt?" Leah asked. The officer wasn't listening. He had turned to talk to a rescue worker.

Frantic and frustrated, Leah looked around and down. For the first time, she noticed smears of blood on the ground. Shoving past the police officer, she ran toward the Amish kids. She was on her knees in front of one of Rebekah's friends, Karen. "Tell me who's hurt." Leah took Karen's hands. "Please. Where's Rebekah Longacre?"

Karen looked at Leah, a mix of shock and horror on her face. "The ambulance took her."

Leah felt queasy. "Was she . . . is she okay?"

Karen shrugged just as Leah felt the police officer's beefy hand on her shoulder. "I told you to stay back," the man barked.

Shakily Leah stood, fighting the urge to scream. "Where did the ambulance go?"

The officer said, "Nappanee Hospital emergency room."

Leah ran back to her car. Her hands were shaking so badly she could hardly get the key into the ignition. When she did get the engine started, she gunned it and made a U-turn in the middle of the blocked highway, heading back toward town. All the way there, she prayed, "Dear God, please let Rebekah be okay. Please!"

• • •

Leah raced into the emergency room. In one corner she saw the entire Longacre family—from little Nathan to the grandparents. In their quaint Amish clothing, surrounded by the high-tech decor of the hospital lobby, they struck a discordant note. Seeing Leah, Ethan came quickly to face her.

Leah grabbed his shirt. "How is she?"

"We do not know yet," Ethan said grimly. "We only just got here ourselves, and the doctors haven't told us anything."

"I was on my way to your place when I saw . . . I saw—" Leah's sobs choked off her words.

"We were working in the fields when we heard the bell. Mama rang it and we came running."

Leah remembered the big bell that hung on the front porch. It was rung for meals and for emergencies. When it sounded in the middle of the day, all the Amish came quickly to see what was wrong. "Oh, Ethan, this is so horrible! Why did it have to happen?"

"Come," he said. "Sit with us."

She followed him to where his father and grandfather stood, their eyes closed, heads bowed. The family had formed a tight circle with chairs, and Tillie Longacre sat ramrod straight, clutching Oma's hand. Charity, Simeon, and Elizabeth were slumped, their cheeks streaked with tears. Sarah, looking very pregnant, held baby Nathan. Her husband paced the floor.

Leah felt like an intruder, but she couldn't be shut out now. She wouldn't allow it. She crouched in front of Ethan's mother. "I'm sorry, Mrs. Longacre," Leah whispered. "Really, really sorry."

"My child is in God's hands now. He will care for her."

Ethan took Leah to one side, and soon Charity joined them. Leah told Charity what she'd heard at the scene of the accident, then asked, "Do you know anything else?"

"Rebekah had her back turned and didn't see the truck coming. She never had time to jump out of the way." Charity's voice cracked.

"You mean the truck ran over her?" Leah thought she was going to be ill.

"We are not sure, but that's the way it looks."

"Then she could be . . . she could be—"

"Do not say the words," Charity interrupted. "Do not even think them."

Leah turned back toward Ethan. "Rebekah's got to be all right. She has to be."

"The produce stand was well made," Charity offered. "It was strong and sturdy. Perhaps it shielded Rebekah somehow."

"Wood is no match for metal," Ethan said bitterly.

All afternoon, the lobby filled with Amish as word spread about Rebekah. Through the sliding glass doors, Leah saw a parking lot full of dark buggies and horses. The men came to Jacob, the women to Tillie. Leah heard one man say, "We are all giving blood, Jacob. Your little one may have need of it."

Leah watched as they rolled up their sleeves and followed nurses down the hall to the lab. She stood. "Maybe I can give blood too," she told Ethan, starting down the hall.

He followed her quickly. "You do not have to do this. There will be enough who give."

"Don't you want my blood? Is it too English?" His face colored, and she regretted her words. "Forgive me, Ethan. I didn't mean it. I just want to do something for Rebekah."

"There is nothing to forgive, Leah. I know how you care about my sister."

At the lab, Leah collected paperwork from a technician and began filling it out. When she got to the box requesting information about diseases or illnesses she may have had, she stopped writing. *Cancer.* The word jumped off the page at her. Her blood ran cold. She took it over to the tech. "Excuse me, but what if I've had one of these problems?"

"Then you can't donate blood."

"But why? I'm sure the problem's gone."

"Sorry. That's the rule. We can't take a chance of passing on serious medical conditions to others." He reached for the paper.

Leah wadded it up, tossed it on the desk and fled the area.

Ethan caught up with her in the hallway. "Stop, Leah."

Crying, she struggled to get away.

"It is not your fault that you had cancer," Ethan said. "Rebekah has plenty of blood donors. Do not concern yourself."

"It's not fair. It isn't, Ethan! There's nothing I can do for her. Nothing."

He held her while she cried. Finally he fumbled for his big handkerchief and wiped her cheeks. "Come. I must get back to the lobby in case the doctor comes to tell us something."

Leah went with him to the lobby, where a doctor in a white lab coat was standing with the family. Flecks of dried blood splattered his shoe coverings. He looked grim, and Leah felt her mouth go cotton dry. He was saying, "We've finally gotten your daughter stabilized and moved up to intensive care."

"How is she?" Jacob Longacre asked, his voice thick with emotion.

"In all honesty, sir, she's in critical condition, with

massive internal injuries. Right now, she's comatose and on a respirator."

"But she is alive," Tillie Longacre said.

The doctor nodded.

"May we see her?" Mr. Longacre asked.

"Yes. ICU is on the third floor. The nurses up there will take you to her." The doctor put a hand on Mrs. Longacre's shoulder. "We're doing everything medically possible for her."

Leah realized that the doctor didn't sound hopeful at all. Mrs. Longacre held her head high. Her eyes were diamond bright with tears. "We will go to her." Calmly, she walked arm in arm with her husband to the elevator, and the rest of the family followed like ducklings. Leah fell into step beside Ethan, hardly daring to take a breath, terrified that she might use up all the oxygen in the room and not leave enough for anybody else.

In the ICU area, a nurse took the group into a glass-walled cubicle where Rebekah lay on a bed, hooked to wires and machines. Green blips trailed across the faces of monitors. Electronic beeps punctuated the silence. And the ominous hiss of the respirator spoke of the fragility of Rebekah's life. Leah stared mutely. Rebekah looked like a fractured china doll. Her face was bruised and her arms were in splints. The tube from the respirator protruded from her mouth, held in place by crisscrosses of papery white tape. An IV bag hung from a pole, a long tube running down to the needle inserted under the skin of her hand. Her tiny body hardly made a mound beneath the sheets.

Seeing Rebekah lying so still and unmoving was more than Leah could bear. Feeling light-headed, she held on to the wall with one hand and moved down the hallway, hoping she wouldn't pass out. Just when she thought she wasn't going to make it, she felt Ethan's strong arm around her waist. "Are you all right?" he asked.

She shook her head, not trusting her voice.

"Sit." He led her to a waiting area and settled her into a chair. "Take deep breaths," he told her.

Leah gulped air and then, finding her voice, managed to say, "Go on back and be with your family."

"I don't want to leave you."

"Please, go on. Your place is with them."

Ethan rose. "I'll be back soon."

Leah watched him hurry away. She hugged her arms and rocked back and forth in the chair. Outside the window of the waiting area, sunlight beat down. She could feel the heat through the glass. Outside, it was summer and the air was hot. But inside, Leah was cold. Very, very cold.

EIGHTEEN

Throughout the long night, Rebekah clung to life. The family was allowed to visit her in ten-minute intervals twice an hour, so everyone took shifts, going in two by two. One of the nurses explained that although Rebekah was in a coma, she might be able to hear, so she suggested that they say positive, encouraging things. "Let her know you love her," the nurse told them.

Leah staked out a place on one of the utilitarian sofas in the waiting area. She didn't care whether the entire Longacre family wanted her around or not. She wasn't going to leave with Rebekah's life hanging in the balance.

Whenever it was Ethan's turn to see his little sister, Leah went with him. She slipped her hand into Rebekah's and squeezed gently. The child's skin felt cool. "Hi," Leah whispered, close to Rebekah's ear. "It's

Leah, your old hospital roommate. Can you hear me? Please wake up, Rebekah."

Only the hiss of the respirator answered Leah.

"You've got to wake up, Rebekah." Leah bit her lip, trying to keep her voice low and calm. "Who's going to take care of your chickens? You're the only one who knows how to really and truly take care of them."

The green line showing Rebekah's heartbeat marched unchanging across the monitor.

"You know I can't tell one chicken from another. How will I know which one is mine if you don't tell me?" Leah asked.

Leah felt Ethan's hand on her shoulder. He crouched beside her, enveloping Leah's hand in his. He whispered something in German in Rebekah's ear. "Come back to us, little one," he added in English. "Do you not know how we love you? Can you not see how we want you to smile at us?"

His quiet voice and simple pleas practically unraveled Leah. "I'll take you for a ride in my car," she promised the child on the bed. "Wouldn't you like that? You can ride up front and wave at all your friends."

"Little sister," Ethan said. "I will let you hold the buggy reins. I am sorry I have always told you no before. But now they will be yours. I will ride beside you and you can make old Bud step high."

Their ten minutes were up. Rebekah had neither

moved nor responded. Shakily Leah left with Ethan and returned to the waiting room. Leah slumped into a chair and buried her face in her hands. "When we were in the hospital together last December, it was different," she told Ethan. "Rebekah was sick, but she could talk and smile. Now she's completely helpless. I'm afraid."

"Many people are praying for her," Ethan said. "There is a constant prayer vigil, day and night."

The news comforted Leah. And it gave her hope. Surely, if so many prayers were being said on Rebekah's behalf, how could a loving God turn a deaf ear to them?

Throughout the next day, Amish friends and neighbors came to check on Rebekah and comfort her family. Women brought food-filled baskets so that the Longacres would not have to buy food in the hospital cafeteria. Church elders came, somber men in dark suits, holding their hats in their hands, offering quiet prayers with Jacob and his sons. Leah watched it all, like a parade that she didn't belong to and couldn't get in step with. She knew she stuck out in her English clothes. But she couldn't leave. And she felt that Ethan wanted her with him. They talked little but simply sat in the corner together, their arms and shoulders touching. It comforted Leah to be near him. She hoped her presence offered him some measure of comfort too.

Jonah arrived around noon. He was dressed Amish,

and Leah realized it was the only time she'd seen him dressed that way. He looked big and rawboned, ill at ease in the confines of the hospital. Charity went to him, and they stared mutely into each other's eyes. Jonah did not go in to see Rebekah, but when Charity returned from a visit, he sat with her, shielding her protectively with his large body.

Several doctors came to check on Rebekah: an orthopedist, a neurologist, a critical care physician, and an internist. Each doctor told the family the same thing. "No change. The next forty-eight hours will be her most critical."

That evening, Jacob sent his exhausted parents home. "Your collapse will not bring Rebekah back to us," he told Opa. And to Sarah, he said, "Go get some rest, daughter. You must think now of your own child." Baby Nathan had been taken away earlier by friends who would care for him until the family returned home.

In the early hours of the morning, unable to sleep on the lumpy sofa, Leah ventured down the quiet halls to the elevator. On the ground floor, she found a small chapel, dimly lit and as quiet as a tomb. Sighing, she slid into one of the short rows of pews and bowed her head. Her mind went blank. She wasn't sure what to say to God anymore. She'd already made a hundred promises to him if he'd only make Rebekah well. Now, in this place dedicated to prayer, Leah felt empty and desolate.

She thought about her stay in the hospital and her terror when she'd been told by the doctors that they wanted to amputate her leg. And she remembered how Rebekah and Charity and Ethan had come into her life and made her less fearful. Now she felt helpless and useless.

"Leah." Ethan's voice interrupted her thoughts. "How are you?" He slipped into the pew.

"Not too good," she answered truthfully. "I'm really scared, Ethan. I'm scared that Rebekah isn't ever going to wake up."

"She hasn't once acted as if she's really here with us," he admitted. "But I will not give up hope."

"I keep thinking about Gabriella and how she kept showing up last December. Where is she now when we need her? She's an angel! So why doesn't she *do* something?"

"What if she wasn't really an angel?" he asked. "What if there is some other explanation?"

Leah shook her head. "I was so sure she was. And you told me that you thought so too."

"All we know for certain is that we cannot explain her strange comings and goings. But even if she is an angel, you cannot expect her to show up in every crisis."

"I'm not asking that she show up in every crisis. But Rebekah needs her now. She should be here. What kind of a guardian angel is she anyway? Why wasn't she on duty when that truck went out of control?"

"Angels are not servants of people. They are servants of God."

"Then God should have sent Gabriella to stop the accident from happening in the first place."

Ethan took a deep breath and smoothed Leah's hair. "But God did not. I do not understand why either. But he did not stop the accident."

Leah laid her head against Ethan's broad chest and began to cry softly.

On Sunday, while the Amish community attended church and prayed for Rebekah and her family, the Longacres remained in the ICU waiting room. Leah stayed also, knowing she couldn't return to her apartment as long as Rebekah was in a coma. The medical tests on Rebekah continued to be discouraging, but still Leah clung to hope. That evening, she called Mrs. Stoltz and quit her job.

"How is the little girl?" Mrs. Stoltz asked.

"No change," Leah said sadly.

On Monday morning the doctors arrived, their expressions unreadable, making Leah feel especially uneasy. She had once seen such carefully guarded looks on the faces of her own doctors before they'd delivered the devastating news that she had bone cancer.

The neurologist held a clipboard and spoke directly

to Jacob and Tillie. "We've repeated tests on Rebekah for days now," he said in a kind but firm voice. "I'm sorry to have to tell you this, but Rebekah has no higher brain activity. She hasn't had much since she was brought in, but still we wanted to give her every opportunity for recovery. Medically, your daughter is brain dead, Mr. Longacre. The only thing keeping her alive is the machines. I want your permission to turn the machines off and let her body join her spirit."

In the stunned silence, no one spoke. Leah wanted to scream at him. She wanted to strike him. She wanted to knock him down and step on him. She stood frozen to the floor and watched Tillie's face crumble with grief and a trail of tears run down Jacob's craggy cheeks. "You are sure of this?"

The doctor held out a long piece of paper with computer-drawn squiggles on it. "This is her EEG, a measurement of her brain activity from the time she was brought in. As you can see, the line gets progressively flatter. And her reflexes are gone. Plus, her pupils are fixed and dilated. All these factors convince me of the diagnosis."

Jacob stared long and hard into the doctor's face. Tillie hung on his arm, as if it were her sole means of support. "We will tell her goodbye," Jacob finally said.

Leah trembled. Why didn't he fight? Why didn't he

yell no? How could he accept the doctor's word so completely? Doctors could be wrong. Tests could be incorrect. Hadn't that been true in Leah's own case?

The doctor said, "Take all the time you need." As Jacob turned to lead his family toward their final visit into the ICU cubicle, the doctor added, "Even if Rebekah had awakened, sir, she would never have been normal. There was simply too much damage."

Jacob nodded, then stepped inside the cubicle.

Leah trailed behind hesitantly, acutely aware that she was not family but only a bystander in Rebekah's life. So she stood outside the enclosure, her palms pressed against the glass, watching. One by one, each member of Rebekah's family bent and kissed the little girl's cheek. They surrounded the bed, hovering like darkly dressed angels, holding hands and bowing their heads. Leah could hear them murmuring in German, and she could see the expressions of quiet acceptance on their faces.

Leah felt numb all over, as if all the blood had been drained from her body and replaced with ice water. She couldn't accept this. It was horrible and undeserved sentence on a sweet, loving child with her whole life ahead of her. Perhaps the Longacres could see it as God's will, but Leah could not. God was unfair!

When the family finished praying, they sang a hymn in German, then touched Rebekah one last time and left.

Leah rode down with them in the elevator. In the parking lot, she blinked in the bright sun. She had not been outside in days. She heard Opa say, "The buggy is over here, Jacob."

As they started toward it, Leah took Ethan's hand, holding him back. "Ethan, please, don't go yet. Tell me what to do. I don't know what to do now."

He stroked her cheek. "Now we go home and prepare for Rebekah's wake and funeral."

"May I come?" she asked in a small voice.

"Certainly, you may come. For now, go home, get some rest. Come to the house tomorrow morning."

"I—I'm not one of you—"

Ethan silenced her by placing the tips of his fingers against her lips. "Rebekah would want you with us," he said. "Charity and I will help you. You will not be alone."

"Should I tell anyone? I—I was thinking of your brother, Eli."

She felt Ethan stiffen. "There is no way to tell him."

"I guess it wouldn't make sense, would it? I mean, he never knew of Rebekah in life. Why should he know of her now that she's—" Leah stopped, unable to say the last word.

The buggy pulled to a stop beside them, and Ethan climbed aboard. His father handed him the reins. Leah heard Ethan say, "*Ya,*" and watched him slap the reins on the horse's rounded rump. She stood in the parking lot, in the hot August-sunshine, and listened to the clop of the animal's hooves on the asphalt. Ethan guided the plain black buggy into the flow of auto traffic. Leah watched it wind its way slowly up the road toward the outskirts of town.

Numb, Leah went to her car. The surface looked dull. She could barely see her reflection in the chrome and mirrors, and what she could see looked distorted. Just as she felt on the inside—deformed and misshapen. Rebekah Longacre was gone. For her there would be no miracle, no restoration of her life to those who loved her. The heavens were silent. God had turned a deaf ear to the prayers and pleas of Amish and English alike. Rebekah was dead. Dead.

NINETEEN

Leah slept fitfully, waking with sudden starts, and, re-membering that Rebekah was dead, cried herself back to sleep. Early in the morning, she gave up on sleep, dressed in dark, somber clothes, and drove out to the farm.

When she arrived, the yard was already full of black carriages. Realizing that her red convertible stuck out like a sore thumb, Leah left it at the very edge of the property, on the far end from where the accident had happened. At the site of the accident, Leah saw that every scrap of wood had been cleaned up. All that remained as witness to the horrible event were the smashed rows of corn.

Leah walked toward the farmhouse. Even so early in the morning, the air seemed stagnant. The heat rose off the ground in waves, making her hair stick to the back of her neck. She found Charity in the front yard, sitting beside the wagon wheel, hugging her knees, her eyes red and puffy. Leah sat down beside her. "Hi. I couldn't stay away any longer."

"I miss Rebekah, Leah. All night, I kept waking up and looking over to her side of the bed. It was empty. Only Rose sat up on the pillow. Like she was waiting for Rebekah to come to bed. I could not bear to even look at her doll."

Fresh tears pooled in Leah's eyes as Charity talked. "I didn't sleep much either." Leah sniffed hard. "Will you tell me what's going to happen? I—I've never been to an Amish funeral."

"The ones I've been to have been for old people. They are expected to die." Charity dabbed at her eyes with a white handkerchief. "But I will tell you what to expect." She sat up straighter. "The Amish undertaker has taken Rebekah's body from the hospital. Papa and Ethan and Opa worked most of the night to build her coffin in the barn. Usually, coffins are made by others, but Papa wanted to make Rebekah's with his own hands."

Leah stared off toward the barn, imagining the sad sound of hammers banging long into the night.

Charity continued. "Other men picked up the coffin this morning and took it to the undertaker's. The hearse will return with it this afternoon for the viewing."

Suddenly it struck Leah that everyone in the community would be arriving to see Rebekah's body lying in the coffin. She shuddered, not certain she could participate in the ritual.

"Many people are helping us now," Charity said. "The men are doing the chores. The women are cleaning the house and setting up for the funeral tomorrow morning. Tomorrow we will have a church service here. Then we will all go to the graveyard at the back of our farm for the burial. Afterward, people will come back here for a meal and help us clear the house of the extra chairs and things. Then everybody will go home."

And life will go on, Leah thought. Chores would be done, cows milked, chickens fed, gardens tilled. Rebekah would be under the ground, and life would go on. She turned to Charity. "You're burying her on the farm?"

"Our family has lived here for many years. In time, all of us will be buried on this land. It is ours."

Leah recalled movies in which cemeteries were portrayed as dark, creepy places where the dead haunted the living. But here, in this land of the Amish, cemeteries were merely resting places for loved ones. There was nothing ghoulish about cemeteries. "What should I do?"

"Just be with us."

Leah plucked a flower from the flower bed and rolled it between her fingers. "Can I send flowers for her funeral?"

Charity shook her head. "That is not done. Amish bury plainly, just as we live."

"Where's Ethan?" All at once, Leah ached to see him, to touch him.

"He is at the family cemetery. He is digging our sister's grave."

Leah followed Charity's directions to the family cemetery, located beyond the barn and the woods, at the back side of the property. She passed the garden and remembered the first day she'd come to the farm and how Rebekah had run to meet her. Leah turned her head. She passed the chicken coop and the barn, remembered the day of the water fight, and felt a lump the size of a fist clog her throat.

Leah skirted the woods and saw a short white picket fence marking off an enclosure of well-kept grass. Within, she saw headstones. She entered by a small gate, covered with an arched arbor, heavy with jasmine and morning-glory vines. She heard the sound of shovels digging in earth and crossed slowly to a pit. There, deep in the hole, stood Ethan, Simeon and Jonah. Emotion almost overcame Leah as she watched them scooping up soil and tossing it up to a pile heaped alongside the grave. "Ethan," she called quietly.

He looked up. Sweat poured down his face. His

homespun shirt was limp and soaked. "Leah! What are you doing here?"

"I—I wanted to see you."

Ethan glanced at Jonah, who said, "Go."

Ethan came up a ladder and swung over the top edge of the hole. Leah stepped closer, but he stepped away. "I am dirty. I will mess you up." Dirt clung to his work boots and hands.

"Why are you doing this?"

"I want to. It is the very least I can do for her."

Leah realized that this was Ethan's way of easing his grief, of sweating off his own pain. The physical labor was good for him. She read it in his expression. "Is there something I can do to help?" she said. "Can I bring you water?"

Ethan shook his head. "We have water with us."

Leah shrugged and glanced around the cemetery. "Whose is the earliest grave?"

"Joseph Longacre. He was the infant son of my great-great-grandparents. He died one winter of scarlet fever."

"Sad," Leah said. "When babies die, it's really sad."

"Dying is part of living," Ethan said. "Nothing can bring my sister back to this life. Now she lives with God, in heaven. I know baby Joseph is playing with her."

Leah wanted to believe it too. How she wished to have Ethan's simple faith! But she was angry at God. He should have allowed Rebekah to live. "I guess I should go back to the house," Leah said.

"We will not be much longer," Ethan told her. "I will clean up and see you there. Many will come this afternoon and evening."

Leah returned to the house and stayed close to Charity. Later in the afternoon, Leah watched through the kitchen window as a lone black horse pulled a simple springboard wagon into the front yard. In the back of the wagon lay an unadorned child-sized pine coffin with two long poles attached to it. Six men, including Ethan, stepped up and pulled the coffin off the wagon, shouldered the poles and carried it up onto the porch, in through the front parlor, and into a small room at the back of the house.

Leah followed Charity and other family members into the room, a room swept meticulously clean, with only a table to hold the coffin, a single chair and a few candles. Both fascinated and repelled, Leah watched as the coffin was set upon the table turned bier. The window in the room was open, but without fans the room felt stifling. Leah left the small, airless room. She pressed herself against a wall, hoping not to faint from either the heat or her burden of grief.

Back in the kitchen, she splashed water on her face from the hand pump over the sink. Minutes later, she felt Ethan's touch on her back. "More people are coming," he said, looking out the window. "To pay their respects."

Leah saw buggies pulling into the yard—a yard cleaned, weeded and clipped to receive friends and neighbors at its very best. Leah murmured, "I—I'm not sure I can go in there and look at her, Ethan."

"It does not matter. Only her body is in the coffin. Her spirit is with the Lord."

"There was a chair in the room. Why?"

"We will keep an all-night watch. It is our custom never to leave the body alone."

She wanted to ask why but decided he probably didn't know. He rarely knew the why of their customs, only that it was always done that way. She looked back to Ethan. "I think I should go."

"You do not have to."

Leah shook her head. "Yes, I do. I don't belong here. I'm the only English."

"That should not trouble you."

Tears filled her eyes. "But it does, Ethan. It does."

Ethan followed Leah outside. The undertaker had gone, but the memory of where his wagon had stood forced Leah to make a wide arc in the yard before she headed toward the road and her parked car. Ethan caught her elbow at the edge of the yard. "What will you do, Leah? Where are you going?"

"Back to my apartment, I guess." She wiped under her eyes. "I should start packing. There was a message on my answering machine from my mother when I got in last night. She and Neil are in Los Angeles and will be flying to Indianapolis today. She plans to come help me get my stuff home next week."

Ethan stared down at her. "I had forgotten. You will be leaving. But . . . so soon! I will miss you." The last was said haltingly, as if he was pulling the words from deep inside.

"You know, two weeks ago, the thought of leaving was driving me crazy." Leah looked over his shoulder at the rambling farmhouse. "Now . . . well, I'm sort of glad. It would be hard to stay, to expect to see Rebekah whenever I came out here." Her voice wavered. "It's best this way. I'll go back to my world. You'll stay in yours."

"You will always be a part of my world, Leah. Because you will always be a part of me."

Her gaze flew to his face. His clear blue eyes were serious, tinged with grief. Was some of it for her? For them? Leah choked down a sob, holding it at bay with steely resolve. "I have to go now. I don't think I can take any more sadness, Ethan. I can't."

He caught her arm once more. "Will you be here tomorrow?"

Leah nodded. "I have to come. I have to tell Rebekah goodbye."

"Yes," he said. "We will all tell her goodbye."

Yet as Leah drove off, she couldn't imagine watching that plain, undersized coffin being lowered into the cool, dark ground. She drove to town, weeping all the way.

TWENTY

It took Leah a long time to decide what to wear to Rebekah's funeral. Anxious that she might be the only English among the mourners, she didn't want to stand out any more than necessary. After much deliberation, she chose a simple black denim jumper and added a white T-shirt underneath. She brushed her dark hair and plaited it into a French braid. She wore no makeup, not even lip gloss.

She drove slowly to the farm, often following black buggies headed in the same direction. When she arrived, she saw a long line of buggies parked in the farmyard and along the country road fronting the farm. Younger kids helped with the horses, tying reins to hitching posts. Leah also took note of several cars. Glad not to have driven the only automobile, she again parked at the far end of the Longacre property and walked to the house.

The first person that she saw in the yard and recognized by name was Martha Dewberry.

Martha's eyes were red from crying. "This is the worst thing that has ever happened," Martha said to Leah. "Rebekah was so sweet. So young."

Leah agreed. She felt no animosity toward Martha. There was no rivalry between them now. In the shared experience of grief, they were only two teenagers, mourning the loss of a friend. "I'll miss her," Leah said.

"She talked about you all the time. She thought you were glamorous." Martha managed a smile. "Like a movie star."

"You're kidding. I didn't know she even knew what a movie star was."

"She peeked in our magazines. The ones we stuff under our mattresses."

"My friends and I used to do the same thing," Leah said. "Hide the things we didn't want our parents to know about."

"It isn't easy growing up Amish. The things of the English are very tempting."

"Your Amish ways are tempting too," Leah said. "I guess neither way is easy."

Leah left Martha and slipped into the house. The furniture had been removed from the dining room and parlor. Wooden benches had been set in long rows. An usher, a young man Leah recognized from Jonah's group of friends, showed her to a place on one of the benches. Rebekah's coffin had been placed at the front of the room, and the Longacre family sat in front of the coffin with their backs to the rows of mourners.

As the mantel clock struck nine, a man stood, removed his hat, turned toward the others, and began to quote Scripture from the Old Testament. Eventually he mentioned Rebekah and the loss of her young life. But the man mostly talked to his audience about living godly lives and preparing themselves for eternal life. He quoted: " 'The Lord gave, and the Lord hath taken away; blessed be the name of the Lord.' " Leah thought it a strange eulogy.

At her grandmother's funeral, the minister had talked about Grandma Hall and her rich, full life. He'd mentioned how much she'd be missed and shared personal things about her life. Leah could only see the back of Ethan's head, but she wondered if he would have liked the minister to say more in praise of Rebekah. Leah certainly wished that the man had. But it wasn't her place to criticize, either.

Once the first man sat down, another stood and spoke. He also had little to say about Rebekah, but instead reminded all the Amish youth, "No person knows the hour of his death, so all must live good lives. Stay away from sinning." Leah shifted uncomfortably. Nothing either man said seemed to address the loss of

Rebekah. She wondered if anyone was receiving comfort from these speeches.

Eventually the second man asked the group to kneel. He read a long prayer in German. Songs were not sung, but spoken in German. And just when Leah thought she couldn't sit for one more minute on the hard, uncomfortable bench, the congregation was asked to vacate the room. The room would be rearranged and the mourners would file past the coffin for one final farewell to Rebekah.

Leah almost panicked. She couldn't look at Rebekah. She couldn't! And yet, when the time came, she found herself in line in front of a young woman who was holding baby Nathan. The child grabbed at Leah's braid, and Leah turned and smiled at him. The baby gave her a slobbery grin. The woman holding him spoke to him sternly, and Nathan's lower lip quivered.

Leah turned back toward the coffin, and with her heart hammering hard against her ribs, she stepped beside the plain pine box and looked down. The lid was formed in two halves. The top half was raised, and inside lay Rebekah. The child was dressed in white, the color for Amish mourning. Her head was covered with a white prayer cap, the ties fastened neatly beneath her chin. Leah wanted to untie them and let them hang loose, as Rebekah always had in life.

Leah's hands began to shake and her knees went

weak. Rebekah looked waxen, like a store mannequin. From behind her, Leah heard Nathan squeal, "Bekah!" She turned to see him open his arms for his dead sister's hug.

The baby's lack of understanding unglued Leah completely. She bolted from the line and darted out the door. She pushed past people standing in the yard and, sobbing, started to run. Leah knew they were staring at her, but she didn't care. Blinded by her tears, she ran. She hit the boundary of the woods. Her heart was pounding, her lungs felt on fire. But she didn't stop running until she came to the great rock in the clearing where Ethan had brought her that moonlit night at the beginning of the summer.

Leah slumped against the great boulder, then slid to the ground. Fighting for breath, she buried her face in her hands. She knew she was missing the procession to the grave site. She knew she wasn't going to see them lower Rebekah's coffin into the ground and cover it with dirt. She didn't care. She couldn't watch anyway.

Slowly her sobs lessened. Her ragged breath calmed, and quiet settled all around her. Above her, she heard a faint breeze whispering through the pine needles. The faint scent of evergreens filled the air. And then she faintly heard someone say her name.

"Leah."

Expectantly she raised her head. Her breath caught in her throat. Less than fifty feet away, at the edge of the clearing, Leah saw Gabriella, dressed Amish. And beside Gabriella, Leah saw Rebekah. She wore the white dress Leah had seen in the coffin, and the prayer cap too. Except that the ties were loose and fluttering. In her hand, she held a lace-edged hanky. Rebekah's face looked radiant, as bright as sunshine. She raised her hand and gave an excited wave, and then, looking up at Gabriella, turned with her, walked away and disappeared behind the trees.

Stunned, stupefied, Leah took several seconds to react. She scrambled to her feet and raced into the woods, calling, "Rebekah! Gabriella! Where are you? Please, come back."

Leah spun in every direction, straining to see shapes in the thick foliage. Long shafts of sunlight hung in the air like yellow ribbons. A lone butterfly circled lazily over a cluster of wildflowers. Otherwise, Leah was alone. Gabriella was gone. Rebekah was gone. All that remained was the faint, sweet scent of pine.

Leah remained in the woods until she was certain the burial was over and the Amish neighbors had gone home. She kept trying to replay in her mind what she'd seen. *Gabriella. Rebekah. Holding hands.* They had had form and substance. They had not been ghosts, nor figments of her imagination. She'd seen them with her eyes wide open.

She left the woods and walked back to the house. Leah stepped up onto the porch and rapped gently on the door. Ethan came, and when he saw her, he opened the screen door wide. "I have been worried about you," he said. "I saw you run away. Where did you go? Are you all right?"

"Yes, Ethan. I'm all right now. I'm sorry I ran off. I've been in the woods. Can I talk to your parents?"

He glanced over his shoulder. "We are having Bible reading and prayer time. Maybe tomorrow would be better."

"It can't wait," Leah said, her heart pounding. "Please."

He took her into the parlor. The room was back in order, with no sign that a crowd of mourners had filled it only hours before. The family sat in a small circle. Baby Nathan played on the floor. Mr. Longacre closed the Bible on his lap and stood. His expression was one of deep sadness mixed with wariness and surprise. "We are in mourning, Leah."

Leah squared her shoulders. "I'm sorry to barge in on you, but something happened today that I must tell you about." Quietly, her voice trembling, she told them what she'd seen in the woods. When she finished, she peered anxiously from face to face. The circle of eyes stared back at her. "Don't you believe me? Please tell me you believe me."

Mr. Longacre cleared his throat. "We have all had a great shock, Leah. Sometimes our minds play tricks on us."

"I tell you, I saw them both."

"Perhaps you fell asleep and dreamed this," Mrs. Longacre suggested with a quavery voice.

Leah shook her head vehemently. "I was wide awake. I saw Rebekah and Gabriella today. I know Rebekah told you about Gabriella and how Gabriella visited us in the hospital last December."

Mr. Longacre looked sterner than ever. "This is a hard thing to accept, Leah. The dead do not appear to the living. We will not see Rebekah again until we meet her in heaven."

Tears of frustration welled in Leah's eyes. How could she make them believe her? "I tell you, I *saw* her." Her voice sounded frantic to her own ears.

"Leah, stop!" Mr. Longacre commanded.

Ethan was by Leah's side instantly. "Papa, do not be angry. I know Leah. She would not make this up."

"Rebekah waved a hanky at me," Leah said, still desperate to make them believe her.

"You should go," Mr. Longacre said.

"Jacob, wait," Oma said, and everyone looked her

way. She stood shakily, her face ashen. "I believe Leah. Early this morning, I had asked to spend a few minutes alone with Rebekah's coffin."

"*Ja*. I remember."

Oma's eyes were bright with tears. "I placed a hanky in her hand. I tucked it in carefully so that no one would see. It was a favorite of hers, and I wanted her to have it with her. No one could have known about the hanky except me. I acted as a foolish old woman, but she was such a precious child to me."

Leah felt suddenly giddy and as light as a feather. She wasn't going crazy. She had not imagined anything. "I—I saw her," Leah repeated softly. "I truly did."

The room was absolutely silent. Finally Jacob Longacre gave a slow nod. "So be it."

Tillie reached for Leah's hand. "Oh, Leah, God has given you a wonderful gift."

"Just as he did last Christmas," Charity added.

"You all believe me?" Leah asked again, relief draining her, making her very bones feel rubbery.

"What you have told us brings us peace," Mrs. Longacre said.

Tears started down Leah's cheeks. "Thank you," she said simply. She felt Ethan squeeze her hand. She turned, and, with head held high, left the room.

TWENTY-ONE

"I think that's about it." Neil slammed the back door of the rented moving trailer.

"I can't believe we got all your stuff into only two cars at the start of the summer," Leah's mother added. "Are you sure you don't mind driving back alone?"

Leah shook her head. "I don't mind."

Neil and her mother had driven up that morning, rented the trailer, and loaded Leah's things for the return trip home. It had been decided that Leah would follow in her car. By now it was late afternoon.

"I could ride with you," her mother said. "We haven't had a chance to catch up, and there's so much to tell you."

Leah glanced down the road leading from the parking lot of her apartment. Would Ethan come to say goodbye?

Neil caught Leah's eye and, with an understanding nod, took Leah's mother by the elbow. "There'll be plenty of time for that, honey, once we get home. Let's get going, and Leah can catch up. We'll be driving a whole lot slower anyway."

Leah tossed him a grateful glance. Neil must have realized that she was dragging her feet. "Sure, you two go on ahead and I'll be along. There are a couple more things I need to do."

Her mother frowned. "I can't imagine."

Leah had briefly mentioned Rebekah's death and funeral, and both Neil and her mother had been very sorry. Sympathy was all they could offer.

Neil opened the car door and guided his wife into the passenger seat. "Drive carefully," he called to Leah as he climbed into the car and started the engine.

"I won't be long," Leah promised. She watched them drive away, the trailer in tow. Alone in the parking lot, she felt foolish. She leaned against her car, unsure what to do.

The last time she'd seen Ethan, it had been at the bus station with his family. They were going to visit an uncle in another part of the state. Mr. Longacre had thought that a short vacation would make them all feel better. Sarah and her husband, along with Jonah, would take care of the farm while they were gone. "My mom's coming next week to get me," Leah had told Ethan.

"I will see you before you leave," he'd promised her.

But the week had passed and he hadn't come. Leah couldn't put off leaving much longer. With only the stuffed bear Ethan had won for her at the fair and the lop-eared bunny glued to her dashboard, she had little else to remind her of him. She had no photos, no snapshots of their summer together. She had only memories.

She thought about driving to the farm for one last look but decided against it. She'd already said goodbye to the farm the day of Rebekah's funeral. With a sigh, she reached for the door handle.

"Leah! Wait!"

Leah whipped around and saw Ethan jogging down the side of the road toward her. She took off running, met him at the end of the block and threw herself into his arms. He scooped her up and hugged her hard against himself. He began kissing her face—her forehead, her cheeks, her eyelids, her mouth.

Leah clung to him, the sweetness of his lips almost melting her bones. "I was afraid you wouldn't make it."

Breathing heavily, Ethan set her back on her feet. "I had problems getting here. I caught the bus yesterday, but it broke down. They sent another bus, but not right away. When I got to the station, I started walking and running."

"I'm glad you made it. I didn't want to go off without saying goodbye."

"Me either."

He took her hand, led her across the street to a small public park, and sat with her on a green bench. A few kids were roller-skating on the sidewalk, and the clickety-clack of their skates over the cracks broke the silence of the warm summer day.

"How's your family doing?" Leah asked.

"We are getting over Rebekah's death slowly," he said solemnly. "Charity cries a lot, but Ma and Oma are there for her. Knowing what you saw in the woods brings us all much comfort."

Leah nodded. "Me too. I'll never get over her dying, but I'm glad Gabriella let me see her one last time." Leah slipped her hand into his. "I really missed you while you were gone."

"All I thought about was you. Papa wasn't happy about my leaving early, but I do not care."

"Will you write me?"

"I will come and visit you."

"You will?" Her heart hammered. This was more than she had ever hoped for. "When?"

"When the harvest is in. I cannot leave Papa with so much work."

"Do you promise?"

Smiling down at her, Ethan asked, "Why do you want me to promise?"

"Because I know you always keep your word."

He kissed her warmly, deeply. "Do you not know, Leah? Do you not know that I love you?"

She started to cry. "I love you too. I have for months." She rested her cheek on his chest and felt the rough fabric of the homespun cloth. It gave her a jolt and instantly brought back all the differences between them. He was still Amish. She was still English. "What are we going to do, Ethan?"

"We are going to be together," he said.

"But—"

He silenced her with another kiss. "I do not know how, Leah. I do not know when. I only know we will."

Looking into Ethan's eyes, Leah believed him. His word was enough.

It was enough.

Until Angels Close My Eyes

This book is dedicated to
Josiah Christian McDaniel,
a lamb of God.

"What is man that you are mindful of him,
the son of man that you care for him?
You made him a little lower than the angels;
you crowned him with glory and honor
and put everything under his feet."

(Hebrews 2:6–8, New International Version)

ONE

"Leah, we need to talk."

Leah Lewis-Hall flicked off the TV and gave her mother her full attention. "What's up?" She knew something was wrong. For days, her mother had seemed edgy and uncommunicative. Most unlike herself. Leah's mother usually had something to say about everything. When Leah had come home from school that day, the house had been empty and there had only been a terse note: *Neil and I will be back before supper.*

Her mother sat down on the edge of the sofa. "I'm sure you've noticed that things haven't been exactly normal around here lately."

"Are you and Neil having problems?" Leah asked, fearing the worst. Since Neil was husband number five for her mother, Leah had reason to feel apprehensive. *Don't let it be divorce,* she pleaded silently. She liked

Neil. A lot. He was the best stepfather she had ever had. Not only that, but she didn't want to be uprooted and moved again. Not in her senior year. It was only October. Couldn't her mother at least gut it out until June?

"Yes, we're having problems," her mother said.

"What's wrong?" Leah's heart sank.

Her mother stood, wrung her hands, and began pacing the living room floor. "Neil had a doctor's appointment last week. Then, today, we went back for a consultation."

"Where is Neil anyway?" All at once Leah realized that Neil was not in the house.

"He's been checked into the hospital."

"What?" Leah's heart began to thud. "Is he sick? What's happened?" She knew a lot about being sick. Almost a year before, Leah had been diagnosed with bone cancer. Leah's mother had all but threatened the doctor with a lawsuit for incompetence and a misdiagnosis. Now her mother looked ghastly pale. Her face reminded Leah of her own excruciating experience.

"I—I never told you something about Neil when he and I first got married," her mother said, her voice quivering. "When Neil and I first met back in Dallas, when we first started dating, I never dreamed it would lead to marriage. He knew I didn't have a great track record when it came to matrimony. But we fell in love. I want you to remember that. I love Neil very much. Even the age difference between us never mattered to me."

Leah thought she might scream, waiting for her mother to get to the point.

"When things first started getting serious between us, Neil confided that he had a serious medical problem. It began even before his first wife died. Leah, Neil was diagnosed with cancer in one of his kidneys."

"*Cancer?* Neil has cancer? What are you telling me?" Leah's voice was trembling.

"Calm down, Leah, please. The affected kidney was removed and he went through chemotherapy to destroy any lingering malignant cells. He's never had another problem. I just assumed he was cured. You know how doctors are."

Leah was reeling, unable to absorb all the emotions that were shooting through her. "You're telling me that Neil Dutton, my stepfather, has had cancer? Why didn't you ever *tell* me? I should have been told, Mother. Especially with my condition."

"We were going to tell you. But the timing was just never right. We were going to tell you when we got back from our honeymoon in Japan. But then you were in the hospital, and Dr. Thomas insisted that you had cancer. We thought it best not to tell you then."

Leah's stay in the hospital had been traumatic. First

the diagnosis of cancer. Then the appearance, to Leah anyway, of the mysterious Gabriella, followed by the strange and seemingly impossible retreat of the cancer from Leah's leg bone. She had undergone six long weeks of chemotherapy and still returned to her doctor for periodic workups and evaluations. "I can't believe this! You had plenty of opportunities to say something about this."

"Neil didn't want to. He thought it best for you to concentrate on getting through chemo. And when that was over, he didn't want to burden you."

By now Leah was on her feet. "Burden me? How can you say such a thing? Even if Neil didn't tell me, you should have, Mom. It was *your* place to tell me!" She stopped abruptly. A new fear gripped her, overshadowing her anger. She turned to face her mother. "So why is Neil in the hospital?"

Her mother's chin began to tremble. "Because it appears his cancer has recurred."

Leah moved around her bedroom as if in a trance, preparing to go with her mother to the hospital to see Neil. She could hear her mother crying in the bathroom down the hall. *This can't be happening,* she kept telling herself.

She stopped at the window and stared out at the twilight. The farm fields stretched into the distance, broken only by a line of trees whose leaves were shot through with red and gold. It seemed all the leaves were on the brink of death.

Leah longed to talk to Ethan. He would help her sort everything out. The clear image of his tanned face, eyes as blue as sky, hair the color of wheat and sunlight, seemed to smile back at her from the window.

"I love you, Leah," he had told her that last afternoon they'd been together in August. But he was Amish, she was English. They were worlds apart in every way—miles apart physically. Yet she ached to see him, touch him. She missed him. She missed the rest of his family, too, especially his sisters Charity and Rebekah. Leah shook her head sadly. She'd never see Rebekah again—at least, not in this world.

Leah leaned her forehead against the cool pane. She had no way of getting hold of Ethan. The Amish had no phones, no computers for E-mail, no fax machines. Only snail mail, the U.S. postal system. Although she'd write him that very night to tell him about Neil, it would take days for him to get her letter and respond. She needed him now. No one at her new school would understand what she was going through. She wasn't particularly close to anybody there. Sure, she had friends, but no one as special as Ethan.

"Are you ready?"

Her mother's question brought Leah back to the moment. "Sure. Let's go."

They didn't talk during the fifteen-minute ride to the hospital. Leah knew what it was like to hear doctors say, "You have cancer." And apparently, so did Neil. At the moment, Leah just wanted to see him with her own eyes.

The community hospital wasn't huge, but it was new. As she stepped into the hospital corridor, Leah's own hospital stay in Indianapolis flooded back to her. The smell was the same: clean and antiseptic.

Leah's mother stepped up to the nurse's station. "I'm Roberta Dutton. Has the doctor been in to see my husband yet?" she asked.

"Dr. Howser is in with Mr. Dutton now," the nurse said.

Leah remembered Dr. Howser, Neil's physician. She had gone to see him when her finger broke for no apparent reason while Neil and her mother were honeymooning in Japan. Dr. Howser had X-rayed the finger, then sent her off to the hospital in Indianapolis. Except for meeting the Amish family she never would otherwise have known, the experience had been horrifying.

Leah's mother stopped in front of a door, squared her shoulders and pasted a smile on her face. She breezed into the room, and Leah followed.

Neil was propped up in the hospital bed. "Hey, girls," he said as Roberta kissed him on the cheek. Neil was sixty-eight, but he had always looked and acted much younger. The beautiful tan he'd gotten aboard the windjammer the past summer was gone. His skin looked sallow and papery. Leah swallowed against a lump in her throat. This change hadn't happened overnight, and she was upset with herself for not noticing it before.

"Look, why don't I let you visit with your family, Neil," Dr. Howser said. "I'll see you tomorrow when I make my rounds."

"As soon as I'm out of here, let's hit a few golf balls." Neil's voice had a forced joviality to it.

"You got it," Dr. Howser said before slipping out.

Leah's mother settled on the bed and took Neil's hand. "How are you feeling, dear?"

"Like a truck ran over me."

Leah noticed big bruises on Neil's arms.

Neil pushed his reading glasses down his nose and looked over them at Leah. "Hi, Leah. How are you?" His voice sounded kind, soft.

Leah felt glued to the floor.

"Come closer, honey."

Stiffly she edged forward. "I'm sorry you're sick," she mumbled.

Neil studied her, then turned to his wife. "Roberta, why don't you go get Leah and me some ice cream in the cafeteria? I couldn't eat much supper, and ice cream would taste good to me now."

The request almost made Leah start crying. She and
Neil sometimes ate ice cream and watched TV together
in the evenings at home.

Roberta glanced between Neil and Leah. "I guess I
could." She stood hesitantly, looking a little lost. Leah
kept staring at Neil. Her tears had retreated. In their
place was a building bubble of anger.

When Roberta finally left the room, Neil held out his
hand. "Come closer, Leah."

She shook her head furiously.

"Please."

Tears formed again in Leah's eyes. She threw her
coat on the floor and hurled herself at his bedside.
"Why!" she exploded. "Why didn't you tell me you had
cancer? Why didn't you tell me the truth?"

TWO

Neil calmly patted the mattress. "Come sit down, Leah. I sent your mother out of the room so that we could talk."

"I don't want to sit down." Leah was shaking. She hugged her arms to herself.

"I want to explain why I kept this from you, but I can't talk to you when you're hating me for it."

"I don't hate you. Please tell me."

"In a nutshell, the timing never seemed right. And don't be mad at your mother—I swore her to secrecy."

It irritated Leah that Neil knew just what she was thinking. She *was* angry at her mother. "I'm angry at you, too," she said.

"I knew you would be." He gave her an apologetic smile. "But please put yourself in my place for a minute. When you were first told about your cancer, you and I were virtual strangers. I'd just married your mother, you weren't happy about being moved from Dallas to Indiana farm country, and I was adjusting to taking on a wife and an almost grown daughter."

Neil's assessment was correct. Leah had hated moving and starting over in another school—especially one out in the boondocks.

Neil continued. "My first wife and I never had children, but I'd always wanted them. Suddenly, in my twilight years, I had a young energetic wife and a lovely stepdaughter. I was a little overwhelmed. I didn't want us to start out as enemies, Leah. I knew I wasn't your biological father, and I knew I couldn't replace him. I had to find my own place with you."

Leah turned her head, not wanting Neil to see how quickly tears had sprung to her eyes at the mention of her father. He'd died years before, homeless and on the streets. Her only link with him had been her Grandma Hall, but she had died too, and the biological link had been forever severed. Leah's mother had married and divorced three more times before marrying Neil. "What do you want me to say?" Leah asked, looking right at Neil. "That I like you better than the others?"

He smiled wryly. "Just that you like me is good enough."

"You know I like you. So if you know it, you should

have said something about your cancer to me. You knew what I was going through."

"It was a judgment call. At the time, the last thing I thought you needed to hear was a lame pep talk, like, 'Oh, by the way, I've had cancer myself, so hang tough and make it through just like I did.' I thought you needed to hear that I cared about you regardless of any health problems, and that your mother and I were going to be around for you no matter what. I see now that it was a poor call. I'm sorry."

"Well, when I started chemo, you should have told me then. I was scared. You could have helped me."

"I almost did," Neil said with a sigh. "But I was afraid of discouraging you. You see, I was so sick during my chemo treatments six years ago that I wanted to die. When I saw you going through chemo, I figured, why tell you about my horrors when you were having hardly any problems with it. I didn't want to jinx you."

Except for some mild nausea, Leah had sailed through chemo treatments. "So that's why you didn't say anything? You didn't want to give off negative vibes?" she said, rolling her eyes.

"You did have a pretty easy time with it, Leah. You never even lost your hair. I was bald as a cue ball for months."

Leah tried to picture Neil without his head of steely

white hair. "All right," she said grudgingly. "What about after my chemo? You could have told me then."

"Again, I could have, but I didn't. I gave you the car to celebrate." He smiled again. "I wanted you to be happy, and telling you then seemed impossible. I wanted to have more in common with you than cancer."

Leah felt exasperated by his explanations. His logic did sound . . . well, logical. However, she was still angry and didn't want to let him off the hook for keeping such a secret from her. "You still should have said something to me."

"I really figured I'd tell you this past summer. Out there on that windjammer, under those stars, a person feels very close to God. And to one's family."

"I wanted to live in Nappanee and work," Leah said defensively. She didn't add that she'd wanted to be with Ethan as much as possible, and that her summer with him had been wonderful.

"And I agreed that you should," Neil said. "Didn't I argue in your favor?"

It was true. It had been Neil who'd gone to bat for Leah with her mother. It had been Neil who'd found her a job and a place to live. "I came home in August," she said, getting in one more dig.

"And you were heartbroken over the death of little Rebekah. How could I have added to your pain?" Neil asked. "I couldn't."

"But now you're sick and I *have* to know. Otherwise, you'd probably never have told me, would you?"

"Probably not," Neil said. "By now, it would have been historical information and totally unnecessary to your well-being. For one so young, Leah, you've had a lot dumped on you in your life. I didn't want to be one more bad thing."

"Will you be honest with me from now on?" Leah asked. "Will you tell me exactly what's going on? Exactly what your doctor says?"

"Yes," Neil said. "No need to shelter you anymore. From now on out, the whole truth, and nothing but the truth, so help me God."

Leah managed a smile for him. *The truth.* She hoped they *all* could handle it.

Later that night, Leah composed a letter to Ethan. After telling him about Neil's previous cancer diagnosis, she poured out her feelings:

> *Weird, isn't it? That Neil and I should have so much in common without me knowing about it until now. I don't think it's right that he and Mom kept the truth from me, but it's been done and I know I shouldn't hold it against them. I believe Neil really thought he was doing the best thing for me. But it would have been good for me*

to know that he'd been through chemo before I started. I was pretty scared about it, and he could have helped me.

I worry about Mom getting through this too. She's not exactly a rock. Neil doesn't want us to worry. He wants us to go on with our lives. But how am I supposed to concentrate every day in school, wondering if he really does have cancer again?

I miss you, Ethan. I wish I could see you and talk to you. You always cheered me up whenever I felt down this summer. I still think about summer, you know. I still remember our being together, and your trying out English things. How are things going with your family? I know you miss Rebekah. I know I do. But whenever I start to miss her big-time, I think about the day of her funeral and what I saw in the woods. That always makes me feel better.

In your last letter, you asked me how my doctor's appointment went in September. Dr. Thomas says I'm doing just fine and that my MRI and X rays look clear.

Leah stopped writing and leaned back in her desk chair. The house was eerily quiet. Outside her window, the night looked black and deep. Her windowpane felt cool. Leah shivered. She reread what she'd written and shivered again. Her X rays looked clear and she didn't have to go back in for a checkup until spring. Yet a hard, cold knot had settled in her stomach. She couldn't seem to get rid of it. Yes, it was true that things looked good for her medically. But then Neil had thought the same thing. He'd thought he was perfectly fine. And now he was sick again.

Leah didn't want anything to happen to Neil. He'd been good to her mother, good to Leah. He was different from the other stepfathers she'd had. He was kind, generous. Neil *had* to get well. She and her mother needed him.

Leah buried her face in her hands and wept.

THREE

"Hey, Leah! Wait up!"

Leah turned to see Sherry Prater, a girl from her English class, coming toward her down the hall. While they weren't exactly best buddies, Sherry was friendly and energetic, and Leah liked her. Sherry was overweight, and therefore not on the social A-list. This suited Leah just fine. Leah had been with the in crowd at her former high school and thought the distinction highly overrated. "What's up?" she asked the out-of-breath Sherry.

"I was wondering if you were going to the football game Friday night. I thought we might hook up and sit together."

"I forgot about the game."

Sherry stared at Leah as if she were speaking a

foreign language. "This game's against Henderson. They're our biggest rival! Everybody's going."

"My stepfather's not well," Leah said. "He's in the hospital." In fact, Neil had been in the hospital for the better part of the week.

"I didn't know." Sherry's brown eyes filled with concern. "Is he going to be all right?"

"I don't know yet. He's going through some tests."

"That's too bad. When you find out what's wrong, will you tell me?"

Leah agreed. "As for the game, I'll let you know if I decide to go."

Sherry looked pleased. "It's not just because everybody's going that I want to go," she confided. "It's because of Dave Simmons." Her eyes took on a soft look. "I think he's so gorgeous."

Dave was Johnson High's primary football star. Leah thought him conceited, vain and even cruel. One boy had been sent to the hospital after Dave had crushed him during a game. The next day, Dave had bragged about it. "You really like him?" Leah asked.

Sherry nodded. "Of course, he'll never notice me, but it's nice to dream."

"I know what you mean," Leah said, thinking of Ethan.

"You've got a guy?"

"He doesn't live around here."

"A long-distance romance . . ."

Leah chuckled over Sherry's dreamy expression. "Actually, he's Amish."

Sherry's jaw dropped. "Are you kidding? The Amish keep to themselves. How'd you even find each other?"

"It's a long story." Leah realized she'd said more than she'd meant to. "Listen, I've got to run." She waved goodbye and hurried out to her car in the student parking lot. The October air smelled crisp and clean, and the sky was a brilliant blue. Yet she felt sad and lonely. Mentioning Ethan had only made her miss him more. She had no idea when she'd see him again. Still, he had promised he would come see her. And Ethan always kept his word. Right now, his promise was the only bright spot in her life.

When Leah got to Neil's hospital room, her mother was there, as was Neil's oncologist, Dr. Nguyen. She was a young, petite Asian woman with black hair held against the nape of her neck by an eye-catching silver barrette.

Neil said, "Doctor, this is my daughter, Leah."

His introduction surprised Leah. He'd called her his daughter.

Dr. Nguyen smiled an acknowledgment. "I've just been going over your father's test results."

Leah caught Neil's eye. The transition had been made. Without ceremony, she'd officially passed from "step" into daughter status. She wasn't sure how she felt about it. At the moment, she didn't have time to dwell on it, because Dr. Nguyen was continuing to talk.

"There is evidence of cancer in your liver, Mr. Dutton."

The words fell like heavy weights. Leah's mother cried, "No!" Leah felt sick to her stomach.

"Everything points to it—abdominal bloating, the tenderness in that area when I examined you, your jaundice, plus the radioisotope scan and the needle biopsy. The pathologist's report shows a clear grouping of cancerous cells."

"I don't believe it!" Leah's mother blurted out.

"I wouldn't make this up, Mrs. Dutton," the doctor said.

Neil took his wife's hand. "It'll be all right, Roberta."

Leah saw tears fill her mother's eyes and her knuckles grow white as she gripped the bed rail. Her mother said, "But they took out his bad kidney years ago. How could he have cancer in his liver now?"

"Some maverick cells escaped surgery and chemo. It happens. The cells get into the bloodstream, travel down the portal vein and metastasize in the liver. They can lie dormant, then activate."

Neil cleared his throat. "All right. That's the worst of it. What are we going to do about it?"

"Chemotherapy is the standard treatment procedure."

Neil winced. "It didn't work before. How about radiation?"

"Unfortunately, radiation is very destructive to liver cells and not very harmful to liver cancer cells."

"What about surgery?" Leah's mother asked.

"Not an option in Neil's case."

"I hate chemo," Neil said sullenly.

Dr. Nguyen put her hand on Neil's arm. "We *have* made improvements in the drugs since you went through it before. The side effects can be much less horrific. I'm going to do a minor surgical procedure to insert a shunt into your abdomen. You'll wear an infusion pump and the chemo will be administered automatically, in small amounts, twenty-four hours a day."

"When do I start?"

"I want to begin treatment at once."

"Will it work this time?" Roberta's question sounded hostile and accusatory, as if Dr. Nguyen was somehow to blame for Neil's diagnosis.

"Second chemo protocols aren't always as successful as the first," Dr. Nguyen said cautiously. "But it's still your best hope."

Leah let her words sink in. By the time she grasped the full meaning, Dr. Nguyen was talking again. "I'm scheduling you for surgery tomorrow morning. I'll get the shunt in and get you regulated. You should be headed home in a couple of days."

"Then what?"

"Then we wait it out, keep testing you for progress and see what happens."

Leah, Neil and her mother all looked into each other's eyes. No one asked the obvious: *"What happens if it doesn't work?"*

Leah went home alone, leaving her mother and Neil to have dinner together in his hospital room. They had asked her to stay, but she excused herself, saying she had homework. In truth, she couldn't stand hanging around the hospital one more minute.

At home, she brought in the mail and found a letter from Ethan. Eagerly she tore open the envelope.

Dear Leah,

I just got your letter and am writing you right away. I am sick inside my heart about your stepfather's illness. I have also told Charity and together we will pray for him. And for you and your mother.

I also miss you, Leah. I, too, think of our summer with each other. Your smile is always before me, inside my mind, making my heart glad. On weekends, I still dress English and go into town to be with my friends. Except it is not nearly so much fun as when you lived in town. I pass by the apartment building where you lived and I want to run up and pound on the door and have you open it and let me inside. But you are not here, no matter how hard I wish for it.

We miss Rebekah very much. Ma cries sometimes when she thinks no one sees her. She and Oma and Charity go to the cemetery some afternoons, just to be with Rebekah, even though we know her spirit is with God and only her body lies under the ground.

I fear that Pa and I are not getting along very well. He wants me to return to church and stop running with "that wild bunch" (as he calls my friends). I tell him over and over that I am not yet ready, but it only makes him angry. It is good that we have so much work to do on the farm to prepare for winter. Hard work keeps us too tired to argue.

Sarah had her baby—a little boy they named Josiah Christian. He is very handsome. I like being an uncle. When he grows up, I will tell him of his aunt Rebekah. She would have loved him. Like a little doll.

I must close now, for it is late and my lamp is burning low. Thank you for your letters, Leah. They make my days happier. I keep the picture of you in my pocket, next to my heart.

Ethan

P.S. Charity says that I am to tell you hello. Hello.

Leah finished reading the letter through tear-filled eyes. The ache within her was so real she was certain it would ooze through her skin and onto the paper. She reread the letter, then pressed it against her cheek, imagining the paper in Ethan's hands, touching his skin.

Leah had returned from the summer believing that with Rebekah's death, the worst was over, that there was no place to go but up. But now Neil had been diagnosed with liver cancer and her mother was falling apart. Leah and Ethan were miles away from each other. She still had to face future checkups for her own health—which, she now realized, was a total unknown.

What about me? Leah wondered. Will I get sick again too?

Like Neil, Leah had convinced herself that cancer was behind her—that either Gabriella had made it disappear or the chemo treatments had succeeded. Like

Neil, Leah thought she was home free. But Neil's cancer had returned like an evil ghost. And now he had to begin his fight against it all over again.

Leah vowed to help him however she could. They were comrades in a battle against a mutual enemy. She'd lost her real father without ever knowing him. She didn't want to lose this one.

FOUR

Leah didn't think twice. The next morning, the day of Neil's minor surgery, she missed school and sat with her mother in the waiting area. She wished the two of them could be anyplace else. "He'll be fine," Roberta insisted. "Neil has the constitution of a much younger man. This won't keep him down for long." Her mother's forced cheerfulness got on Leah's nerves. Roberta was the picture of health. She didn't know what it felt like to be shattered by the three words *You have cancer*.

"I just want him to be okay," Leah said with emotion. "It isn't fair he has to go through this twice."

"No, it isn't," her mother agreed. "But then, when has it ever been fair?"

Neil needed several more days in the hospital after the surgery, but by the end of the week he was sent home to recuperate. He wore sensors, wires and tubing that controlled the constant flow of chemotherapy drugs into his body. A special belt around his waist held a small black monitoring device that resembled an overgrown pager. It beeped if a line clogged.

"How's your stepfather doing?" Sherry asked Leah after school a few weeks later. They were putting their books in their lockers.

"He's hanging in there. He sleeps a lot, and he's sick to his stomach, but his doctor says he'll gradually adjust and then he'll feel better."

"It's so awful that he's got cancer. It's such a scary disease."

Leah thought, *You don't know the half of it,* but said, "Neil can handle it."

"Are you going to the Harvest Ball?" Sherry changed the subject. Next to the prom, the Harvest Ball was the biggest event of the high-school year.

"I don't think so." Leah shut her locker and twirled the combination lock. "I really don't want to."

"Is it because of that guy you told me about? The Amish one?"

"Even if Ethan weren't in my life, there's still nobody I'd like to go with." Leah had gotten only two more letters from Ethan. She made excuses for him to herself—that he was busy with farmwork and exhausted by day's end—but she couldn't get Martha Dewberry out of her mind. Martha had all but told Leah last summer that once she was out of the picture, Ethan would come back to Martha, the Amish girl his parents wanted him to marry. Leah hoped it wasn't true, but she and Ethan were so far apart and weren't getting any closer.

"I'd give anything to be asked," Sherry said with a sigh.

"Maybe someone will ask you."

"Right. And maybe there really is a Santa Claus."

"Stop putting yourself down. You're a great person, Sherry. A guy would be lucky to go out with you."

"If only boys thought like girls instead of boys," Sherry said. "I know I'm not pretty." She gave Leah a wistful smile. "Anyway, it's nice of you to say that, Leah."

By the time Leah got to the parking lot, most of the cars were gone. Her red convertible sat by itself in the sunlight. She was about to get inside when she heard someone call her name. She turned to see Dave Simmons coming toward her.

"Wait a minute," he said. "I've been waiting for you."

Leah saw Dave's car sitting near the back of the parking lot. Several of his football buddies were lounging against it. "What is it?" she asked.

Dave's neck was as thick as a bull's, his hands as large as ham hocks. His head was shaved except for a brown tuft on top. Because of his sheer size, he reminded Leah of Jonah Dewberry, Ethan's friend whom she hadn't liked too much.

Dave glanced over at his friends. "I want to ask you to the Harvest Ball."

Leah stared at him blankly.

"You haven't been asked yet, have you?"

Leah shook her head, trying to assemble her thoughts. "I hadn't planned on going," she finally said.

Dave grinned. "Then plan on going with me."

He tossed another look toward his friends, which irritated Leah. "Thanks, but no thanks."

He stared at her as if he hadn't heard correctly. "But I want to take you."

Looking at this boy brought back memories of Ethan, of his gentleness and his quiet, unassuming manner. Dave figured every girl in the school was dying to be noticed by him, and it irked her. "Look, if you want to ask somebody, ask Sherry Prater."

"Who?"

"Sherry. You must know her. The girl whose locker's next to mine."

"That cow?" Dave shook his head. "No way."

Leah saw red. "She's a nice person, and you have no right to call her names." She jerked open her car door and swung into the seat.

"Hey!" Dave looked startled. "I asked *you* to go to the dance with me."

"Not if you were the last person on earth." Leah

threw the car into gear and drove out of the parking lot, leaving Dave Simmons standing on the asphalt.

Leah's rejection of Dave's offer became the talk of the school. Even Sherry asked, "Why did you say no? I can't believe it. Was it because you knew I liked him?"

"He's not my type." Leah vowed she'd never tell Sherry what Dave had said about her.

"Well, I'd give anything if he'd asked me. Course, we both know he never would."

"Don't waste yourself," Leah said. "You're too good for him."

"A girl can wish, can't she?" Sherry asked.

"Sure," Leah said with a shrug. "Dreaming's free." She dreamed about Ethan, but dreaming hadn't brought him any closer. And she had once dreamed of belonging to a nice little family, but with Neil's illness, that dream was caving in on her too.

Over the next few weeks, Neil slowly rallied as he adjusted to his chemo dose. It was mid-November when he asked Leah, "Would you walk with me out to the barn?"

"Sure." The refurbished barn was where Neil kept his collection of antique automobiles. He had once enjoyed polishing them, tuning up their already perfect engines, and sometimes taking Leah and her mother out for a drive in the countryside. But his medical ordeal had kept him preoccupied and away from the old machines.

When they reached the barn, Leah slid open the door and turned on the light. Large tarpaulin-covered mounds peppered the clean cement floor. How different this barn was from the one on Ethan's farm, where the smell of hay and livestock filled the air.

Neil walked over to one of the hulking mounds and peeled back the cover to reveal a shiny maroon-and-chrome hood. He patted the metal surface as if it were a pet. "I've collected these cars all my life. They're worth a great deal of money. I've been thinking that maybe it's time to start selling them."

"You can't do that," Leah declared, alarmed by the resignation in Neil's voice. "You love these cars. Who'll take care of them the way you have?"

"Any number of enthusiasts," Neil said.

"Well, I think it's a bad idea. You're going to regret it if you do."

"I can't keep them up the way they should be kept," Neil said sadly. "I feel lousy."

"I could help you," Leah offered.

Neil smiled at her. "You don't know a crankcase from a tire iron."

"I could learn."

"I wouldn't ask that of you, Leah. No, you're young

and you should be dating and having fun. High school is fun for you, isn't it?"

Leah shrugged.

"You ever think about what you want to do after high school? How about college? You make good grades. How'd you do on those SATs?"

"My scores aren't in yet," Leah said. If the truth were known, Leah had no burning desire to go to college. She'd never been interested in any particular subject in school and figured that without some purpose for going, college would just be a waste of time. She said, "Maybe I'll just get a job when I graduate."

"You could take a job aptitude test. We gave them all the time when I worked in Detroit. It helped us fit the applicant to a job. It might help you define your goals."

This was more than she wanted to think about right then. "Maybe later," she said evasively. "I don't like talking about the future very much."

Neil studied her kindly. "Is that because you're afraid that what's happened to me could happen to you?"

With uncanny insight, Neil had looked inside her and uncovered her deepest, most nagging fear. "Maybe."

"Just because my cancer returned doesn't mean yours will, Leah. You can't equate the two. Besides, let's not forget your mysterious friend, Gabriella. She played an important role in your recovery."

Aside from Ethan and Charity, only Neil had believed that something supernatural had happened to Leah through the mysterious Gabriella. "I don't know what to believe anymore," Leah said. "If Gabriella really cared about me, where is she now? You could sure use a little divine intervention."

"God doesn't owe people miracles, Leah."

"Well, I don't think it's fair. You'd think God would be nicer to the people who believe in him. You'd think he'd show some pity."

"Fortunately, God doesn't play favorites. If he did, we'd all be striving to earn his attention, just to get the perks."

Leah had no rebuttal. She turned her attention back to the cars. "Please don't sell all your cars, okay? I'll help you take care of them, but please don't sell them."

Neil rubbed his temples wearily. His skin had suddenly taken on a sickly gray pallor. "I guess I could hang on to them for a while longer. Maybe I won't always feel this crummy." He took her arm. "Will you walk me back to the house? I'm feeling a little woozy."

Leah let Neil lean against her, and together they returned to the house.

FIVE

Right before Thanksgiving, Dr. Nguyen said that there was evidence that Neil's cancer was responding to treatment. Neil was feeling better too, and to celebrate, he took Leah and Roberta into Chicago for holiday shopping and the theater. Leah loved the hotel Neil chose, especially since she had a lavish room all to herself. Her window looked out onto State Street, where Christmas decorations sparkled and glittered from lampposts, and colorful storefronts with animated displays attracted throngs of tourists.

The three of them ate Thanksgiving dinner, with turkey and all the trimmings, in an elegant restaurant. On Friday, while Neil rested, Leah and her mother went Christmas shopping. On Saturday, her mother took her into a photographer's studio. "I thought we could give Neil a picture of us together for Christmas," she told Leah.

A makeup artist and hairstylist prepared them for the shoot, which took hours. But Leah enjoyed the session, and when they headed back to the hotel, she told her mother it had been a good idea.

"I want Neil to be happy," her mother responded. "He's kind and loving, and I . . . I . . ." Her voice broke.

Leah studied her with some surprise. Lately she had not given much thought to the way Neil's illness was affecting her mother. Suddenly Leah saw that in spite of her mother's apparent cheerfulness, it had all been a terrible strain on her. "He's got good doctors," Leah offered awkwardly.

"You and Neil are all I have," her mother said. "You're all I want to have."

Was her mother concerned about her, too? She usually acted as if Leah's diagnosis had been some huge mistake, some medical blunder. But now, with Neil's health in doubt, she seemed much more frightened. "Don't worry," Leah said as casually as she could. "We'll both be fine."

Her mother reached over and squeezed Leah's hand, and Leah was amazed at how comforted she felt by this simple act.

On Sunday they drove home, the car and its trunk stuffed with gifts and goodies. Leah's mother chattered all the way. Neil nodded and mumbled "Hummm" a lot, and Leah stared out at the brown and dreary country-side, thinking. Here she was, seventeen years old, and for the first time in her life she felt like a member of a family—the kind of family portrayed on TV and in magazine stories. All the holidays of her past stretched behind her like a road paved with half-formed bricks. She'd never had a stepfather like Neil. The others had been imitations, men who had been indifferent to her—or worse, overly friendly. None of them had showed her the kindness and acceptance that Neil had.

But Leah couldn't help wondering what it would have been like if her real father had stayed with her and her mother. Would he have been the kind of father Neil was to her? She would never know. All she knew was that she wanted Neil to be well. Like her mother, she wanted him around for a long, long time.

Two weeks before Christmas break, Leah was hurrying down the hall at school, not looking where she was going, when she ran smack into Dave Simmons.

"Whoa," he said as she jumped back, dazed. "Is there a fire drill?"

"Sorry," Leah said. Ever since their encounter in the parking lot, they'd given each other a wide berth. She bent to pick up the books she'd dropped.

Dave crouched next to her. "You know, with football

season over, I have more time for hanging around. I thought I'd give you another chance to date me."

Leah arched an eyebrow and asked, "You're joking, aren't you?"

His eyes did look amused, and he wore a half grin. "Maybe a little." He stood and hauled her to her feet. "I'd like to start over, though. So how about we go out Saturday night?"

"It's nothing personal," Leah said, telling him a half-truth, "but I really don't want to."

Dave looked incredulous. "You already have a guy? Is that it?"

"Yes. He doesn't live around here, though."

Dave's eyes narrowed. "It seems to me like you're wasting your time, then. If he's not around, why not date someone else? He probably is."

"I'd rather not."

Dave shook his head and smirked. "Suit yourself. But this is your last chance with me."

"Thanks for the warning." Leah heaved her books onto her hip and hurried off to class just as the bell rang.

She couldn't concentrate the whole hour. Not only was she angry about Dave's arrogance, but she was also worried. What if Dave was right? Leah knew how tight the group of Amish kids was. Certainly Ethan was around Martha every weekend.

Letters weren't cutting it anymore. Leah wanted to see Ethan. She wanted him to hold her and say the things he'd written in his letters to her face. A plan began to form. With Christmas break coming, maybe she could drive up to Nappanee and visit him. Even a few hours with him would be better than nothing. And what if she went and stayed the week after Christmas? *But where?* She couldn't stay with Ethan's family at the farm. Mr. Longacre had never made a secret of his feelings toward Leah's friendship with Ethan. Then she remembered Kathy, the girl she'd worked with at the inn all summer. Would Kathy let Leah stay with her?

It took Leah two days to screw up her courage, but on Saturday she called Kathy and casually outlined her plan. She was rewarded by Kathy's enthusiastic endorsement of the idea. Kathy thought it "so romantic" and assured Leah that she'd be welcome.

Leah told her mother about Kathy's invitation, choosing her words carefully. Surprisingly, she met with little resistance. "Neil and I are going to Detroit a few days after Christmas," her mother said. "Some of his old friends are throwing a huge party New Year's Eve. You're welcome to come along, but if you'd rather do something with your friends, that's all right."

Leah sat down and wrote Ethan, mailed the letter, and spent several days nervously awaiting his reply.

What if he wrote her not to come? Then what would
she do?

Three days before Christmas, Ethan's reply arrived
in the mail. Clutching the letter, Leah threw herself on
the living room sofa and tore it open.

Dear Leah,

   *I could not believe my eyes when I read your
letter. You are coming. I will see you face to face.
I cannot tell you how this news makes my heart
happy! I have been thinking of many ways that I
could come see you. Now you will be here and
we will be together.*

   *Leah, I have much to tell you. Papa and I
have harsh words almost every day. This makes
Ma cry. Charity, Elizabeth and even Oma cry
too. I do not like to make my family unhappy. I
am very mixed up. I do not know who I am anymore. I do not know where I belong.*

   *But this is not what I want to say now. I will
talk to you when you come after Christmas. I
think of last Christmas. You were in the hospital—not a happy time for you, but a happy time
for me because I met you. Leah, have a good
Christmas, then come and see me. I will be
waiting.*

                                          Ethan

Thoughtfully Leah folded the letter. What did he mean by "I do not know who I am"? This didn't sound like Ethan at all. For her, Christmas couldn't come and go fast enough.

On Christmas morning, Leah handed out presents to Neil and her mother from the mountain of gifts heaped beneath the ornately decorated tree in the living room. Leah's favorite gift was a gold charm bracelet from Neil. "Oh my gosh!" she cried, trying it on. "This is so gorgeous! Thank you."

Neil looked pleased. "I picked it out myself. I chose a few charms, but there's plenty of room for more. I think the idea is to add one every time something significant happens in your life."

"Like little milestones," her mother said. "Charm bracelets are very fashionable, you know."

Leah examined each tiny charm. There was a silhouette of the state of Indiana, replicas of a vintage car and an Amish buggy, and a charm symbolizing Chicago— for the vacation they'd had there together. But the charm that made a lump rise in Leah's throat was an angel. The angel's face was a diamond chip. Leah locked eyes with Neil. He offered a knowing smile. "So you'll always have an angel with you," he said.

Leah jumped to her feet. "This one's yours. We saved it for last." She dragged a large, square object from behind the living room curtain and set it in front of Neil.

Neil tore off the paper to discover a framed photo-graph of his wife and Leah. "Beautiful," he said. "Absolutely beautiful. Thank you."

Leah's mother bent down and pulled another box from beneath her chair. "This goes with it."

The box held a photo album, and every page held pictures of them, some from the recent photo session. Leah looked over Neil's shoulder as he thumbed through it. "I'm the luckiest man in the world," he said. "And I have two of the most beautiful women in the world to prove it."

Leah fingered the charm bracelet and held it up. The diamond-faced angel caught the lights from the tree and winked at her. Leah wondered if Gabriella might be watching—and feeling pleased.

Leah was ready to go early the next afternoon for Nappanee. The day was cold, the skies cloudy, but there was no snow in the forecast. "You drive carefully," her mother told her. "And call us the minute you get to Kathy's house."

"You and Neil have fun in Detroit," Leah said. "See you on New Year's Day."

When Leah arrived in Nappanee at dusk, she drove down familiar streets. The front of the inn where she'd worked resembled a picture on a Victorian Christmas card. As she pulled into Kathy's driveway, Kathy came out to meet her.

"Leah, you look great!" Kathy said. The dark-haired girl was bundled in jeans and a bright red sweater. Little Christmas tree earrings dangled from her ears.

"You do, too," Leah said, hauling her duffel bag from the car.

Leah followed Kathy inside and up to her bedroom. She tossed her bag onto a cot cluttered with stuffed animals.

"Remember this?" Kathy held up a picture of Leah and herself. They were standing in front of the inn in their uniforms, holding up mops and brooms.

"I forgot these were taken. Boy, those were ugly uniforms."

Kathy laughed. "I'm working there again this summer. How about you?"

"Who knows?" Leah said with a shrug.

"Only six more months of high school, then I'm off to college. I can't wait."

"I'm not sure what I'll be doing yet. Where are you going?"

"Boston College. I want to study physical therapy."

There was a knock on the bedroom door, and one of Kathy's sisters stuck her head inside. "Leah, there's someone at the front door for you. It's a boy."

"Go, girl!" Kathy said, giving Leah a shove.

Leah hurried down the stairs. The foyer was empty.

"He's on the porch," Kathy's sister whispered. "He wouldn't come in."

Leah opened the door. A blast of cold air struck her face. Ethan was standing in a pool of light. "Hello, Leah," he said. Leah flung herself into his open arms.

SIX

Ethan cradled Leah's face between his palms and said, "You are as beautiful to me as ever."

Just looking up into his blue eyes made Leah's knees go weak. "Oh, Ethan. . . . I've missed you so much."

His lips found hers. The warmth of his mouth broke through the icy chill of the night air. His kiss lingered; then he hugged her hard against his chest. He was dressed English. Even through the layers of coat and sweaters he wore, she felt his heart thudding. He smelled clean like soap and tasted of cinnamon candy. She wrapped her arms around him tightly.

"I could not wait until the morning to see you," he said. "I had to come tonight."

"How did you get here?" Leah peered around him, half expecting to see his Amish buggy and his horse, Bud. What she saw was Jonah's old beat-up green car.

"I have learned to drive," Ethan said. "I have my license now."

Leah was shocked. "You never told me that in your letters."

"I wanted to surprise you."

"What's your father say about it?"

"He does not know."

This wasn't typical of the Ethan she knew. The old Ethan never would have gone against his father's wishes or acted behind his father's back. "Do you like driving?"

"Yes. And getting places takes less time. I like that too."

"But you still live at home?"

"Only during the week. On weekends I stay in town at Jonah's. He has a job in town now. And his own apartment. Many new friends, too. It is often like one big party."

Leah realized that many changes had occurred in the few months she and Ethan had been apart. "Jonah always told me he'd stay Amish, that English ways were for fling-taking only."

"He is still Amish. We are all Amish." Ethan sounded defensive. "Trying out English ways will not change who we are."

"How does Charity feel about Jonah living on his own? Does she come to his parties?" Ethan's sister had once confided to Leah that she expected one day to marry Jonah.

"She has come to a few parties, but before Christmas she told Jonah she would not see him again unless he changed his habits and came back to the Amish way."

"I'll bet he didn't take that too well."

"He got very drunk. And very sick." Ethan smoothed Leah's hair. "I do not want to talk about Jonah and Charity. I want to talk about us."

"What about us?"

"You will be here only a week, and I want to spend all of my time with you."

"What about your farm chores?"

"The heavy work is done until spring. Simeon is expected to take on more of the easier work I have been doing. I have thought about getting a job in town for the winter."

Leah stepped back. "Can you do that?"

"It is something we Amish often do during the wintertime to earn extra money."

"What would you do? What can you do?"

Ethan's eyes took on a mischievous sparkle. "Do you think I have no talents except pitching hay and mending fences?"

Leah felt her face redden. Ethan had gone to school

only through the eighth grade, and she wasn't sure what kind of job skills he possessed. "Of course not. I was just wondering, that's all."

"I am a good carpenter. And there are Amish farmers who have no sons or who do not stay with the old ways. They have machinery to make jobs easier. I can work at one of these farms."

"Is this what you want?"

"What I want," Ethan said quietly, "is to spend every minute of this week with you. I will be staying at Jonah's here in town all week long so that we can be together."

She tightened her arms around his waist again. "All right. But I want to see Charity, too. Is it okay if I go out to your farm?"

"Certainly it is all right."

"Then I'll go in the morning."

"I will go with you," he said. He gave her Jonah's address. "Come and get me when you are ready."

He kissed her goodnight. Leah watched him return to Jonah's old car and drive away. She felt unsettled. She was so out of step with Ethan's life. When she'd left in August, he had been testing the limits of his Amish upbringing—but just slightly. Now, only a few months later, he was driving and talking of taking a job. Ethan hadn't been kidding when he'd written, "I do not know where I belong."

• • •

Leah was up early the next morning and ate breakfast with Kathy and her sisters. Once their parents had headed off to work, Leah drove over to Jonah's apartment. Kathy was very understanding. Leah was grateful that she could just go and be with Ethan.

Ethan opened the door at her first knock. "Good morning, Leah!" His smile lit up his face.

Kissing him lightly, Leah stepped into a living room area littered with newspapers, magazines, videotapes and old pizza boxes. Pillows were scattered on the floor, and plastic cups, some half filled, dotted the tops of a coffee table and two lamp tables. "Boy," she said. "Your livestock lives better than this."

Ethan laughed. "We are not very tidy. The others are at work now. There will be a party tomorrow night. Come and meet them."

Leah had gone to Amish parties before and had felt like an outsider. "Will I be the only English?"

"No. I have told you, Jonah has many new friends. Most are English."

"But will any of your Amish friends be here?" Leah was thinking specifically about Jonah's sister, Martha.

Ethan nodded. "We Amish still do many things together. We have been friends a long time. Jonah invites everyone, but not everyone comes."

Leah felt sure that Martha would show up, but she decided not to let the thought upset her. After all, Ethan had made it quite clear that it was Leah he wanted to be with all week.

The drive out to the farm along the flat, familiar country road brought memories of summer back to Leah. The fields had been green, a sea of cornstalks. Now the corn had been harvested and the stalks were brown, dry and broken. Patches of snow dotted the roadside, and puddles of water were iced over.

Leah came to the fence that marked the boundary of the Longacre farm and slowed down. She could hardly stand to look upon the place where a truck had plowed into the produce stand, flattening the fence behind it and killing Rebekah, who had been in its path. "The fence looks as if it was never hit," Leah said.

"It does not take wood long to weather," Ethan said.

Or for little girls to die, Leah thought. The pain of Rebekah's death struck her hard and deep. She could only imagine what it must feel like for Ethan to pass this place every day.

Ethan peered through the windshield at the gray sky. "We will have snow by midmorning."

"You can tell that just by looking at the sky?"

"I have been reading the signs of coming weather all my life. The winter will be hard this year."

"How do you know?"

"The woolly caterpillars grew extra-thick coats last fall. When they do, winter will be very cold."

"Gee . . . and all this time I've been watching the Weather Channel."

Ethan gave her a puzzled look, then slowly smiled. "You are making a joke. I understand because I've seen this Weather Channel on Jonah's TV."

Leah returned his smile. There had been a time when Ethan hadn't caught on to her humor, because it was English. She said, "You really are different these days."

"Only in some ways," he told her.

Leah turned into the long, rutted driveway to the house. Except for the colors of winter, the old farmhouse was exactly as Leah had remembered it. The weathered wooden roof and siding looked stark against the sky, much as she believed they had a hundred years before when first built. No electrical or telephone wires tethered them to the present. One shutter had come off its hinge.

"I must fix that," Ethan said. "For Ma." His expression looked brooding.

Leah parked and shut off the engine, half expecting Rebekah to come flying out the door to meet them. The door swung open and instead Charity stepped onto the porch. She wore a long black Amish dress and a prayer cap. A woolen shawl was tied around her shoulders. "Leah!" she cried, hurrying to the car.

Leah got out and embraced her friend. "Surprise! I couldn't stay away."

Charity glanced at her brother, and Leah could have

sworn she saw a shadow of sadness flicker across
Charity's eyes. The look vanished as Charity grabbed
Leah's hand. "Come inside where it is warm. I have tea
and fresh bread made."

Inside the kitchen, Leah felt the warmth from the old
woodstove in the corner. The room smelled like baking
bread and warm apples. Tillie Longacre, Charity and
Ethan's mother, greeted Leah, asked a few polite questions, then cut some warm bread, placed it on a plate,
and carried it out of the room.

"Oma has a bad cold," Charity explained as she
poured Leah hot tea, "so Mama is taking her a snack."

"I hope she'll be okay," Leah said. Oma had sometimes reminded Leah of her grandma Hall.

"I will look in on her," Ethan said.

When Leah was alone with Charity, she asked,
"How are you doing?"

Charity sighed. "Winters are very long. I miss
Rebekah very much."

"So do I."

"But Sarah's new baby is precious." Charity brightened. "I spend many afternoons at Sarah's helping with
little Josiah. He is most adorable."

"Listen, Ethan told me about you and Jonah." Leah
changed the subject, not knowing how long the two of
them would be alone. "I'm sorry. I know you liked him."

"I still like him, but I cannot be with him when he is

so wild. Until he returns to the community and Amish ways, I will have nothing to do with him."

Charity looked sad. Leah wondered how much of Charity's decision was hers and how much of it was her family's. "I'm sure Jonah will come around," Leah said. "He always told me that he would have his fling and return to Amish ways."

"He did?"

"Well, yes—" Leah got no further. The outside door opened and Mr. Longacre stepped into the room. His expression looked grim. He took one look at Leah and walked straight past her without saying a word.

SEVEN

Charity rose from her chair, looking shocked, then turned toward Leah. "I—I'm sure Papa was in a hurry," she stammered.

Leah felt her cheeks begin to burn. Mr. Longacre had snubbed her on purpose. "Maybe I should go."

"No, Leah. I know Papa didn't mean to offend you. Ever since Rebekah's accident . . ." Charity didn't finish the sentence. "Please, do not take offense," she said.

Before Leah could respond, Mr. Longacre swept back into the kitchen, his wife on his heels. "Hello, Leah," the man said stiffly.

"Hello, sir," Leah answered, her heart pounding. She saw Ethan slip into the room through a different door.

"I saw your car parked in my yard," Jacob said. "I thought something might have happened."

"I'm only visiting for a few days," Leah told him. "I'm staying in town with a friend."

"Would you like some tea, Jacob?" Tillie asked.

"No. I have things to do in the barn." He turned to Ethan, and the look that passed between them made Leah's stomach knot. "You will come to the barn before you leave," Mr. Longacre said. It wasn't a request.

"I will come," Ethan answered, his expression grim.

"Have a nice visit," Mr. Longacre said in Leah's general direction. In another second he was out the door, shutting it firmly behind him.

Tillie stepped forward and took Leah's hands in hers. "It is good to see you, Leah. Rebekah spoke of you often. You were a favorite of hers."

Tears sprang into Leah's eyes. "Thank you. She was a favorite of mine, too."

"Will you have more tea?" Tillie asked, looking inside the teapot.

"No, thank you. I really should get back to town to spend some time with my friend."

"I will walk you to your car," Ethan said.

Once outside, Leah asked, "Aren't you coming with me?"

"I must go see Papa." He didn't look happy about it.

"I'll wait for you."

"No, do not wait. But before you go, walk with me into the woods." Ethan took her gloved hand in his.

Leah understood. Ethan needed to collect himself, and the woods on the back portion of the property was where he usually went to find solace. She took a deep breath. She had not been there since the day of Rebekah's funeral. But, once surrounded by the towering trees and whispering pine needles, her heart felt more at ease.

"I'm sorry I upset your father," she said.

"It is not you, Leah. It is me who displeases him."

"Because you're taking your fling?"

"I think he was certain that I had gotten over my fling by the end of last summer. I have told you how Pa does not like me to run with Jonah and his crowd."

"Or date English girls," Leah said.

"I am mixed up, Leah." Ethan turned to face her. "I have tried to care for another, but I cannot get you out of my mind. Or my heart."

Leah felt a pang of jealousy. She didn't want him to care for another. She wanted to be the only girl in his life. "I've wanted to talk to you a hundred times these past few months," she confessed. "What with Neil and all."

"Is he better?"

"He seems to be on the mend—for now. I really like Neil, Ethan. I don't know what Mom and I would do if something happened to him. Especially Mom. She and Neil get on really well together. I've never seen her happier. But this has really messed things up for all of us."

"I am sorry about all your family is going through, Leah, but you are well, and this makes me happy."

"I hope you're right."

His expression sobered. "Did you not have a good checkup when you last went for tests?" Ethan had gone with Leah to her doctor's appointment during the summer, and her mother had accompanied her to the fall appointment.

"So far, so good. But who's to say it can't all blow up in my face? Neil thought he was finished with cancer too, and look what's happened to him."

"But an angel touched you," Ethan reminded her.

"That's what you and Neil and I think, but Mom and my doctors don't believe it. Mom thinks it was a misdiagnosis, and Dr. Thomas calls it spontaneous remission. I wish I could talk to Gabriella face to face and ask her once and for all."

"You must have faith," Ethan said.

"Don't you think I'm trying to have faith? But every time I feel as if I do, something terrible happens. Rebekah dies. Neil gets sick. I just don't get it. Why do terrible things happen to nice people? Doesn't it make you mad about Rebekah?"

Ethan put his arms around Leah and rested his chin on her head. "It makes me very sad. I do not know the answers to your questions, Leah. I do not know where to go to get the answers. All my life, I grew up going to church, believing the things I was told. I accepted Amish ways, even when they did not make sense to me. Yet, today, my sister is dead and my brother Eli is gone."

The mention of his older brother made Leah pull back and study Ethan's face. He looked tormented. "Ethan, I'm sorry. Let's forget all this serious stuff and think about this whole week of being together and having fun."

He smiled. "This is a good suggestion. Right this moment, I want to think about kissing you."

Leah rose on her tiptoes. "Why think about it?"

He lowered his mouth to hers.

Around them huge, fat, wet snowflakes began to fall.

Leah left Ethan at the farm and returned to Kathy's. She found Kathy in her room, organizing her clothes closet. "I'm trying to see if my new stuff works with any of my old stuff," Kathy explained. She shut the door. "How's your boyfriend? Is the magic still there?"

"More than ever."

"Gee, Leah, liking an Amish guy is risky. They stick to their own kind."

"Not always," Leah said defensively. "Actually, Ethan's brother left the community," she confided.

Kathy didn't seem impressed. "Just watch out. Don't get hurt."

"I don't plan on getting hurt. Ethan may not know a

lot about English ways, but he's the kindest, nicest guy I've ever met. The guys back home are such losers compared to him."

"But this is *his* world, Leah. How would he fit into yours? How would he get along with your regular friends? Picture him with *your* crowd."

Kathy had a point. Up until now, Leah had only been with Ethan in his hometown, in his Amish world. "In the first place, I don't hang out with any special group at my school. For that matter, I don't care to. Except for my friend Sherry, I'm not close to anyone. I'm just not interested in any of their little cliques."

"I know what you mean. Sometimes high school is just so lame. College will be my big breakout." Kathy grew thoughtful. "Still," she said, "hooking up with an Amish guy may not be the smartest thing you can do. Amish don't fit anywhere but in their small world, Leah."

"I don't care," Leah said stubbornly. "Ethan is the only guy I want in my life, period."

Kathy shrugged. "Then good luck, girl."

Ethan caught a bus to Kathy's, and after supper Leah drove the two of them back to Jonah's. Ethan was quiet, almost withdrawn, during the short drive, making Leah realize that things had not gone well between him and his father. "Do you still want to go to the party?" she asked, half wishing he'd say no.

"Yes," Ethan said. "I want us to have a good time tonight. I want to show you off to everyone there."

The party was in full swing. Ethan headed toward the kitchen for a snack, leaving Leah alone for a moment.

From the corner of her eye, Leah saw Martha dancing with a lanky, dark-haired guy. She was dressed in tight jeans and a fitted sweater—a far cry from the Amish clothing Leah had last seen her in at Rebekah's funeral.

Martha walked over. "Ethan said you'd be coming," she said above the wail of the music. "It is good to see you."

Leah didn't believe her, but she smiled anyway and said, "It's good to be back. How have you been?"

"Busy," Martha said. "I have a job in town now. I work in a bakery selling Amish breads and making lunches for customers."

Martha sounded pleased about her independence. "Do you live in town, too?" Leah asked.

"I live at home. Jonah comes and picks me up and brings me into town to my job."

The boy Martha had been dancing with came up beside her and slipped his arm around her waist. "Let's dance."

Leah smelled beer on his breath.

"Todd, this is Leah," Martha said. "She's Ethan's girlfriend."

Todd grinned, and Leah urged them, "Go dance." As

she watched them walk away, she noticed Todd shoved his hand into the back pocket of Martha's jeans. Leah realized she'd been introduced as Ethan's girlfriend. Did that mean Martha was relinquishing her claim on Ethan?

Ethan returned with sodas. "The music is too loud. Come with me."

Leah followed him outside onto the balcony. "Leah, there is something I want to ask you," Ethan said quietly.

Instantly on alert at the tone of his voice, Leah said, "Sure, ask me anything."

"I want to see my brother Eli again. Please, will you help me find him?"

EIGHT

"Help you find Eli? What makes you think I can do that?" Ethan's request had taken Leah totally by surprise.

"You are English. You know the English world. I thought that you might know about such things."

"But I wouldn't know where to begin."

Ethan's face fell. "I am sorry. I did not know who else to ask."

Leah's heart went out to him. "Oh, Ethan, don't be sorry. I want to help you. I just don't know if I can. I mean, you've told me that Eli dropped out of sight years ago. He could be anywhere."

Ethan had confided in her the previous summer about his older brother Eli. Amish kids often quit school to help in their homes and on their farms, but Eli had wanted more education. He had attended high school, and he had won a college scholarship. Against his family's wishes, and against Amish traditions, he had left home to pursue his dreams. His leaving had forced a permanent wedge between him and his family. It had also left Ethan, who had been only ten at the time, with Eli's responsibilities. To this day, no one spoke Eli's name. To his family, it was as if Eli were dead.

"I cannot stop thinking about him." Ethan's voice sounded tormented. "I see him in my dreams—the way he was the last time I saw him. I wonder what he's doing and if he's happy. I think of how he never even knew Rebekah."

Rebekah had been born after Eli had left home. Now it was too late for them to know each other. Leah said, "Last summer, you acted as if you accepted your father's decision about Eli. What changed your mind?"

"I have been troubled about many things." Ethan shook his head sadly. "This does not seem right to me. Eli was not even a member of the church. He was never shunned, and yet he is as lost to me as Rebekah."

The Amish custom of shunning was reserved for noncompliant church members, but, according to Ethan, Eli had never been baptized, so his ejection from the Longacre household was purely the result of their father's unwillingness to allow him the freedom to be his own person.

Leah warned, "Your father won't like your contacting Eli, you know."

"I would not tell him."

"But how could you keep such a secret?"

Ethan shrugged. "I do not know. I only want to see my brother again. I do not want to think about why I should not."

Leah chewed her bottom lip thoughtfully. "I really don't know how to start searching for him. But I'll bet Neil could help. He knows everything."

The fire of hope leaped into Ethan's eyes. "Would he do such a thing? He does not even know me."

"He's never met you, that's true. But Neil would help if I asked him." Neil had been feeling good since Thanksgiving, and this type of project might be one he would be willing to take on—or at least be willing to advise her and Ethan about.

Ethan looked relieved and grateful. "Thank you, Leah. I will not forget your kindness. This has been on my mind for days, and I could not keep it inside any longer."

"No problem," Leah said, her teeth chattering. "I'm glad you told me."

Ethan slid open the glass door and a blast of heated, smoky air rushed out at them. Leah wasn't sure what was worse—freezing on the balcony or suffocating in the apartment. She stepped inside and immediately saw Jonah. He was leaning against a wall, smoking, holding a beer can and watching the dancing couples with brooding, heavy-lidded eyes.

When he caught sight of Ethan and Leah, he shoved away from the wall and sauntered over. "Hello, Leah," he said without warmth.

"Back to you," she said with more cheeriness than she felt.

"I'll get us sodas," Ethan said, and made his way toward the kitchen.

Alone with Jonah, Leah wasn't sure what to say. Jonah had never been happy about her friendship with Ethan. "Looks like this is the place to come for Amish or English," she said, trying to sound friendly.

Jonah shrugged. "My friends know they can come here whenever they like."

"And do whatever they want?"

"Yes, until the police show up. Or until the elders ban everyone from being friends with me." He sounded bitter.

"I went to see Charity yesterday," Leah said, offering the name like bait. She watched Jonah's expression harden.

"She is a silly girl—not person enough to think for herself."

"She's lonely and confused," Leah corrected. "And for reasons I can't begin to figure out, she cares about you."

Jonah took a long swig of his beer. "Well, I no longer care for her."

"Too bad. She misses you."

Jonah turned and brought his face close to Leah's. "Do not involve yourself, English. You do not know what it means to be separate."

"Separate" was how the Amish referred to themselves. They kept themselves separated from the rest of the world, following the Bible's mandate to be in the world but not of the world. Leah felt a surge of anger because Jonah had no idea where she was coming from. If he thought Amishness made a person separate, he should try having cancer. Now, *that* was separation. Leah squared her jaw. "You don't look very separate to me, Jonah. You look just like some kids I used to know in Dallas. All they did was drink and party, too. What's so separate about that?"

Jonah straightened. "If you do not like my party, Leah, then leave." He jiggled his beer can. "Empty." He crushed it in his fist. "I need a refill."

Leah watched him swagger away and felt pity for him. Jonah was caught between two ways of life. He had a foot in both, but he seemed stuck, unable to make up his mind where he wanted to stand. It scared her that Ethan might get caught in the same web of confusion.

•   •   •

As the week dwindled, Leah and Ethan became inseparable. Kathy's mother even invited him for dinner one night, and later Leah heard Kathy's mother tell Kathy, "What a nice boy. You should date a boy like him."

Leah heard Kathy say, "He's Amish, Mother. How many of them mingle with us in the first place?"

"Amish! I'll bet his parents are fit to be tied."

"Leah knows what she's doing," Kathy said. "She's not an idiot."

Leah was glad that Kathy had defended her, but she wasn't so sure about Kathy's conclusion. Maybe she *was* an idiot. Loving Ethan was risky. What could really ever become of it? And now that he'd asked her to help locate Eli, she felt a greater turmoil. She didn't want to let him down.

The thought of returning to school, to boring classes, was even less appealing. She could not get Neil's or her own health problems off her mind. What if Neil had a relapse? What if *she* had one? How could her mother handle both of them being sick? How could Leah turn to Ethan for support when he was hundreds of miles away? And if he lived with Jonah, would he turn into a Jonah clone? Leah could hardly stand to think about any of it.

Ethan took Leah to their favorite pizza parlor after they'd spent the afternoon ice skating. The parlor had

Happy New Year banners hanging along the walls, reminding Leah that she had only two days left before
she'd have to return home. She thought of Neil and her
mother on their way to Detroit for the upcoming round of
holiday parties with Neil's old friends.

She and Ethan both were in low moods as they nibbled halfheartedly on the food. "I don't want you to
leave," Ethan said.

"And I don't want to leave," Leah confessed.

"Then don't."

She gave a mirthless laugh. "Where would I stay? In
my car?"

He stared morosely out the window. "What can we
do, Leah?"

Suddenly she sat up straighter. Like a bolt of lightning, an idea struck her. "You know what, Ethan? I just
had the craziest idea. I can't stay here, but you can come
home with me. Why don't you?"

NINE

Ethan asked, "Go home with you? What do you mean?"

"Just what I said. Why should you stay here? You told me you wanted to get a job. Why not get one where I live? A job's a job." Leah's excitement mounted as she tossed out possibilities.

"Where would I live?"

"With me—us," she corrected. "Me, Mom and Neil. The house is huge. Why, there's a whole other house in the basement—bedroom, bath, family room. We never even go down there. Mom hates basements." Leah waved her hand dismissively. "We have the space, and you could live in it."

"My father would not allow—"

"You're eighteen, aren't you?" Leah interrupted him. He'd had his eighteenth birthday in October. "When you're eighteen, you don't need your father's permission. You can just leave."

"That is what Eli did." Ethan looked concerned. "It hurt Pa deeply."

"And that's another thing. If you want to find Eli, it will be easier if we look for him together. No telling where he is or how hard it's going to be to find him. But this way you can get the information more quickly because you'll be right there when Neil gets it. You won't lose days waiting for my letters."

Leah could tell that Ethan was pondering her suggestion. Having him close by her again was just what she'd dreamed about all these long months.

"What will your mother say?" Ethan asked.

Leah knew it would be a tough sell, but if Ethan was already there, it would be harder for her mother and Neil to say no. "Look, Ethan, let me worry about my family."

"I don't know, Leah." His brow puckered.

She suddenly remembered Neil's barn full of antique autos. Perhaps Ethan could help Neil maintain them. "Neil can't handle even simple chores around the house anymore. Maybe you could help out. There's lots of stuff for you to do."

Ethan nodded slowly. "Yes. I would have to help somehow."

"I'll be in school all day. And once you get a job, you'll be working, so it's not like we'd be in each other's way or anything. We'll be apart but still together." Leah shot him a broad smile.

"And if we cannot find Eli?"

"Don't give up before we even start," Leah chided.

Ethan leaned back in his chair, hooking his hands behind his head. He stared out the window for a long time. Leah's heart thudded. She knew he did nothing in haste. But the more she considered her plan, the more sense it made. They could search for Eli without the frustration of distance between them. And she could have Ethan in her world. She had lived among the Amish. Now it was Ethan's turn to live among the English.

"When would we leave?" Ethan asked quietly.

Leah licked her dry lips. "The sooner, the better, I think. I have to start school the day after New Year's, and you need to get settled in. You know, adjusted." She didn't add that she really wanted to get home before her mom and Neil returned from Detroit. If Ethan was already moved in by the time they returned, it would be harder to throw him out. It was urgent that she get to her mother first thing, before she had time to blow a fuse.

"I want to go with you, Leah."

Ethan's simple acceptance startled her. She had expected more resistance. "Well. Okay then. You'll drive home with me. If we leave tomorrow, we can spend New Year's Eve at the house. We can watch the ball drop on TV."

He looked puzzled. "What ball?"

While she was growing up, Leah had sometimes stayed up until midnight to watch the Times Square crowds in New York welcome in the New Year. Of course, Ethan didn't know about the yearly ritual. "I'll tell you about it on the drive home."

Ethan stood. "Come."

"Where to?"

"To go tell my parents."

Leah felt a jolt as reality hit. "Ethan, I don't know if you should tell them."

"I cannot just sneak away."

"But they may get angry and try to stop you. Maybe you could just write them after you get home with me."

"I cannot. I must tell them to their faces. And you must go with me."

She swallowed hard. "I could wait in the car. Keep the motor running."

He gave her a little smile. "No, Leah. You must be by my side. And you must tell them of your offer of a place to stay."

"But not about Eli?"

"No. That will be our secret."

Nervously Leah stood. "Are you sure you want to go tell them right now?"

"They are together tonight. It is best to go now."

With her heart thudding like thunder in her ears, Leah followed Ethan out into the cold, dark night.

Leah fought an intense internal battle as she and Ethan drove out to the farm. Now that she was about to get her way, she was scared. Was she being selfish? Would Tillie hate her? She'd come into Ethan's tidy little world and turned it on its edge. She was English, everything the Amish held in low regard. Now she was luring Ethan away from his family and the only way of life he'd known.

By the time they arrived at the farmhouse, Leah felt sick to her stomach. But she couldn't turn back now. She'd made Ethan promises, and she had to keep them.

They found his parents alone in their kitchen beside the woodstove. Jacob Longacre had the big German Bible open on his lap, and Tillie was sitting in an old rocker doing cross-stitch by the light of an oil lamp. Startled by Ethan and Leah's appearance, Jacob asked, "Has something happened?"

"Nothing bad, Pa," Ethan said. He glanced around the shadowed room. "Where are the others?"

"Oma and Opa have retired. The children are visiting Sarah," Tillie answered.

Leah held on to the edge of the countertop, certain her knees would give way if she didn't. She saw Jacob scrutinize his son and realized that Ethan was dressed English.

Without preamble, Ethan announced to his parents, "I have decided to go away."

The room was silent except for the wood crackling in the stove.

"Where will you go?" asked his father.

"Leah has asked me to her place. I am going."

Leah expected an explosion of temper, but she was surprised. Mr. Longacre simply studied his son with resigned, contemplative eyes.

"Neil and my mother will take good care of him," Leah offered in a breathy voice.

"And who will care for his soul, Leah?" Mr. Longacre leveled a blue-eyed gaze at her.

"We're not heathens, you know. He'll be all right with us."

"Do you know for how long you will be gone?" Jacob asked, ignoring her outburst.

"I cannot say."

Jacob stood, folded his reading glasses, closed the Bible and placed it under his arm. "Do what you must do, Ethan. I cannot stop you."

"As for my work"—Ethan gestured to his surroundings—"Simeon is young and strong. He is good help. Do not let Opa work too hard."

Mr. Longacre nodded. "We will manage."

"I love you, Papa." Ethan's voice was firm.

Jacob sighed deeply. Wearily he walked over to stand in front of Ethan. Leah was close enough to see that his eyes glistened with tears. His hands were big, work-worn, covered with calluses. A lump of emotion clogged her throat.

Jacob placed his free hand on Ethan's shoulder. "And I love you, Ethan. Be careful among the English."

Jacob turned and left the room. Ethan followed his father with his gaze.

Tillie rose from her chair and set her sewing on the counter. Leah remembered summer days when they canned fruit and vegetables together, of a kitchen alive with laughter and women's voices. She saw Rebekah's sweet face reflected in Tillie's features.

Ethan reached for his mother's hand. "I will be fine, Ma."

She came closer, touched his cheek lovingly. "You are a man, my son. You must make your own way in the world. But do not forget your youth and all that we have taught you."

"I will not forget."

"Remember the words of our Lord," she said. "'You are the salt of the earth, but if the salt loses its saltiness, how can it be made salty again? It is no longer good for anything, except to be thrown out and trampled by men.'" Tillie smiled wistfully. "It is God who calls each man whom he wants for his own. You must know if you, Ethan Longacre, have been called by God to be separate."

Tillie turned to look into Leah's eyes. "You were touched by an angel, Leah. You were blessed. But my Ethan must search his heart and discover what it is that God requires of him. Do you understand?"

Leah nodded, unable to speak.

"I will not be cut off from you, Ma," Ethan said. "I will not allow us to become strangers."

Leah heard his words as a veiled reference to Eli. She thought it extraordinary that even now, neither could speak the name aloud.

"I will always hold you in my heart," his mother said. "Just as I hold all my children there."

"I love you, Ma."

She cupped Ethan's chin. "You are my beloved son. I have lost two of my children already. I do not want to lose another."

"Ma." The word sounded strangled in Ethan's throat.

"Take good care of yourself, Ethan." Tillie picked up the oil lamp. It lit her face with an ethereal light. The ties of her prayer cap trailed to her shoulders. In her dark Amish dress, with only the lamp's light on her face, she reminded Leah of a dark ghost.

For a trembling minute, Leah thought Ethan was going to turn and tell her to go away without him, but slowly he squared his shoulders. "I must get some things from my room."

"Of course." Tillie stepped aside. Ethan bolted out of the kitchen.

Left alone with Ethan's mother, Leah almost fell apart. "I'll watch after him," she whispered hoarsely. "I promise."

"I know you will, Leah, for I know you love him too."

Leah nodded mutely, stunned by this serene woman's ability to calmly embrace whatever adversity life gave her. *So unlike my mother,* Leah thought.

In minutes Ethan was back, a homespun sack over his shoulder. "Tell Simeon and Charity and Elizabeth I am sorry I did not get to see them. Tell them I will write to them."

"I will tell them."

He took Leah's elbow and started toward the back door.

"Son," Tillie called. They turned and she held up the lamp. "Each night you are gone, I will set this in the window of your room. It will burn for you, a light to show you the way back home if you want to come."

Ethan nodded and led Leah into the night.

In the car, Leah laid her head against the headrest and allowed the bottled-up tears to flow unchecked.

TEN

Early the next morning, Leah told Kathy's family she was leaving for home. She had the perfect excuse. Bad weather had been forecast, and she thought it best to beat it home before New Year's Eve. She thanked them for allowing her to stay and gave them the small gifts she'd bought for them. She hugged Kathy goodbye, then drove straight to Jonah's, where Ethan was waiting for her.

"Is that all you're going to take?" Leah asked incredulously.

All Ethan held was a small duffel bag, a battered suitcase, and the sack he'd carried from home the night before.

"It is all I own," Ethan told her. "Too many possessions make a person prideful. And material things are not what is important in life."

"Wait till you meet my mother," Leah said, half under her breath. Leah's mother was a collector of beautiful things—clothes, furniture, jewelry.

Ethan tossed his belongings into the car and got in. He looked tired. Leah felt sorry for him. Ethan was leaving behind him all he had ever known. It was a huge step. But she was excited, too. Ethan was coming home with her. They could be together whenever they wanted.

Ethan did not sleep during the trip but stared broodingly out the window as the miles slipped away. Icy cold rain fell in globs, smacking the windshield with squishy sounds, slowing them down and making the trip twice as long as usual.

By the time Leah turned into the long driveway leading to her house, it was dark and the sleet had turned into heavy, wet snow. She pulled into the garage and exhaled with relief. "Let me turn off the security alarm." She quickly punched in the code and led Ethan inside the house. "Wow, it's cold in here."

Ethan followed her tentatively. She flipped the light switch, but nothing happened. "Oh no! The electricity's out."

"Really," Ethan said. "How will we manage?"

The silliness of the problem made Leah giggle. The Amish didn't use electricity. "Okay, I get your point. But with no electricity, there's no heat." Without power, Leah felt marooned. Outside, the winds had picked up.

Driving snow pelted the house. "This blizzard could last a while," she said.

"Would that be so terrible?"

"I guess not." Her mother and Neil wouldn't be home until late on New Year's Day—or later, if the roads became impassable. Still, they wouldn't be worried about her because they thought she was at Kathy's. Two days alone with Ethan. Leah was certain she could handle it.

"Do you have a fireplace?" he asked.

"In the living room."

"Firewood?"

"In the garage."

"I will build you a fire, Leah."

She found a flashlight, several candles and a stash of matches. Ethan laid a fire in the stone hearth and lit it. Soon the flames danced and warmth seeped into the large room. Leah collected blankets, afghans and pillows and made a nest in front of the crackling fire. "Now, if we just had some food, it would be perfect," she told him.

In the kitchen they rummaged through the refrigerator and pantry and came up with hot dogs, chips, sodas and a can of baked beans. Ethan fashioned cooking sticks from wire coat hangers, and soon the aroma of cooking hot dogs filled the air. He warmed the beans deftly in a pot over the open flames.

"Who ever thought we'd have a picnic in December?" Leah asked as they ate.

"Who ever thought I'd be so far from home in December?"

"Are you all right about this, Ethan? I mean, do you wish you hadn't come with me?"

"No. I wanted to come. You would have starved without me," he teased.

"Probably." She glanced around the room. The flickering flames sent shadows dancing against the walls. The wind howled outside. "Tomorrow's New Year's Eve, but I don't think we're going to party it in."

"I will not miss the party. I am with you. That is all that matters to me."

Leah felt a tingle up her spine. "I guess we'll have to sleep here in front of the fireplace," she said, fluffing a pillow and stretching out.

"We can do as the Amish do," Ethan said. "We can bundle."

"How do we bundle?"

"It's an old Amish custom, not always approved of by parents and elders. But when dating, a boy and his girl will lie in bed together. They do not remove their clothes, but they spend the night in each other's arms."

Leah's jaw dropped. "This is an *Amish* custom?"

"Sex without marriage is forbidden," Ethan quickly added.

"I'd guess so. But—wow—doesn't bundling sort of invite trouble?"

Ethan chuckled. "Winters are long and very cold. Amish couples do it to keep warm."

Leah rolled her eyes. If any guy but Ethan had fed her such a line, she would have laughed at him. She thought that lying in bed with a person you love all night long without going all the way would be a temptation too hard to resist. "What happens if a couple gets carried away? What if they mess around and get into trouble?" In a way, Leah found it embarrassing to discuss such ideas with Ethan, but the subject of bundling was so unexpected from the morally upright Amish, she wanted to know more.

"If a girl is with child, then they must confess their sin before the entire church and ask forgiveness."

"You mean they have to stand up in front of everybody and tell them if she gets pregnant? If that's the case, then maybe they should keep quiet and just get married."

"They usually do marry," Ethan said. "Yet they must still make a public confession."

Leah made a face. "That's awful! It sounds pretty humiliating to me."

"In God's eyes, sin is sin. It does not matter which of God's laws we break. Sinners must repent."

"Does everybody forgive them?"

"It is required to forgive."

Leah had seen how difficult it had been for Ethan's

father to forgive his son Eli for leaving. "Really?" she asked.

A slow smile spread across Ethan's face. "Maybe not as quickly as it should be done," he admitted. "But that is what is supposed to happen."

Leah hugged her knees and stared into the fire. "Will your father forgive you for leaving?"

"Perhaps he already has."

"I'll be honest," Leah said, still gazing at the flames. "I felt sorry for your parents last night. And I expected your father to put up more of a fight to make you stay. Why didn't he?"

Ethan got up, threw two more logs on the fire, then returned to sit beside Leah. "He has known for a long time that I have been unhappy. We have had many talks about it. And I think that losing Rebekah wounded his heart deeply. He has said that perhaps her death was God's punishment for him."

Leah thought back to Rebekah's funeral. Even then she had disliked the stoic that's-the-way-it-is mentality of Ethan's family. She had been angry over Rebekah's senseless death. Her discussion with Ethan at the time had brought her neither understanding nor comfort. "Did he mean he feels he's being punished over the way he treated Eli?"

"Yes. His heart was proud at the time. He showed Eli no mercy."

Slowly a light of understanding flickered on inside Leah's mind. "That's really why you came, isn't it? You don't just want to see Eli again because you miss him. You want to make things right between Eli and your father."

"I want to see my brother. I want to talk to him face to face. If I can persuade him to return home, even for a visit, then perhaps he and Pa can start anew."

Disappointment hit Leah hard. She had hoped that Ethan had come mostly because of what he felt for her. "Sure," she said. "I get it now."

Ethan rose on his knees, took her hands in his and forced her to look into his eyes. "I have many questions, Leah, inside my heart. Not only about Eli, but also about you and me."

Had he read her mind? She returned his gaze. The light from the fire burnished his cheek, turning his skin a warm copper color. The reflections of the flames flickered in his eyes. She could drown in those eyes. "I don't have any answers for you, Ethan."

"We will find the answers together." He traced a finger down the length of her face, sending shivers up her spine. She wanted to lie in his arms, but she was afraid. "I will not dishonor you, Leah," Ethan said. He had made the same promise to her in the summer at the campout. But now the winter winds howled, and the night was dark and long. They were alone.

"That's the problem," Leah confessed. "I don't much care about my honor right this minute."

He sat down behind her and wrapped his arms around her, nestling her back against his chest. She fit perfectly within the curve of his body. "I love you," he said into her ear. "And it is because I love you that I will do nothing to shame you."

He made her feel cherished, respected. The strength of his embrace, the warmth of the fire, the softness of the pillows and blankets covering them, combined to make Leah's eyelids grow heavy. She listened to the wail of the wind and the rhythm of Ethan's breathing. "I guess we're bundling," she murmured. "A nice custom, Ethan. I like it very much."

In the safety of Ethan's arms, Leah drifted off to sleep.

ELEVEN

By morning the storm was over and sunlight flooded the house. Ethan had kept the fire burning all night, and Leah stretched lazily, feeling warm and snuggly beneath the pile of blankets. The smell of coffee forced her eyes open. "Is the electricity back on?" she asked sleepily.

"No, but I found coffee in your kitchen and have made it for us in the fireplace."

She took a mug from him and sipped it, making a face. "This stuff always smells better than it tastes." She smiled at him shyly. "Thanks for taking care of me all night."

"A pleasure," he said with a twinkle in his eye.

She blushed, remembering the night before. She had felt comfortable in his arms, but in the clear light of the day, she was glad he had respected her enough to not take advantage of their situation. "So," she asked, "are you hungry?"

He grinned. "Are there more hot dogs?"

"We can have cereal," she said.

She wrapped the blanket around herself and padded into the kitchen. Ethan followed, and together they prepared bowls of cereal and returned to the warmth of the fire.

"I will shovel the driveway," Ethan said. "It will be clear for your mother's return."

"Once the electricity comes back on, we can do lots of things," she said. "We have a big collection of videos. And tonight is New Year's Eve."

"And we can watch the ball drop?"

She laughed. "I'll tell you all about it."

Ethan stood. "I'd better get busy. The walkway is long and the snow deep."

After he had worked an hour, Leah went outside to join him. "Time for a break," she said. She lugged her large yellow plastic snow dish from the garage.

"But I still have much to do."

"So what? I'm bored and I think we should play."

He jammed the shovel into a snowbank. "With that?" He pointed at the bowl-shaped disk. "What is it?"

"You'll see. Come around back, where there's a hill."

The hill was at the back of the giant yard. So much snow covered it that it was hard to see exactly how steep it was. Leah tossed the dish down, lay across it on her stomach and gripped the short nylon handles on either side. "See ya!" she shouted, then scooted the disk forward. It slipped downward, picking up speed and making her squeal. At the bottom she coasted to a stop and jumped off. She trudged back up the hill and handed Ethan the dish. "Your turn."

His eyes danced. He took the disk and zipped down the hill, his laughter flowing behind him with the sprays of snow. By the time he climbed back up, she had a snowball hidden behind her back. "At home we use cardboard for such rides," he said. "And the ground is not so steep."

She tossed the snowball in his face, snatched the dish with her free hand, leaped onboard, and flew down the hill, laughing as he sputtered and wiped snow out of his eyes and mouth. "Gotcha!" she yelled.

He started down the hill after her, clomping through the snow, getting stuck in areas that were waist high, struggling against the snow's heavy wetness. Leah kept laughing. When he arrived at the bottom he doubled over, gasping for breath. "I thought you'd be in better shape," she teased, "you being a farm boy and all."

"You flirt with danger," Ethan said, lifting his gaze to hers.

"I don't think so," she needled. "You're a wimp."

He pounced on her. They rolled in the snow. Ethan

stuffed handfuls of it down the front of her jacket and sweater. Leah squealed, trying in vain to fend him off. "You'll pay for this!" she promised.

He pinned her on her back, grinned and plopped a fistful of snow in her face. "How will you make me pay?"

"I'll poison your food!" she sputtered.

"How? You don't cook without electricity."

"I'll find a way." She squirmed as he tossed another heap of snow at her face. "Get this stuff off me. It's freezing!"

He paused, looking down at her with a smile that lit up his face. "I know a good way to get the snow off." He tugged off his glove and brushed her cheeks with his bare hands. Then, holding her wrists, he bent over and kissed her with such an intensity that she was certain the snow would melt from the very heat of his mouth.

By midafternoon the electricity was back on, and Leah took a long, hot shower. Afterward she showed Ethan around the house, including the basement rooms where he would be living. He stashed his few belongings in the closet and went back upstairs with her to the kitchen.

"I have my grandmother's recipe box," she said. "I'll bet I could fix us something special for supper."

"I *am* hungry," he confessed.

"Ethan, you were born hungry," she said as she riffled through the box. Her grandmother's familiar

handwriting made Leah feel linked to the woman she had
loved and lost when she was still a child. Leah pulled up
a card. "This one looks easy. If Mom has all the ingredi-
ents, we'll be eating in a couple of hours."

Leah studied her grandmother's neat writing and
swallowed a lump of emotion. She set to work on the
beef stew.

Leah and Ethan ate in front of the fireplace, where Ethan
had laid fresh logs. He wolfed down three bowls of stew,
and three slices of bread, topping off the meal with two
glasses of milk and half a bag of vanilla wafers.

"Get enough?" Leah asked, slightly awed by the
sheer quantity of food he had downed.

"Is there more?"

She threw a pillow at him. "Eat this."

Later Leah made popcorn. Close to midnight, she
stopped the video they were watching and switched over
to network television. Crowds of people were partying in
Times Square. Leah found a bottle of sparkling grape
juice in the refrigerator. Neil and her mom often liked
wine with their dinner, but with Neil's chemo he couldn't
drink alcohol, so her mother sometimes served the bub-
bly grape juice instead. Now Leah filled two of her
mother's good wineglasses for her and Ethan.

"Watch, watch!" she said as the great, glowing ball
began to descend and the crowd began the countdown.

"They all seem very happy," Ethan observed.

"The start of every year means starting fresh. People like that."

"I am starting fresh, too."

The ball hit the bottom, an orchestra played "Auld Lang Syne," and Leah clicked her glass to Ethan's. "Here's to us."

He sipped the juice while gazing at her over the rim of the glass. "Now what?"

On TV people were hugging and kissing. "We're supposed to kiss for good luck. And wish each other Happy New Year."

He set his glass down and pulled her into his arms. "Happy New Year, Leah."

"Happy New Year to you," she whispered as their lips touched.

"This is a good custom among you English," he said.

His wording jarred her. *You English*. For a while she had forgotten their differences. She warned herself not to forget again. "Well, back to our movie." Her hand was shaking as she clicked the remote. She settled into the heap of pillows and blankets still strewn in front of the fireplace.

"Maybe we should go to our beds. The electricity has warmed the house."

"Maybe later," she said stubbornly, not wanting their time of togetherness to end. "We'll watch some more films—we've got a bunch more." She gestured toward the stack on the floor.

"We would have to stay awake all night."

"So what? We can sleep all day tomorrow."

"Sleep through the day?" He sounded scandalized.

"Okay—half the day. At least until you need another feeding."

He laughed. "It is different not to have cows to feed, chores that must be done. I'm not used to this."

"We have goldfish," she said. "Want to get up at five in the morning and feed them?"

"No," he said, stretching back against the pillows. "I want to watch movies all night with you. It is a brand-new year, is it not? We can begin it however we please."

Leah had faced the start of other years before, but never had she felt that one could hold so much potential for happiness along with so much room for tragedy. The possibilities whirled in her head. Would her cancer remain in remission? Would Neil win his battle for good health? Would Ethan love her enough to stay in her world? She chased away the list of questions and punched the Play button.

Leah woke with a start. Electronic snow filled the TV screen. It was daylight, but the day looked cloudy, the skies dreary. Beside her Ethan was on his stomach, fast asleep. Groggily she reached for the remote and clicked off the VCR. What time was it anyway?

She heard a noise. With a start, she realized it was a key in the front door. *"Oh, no!"* This wasn't the way she wanted to be found. "Ethan! Wake up!" Leah shook his shoulder.

"Leah! Honey, we're home," she heard her mother call. "Where are you?"

"Hurry!" Leah urged Ethan.

Leah scrambled up. Ethan rose beside her just as Leah's mother and Neil came into the room.

Her mother stopped dead in her tracks. Her mouth dropped open as her eyes swept over the pillows and blankets in front of the fireplace. Her gaze halted on Ethan. For a stunned moment, no one spoke. Finally, in her frostiest tone, her mother said, "Just what is going on here, young lady? I want an explanation, and I want it now."

TWELVE

"I—I can explain," Leah stammered.

"I'll just bet," her mother snapped.

Neil stepped forward. He looked shocked, as if Leah had struck him. His look cut her deeply. She'd rather have done anything than upset Neil. "Is this your friend Ethan?" he asked.

Ethan held out his hand. "I am Ethan."

Neil took Ethan's hand, but before he could say a word, Leah's mother stormed over, picked up a blanket and shoved it at Leah. "Is this what you do behind our backs? Tell us you're visiting a friend, then shack up with your boyfriend?"

Leah felt her face burn with embarrassment. "That's not what happened, Mother—"

"I trusted you!" her mother exclaimed. "Is this how you pay me back?"

"If you'll let me explain—"

"I can't believe it, Leah. How could you do this to us?"

Neil put a hand on his wife's arm. "Calm down, Roberta."

"Calm down? She's not your daughter, Neil. She—" Leah's mother stopped her tirade. "I didn't mean that," she amended quickly. "I'm just so upset."

Neil looked at Ethan. "Why don't I take Ethan and show him my car collection? That'll give you and Leah a chance to clear the air."

Grateful for Neil's offer, Leah nodded vigorously. Neil had a knack for knowing what to say and do in a crisis. And this was a crisis.

"I should stay," Ethan said, looking bewildered. "This is my fault, too."

Leah turned toward him. "Go on with Neil, Ethan. You wouldn't want me around if it were your father's and your discussion. I need to talk to my mother alone."

Ethan hesitated, then said, "All right, I will go. But if you need me, call for me."

She watched Ethan and Neil leave, waited for the click of the front door, then spun on her mother. "That was so embarrassing! You shouldn't have said those things in front of Ethan."

"Well, pardon me," her mother mocked icily. "I always expect to come home from a holiday and find my daughter and her boyfriend sleeping together."

"We were *not* sleeping together!" Leah stamped her foot. "We fell asleep in front of the TV watching movies."

Her mother rolled her eyes. "Oh, please, Leah. Give me some credit. You've been crazy about this boy for over a year. You spent a summer with him." Her eyes grew wide, then narrowed. "Did he spend nights at your apartment? Did we fund your little love affair all summer long?"

On the verge of tears, Leah cried, "How can you think such a thing? I've never slept with Ethan. Sure we've had the opportunity, but we never did. He respects me. He loves me."

"Loves you? What would a seventeen-year-old like you know about love?"

Leah saw red. "I know lots about love, Mother. I know you don't have to marry five times to find it." Color drained from her mother's face, but Leah didn't back down. "I know that love is caring enough about a person to stick around when things get tough. I know that love is letting your daughter see her grandmother. And helping her keep in touch with her real father."

Where did all that come from? Leah wondered. She hadn't meant to say those things. She'd meant only to tell her mother about her and Ethan.

Her mother stiffened, but she kept her voice controlled when she spoke. "I'm not going to discuss ancient history with you, Leah. This is neither the time nor the place. I won't allow you to distract me from the real situation—finding you and Ethan alone and unsupervised in this house."

Leah heard the subtle shift in her mother's words. At least she was no longer flinging wild accusations. Leah swiped at the tears rolling down her cheeks. "I know how it must look, but nothing happened between me and Ethan. You've got to believe me."

"So you say. How can I believe you when the evidence is all over the floor?"

"Don't you think if we were sleeping together, we'd have tried to hide it from you? Not leave ourselves out in the open for you to trip over?"

"I don't know what to think." Her mother rubbed her temples as if fighting off a headache.

"Here's what happened, from start to finish. Just listen." Leah told her mother about the storm, the power outage, their watching TV and falling asleep. When she finished, she said, "That's why we were on the floor. We just conked out."

"That explains the physical situation," her mother said. "But it doesn't tell me why he's here in the first place."

"That's going to take a little longer." Leah sat on the sofa. Her legs ached from holding her body rigid. "He's here because I invited him to stay with us for a while."

"Oh, Leah! How could you? Neil and I don't need some teenage boy underfoot. Especially now."

"Just listen," Leah said. "Please. I told him Neil could help him find his brother." Leah patiently explained about Eli, the estrangement between Eli and Jacob, the terrible sense of loss Ethan felt over the death of his sister and the disappearance of his brother. "I know what it's like to feel alone, Mom. I know what it feels like to want your family intact."

"Is that another slam about the way I raised you?"

"No." Leah sighed. "I'm just telling you what I felt growing up . . . about how much I wanted a family around me."

"*I* was your family," her mother said sharply.

"You worked."

"I had to put food on the table. I had to take care of us."

Leah was tempted to remind her mother again about her tendency to marry any man who came along. She thought better of it. At least her mother had calmed down and seemed to be listening to her. "Look, right now Ethan needs to get some things settled. I offered to help him. I don't see how that's going to interfere with your life."

"Dare I remind you that Neil's recovering from cancer?"

"Well, so am I," Leah said. "And I know that having Ethan around is good for me. Why don't I talk to Neil and tell him just what I've told you and let him decide about letting Ethan stay?" Leah felt confident that Neil would be more sympathetic than her mother.

"I don't want to burden Neil. He—He isn't feeling all that good."

The news jolted Leah. "He's sick?"

A shadow crossed her mother's face but quickly disappeared. "No, I'm sure he's fine. But he's tired all the time. He just hasn't gotten his strength back from all that chemo yet."

Neil's chemo had ended weeks ago. "He was feeling all right at Christmas and before your trip."

"It was probably just the trip," her mother said dismissively. "We were very busy and went to parties with many of his old friends. He's just overextended himself, I'm sure."

Leah stood, suddenly anxious to talk to Neil. "I'm going out to the barn."

"I'm not finished discussing this."

"I want to talk to Neil about it," Leah said stubbornly.

"Oh, all right." Her mother sounded tired and cross. "But this isn't over—not by a long shot. I'm going to unpack. And then there's a meal to think about fixing."

"There's some leftover stew in the fridge. I made it last night from one of Grandma Hall's old recipes. She used to make it for me when I was little, before—" Leah broke off. "Well, anyway, I liked it a lot."

Leah started for the garage, where her coat and boots were.

"Leah," her mother said, "I know you have plenty of questions about the past."

Trust her mother to state the obvious. "You're right. I do."

"Well, be careful. Don't be so eager to dig around in the mud. You might not like what you find."

Without another word, Leah left the house.

In the barn Leah found Ethan and Neil inspecting the cars. Several of the tarpaulins had been pulled back, exposing the fine old machines. Looking keenly interested, Ethan told Leah, "These are very beautiful."

"Not like Amish buggies, huh?"

"Did you pacify your mother?" Neil asked.

"For the moment."

"Ethan explained to me what happened."

Leah studied Neil's face. He looked thinner. "Do you believe us? We weren't doing anything wrong, Neil."

"I believe you both. And don't be hard on your mother, Leah. She's just concerned for you."

Leah said, "Mom and I have some things to work out. But it has nothing to do with you. I'm sorry about her crack about me not being your daughter."

"I know she didn't mean it."

"Which is a big part of her problem. She often says things before she thinks. It hurts people's feelings."

Neil gave Leah a sympathetic smile. "It's a problem for most adults. Especially when they love their kids."

Leah didn't feel like arguing the point. She stared hard at Neil, studying him for a long moment. "Mom said you haven't been feeling great."

"A little tired," Neil said. "Lingering effects of the chemo, I guess."

"It made me tired too, but once it was over, I snapped right back."

"You're younger," Neil said with a grin. "It takes a little longer these days."

"When do you see your doctor again?"

"End of the month."

"Maybe you should——"

"Oh, quit your worrying," Neil patted Leah's hand. "I'm fine. I just need a little rest." He turned toward Ethan, who was listening intently to the conversation. "I know you didn't come all this way for a New Year's Eve party, Ethan. Why did you come home with Leah?"

"I want to find my brother."

Ethan explained his situation; then Leah explained how she was hoping Neil could help him. "There's no big rush," she added. "And we'll do all the work. But we don't even know how to begin."

Neil looked thoughtful. "I'll have to give it some thought myself."

"Not right this minute," Leah said hastily. Neil looked exhausted. "I figured Ethan could stay in the basement, in the extra room down there."

"And I will work, sir," Ethan said. "Anything you need done around your property. I'm a good worker. Plus, I'll get another job to pay for my room and food."

"Oh, I don't think that'll be necessary."

Ethan shook his head. "No. I must work."

Neil nodded. "We can talk about it later. Don't think I didn't notice the clean walk when we drove up. You did a good job."

"Thank you," Ethan said.

"There are lots of little things around the house that need doing. I can do them, but . . . well, my energy level isn't up to par."

"I will do whatever chores you want done."

"Keeping the cars up is important to me."

"All you must do is tell me how."

Neil smoothed his hand over the fender on the nearest car. "I'll be glad to. Forgive an older man's vice, but I love these big hunks of metal."

"I feel the same affection for my father's horse and buggy."

Neil flashed Ethan a big grin. "Then we're not so different after all. You've got a job, Ethan."

Leah watched the two of them shake hands and felt relieved. Ethan was staying.

THIRTEEN

Ethan moved into the basement area of Leah's home, Leah returned to classes and schoolwork, and by the end of the first week, Ethan had proved himself nearly indispensable to the household. While Ethan still didn't have a full-time job, Neil managed to keep him busy caring for his cars and doing minor repairs around the property.

"That young man can fix anything," Neil told Leah.

"And he'll eat anything, too," Leah said. "He eats Mother's cooking as if he actually likes it."

Neil chuckled but admonished, "She's not *that* bad a cook."

Leah didn't argue, but she looked forward to the nights when take-out food was on the menu.

At school Leah settled back into classes, but as soon as the final bell rang, she headed straight for home—and Ethan. He had been with them only a couple of weeks when the two of them drove into town for a movie. They were in the ticket line when Sherry bumped into them.

"Hi," she said, giving Ethan a curious stare.

Leah introduced them. "Want to sit with us?" she asked.

"Love to," Sherry said with a grateful smile.

After the movie they went for hamburgers. The minute Ethan left the table to order more food, Sherry leaned toward Leah. "So this is the Amish boyfriend you used to mention?"

"That's right."

"And you talked your mother into letting him move in with you?"

"It's just for a while. Until he gets some things worked out." Leah didn't tell Sherry about the search for Ethan's missing brother, only that Ethan had some family problems.

Sherry leaned back in the booth and gave Leah an admiring look. "I'm totally impressed. Have you ever thought of politics as a career choice? I mean, if you can persuade your mom to let the guy you're dating live with you, you must be some talker."

Leah laughed. "It wasn't an easy sell, believe me. But Ethan's so nice and he helps around the place so much, even my mother is beginning to depend on him."

She frowned. "Still, it would be good if he could get a real job. I know it's starting to bother him that he isn't giving Neil and Mom money for his keep."

Sherry stirred her milkshake with a straw. "Maybe my dad can use him."

"Really? What's your dad do?"

"He's a veterinarian. He has a practice out on Mill Road. He takes care of farm animals—and house pets, too. I help out in the summers, but lately he's been talking about getting someone to help him in the field. Birthing season is just beginning for the farmers. Since Ethan's Amish, he probably knows a lot about animals."

Leah nodded enthusiastically. "He knows tons. Would you ask your dad about giving Ethan a job?"

"Sure. And I'll call you."

"That's really nice of you, Sherry."

Sherry shrugged self-consciously. "It's no big deal. You're my friend. I'd like to help you out. And besides, Ethan's nice. Not to mention totally gorgeous."

"I'll tell him you said so."

Sherry shrieked and her face turned red. "Don't you dare!"

" 'Don't you dare' what?"

Both girls started, then looked up to see Dave Simmons, who had appeared beside their booth.

Leah stiffened, remembering their last encounter. "Private conversation," she told him. "Don't eavesdrop."

Dave held up his hands in mock surrender. "Well, excuse me. The princess has spoken. Let the world stop spinning."

Sherry sat mute as a post, her face reddening even more.

"Leah? Is there a problem?" Ethan had come alongside the table. He set his food tray down.

Dave turned, then gave Ethan a hostile gaze. "Who are you?"

"Ethan Longacre."

Dave looked Ethan up and down. "You aren't from around here. Where do you go to school?"

"I do not go to school."

Leah's heart thundered. She didn't like Dave's attitude. Ethan didn't understand the threat Dave represented.

Dave said to Leah, "I never figured you for falling for a dropout. Or is he just stupid?"

"Get lost," Leah told him.

"I am Amish," Ethan said, as if that would explain everything.

Dave rolled his eyes. "Even worse."

Suddenly Sherry's milk shake slopped across the table, landing on the front of Dave's jeans.

"Whoops!" she cried, looking horrified.

The pale white glop rolled down his pant leg. Dave jumped back, swearing.

Ethan stared at him. "You are rude," he said to Dave. "And we do not want your company."

"Go away," Leah said, "before I call the manager."

People's heads turned in their direction and conversation fell off. Desperately Leah hoped Dave would notice and not cause any more of a scene.

Dave glared menacingly, swore at Ethan and Leah and stalked off. He stopped, grabbed a handful of napkins and mopped his pants. He turned long enough to say, "Listen, Amish boy, if you know what's good for you, you'll stay out of my way."

Ethan turned his back on Dave. "He is not nice."

Leah's hands were shaking. "He's mean, Ethan. Don't mess with him."

Ethan grinned. "He is like a dog locked behind a fence. He barks but has little courage."

Leah started to argue her point, but then she remembered Sherry. "You all right?" she asked.

"Sure," Sherry said, looking acutely embarrassed.

Leah was fuming. "Dave's a jerk. He shouldn't have said those things. Good thing you had that accident."

"It wasn't exactly an accident," Sherry said with a sheepish grin.

Leah returned her smile gleefully. "Good for you. Too bad you couldn't have dumped it on his head."

"I will buy you another," Ethan said.

"No. . . . It's okay. Really. I've lost my appetite." Sherry stood and slipped on her coat. "I've got to be going anyway. Leah, I'll call you after I talk to my dad. And Ethan, it was nice meeting you. I'm sorry Dave was so rude. We're not all that way."

Leah and Ethan watched her leave. When they were alone, Ethan said, "I am sorry for your friend's feelings. What is Dave's problem?"

"He doesn't like you."

"He does not even know me."

Leah briefly explained how she kept turning down dates with Dave. "A guy like him thinks he's God's gift to the world. He can't take no for an answer. Still, I'd have thought he would have gotten over it by now."

"His anger is foolish, but it does not bother me."

"It bothers me," Leah said. "You be careful, Ethan. Stay far away from him."

"I do not fear him."

Leah knew it was the truth, but she feared for Ethan. In his heart he was still a plain person, but the world around him was different from his world in Nappanee. In her area, kids might not understand about the Amish. And they might not treat them with kindness. "Just be

careful," she said again, feeling the gulf between her and
Ethan opening up once more.

On Sunday evening, while Leah and Ethan were playing
Monopoly, Neil came and sat down at the table.
"Who's winning?"

"Ethan," Leah grumbled. "He has the best luck.
Look, he owns all the railroads, plus Boardwalk and
Park Place."

Ethan's blue eyes studied the Chance card he'd just
drawn. "I have gotten an inheritance of five hundred
dollars."

Leah groaned and counted out five Monopoly bills
from the bank.

"Let's take a break," Neil said. "I want to talk to you
about finding this brother of yours."

Ethan leaned forward. "Yes."

"I've been giving it a lot of thought," Neil said. "Tell
me everything you know about him."

"I know nothing."

"Wait," Leah interjected. "Didn't you tell me you ran
into one of his old teachers once? You told me she said Eli
was finishing college and going to become a teacher."

Neil said, "Did he become a teacher?"

"I do not know."

Neil considered the dilemma. Watching his face,
Leah was again struck by how thin he looked. "I'll call

the Indiana State Board of Education and ask if there's a teacher in the state named Eli Longacre," Neil said.

"And if there is not?"

"Then I'll contact teaching organizations in surrounding states. If that turns up nothing, we'll try national groups."

"But what if he is not a teacher?"

"There are other ways of finding people," Neil said. He found a yellow pad of paper in a desk drawer. "Right now, I want you to tell me everything you can remember about your brother." He took notes while Ethan answered his questions. Once he was satisfied, he said, "I won't give up, Ethan. We'll find out something about Eli."

"Thank you for your help. I am in much debt to you."

Neil shook his head. "No debt, Ethan. I know what it's like to want to know about your family. My parents are dead and my only brother died in World War Two. Except for Leah and her mom, I have no family at all. But I've always wanted one. The bigger, the better."

Leah rose and gave Neil a quick hug. His cheek felt dry and papery against hers. "Well, I want to thank you, too. I knew you could help Ethan."

Neil patted her back. "We all need help now and again. I'm glad to be able to offer it to you. You're a good man, Ethan. I hope you find your brother, and I hope you won't be disappointed in what you find."

"How do you mean?" Ethan asked, looking puzzled.

"People change," Neil said. "Sometimes for the worse."

Up until that moment, it had never occurred to Leah that finding Eli might not be a pleasant experience. She locked gazes with Ethan and saw instantly that it had not occurred to him either. Her mother's words from New Year's Day came back to her: "... *be careful*.... *You might not like what you find.*"

FOURTEEN

At school Sherry told Leah that her dad wanted to interview Ethan for a job, so on Wednesday afternoon, Leah drove Ethan out to Dr. Prater's animal clinic on Mill Road. She parked and was about to get out of the car when Ethan stopped her. "I am not sure this is a good idea, Leah."

"But why? I thought you wanted a job."

"I must have a job. But this is so far from your home. How will I get here if I am even hired?"

Leah sank back into the car seat. "Gosh, I didn't think of that."

"Maybe I should just forget about finding Eli." Ethan sounded discouraged.

"You can't give up already. Neil's hardly gotten started in his search."

"Neil is not well. I can see it whenever I look at him. He does not need my problems."

"But he likes doing this for you, Ethan. And I think he needs to do it. It makes him feel useful. Even my mother is glad for him to have something to do."

Leah was telling the truth. Her mother had done an about-face concerning Ethan's stay at the house. "Having Ethan around makes Neil feel good," Leah's mother had confided to Leah. "It gives him some comfort knowing that little things are being taken care of. Ethan listens to Neil and seems to respect whatever he says."

Leah saw the results of Ethan's handiwork almost every day when she came home from school. In the weeks he'd been living with them, he'd fixed leaky faucets, painted the living room and kitchen, cleared out the garage, and helped Leah's mom sort through boxes full of stuff in the attic and garage. And he took care of Neil's antique cars.

"Don't worry about getting here if you get the job," she told Ethan. "We'll work something out. Even if you have to take me to school every day and use my car."

Ethan nodded, but Leah could tell he wasn't crazy about her offer. It wasn't the Amish way to be indebted to people.

Inside the building, Dr. Prater showed them around. He and Ethan talked about farm animals and what would be expected from Ethan. By the end of the interview, Dr. Prater seemed very satisfied with Ethan's abilities and offered him a job on the spot. "I'll need you five days a week, from eight in the morning until around four o'clock, and half days on Saturdays," Dr. Prater said. "Especially during the upcoming calf-birthing season."

Ethan hesitated, then agreed.

"Good," Dr. Prater said with a smile and a handshake. He went to a file drawer and handed Ethan a sheaf of forms. "Fill out the necessary paperwork, and you can start this Saturday."

At the dinner table that night, Neil and Roberta congratulated Ethan on getting the job, but Ethan shook his head. "I must call Dr. Prater back and tell him I cannot take this job."

Alarmed, Leah set her fork down.

"Why?" Neil asked.

"The papers the doctor gave me asks for numbers I do not have."

"Such as?"

"I do not have a social security number."

"But everybody has one," Leah's mother said. "You can't get a job in this country without one."

"I have only worked on my father's farm. I do not have this number."

Neil leaned back in his chair. "The Amish don't pay

social security taxes," he said. "I remember now. They're exempt by congressional order because they don't accept any of the benefits. They take care of their own and have no need of government handouts."

Leah hadn't known this, but it didn't surprise her.

"It is our way to care for one another," Ethan explained.

"Take the job," Neil advised. "We'll apply for a social security card and tell the doc it's coming." He drummed his fingers on the table, a thoughtful look on his face. "This gives me an idea about finding your brother. If he's working, he has to have a social security card, too. That might be a way to track him down."

As long as Neil was in a problem-solving mood, Leah thought she'd bring up Ethan's need for transportation. "He can use my car," she added, "but he'll have to take me to school every day."

"No need for that," Neil said. "He can use my old pickup. You do have a license, don't you?"

"Yes."

"Good. Then it's settled. You can go to work."

"You are too generous. I will not forget all you are doing for me."

Neil dismissed Ethan's thanks with a wave of his hand. "You just pay your insurance and gas. The old truck will need a tune-up before you can drive it, however. I'll take it into a garage tomorrow. There was a time when I could tune that baby up myself, but not now." Neil sounded sad about it. "I could teach you, Ethan, but I guess you don't want to learn how to be a mechanic."

"I would learn—for you. But animals are more to my liking."

Once the truck was mechanically sound, Leah and Ethan went their separate ways each day. Leah missed being with him when she returned home from school, but she made herself do her homework then so that she could have free time with him during the evenings.

Leah arrived home one afternoon to find her mother crying at the kitchen table. "What's wrong?" Leah dumped her books on the floor and hurried to her mother's side.

"Neil's white count is up," her mother said between sniffs. "More than up. It's very high. His doctor wants to put him back on chemo."

Leah felt her stomach sinking. An elevated white blood cell count was ominous in Neil's case.

"It's an experimental drug, part of a test program," Leah's mother said. "They want Neil to try it, although Dr. Nguyen warned us that there may be some adverse side effects."

"What kind of side effects?"

"Nausea, vomiting—there's a whole list. But she wouldn't have recommended him for the program if the other therapy was working."

Leah's stomach churned. She was afraid she might throw up. "When will he start?"

"They'll reinsert the infusion pump tomorrow. He'll have to go for weekly testing, and if he can't tolerate the drug at all, he'll have to go off it." Roberta's gaze flew to Leah's face. "I don't know what I'll do if anything happens to Neil."

Leah was at a loss for words. Her mother was begging her for reassurance, but Leah didn't know how to give it to her. "We'll just have to hope the new drug works," she said lamely. "How's Neil taking the news?"

"He's trying to act cheerful, but he's devastated. I can tell. We both had such hope that the other chemo had worked. Leah, it's been less than three months since he was in remission. I never dreamed he'd have a relapse. And so soon!"

Leah trembled over the note of desperation in her mother's voice. "Where is he?"

"He walked out to the barn. The news has really shaken him up."

A raw February wind whipped Leah's hair as she hurried to the barn. She found Neil inside, seated on the hood of an old Desoto, his head bowed and his elbows propped on his knees. He looked up when Leah came inside. She said, "Mom told me."

Neil managed a crooked grin. "So now I'm a guinea pig." Tears slid down Leah's cheeks. Neil fumbled for a tissue in the pocket of his jacket. "You girls, honestly. You cry like babies, but you never have a tissue handy."

Leah wiped her eyes. "Yeah . . . Imagine crying about you relapsing and going into a high-risk drug program. Go figure." She blew her nose.

He offered a wry smile. "Point taken. Listen, kiddo, these next few months are going to be tough sledding. I don't have any false illusions about this new stuff helping me a whole lot."

"You talk like you don't expect this to work."

Neil sighed. "It's a long shot, honey. A real long shot."

Leah's chin trembled and fresh tears pooled in her eyes. "I don't want you to die."

"I'll stick around as long as the good Lord lets me. I want to live. And I want to stay out of the hospital."

"What can I do to help?"

"You may have to let your mother lean on you a bit."

"Her lean on me?" Leah thought the idea preposterous.

"You know how she sometimes lapses into denial: 'If I don't think about it, then maybe it isn't happening.' " Neil said. "She doesn't mean anything bad by it. It's just the way she copes. You know?"

Leah sniffed. "What do you want me to do?"

"Just be sensitive. Help her adjust." Neil shifted on the hood of the car and lightly slapped the fender beside him. "Hop up."

Leah settled next to him.

"She loves you, Leah. She depends on you."

Leah was skeptical. "Mom's always had someone else in her life to lean on. I sometimes thought she'd be better off if she'd never even had me. I felt in the way."

Neil shook his head. "Not true. Everything she did, every marriage she entered into, was with you in mind."

"Well, except for you, she had bad taste."

Neil chuckled. "Thanks for that." He patted Leah's hand. "Did you know that she never finished high school?"

"She never told me that!"

"She's never told you a lot of things."

Leah was irritated that Neil knew things about her mother that she didn't. "Did she ever tell you why she dumped my father? Or why she hated my grandmother?"

Neil didn't answer right away. When he did, his tone was serious. "Your father suffered from paranoia. Do you know what that is?"

Leah had heard the word used loosely but couldn't remember what it really meant. "I'm not sure."

"It's a kind of mental illness. The victim often suffers from delusions of persecution. He thinks someone's out to get him, that he's the focus of a conspiracy. He hears voices that tell him to do bizarre things. Often the victim seems perfectly normal and completely functional. Then something happens that triggers an episode and he turns into some sort of deranged person."

Leah stared at Neil, stunned by what he was telling her, unable to fully absorb it. "*My* father? You're talking about *my* father? He—He was crazy?"

"He was sick, Leah," Neil corrected.

"Didn't he go to a doctor?"

"Back then there wasn't much that could be done for a person with paranoia. Over time your father got worse, and your mother was afraid. She divorced him because she was afraid he might harm her. Or you."

"And Grandma Hall? What about her? What did Mom say about her?" Leah was shaking. She felt angry and defensive. Parts of her universe were fragmenting in front of her eyes. She'd known that something had been wrong between her parents, but she'd never suspected this. Why hadn't her mother told her?

"Your grandmother had a blind spot when it came to her son. Mothers sometimes do, you know. She refused to accept her son's illness. She blamed your mother. When your father took off, your grandmother tried to get custody of you and failed. It left your mother bitter. She married the first guy who came along out of self-preservation."

Neil took Leah's hand. His hand felt warm; hers was icy cold. "I've begged your mother to tell you all this, but she keeps saying, 'I'll tell Leah someday . . . when she's older.' I think you're old enough, and I'm telling you because she's going to need you to help her through

whatever happens to me. I'm also telling you because I
didn't confide in you about my previous cancer. I saw
how much that upset you."

Leah felt as if she had heard a story about somebody
else. It was as if Neil were telling her something he'd
read or seen on television. It couldn't really be her life
they were discussing. "I—I'm glad you told me," she
said, numb from the weight of the information.

Neil said, "I know I've dumped a lot on you, Leah,
but you need to start seeing your mother through new
eyes, to begin to understand her life and the choices
she's made. Most everything she did was for you. Even
marrying me."

Leah whipped around to face him.

"Don't be shocked," Neil said. "I've always known,
and it's never bothered me."

"But she loves you." Leah's voice sounded small,
childlike. "She's told me so."

"I know." Neil smiled. "That's the best part of all.
That's how I know she'll be here for me no matter what
happens. No matter how bad it gets. We're a family,
Leah. For better or worse, we are a family."

FIFTEEN

Neil went into the hospital the next morning and straight into surgery for the reinsertion of the infusion pump. At Neil's insistence, Ethan went on to his job, but Leah skipped school so that she could hang around the waiting room with her mother. Leah had hardly slept the night before. Her mind spun. Not only was Neil facing medical uncertainty, but also, she wondered what the failure of his chemo protocol might mean for her. If she relapsed, would she also have to endure an experimental drug program?

The revelations about her father, mother and grandmother haunted her. How could she have never known the truth? Why hadn't anyone told her until now?

Leah and her mother sat together in an empty waiting room. Her mother sipped coffee and stared out the window at the bleak February landscape. Leah fidgeted, wanting to talk to her mother and not knowing how to begin.

Her mother relieved her of her dilemma when she said, "Neil told me he talked to you yesterday in the barn. He told me everything the two of you talked about."

"You should have been the one to tell me," Leah said, knowing she sounded hurt. "Why am I always the last to know about everything in this family?"

"It isn't a conspiracy, Leah. I was going to tell you about your father. I just never knew how."

"The same way you told Neil. You just say it." Leah paused as another thought occurred to her. "You're not mad at Neil, are you? Because if you are—"

"I'm not mad at Neil," her mother said. "He wouldn't do anything to hurt either of us."

Leah stood, unable to sit still one more minute. "I know what Neil told me, but I'm mixed up. *You* once told me that the reason you wouldn't let me see Grandma Hall was because you were mad at Dad for not being able to take care of us. You said that you were bitter and that you took it out on her." Leah recalled as if it had been yesterday the conversation she'd had with her mother when she'd been hospitalized. "So which is it?"

"I also told you that your father wasn't well psychologically. That's the closest I ever got to telling you about how sick he really was. I should have told you everything then, but I didn't."

"Why not?"

Her mother shrugged. "If you could have seen the look that crossed your face when I told you as much as I did, you'd know why. You looked horrified. And then hostile, as if you'd never accept anything negative about him from me. You had him built up in your mind to god-like status. You were also being told at the same time by your doctors that you had cancer and that you might lose your leg. I couldn't trash your father to you. It wouldn't have been right. You needed to concentrate on the future, not the past."

"Why is everybody always trying to protect me instead of being honest with me? Neil said you divorced Dad because you were afraid for our safety. Is that true? Did you think Dad would have hurt us?" It pained Leah deeply to think such things about her father.

"You idolized your father, Leah. You were Daddy's little girl from the time you were born. In spite of everything that happened, I wanted you to have that illusion."

"But it was all a lie!"

"No," her mother said. "When he was in his right mind, it was true. But when he had an episode, when he heard voices telling him to protect you, even if it meant running away with you or hiding you, I panicked. One night I came home from work and he thought I was the Angel of Death come to snatch you away. That's when I moved out. I didn't have anyplace to go—my parents were dead, and Grandma Hall thought I was a horrible person for deserting her son. I found us a dumpy little trailer in a crummy trailer park, but it was all I could afford. I worked nights, and a neighbor watched you. I married Don when you were five."

Leah remembered the trailer more clearly than she did her first stepfather. He took off when she was six. The trailer remained her home until she was almost seven. When Leah's mother would go to work, Leah would lie alone in the dark, terrified, listening to the sounds of the night outside her window. They had moved from the trailer into an apartment when Leah's mother married her third husband. That marriage, too, had ended in divorce. Leah had been nine. But when Leah was ten, her real father died, homeless and alone in an alley far away in Oregon. Then Grandma Hall died and Leah's mother married for the fourth time.

Leah's fourth stepfather was years younger than her mother, and Leah had disliked him intensely. He left them less than a year later. Then she and her mother lived alone for two years. Finally Neil had entered their lives and had given them both a sense of being cared for. Leah had thought the hard times were finally over. But she was wrong. Now they might lose Neil to cancer.

Leah turned to face her mother. "Neil said Grandma Hall tried to get custody of me. Is that true?"

"She threatened me with a custody battle right after

your father and I separated," her mother replied. "Voices had told him that a mysterious stranger was stalking him and was going to kill him. It wasn't true, of course, just another one of his delusions. But he left me with a pile of bills, a child to raise, and no money. I was angry. When your grandmother tried to take you away, I freaked. Of course, we never went to court, but I swore that she'd never see you again."

But she did, Leah thought. Her grandmother had sneaked into Leah's day care centers and schools to visit her. Even now, Leah couldn't bring herself to tell her mother that. "But when she got sick, you took me to the hospital to see her."

"I did," her mother said with a sigh. "I felt sorry for her. She was alone. Her son—your father—was dead. She had no one else in the world but you. And I didn't want her to die without making my peace with her."

Leah realized that many of her notions, ideas and impressions of her childhood were not correct. She'd thought her father had been a sad and lonely man, driven off by her mother. Her recollections of her mother's and grandmother's animosity had been true enough, but now Leah understood their enmity. Maybe her grandmother had meant well, but wouldn't any mother fight to keep her only child?

Even her mother's many marriages took on new meaning for Leah. Her mother had married to improve her lot in life. Using marriage to better oneself seemed distasteful to Leah, but she realized that her mother had probably considered herself resourceful each time. Leah began to understand why her mother had always worked at menial jobs. Without a high-school diploma, she'd probably had no choice.

From the nurse's desk down the hall, Leah heard a doctor being paged. Weak February sunshine pooled on the toe of her boot. The smell of old coffee hung in the air. A nurse's aide rattled bedpans as she walked down the hallway.

"So is that it?" Leah asked quietly. "Is that everything there is for me to know about my dad, about the past?"

"Yes," her mother answered. Then she added, "Just one other thing. You may not understand a lot of my choices. You may be angry about the way things went for you as you were growing up. But until you have a child of your own—until you have to make choices and decisions for your child's welfare—please hold back judgment on the way I've handled things."

Leah stared at her mother. At the moment, she couldn't imagine having a child of her own. At the moment, she couldn't imagine even wanting one.

The experimental drug was not kind to Neil. He became deathly sick. His hair fell out. Sores erupted on his body.

He lost so much weight that he couldn't wear any of his clothes, and Leah's mother had to buy him a new wardrobe. Once Dr. Nguyen allowed him to go home, Neil stayed in bed, too ill to get up. Leah watched a few of their favorite television shows with him at night, but Neil usually fell asleep. Sometimes he felt so nauseated he had to be helped to the bathroom.

Ethan continued to be invaluable to the household. He did every chore Leah's mother asked him to and continued to keep Neil's cars clean and polished—all while he worked days at Dr. Prater's. His presence brought calm and eased tension in the house. Leah's mother was less likely to fly off the handle when Ethan was around. Leah was more likely to be nice to her mother in Ethan's company. Neil kept saying how grateful he was that Ethan was looking out for them.

Neil apologized to Ethan over his inability to continue the search for Eli. Ethan assured him it was all right. "I'll get back to it when I'm feeling better," Neil promised.

Ethan received letters from his family, and he occasionally wrote letters home. He never shared the contents of his mail with Leah, except to say, "Charity sends a hello to you." It hurt Leah that he didn't, but then she had not told him of her talks with Neil and her mother, either. She wasn't trying to hide the information about her childhood from him, but she knew it was totally out of his Amish frame of reference. How could he ever relate to a father gone mad? Or to a childhood filled with a regiment of stepfathers? Or to marriage vows broken with the rap of a judge's gavel?

In March Leah received her SAT scores. She was stunned to learn that she had scored high enough to rank nineteenth in her senior class of 321.

"Wow," Sherry said in awe. "I didn't know you were so smart. No offense."

"None taken," Leah said with a laugh. "I didn't know either."

The news gave Neil a spurt of energy he hadn't had in weeks. "Good for you, kiddo," he said from his bed when she told him. A smile lit his haggard face.

Her mother acted especially pleased about her scores. "I always knew you were bright. I read to you every night before bed when I didn't have to go to work."

Leah was ashamed to admit that she didn't remember.

Leah's school counselor called her in to discuss her scores. "Surely you've chosen a college by now," Mrs. Garvey said.

Flustered, Leah answered, "No. I—I'm not even sure I'm going to college."

Mrs. Garvey leafed through Leah's records. "I know that your grades aren't exemplary, but you've brought them up steadily over the past year, and now your SATs

prove that you're college material. You really should consider going, Leah. There are many fine colleges and
universities in Indiana, if going too far from home is
a problem."

Leah had too much on her mind at the moment to do
more than nod, thank the counselor and take a sheaf of
brochures from her.

In late March, the high school sponsored the Spring
Fling, a week of activities that culminated with a carnival on the school grounds. A boy named James asked
Sherry to go to the carnival, and Sherry begged Leah to
bring Ethan and double-date with them. "I'm scared,"
Sherry told Leah. "I've never had a date before, and I'd
just feel better if you were with me for moral support."

Leah agreed, even though she didn't really want to
go. On the night of the carnival, she and Ethan met
Sherry and James in the gym parking lot. The four of
them headed to the football field, where an enormous
tent had been erected. It was packed with kids, teachers
and guests. Along the sides of the tent, booths had been
set up with games of chance. Proceeds would go toward
buying library books and new sports equipment for the
high school—"after we split the money with the carnival
owners," James said in a tone that assured the others he
had privileged information. "And everybody knows
these games are rigged in the carnival owners' favor."

"Is that a fact?" Ethan asked innocently.

"Absolutely," James said, pulling his baseball cap tight against his head. "No one can win."

"Then we shall have to un-rig them," Ethan said, heading over to the nearest booth.

"What's he going to do?" Sherry asked.

Leah flashed a smile. "Come see for yourself."

They walked over to a booth where rows of wooden bottles were stacked. "Try your luck," said the man in the booth. "Three balls for a dollar. Knock 'em down and win a prize for the little lady." Leah had gone to a carnival with Ethan in the summer, and she knew how talented and clever he was at the game. The booth tender hadn't a clue.

"Yeah, Ethan," a voice boomed from beside them. "Win the little lady a great big prize."

Startled, Leah jumped. She spun to see Dave Simmons's mocking grin and malevolent glare.

SIXTEEN

Leah stiffened. Dave was the last person she wanted to be near. Cory Nelson, one of the school's more popular cheerleaders, was hanging on his arm.

Ethan offered an open, friendly smile. "Would you like to try first?" he asked Dave.

Sneering, Dave said, "I'm sure I can do better than you, choirboy."

Three of Dave's buddies, who were standing behind him, laughed. Leah wondered if Dave ever did anything without an audience.

Ethan held out the three balls. "You can buy the next set."

Dave took the balls and turned to Cory. "What prize do you want?"

Cory studied the grouping of stuffed animals, then

pointed up at a large, bright green dragon. "That would look cute in my room."

Dave nodded, shouldered up to the booth, aimed and threw a ball with such force that it nearly made a hole in the back of the canvas. But his pitch missed the bottles entirely. "Hey, watch it!" the booth tender growled.

Dave glared at him and heaved a second ball at the next stack of wooden bottles. Only the top bottle fell. His friends clapped him on the back and said, "Way to go!"

Dave's third pitch toppled only one more bottle from the third grouping. Dave stared in dismay. "Hey, this thing is rigged!"

Ignoring Dave's outburst, the booth tender asked, "You going to try again? If not, move aside. There's a line behind you."

Ethan stepped up to the booth and looked at Dave expectantly. Dave cursed but pulled out a crumpled dollar bill and slapped it down. "Your turn, choirboy."

Ethan took the balls the man handed him, eyed the bottles, then lofted a ball toward the first stack. It tumbled backward. He did it two more times, each time toppling a pyramid. Dave and his friends stared open-mouthed at Ethan's effortless accomplishment.

The booth manager said, "You did it, kid. What's your pleasure?"

Ethan looked at Leah. She pointed to the dragon. When the man handed it to her, Leah held it out to Cory.

"Ethan wins this stuff for me all the time. Take this from us," she said sweetly.

Dave's expression looked murderous, but Cory, oblivious to the tension among Leah, Dave and Ethan, squealed and grabbed the stuffed animal. "Too cool. Thanks, Leah."

Leah hooked her arm through Ethan's and walked away. Sherry and James, who had watched from one side, joined them. Sherry said, "I think you made Dave mad."

"But why?" Ethan asked. "It was a fair contest."

"Dave doesn't play fair," Leah said. "But so what? He's a creep and I'm glad you beat him."

Ethan stopped. "I did not act kindly toward him. I knew I could win and I forced him to go against me. I did not play fair either."

James snorted. "Quit with the attack of good conscience already. The guy would have humiliated you if he'd won."

"He's right," Leah told Ethan.

"Still," Ethan said, "I should have been a better person. I have been taught, 'Do unto others as you would have them do unto you.' "

"Don't you mean, 'Do unto others *before* they do it to you'?" James laughed at his own joke.

A frown creased Ethan's brow, but he said nothing else.

The four of them continued to stroll around the

carnival, but Leah could tell that Ethan wasn't having a very good time. After thirty minutes, she said, "Maybe we should go home. I told Neil I'd be back before he went to bed." It was a half-truth. She knew Neil rested better once she was home for the night, but she also was not much in a party mood. She offered Sherry an encouraging smile and headed outside with Ethan.

By now it was dark, and the March air felt damp and cold. Leah pulled her jacket closer. Ethan slipped his arm around her shoulders. "You are unhappy," he said. It was a statement, not a question.

"I guess the business with Dave upset me. Guys like him should have a belly button check just to make sure they're really members of the human race."

Ethan laughed. "You say funny things, Leah."

"Well, you shouldn't feel bad about winning the game. What's wrong with winning?"

"Nothing. Still, it is a matter of the heart. My heart was not generous toward him. That was not right."

By now they were at Leah's car. She fumbled in her purse for the keys, but before she could find them, bodies materialized from the shadows. In moments she and Ethan were surrounded by the hulking forms of Dave and two of his buddies. Leah gasped and pressed herself against the cold metal of the car. "What do you want?" she cried.

"I just want to talk to your friend here." Dave's voice sounded low and menacing.

"Go away," Leah said, looking around. The parking lot was dark and deserted. With their backs against the car, there was no place to go.

"I'm not talking to you," Dave said sharply. He leaned toward Ethan. "You know what? I don't like you."

"You do not know me," Ethan returned.

Leah didn't think Ethan sounded frightened. Obviously he didn't realize the danger.

"I don't want to know you," Dave said. "I think you're a wimp."

Ethan said nothing.

"Yeah," Dave said, glancing at his two friends. "This guy's a real weenie."

Dave's buddies grunted.

"And you're a jerk!" Leah blurted out. "Leave us alone."

Dave threw up his hands in mock surrender. "The princess speaks." His tone turned nasty as he added, "But I'm not talking to you, Leah. I'm talking to the choirboy." His body tensed and his hands clenched. "Why don't we see what you're made of, choirboy?"

Still Ethan said nothing.

Alarmed, Leah stepped between them. "Please, go away. Ethan's done nothing to you."

Dave shoved Leah out of the way. One of his friends caught her and held her arms behind her back.

"Let her go," Ethan ordered.

"Why? You going to do something about it?"

Leah struggled, but she was held fast. Her fear gave way to anger. "Let go of me!" she bellowed. "He's just trying to provoke you, Ethan. Don't let him."

Dave shoved hard on Ethan's shoulder. "Your girl-friend always tell you what to do?" he asked. "You let a girl run your life?"

Ethan didn't move, even with Dave's shove. It must have maddened Dave because he shoved him harder. Ethan stood like a rock, his hands hanging loosely at his sides. With an open hand, Dave slapped Ethan hard across the face. Leah cried out, but Ethan still didn't budge.

"What's the matter?" Dave snarled. "Can't you make a fist?"

"I will not fight you."

Lightning fast, Dave smacked Ethan's face harder. The sound of the slap crackled in the cold night air.

"Stop it!" Leah cried. Why didn't Ethan defend himself?

Dave jabbed at Ethan's face. Ethan bobbed his head to miss the blow. Dave jabbed again. This time, the blow connected. Ethan's head snapped back hard, but he still did nothing to defend himself. "What's the matter?" Dave asked. "You too chicken to fight?"

"I do not fight," Ethan said.

"Then I'll beat the crap out of you where you stand," Dave said, moving forward, fists jabbing at Ethan's head. Braced against the car, Ethan couldn't get out of Dave's way. "You're a coward," Dave said, dancing and jabbing. "Come on and fight!"

Leah brought the heel of her boot down hard on the toe of the boy who held her. He yelped and loosened his grip, and Leah started swinging. She clobbered Dave hard on the side of the head.

"Why, you—" He started toward her.

"What's going on here?" A voice boomed from the darkness.

All movement stopped, and the football coach hurried up to the group. "I asked what's going on. Simmons? What are you doing?"

Dave leaped back, brushing his knuckles on his jeans. "Nothing."

Leah was shaking so hard that she could barely make her voice work. Her hand throbbed from striking Dave. "He attacked us," she said.

The coach stepped forward and peered at Ethan. "Is that true? Are you all right?"

"I am all right," Ethan said quietly.

The coach spun toward Dave. "I don't know what happened here, but I do know that fighting on school grounds is forbidden. You're up for several athletic scholarships, Simmons. Don't make me put this on your record. You save the hostility for the football field, you hear me?"

"Yes, sir."

The coach looked at the other two boys. "I expect to see all three of you in my office first thing Monday morning. Then I'll decide what your punishments will be. Now, the three of you get out of here." Dave and his friends backed away. "This is finished," the coach added. "Do I make myself clear?"

Shaking with anger and frustration, Leah watched Dave and his friends go. "I hate them," she said.

"I'm sorry," the coach said. "But don't worry; I'll deal with them. You two sure you're not hurt?"

"We're okay, I guess." Leah sniffed hard. When the coach left, she turned to Ethan.

"Let's go," he said.

Inside the car, with the dome light on, she saw that his lip was bleeding and his eye was beginning to swell. "You're hurt."

Ethan blotted his lip on his sleeve. "It is nothing."

"Why didn't you stop him?"

"Amish do not fight."

"I know that, but you could have at least defended yourself."

"I will not fight, Leah."

"Not even to defend yourself? Or someone you love?"

He shook his head. "Leah, my feelings about violence cannot vanish simply because I am threatened. What good is a virtue if it is untested? What good is a belief if any challenge causes us to toss the belief aside?"

"But you could have been really hurt!"

"Often God provides a way out. Tonight the coach showed up."

"But what if he hadn't shown up?"

"But he did," Ethan said.

"Well, you almost got your teeth knocked out." Leah started the car and gunned the engine. "And I can't believe you Amish don't make allowances for hitting a bully like Dave who's about to do you bodily harm. You'd think you could at least defend yourselves!"

"It is our way, Leah." Ethan's tone sounded patient, as if he were explaining something to a child. "It has always been our way. It always will be."

She gritted her teeth, afraid to answer him because she was so angry. How could anybody stand by and let some idiot pound him into the ground and not lift a finger? Some things about the Amish made no sense to her at all. "I'll put some medicine on your lip when we get home," she said. "Or is that against your rules too?"

He said nothing. They didn't speak for the rest of the ride home.

SEVENTEEN

Scuttlebutt at school the next week had it that Dave and his two friends were in deep trouble. They could have been suspended, but the coach intervened and they were spared. For punishment, they had to pick up trash and paper from the school grounds every day after school for two months. They steered clear of Leah, which suited her fine. But she couldn't forget the fear she had felt and Ethan's absolute refusal to do anything to protect them.

"Would it have been better if he had fought and gotten pounded to a pulp?" Neil had asked her when she told him her feelings.

Leah shuddered at the image of her tender, gentle Ethan after a bashing by Dave. "Of course not. But what about the next time some jerk comes along and threatens him? Will he never stand up for himself? I see bad stuff every day on TV. Sometimes a person has to fight. Or die."

Neil sighed. "I agree—the world's a mean place. But the Amish are pacifists and always have been. They don't fight in wars. If they must serve in the military, it's in a noncombat support role."

Ethan had once told Leah the same thing, but at the time she'd hardly paid attention. Now she couldn't shake her fear that something awful might happen to Ethan if he never did anything to protect himself.

Neil added, "This is one of the reasons that the Amish keep to themselves—so that they won't have to fight and quarrel. Their world and ours don't mix. You've known that all along."

Yes, Leah had known it, but now the disparities between her and Ethan's worlds had taken on a sinister note. This time it was more complicated than not using electricity or modern conveniences. As for Ethan, he went about his everyday life as if nothing had happened. Neither Leah nor Ethan spoke of it again.

Leah was out in the barn helping Ethan with the cars late one afternoon when Neil came in to see the two of them. His gait was little more than a shuffle and he was slightly stooped, but Leah could tell he was excited about something. "What's going on?" she asked.

Neil waved a piece of paper. "Ethan, I think we've found your brother."

Ethan dropped the rag he was using to polish chrome and hurried up to Neil. "Eli? You've found Eli? Where is he? Can I go to see him?"

"Whoa . . . One thing at a time." Neil thrust the paper into Ethan's hand. "This is a report concerning him. It appears he changed his name to Elias Long. That's why it took so much time to track him down. I hadn't thought about his renaming himself, but he did."

"This will shame Pa," Ethan said, shaking his head.

"I'm sure Eli had his reasons. Anyway, here's the good news. He's a schoolteacher, and he's employed in the southern part of the state, in a small rural school district not far from the Kentucky border. His address and phone number are in the letter."

Ethan stared at the paper, but Leah saw a slight tremble in his hand. It was Ethan's only outward sign of excitement. "Do you want to call him?" she asked.

"No. I want to see him. With my own eyes, I want to look into his face. Will you come with me, Leah?"

Leah and Ethan left on Saturday. Since the trip was about two hundred miles, Ethan asked off from work and Dr. Prater excused him. Ethan said little during the drive down the interstate. He drove while Leah watched the countryside fly past as they headed south. Pale pink blossoms adorned plum trees, and new leaves sprouted from trees like insets of green lace. Tulips and daffodils pushed through the hard, dark earth in spikes of brilliant color. Even the cold air was tinged with the scent of spring.

"Are you excited?" she asked.

"I have dreamed of this for years, but now that it is about to happen, I feel . . . well, like there are butterflies inside my stomach."

"He's probably missed you as much as you've missed him."

"I am not so sure. If he wanted to see me again, he would have come home."

Leah had no reassuring words to offer.

Once they were off the interstate, Leah checked the map and the directions a gas station attendant had given them. "I think that's it up on the right," she told Ethan. A lone mailbox stood by a gravel driveway that led to a house set far back on the property. "Yes, this is the place," she said, checking the number on the mailbox.

Ethan turned onto the driveway.

"It sort of looks like your place," Leah said. "Not the house, but the property." A garden could be seen off to one side, and clusters of trees dotted the land.

"I am surprised," Ethan said. "Eli always hated working in the garden." He stopped the car behind a pickup truck parked in front of a garage. His knuckles looked white on the steering wheel.

A dog bounded from around the side of the house

and started barking. Fearlessly Ethan got out of the car. Leah waited patiently while Ethan made friends with the big black Lab. When she thought it was safe, she got out and, with Ethan, walked up to the house. The dog trotted at their heels.

The front door opened and a man stepped out onto the porch. He was tall and thin and dark-haired. His eyes were blue, like Ethan's. His features were hauntingly familiar to Leah, although she'd never seen him before in her life. Leah knew he was around twenty-five, but he looked much older. He asked, "What do you want? Are you lost?"

"Eli?" Ethan said.

The man stared. Color drained from his face. "E-Ethan?" he stammered. "Is it you, Ethan?"

"Hello, my brother."

"Dear Lord. It *is* you." Eli staggered backward. "I never thought . . . I mean . . . How are you? What are you doing here? How did you find me?" His flood of questions stopped abruptly. "Is it Pa or Ma? Have they—?"

"They are well," Ethan interrupted. "I have come on my own. I have come to see you."

Suddenly Eli swept Ethan into his arms, buried his face in Ethan's neck, and began to cry.

Fifteen minutes later Leah and Ethan were inside the house sitting on a worn sofa. Ethan had explained about

Leah, about Neil's search, and about his coming into the English world with Leah's help. "It took a very long time to find you because you changed your name," Ethan said.

"I wanted to be more like the English," Eli said, his eyes still shining with emotion. "It was easier to fit in if I used a more English-sounding name. And at the time, I didn't want anything to do with the Longacre name."

Leah saw that the confession hurt Ethan. "And are you like the English?" he asked.

It was a needless question. A television set in a bookcase, piles of books and videos, wall-to-wall carpeting, lamps and a computer on a desk painted a clear picture. There were also toys, blocks and a game board scattered in one corner of the room.

"Nice place," Leah said, smoothing over the awkward moment. She pointed to the toys. "Do you have kids?"

"Sure do. My wife, Camille, and the two boys, Jason and Timmy, are grocery shopping. They should be back any minute now. Hey, would either of you like something to drink? Soda? Coffee?"

They both accepted a cola.

"You look great, Ethan," Eli said, handing him a can. "You've grown up."

"You have changed also," Ethan said.

"Yeah, I guess so."

"How long have you been married?"

"Five years now. Camille works at a day care center. Jason's almost four and Timmy's just turned two. I'm a teacher. But you know that." Eli grinned self-consciously. "I teach high-school English, and I'm planning on graduate school as soon as the boys get a little older. I want a Ph.D. in education. I'd like to teach college someday."

"You have many plans," Ethan said.

Eli cleared his throat. "What about you? School?"

"I am finished with school. I was not a student like you. Or Charity."

"Charity!" Eli exclaimed. "How are our sisters?"

"They are well. Charity is very pretty—almost grown. And Elizabeth is already thirteen. Sarah is married and has a new son. Simeon is growing tall."

"Simeon was Timmy's age when I left." Eli got a faraway look in his eye. "Is he still as blond as you?"

"Yes," Ethan said. "And there is also Nathan."

"Ma had another baby?"

Ethan nodded. "Ma also had Rebekah. She died last summer, when she was six."

"Died!" Eli looked stricken. "But how?"

Briefly Ethan told Eli about Rebekah's short, sweet life. "We miss her very much," he added.

"That's how Ethan and I met," Leah said. "Rebekah and I were in the hospital together, and we got to be friends. I'm sorry you never knew her. She was the sweetest, nicest little girl in the world."

Eli raked a hand through his hair. "I'm sorry too," he mumbled. "And—um—the others?"

"Oma is ill. The winter has been hard on her," Ethan said.

"Pa never got electricity in that old barn of a house, I guess." Eli's expression hardened.

Ignoring Eli's question, Ethan continued, "Opa still works with Pa. The crops have been plentiful these past two years. Yet the old ones are predicting a hot summer—maybe a drought."

Just then the door banged open and a small boy hurtled into the room. "Daddy!" he yelled. He stopped abruptly when he saw Leah and Ethan.

A younger boy trotted through the open door, followed by a long-haired woman carrying a sack of groceries. "Whose car?" she asked.

"Camille," Eli said, "I want you to meet my brother, Ethan."

Camille allowed the grocery sack to slide to the floor, her expression wary. "Hello," she said. "Eli's told me about you."

Leah watched Camille as Eli explained what was going on. It was obvious that Camille wasn't thrilled to see Ethan. She was a small woman with plain features, and she wore a tiny cap on her head. Leah had spent enough time in Nappanee to recognize that Camille was Mennonite, a member of a more liberal religious group than the Amish. While the Mennonites held to many of the traditional Amish values, they believed in using modern conveniences and didn't mind mingling with the English.

The toddler, Timmy, started rummaging through the forgotten sack of groceries. Jason hung on to his father's pant leg, peeking around it with serious blue eyes. Leah saw the family resemblance in Eli's sons. Both boys looked like their father, who looked a lot like Mr. Longacre.

Eli took both boys by their hands. "I want you to meet your uncle Ethan."

Ethan crouched so that he was face to face with the children. "Hello, Jason. Hello, Timmy."

Jason continued to act shy, but Timmy grinned and gave Ethan a hug. The gesture tugged at Leah's heart. With his winsome, open smile, Timmy reminded her of Rebekah.

"You must stay for supper," Camille said in a tone that told Leah she'd rather they wouldn't.

"Yes," Ethan said. "This would be good. I have much to learn about these years we have been apart."

"You could stay the night," Eli said. "We'll put the boys in with us. Leah can have their room. Ethan can take the couch."

"All right," Ethan said without hesitation.

"I'll call Mom and Neil and let them know," Leah said.

"Well, let's help unload the groceries," Eli said cheerfully.

A look passed between Eli and Camille that Leah caught. She'd seen her mother pass enough such looks as she was growing up and read it instantly. It said: *Why are you doing this? I don't want them here.* Leah felt instant rejection but also firm determination. Ethan had come too far and worked too hard to lose his brother now. He deserved to get to know Eli—whether Eli's wife liked it or not.

EIGHTEEN

Later Leah found herself sitting on the sofa with Ethan, listening to Eli tell of the years between his leaving home and the present.

"College was difficult," Eli said as he flipped Timmy's sponge basketball from hand to hand. "Not because of the studying, but because I didn't fit in anywhere."

"I do not understand," Ethan said.

Leah understood perfectly, but she listened to Eli's explanation without commenting.

"When you're raised Amish, you just don't slide into the English world so easily."

"But so many of your friends were English back home."

"True, but they were also small-town and raised

around an Amish community. I wasn't quite prepared for dorm life, for all-night parties where everybody got blasted, or for drugs."

"You took drugs?" Ethan looked appalled.

"I tried them, but they weren't for me." Eli gave a sardonic chuckle. "You know what they say, 'You can take the boy out of Amish country, but you can't take the Amish out of the boy'—or something to that effect."

"Why did you hate our way of life so much? How could you leave us and never write? Never come home?"

Eli flipped the basketball across the room and sank into his chair, his fingers laced in his lap. "You know as well as I that when you leave, you aren't welcomed back."

"You could have come home. Pa and Ma would have forgiven you."

"I couldn't go back, Ethan. I hated the farm. I hated living in the eighteenth century instead of the twentieth. I was never accepted by the other Amish boys. Books were my only true friends. When I opened a book I could escape into other worlds by myself. I sailed with Ulysses. I climbed Mount Everest. I traveled to other planets—all within the pages of books. I didn't like slopping out pig-pens, pitching hay, plowing fields. I hated the long, boring church services. And most of all, I hated the hypocrisy in our community."

Ethan's face colored. "I, too, have disliked some of the rules, but it is not so bad."

"It was bad for me. Do you remember Jonathan Meyers?"

Ethan shook his head.

"He was the blacksmith until he was shunned."

"Shunning is only done to bring a person back into fellowship."

Eli rolled his eyes. "That's the party line. Do you know what his crime was? His hat brim was one inch wider than the bishop allowed. And for that 'crime' he was ostracized. He was driven away by his neighbors, forced to sell his farm and move."

Leah was shocked. The size of a man's hat brim hardly seemed like a reason to destroy his life. This was the part of Amishness she could never accept—the complete smothering of individuality.

"He had only to repent—"

Eli thrust out his hand. "Don't start, Ethan. How could this be a crime? How can we, whom the church teaches not to judge, judge so harshly?"

"It was his pride that set him apart. It is pride that can get a man shunned."

Eli scoffed. "Well, I liked Brother Meyer. I liked his daughter, Ruth, also. I was in seventh grade and madly in love with her." A smile of remembrance touched his face. "When she moved away, I thought the world would end."

"I do not remember this," Ethan admitted. "But we have a new bishop now. He is not so traditional as the old one."

How so?, Leah wondered, but she kept quiet.

"Ethan," Eli said with a sigh, "it does not matter. I didn't want to live among such people. I threw myself into schoolwork. I was happy inside my books. I was smart, and in the English world I was admired just because I was smart. At home I was considered prideful and rebellious. You know how Pa can be."

"He allowed you to go to high school."

"So what? We argued about it all the time. But by that time I knew I didn't want to remain Amish. I was ashamed of my backward family and their simple ways." Eli shifted forward, leaning toward Ethan and Leah. "Look at you, Ethan. You are dressed English. You are with an English girl. I know you've had the same feelings."

Leah stiffened. She had often felt guilty about Ethan's decision to take his fling. If it hadn't been for her, perhaps . . . "I wanted to help Ethan," she said defensively. "He wanted to take his fling."

"Trying out English things and leaving Amish ways forever are not the same thing," Ethan said. "And as for Leah"—he turned toward her on the sofa—"she means much to me. She has made my life happy and good."

"But I'm not Amish," Leah added. "You don't have

to keep reminding me." Turning to Eli, she said, "I've had to deal with your leaving too, Eli. Your father's very distrustful of everybody English. The only reason your family allowed me to come around last summer was because of Rebekah."

"She must have held extraordinary power over him to have persuaded him to let you within a hundred yards of his precious farm," Eli said.

"Pa is changed," Ethan insisted. "He has suffered much over your leaving—and Rebekah's dying."

"I'm sorry about my little sister. I can't change that. But as Jacob Longacre's eldest son, I don't believe Pa will ever forgive me. I do not want to be a farmer, Ethan. I can't be what he wants me to be. I never could."

"Yet you have chosen what most Amish men choose. You have a wife and a family," Ethan pointed out.

"Do you really think Old Order Amish would accept my Mennonite wife?" Eli shook his head. "I don't think so."

"You will not know unless you take your family back home."

Eli stood abruptly. "No way." He left the room.

Later, while the boys watched a video and Camille prepared dinner, Leah and Ethan took a walk. "I guess you didn't persuade Eli to go home for a visit," Leah said.

"I did not." Ethan looked dejected.

"But still, you've gotten to see him again. Isn't that what you wanted?"

"Yes. But I also wanted him to return home. It would mean so much to Ma. And to Oma, too. She is sick and old. I know it would make her happy to see Eli before she goes home to the Lord."

In truth, Leah felt pretty down herself. She didn't know what Ethan was thinking or what was going to happen now that he had accomplished his goal of reuniting with Eli. "Have you ever felt like Eli did? I know your father didn't want you to take a fling. I know he wasn't thrilled about your seeing me."

"I have had many arguments with Pa, but taking a fling is my right. Seeing you is my pleasure."

"And you don't see how this is a double standard? That you're going against Amish convention?"

Ethan turned, took Leah by the shoulders and pulled her close to him. "I do not know how it will all turn out, Leah. I only know I love you."

She threw her arms around him and buried her face in the hollow of his neck, where his pulse throbbed and sent her pulse soaring. "What's going to happen to us, Ethan? What are we going to do?"

He did not answer.

•   •   •

After supper, while Eli bathed the boys, Leah helped Camille wash the dishes. The kitchen was small and painted bright yellow. Jason's and Timmy's drawings hung on the refrigerator, attached with colorful letter magnets. Someone had spelled out *cow, cat, dog.* "Jason?" Leah asked.

"Timmy, actually," Camille said. "He's only two, but can already pick certain words off the pages of books. He's going to be smart like his father."

"Where did you meet Eli?" Leah asked.

"College. We both have education degrees. I'll go to work once the boys are in school so that Eli can return for graduate work."

"Sounds like you have everything planned out."

"I like having a plan." Camille put a pot into the suds. "How about you? What are your plans?"

"I don't have any." Leah told Camille about Neil. "I think I should hang around until I see how it's going to work out."

"Are you thinking that you might have a life with Ethan?"

Camille's question was unexpected and made Leah stammer. "I—I don't know."

"Well, take it from me, Leah, living with an Amish man is not easy."

"You do it."

"And it has been difficult. Eli has such guilt about

not seeing his family. Despite his feelings about his Amish upbringing, he is not free of it. He tries to be English, but he can't quite let go of his Amishness. He is caught between the two societies, and I tell you, on some days it has threatened his sanity."

"This afternoon he talked as if he hated everything Amish."

Camille wiped her brow, leaving a trail of suds near her hairline. "What he hates is not being able to get rid of it. If it were a tumor, he could go to a surgeon and have it cut away. But it's imbedded in him, even now, after all these years of being away. It would be the same for Ethan. No matter how much he loves you, he will always be bound to his culture."

Leah felt her cheeks growing warm. Until now, no one had ever paired her and Ethan in a permanent way. Even she had hesitated to project a future for them. "Do you hate the Amish?" Leah asked.

"I grew up in Ohio, near an Amish settlement. I am Mennonite—a people sometimes not regarded highly by Amish because we rejected many of the old ways decades ago. I have seen firsthand how conflicted the Amish children are when they attend English schools. Our sons and I have suffered with Eli as he has tried to find his way between the Amish and English worlds." Camille paused, staring gloomily out the window over the sink into the blackness of night. "Still, I do believe it's not good for Eli to totally reject his family. I have suggested many times that he make peace with his father and go back for a visit. Perhaps seeing Ethan again will help him decide to do it."

"I know it would mean a lot to Ethan."

"Well, if you love Ethan, Leah, be careful. Don't think you can make him forget his past. Don't think your love can make up for all that he holds dear in his heart. If you do, you will only find your own heart broken."

Leah slowly dried the glass bowl she held, not daring to respond to Camille's comments. Ever since she'd first met Ethan, she'd been attracted to him—and to the sense of family he brought with him. The Longacres were close-knit and involved with one another, not estranged and cut off as she'd often felt in her own family. That is, at least until Neil had become a part of her and her mother's lives and offered a stability Leah hadn't known before.

Over the summer, Leah had lived among the Amish, but she knew she'd not been fully accepted by them. A part of her found their lifestyle attractive, even compelling. Another found the Amish full of contradictions. They were a people of great personal integrity and strong family values.

But poor Ethan! She didn't want him to end up like Eli: torn and divided, unable to make his peace with either the world of the Amish or that of the English. Neither did she want to feel forever like an outsider herself, as Camille did. Leah found it difficult to think about a future with Ethan, and even more difficult to see her future without him.

NINETEEN

That night Leah slept fitfully. She was glad when the aroma of brewing coffee drifted up from the kitchen. She got up, dressed and went downstairs, where she found Eli and Ethan sitting at the kitchen table.

"Good morning," Ethan said with a smile. "I have told my brother that we will leave this morning. I must work tomorrow, and you have school."

"Do you like school?" Eli asked Leah politely.

"It's all right."

"Leah scored high on those SATs," Ethan offered. "She is near the top of her class."

"Good for you," Eli declared. "Where are you going to college?"

"No plans yet. I've never loved school the way you do."

"Don't waste your talent," Eli said. "I see many

students who are smart but unmotivated. They're headed for dead-end lives. College helps you focus on your future."

Leah wasn't in the mood to discuss her future. "I'm thinking about it," she said, pouring herself a cup of coffee. It gave her something to do with her hands. "I'm sure Ethan's told you about my stepfather, who is so ill. I'm not sure I should make too many plans." She didn't mention her own medical baggage. "Anyway, I haven't decided what I'm going to do yet." She sat down at the table. "You know, Eli, you have nice kids. And back in Nappanee, you have some really nice brothers and sisters. That means that Jason and Timmy have some pretty neat aunts and uncles. Because I grew up alone, I think it's cool to have a big family. I think you and Ethan are both lucky to have that. For what it's worth."

Eli wrapped his hands around his coffee mug. "I'll take your comments under advisement."

Leah smiled sweetly. "Just as I'll take yours about college for me."

Timmy and Jason swooped into the room, clamoring for breakfast, and soon Camille joined them. She prepared a big batch of pancakes, which the group wolfed down, and once the dishes were cleared, Leah and Ethan prepared to depart for home. Soon Ethan and Leah were standing in the driveway and Eli and his family were clustered around them.

Ethan opened the driver's side door and got in.

"So you have your license," Eli said. "Does Pa know?"

"No," Ethan admitted.

Eli shook his head. "He's still as hard as ever."

"No, he is not," Ethan insisted. "Go home and see for yourself. You will be surprised."

Eli leaned into the window. "I can't do that, brother. I can't let him subject my family to his unbending, unyielding attitudes. It would confuse my sons and undo everything I've spent these years trying to forget."

Leah leaned over to look Eli in the eye. She said, "He didn't put up a fight when Ethan made up his mind to come home with me in January. It upset him, sure. But he let Ethan go without any yelling or arguing. I think you should know that."

"That's hard to believe."

"It is the truth," Ethan said.

Leah added, "I always wished I'd had a grandfather, but both of mine were dead by the time I was old enough to know what one was."

Eli straightened. "I'm glad you came, Ethan. You are a fine man. I have missed you."

"And I you."

"Will you write?"

"I will."

"You are welcome to come again," Camille offered, hooking her arm through Eli's. "Both of you."

Eli nodded. "Yes. Now that we've rediscovered one another, please don't lose touch." Leah saw moisture in Eli's eyes and felt sorry for him.

"You are my brother, Eli. Nothing will ever change that. Not ever."

As the car pulled out of the driveway and onto the highway, Leah watched through her window until Eli and his family vanished from sight.

When they reached home, it was night and rain was falling. The house's windows were dark. "Wonder why Mom hasn't turned on any lights," Leah said. "She knew we were coming home."

Ethan raised the garage door. Roberta's car was gone. They went into the house, but the silence told Leah that no one was home. In the kitchen, she found a scribbled note taped to the refrigerator door: *Neil took very sick. Ambulance came. I went to hospital to be with him. Come ASAP.*

Leah's heart sank, and nausea gripped her stomach. "Something's wrong with Neil, Ethan. We have to get to the hospital. Hurry!"

Together they ran out the door into the rain.

• • •

Leah found her mother in the emergency room waiting area. "Mom! What happened?"

Roberta grabbed Leah's arms. Her face looked pinched and white. "I went to take Neil his supper tray. I couldn't wake him up. I was scared. I called nine-one-one and an ambulance brought him here. He's unconscious, Leah. They won't tell me anything."

"They will when they know something," Leah said. "You'll see. Is Dr. Nguyen with him?"

Roberta nodded and looked at Ethan. "I'm glad you're here too."

"I will stay for as long as you need me."

Leah began to tremble. She couldn't get warm despite the jacket she wore. She kept remembering last summer and the frantic hours of waiting for word on Rebekah.

"I thought he was doing better," Leah's mother said, half under her breath. "I really did."

They waited almost an hour longer before Dr. Nguyen came through the swinging doors of the emergency room's triage area. Roberta sprang to her feet. "What's going on?" she cried. "How's my husband?"

"We've finally gotten him stabilized," the doctor said. "I've transferred him up to a room."

"I have to see him."

Leah's mother almost bolted, but the doctor stopped

her, saying, "Neil's condition is extremely critical, Mrs. Dutton. His liver function tests are poor. His liver is failing."

Leah said, "But without his liver working—" She stopped as the implications slammed into her.

Leah's mother shook her head. "I won't accept this. What about that fancy new drug he was taking? He was doing better on it. He was."

"The drug didn't have the efficacy we hoped it would."

Leah wondered why doctors always resorted to using complicated words when they wanted to sidestep an issue. "You mean it didn't work," she said.

With a slight nod, Dr. Nguyen acknowledged and accepted Leah's remark.

Roberta snapped, "We'll talk more later. Right now, I want to see Neil. Where is he?"

Dr. Nguyen gave them Neil's room number, and with a swish of her coat, Roberta stalked to the elevator.

Neil lay on a hospital bed hooked to IVs and lead wires attached to monitors. His skin, stretched over his thin frame, was the color of mustard. Even the whites of his eyes were yellow. Yet he managed a wan smile when Leah, her mother and Ethan came into his room.

"I'm not too pretty, am I?" he asked.

Roberta bent and kissed his cheek. "You look good

to us. Goodness, you gave me a fright. When I came in and couldn't wake you . . ." She didn't finish the sentence.

Neil held out his hand to Leah. "I'm glad you're back and can be with your mother." To Ethan he said, "How'd it go with your brother?"

"It was a good visit. Thank you for all your help."

Neil nodded, shut his eyes and grimaced with pain. "Sorry," he said moments later. "They've given me enough morphine to stop an elephant, but it still hurts."

Leah thought she might burst into tears. "Mom only got to talk to Dr. Nguyen for a few minutes. She said the drug you've been taking hasn't worked."

"I know. It doesn't look good for me, honey."

"Stop that kind of talk!" Roberta said with a stamp of her foot. "Your doctor will think of something. I'll make sure she does."

Leah saw resignation on Neil's face. He turned his head toward Ethan. "I need you to watch out for things at the house while I'm laid up."

"I will be there."

"If you need anything—if anybody needs any-thing—you call Harold Prentice, my attorney. You understand?"

"We will," Leah said.

"Now, you all go on home tonight. I don't want you hanging around this place."

"Fat chance!" Roberta dragged a chair over to Neil's bedside. "I'm spending the night right here with you."

"You need your rest, Robbie."

Ignoring Neil's words, Leah's mother said, "Leah, I do want you and Ethan to go back to the house. Both of you stick to your regular schedules. School tomorrow for you, young lady."

Infuriated, Leah shook her head. "I want to stay, too."

Her mother stood, took Leah by her elbow and dragged her into the hall. "I won't have Neil thinking we're on some kind of death watch."

"But what if—"

"I'll call you if there's any change. You can be here in a matter of minutes. Now please, do as I ask."

Leah felt torn. She knew her mother was right. Neil needed the kind of moral support that came with people going about their normal routines. "All right," she said reluctantly. "But call me if anything happens."

Leah and Ethan said goodbye and left the hospital, but once back home, Leah got scared. "What if he dies?" she asked Ethan. "What if I can't talk to him again?"

Ethan put his arms around her and rested his chin on her bent head. "Do not think such terrible thoughts, Leah. Neil's in God's hands, and God will decide what's best for him. I have an idea," he added softly. "Why don't we bundle tonight? Just as we did on New Year's Eve."

"Here, in front of the fireplace?"

Ethan lifted her chin with his forefinger. "I would like to hold you tonight, Leah. I would like to be close to you and feel you close to me."

Without hesitation, she nodded. Some Amish customs made perfect sense, and on this night she wanted to be in Ethan's arms more than anything. "Hold me, Ethan," she whispered. "I'm so cold. Please, hold me."

TWENTY

As the days dragged by, the three of them fell into a routine. Leah's mother spent nights at the hospital on a cot in Neil's room, remaining through the day until Leah got out of school. Then Leah relieved her mother, who went home to rest, freshen up and deal with phone calls and mail. In the evenings Ethan drove Roberta back in her car and visited until ten o'clock; then he and Leah drove together to the house in Leah's car.

Leah could hardly concentrate on her classes, but fortunately her teachers cut her a lot of slack. Sherry sent her cheerful notes at school and mailed a card to the house. Leah began to appreciate what a good friend Sherry was and swore she'd be more available to do things with Sherry once Neil had returned home.

However, Dr. Nguyen gave them little hope that Neil

would ever go home. "His liver function keeps falling," the doctor said outside Neil's room on Thursday.

"Do something!" Roberta demanded.

"We've done all we can," the doctor said, looking upset. "The cancer's invaded other parts of his body. It's everywhere now, and we can't stop its progression."

Roberta stifled a cry. Tears swam in Leah's eyes. Ethan gripped Leah's hand so hard that it throbbed. "I just can't believe there's nothing else you can do," Roberta said.

"I wish there were. Doctors like to heal patients, Mrs. Dutton, not watch them die."

Leah's mother looked resigned. "What's going to happen now?"

"He'll gradually slip into a coma," Dr. Nguyen said, "which may last a day or a week. But eventually he'll simply stop breathing. I'm sorry. So very, very sorry. He put up a good fight."

"A fight that he can't win is no fight at all," Leah's mother said bitterly.

One afternoon Leah was alone in the room with Neil when she heard him say her name. She dropped the magazine she was reading and leaned over his bed. "Yes? Are you in pain? Do you want me to call a nurse?"

"No. I want to talk to you."

"I'm listening."

"It won't be long now, Leah."

"Please, Neil, no—"

"Now, don't you fall apart on me. I'm not afraid to die, Leah. I know where I'm going from here. But I sure hate leaving you and your mother alone." He sighed deeply. "I need you to watch out for your mother once I'm gone."

Leah wanted to say, "Mom's able to take care of herself," but didn't.

"I know you think she's strong, but she needs you. I love her," Neil said softly. "And don't you ever doubt for a minute that she loves you. She may not have always expressed it in ways you understood, but she's tried to do what was best for the two of you."

Leah had to admit that she and her mother had gotten along much better since Leah had learned the truth about her real father and grandmother. Hearing about her mother's early struggles had helped Leah to understand her mother's proclivity for marrying and divorcing. "You helped make her different," Leah said. Neil had made *both* their lives different.

"No," Neil said. "I only helped make her feel safe." He closed his eyes and Leah thought that he might have fallen asleep, but soon his voice came again. "And watch out about Ethan, too."

"But why?"

"He's Amish, honey. It's in his blood." Neil reached for her hand. "I don't want your heart broken."

"Ethan wouldn't do that to me."

"Not intentionally. But sometimes circumstances come up against us like a brick wall. Circumstances we can't do anything about."

"I know," Leah said. "Like getting cancer." She recognized those kinds of circumstances all too well. But loving Ethan was her choice. "Are you saying falling in love is like getting sick?"

Neil smiled. "Sometimes it seems that way . . . but no. Falling in love is a good thing."

"I know that Ethan and I have a lot of things going against us. I didn't set out to care about some Amish guy, you know."

"I believe you. Too bad we don't always get to pick who we love. Sometimes love just happens to us, whether we're looking for it or not. But finding the right person at the wrong time can be a problem. Lots of things have to come together before love, and the person we love, are just right for us."

Leah wanted to keep talking about herself and Ethan, but she knew Neil didn't have the strength for it. "Maybe you should rest."

"Not yet." His breathing sounded labored. "One more thing." He gestured toward the drawer of his bedside table. "Open it."

Leah discovered a small wrapped box. "What's this?"

"Part of your graduation gift. I had your mother bring it here so that I could give it to you."

"But I don't graduate for two months."

"I won't be there, Leah."

"Maybe you will," she countered stubbornly. "You could fool your doctors and go into remission again."

He slipped his hand over hers. "That's not going to happen, honey. I won't be around for a lot of things in your life. I'll miss your wedding day when that rolls around. But I promise I'll be looking in on you when you walk down that aisle."

Until then, Leah had never considered that she'd have no father to give her away. Tears of sadness and regret filled her eyes. "Then I'll walk alone."

"Sh-h-h. Don't cry now. Just open that box while I can still see your face."

With trembling fingers, Leah opened the box. Inside was a gold charm of a diploma, sparkling with a ruby chip. "For your bracelet," Neil said.

"Thank you. It—it's beautiful."

"No—thank you," he said with difficulty. "I'm so proud of you, Leah. You're smart. You have a good, kind heart. Do something wonderful with your life."

Neil drifted off to sleep, and Leah bowed her head and cried.

• • •

Leah and Ethan went to the hospital coffee shop that evening, ordered hot chocolate and sat at a corner table. Leah felt weary to her bones. Neil had not awakened again all afternoon or evening.

"I'm sorry," Ethan said. "I know this waiting cannot be easy for you."

"It isn't easy for you, either," Leah said. "I keep thinking back to Rebekah's death. It happened so suddenly. And with Neil, we've known for months that he was sick, but I'm not any more ready for him to die than I was for Rebekah."

Ethan reached across the table and laced his fingers through hers. "We cannot change what God has ordained, Leah. We may not understand why, but even if we knew why, knowing would not stop it."

"It just isn't fair. And it makes me mad," she said.

Ethan smoothed her cheek with his palm. "But miracles happen also. You are proof of that."

Ever since Neil's hospitalization, Leah had suppressed fears about her own health. She would go for another checkup at the end of May. "But what if—?"

Ethan silenced her with a shake of his head. "You will be fine. I believe this with all my heart."

Not wanting to speculate about it, she asked, "Tell me something to make me happy. I'm so tired of talking about cancer and dying."

Ethan looked thoughtful. "Dr. Prater has offered to

send me to a special school this summer in Indianapolis so that I can learn more about veterinary medicine."

Leah sat up straight. "Really? Why didn't you tell me sooner?"

"He only just mentioned it yesterday."

"Indy's not that far away. Hey, you could even commute from our place." She felt a mounting excitement.

Ethan grinned. "You are like a horse with a bit in its teeth—off and running. I am not sure I will go."

"Why not? It sounds like a good idea. You like working with animals. Maybe you could be a vet like Dr. Prater."

"It is much like college for you—a choice, but not one I'm sure I want to make."

"You should seriously think about it," Leah said, her heart hammering. Ever since their visit to Eli's, she had been afraid Ethan would leave. Now it appeared that he had a perfect reason to remain. Besides, the Amish needed veterinarians, so it wasn't as if he could never return to his community. Why, she believed that even Jacob Longacre might approve of Ethan's becoming a doctor for animals. If Ethan stayed the summer and attended the school, then continued working with Dr. Prater, she could stay around too. They would be together.

Leah cleared her throat. "Well, I think it's a great opportunity, and you should really think hard about it."

Ethan stared pensively out the window. "I will, Leah."

• • •

On Friday Neil slipped into a coma. Leah got the call at school. She ran out of the building, hopped into her car and sped to the hospital. Ethan arrived less than an hour later, still muddy from a field. "I was helping Dr. Prater with the birth of twin calves," he explained.

Roberta took Neil's hand into hers and kissed his palm. "We're here, honey," she told him. "We'll be here until you leave."

Leah experienced déjà vu. Hadn't she just stood by Rebekah's deathbed only months before? Hadn't she felt these same emotions, numbness, anger, fear, and unbearable sadness? How much grief could a person take?

She asked Ethan, "What should I pray for?"

"Pray that his passing is gentle. And quick."

She bowed her head but couldn't form the words— not even mentally. She didn't want Neil to die. She didn't want to let him go.

The three of them stationed themselves around Neil's bed. They talked to him, touched him, watched his body shut down. Machines performed the tasks of his diseased organs. Time became fluid as the hours melted into one another. Still there was no change in Neil's condition. Nurses brought two sleeping chairs into the room for Leah and Ethan, and then very early in the morning, Leah was startled awake by the high whine of Neil's heart monitor. She leaped to her feet to join her mother, already bent over Neil's motionless body.

A nurse rushed in and flipped off the monitor. The silence seemed deafening. The nurse felt for a pulse. "He's gone," she said.

Leah crumpled onto the bed, sobbing, her lips pressed against Neil's ear. "I love you, Neil." Suddenly the words were not enough. And they were the wrong words. "Daddy," she choked. "I love you, Daddy. I love you."

TWENTY-ONE

Dawn had broken when Leah and Ethan walked out into the cold spring air. Leah's mother had remained to fill out paperwork and told them to wait for her in the lobby. But Leah couldn't stand being in the hospital one more minute. Outside she shivered, and her cheeks, still wet with her tears, felt stiff and frozen. Ethan put his arm around her and they stood huddled together.

Leah said, "I half expected Gabriella to show up and save Neil. Wasn't that stupid of me?"

"How do you know she didn't?"

"I sure didn't see her. Did you?" Leah didn't hide her sarcasm.

"Just because she did not show herself to you does not mean she did not come. I believe she came to take Neil's soul to heaven."

"Why do you think that?"

Ethan pulled back and gave Leah an inquiring look. "Do you not know what today is, Leah?"

"I—I don't even know what day of the week it is."

"It is Sunday. Easter Sunday."

Astounded, Leah asked, "It is?"

"Yes. It is a day for resurrection. It is a good day for angels to come and take Neil home."

Later Leah and Ethan went to the funeral home for the viewing. Leah sneaked off to an unused room and sat, feeling numb and overwhelmed.

Ethan came into the semidarkness and sat down beside her. "I missed you."

"I couldn't stand it in there one more minute. I had to get out."

"So many tears," he said. "So much sadness."

Leah turned to him. "You're thinking about Rebekah, aren't you?"

"Her memory is all around me," Ethan confessed. "Amish, English—the pain is just the same."

"You liked Neil, didn't you?"

"*Ya*, he was a good man, Leah. Yet today, it is not just Rebekah and Neil I am thinking of. I am also thinking of Eli. He is alive, but he acts as if he is dead to us."

"That's the way it was for my real father for so many years. He was alive, but he might as well have been dead for all the good it did us. I wanted him to come home so much." The memory brought on fresh tears.

"Home," Ethan said, with a longing in his voice that made Leah's breath catch.

She reached out and held tightly to his arm. "Stay with me, Ethan. Please, don't leave me now."

He touched her cheek tenderly. "I will not leave you, Leah. I will not."

After the funeral the next day, Leah's mother cried softly into a handkerchief. "I miss Neil so much. I feel so alone without him. Like part of me is missing." She sounded desolate.

"We'll be with you," Leah offered.

"Yes," her mother said, as if seeing her for the first time. "Yes, you will. It's just us again, Leah. Only you and me."

Leah wasn't sure how to respond. Neil's death had left a hole that neither of them knew how to fill. They got into the car and rode home in silence.

Guests arrived bearing casseroles and baskets of food and flowers. Leah and Ethan escaped to the solitude of the barn, and being around Neil's cars brought Leah a measure of comfort. Ethan began to methodically polish the steel and chrome of the old automobiles.

"Neil won't be back to inspect them," Leah said forlornly.

Ethan glanced at her with sad blue eyes. "This is true. But I know he would want them cared for if he were here. I will keep them up for him."

How like Ethan, Leah thought. He did his duty with such a sense of purpose. She felt purposeless, adrift, like a sailor marooned on a far-off island. What was going to happen to her and her mother now?

She watched Ethan polish the cars until it was dark and all the people had left the house.

Two days after the funeral, Roberta came into Leah's bedroom, where Leah was lying on her bed. Her mother asked, "Can I sit for a minute?"

Leah moved over to make room.

"I've just returned from Mr. Prentice's office—you know, Neil's lawyer." Leah said nothing, and her mother continued. "We went over Neil's will. He left everything to me."

"Congratulations," Leah said without emotion. "What will you do with it? Move?"

Her mother looked surprised. "This is home, Leah. I'm staying right here."

"Oh." Leah wasn't sure what she'd expected her mother to say, but she was pleased her mother was staying put, relieved that this would still be home.

"Neil left you something too, Leah."

Leah propped herself up on her elbows. "He did?"

Her mother held out a small gift wrapped in colorful tissue. "Neil wanted me to give you this after . . . well, after he was gone. It's a graduation present."

"He gave me the gold charm at the hospital."

"This is something else he wanted you to have."

Leah unwrapped the present and found a small key. "What's this?"

"It's a key to a safe-deposit box. In it are the titles to all the cars in his antique auto collection."

"What am I supposed to do with his cars?"

"He left instructions that the proceeds from selling the cars should be used to set up a trust fund for you. Those cars are worth a great deal of money, and all of it will be yours to use however you want."

Stupefied, Leah stared at the small key. "Neil did that for me?"

"Yes. He loved you like a daughter. Naturally, it will take some time to find buyers for all the cars, but eventually you'll have quite a nest egg." She paused. "You know, Leah, it was always Neil's hope that you would go to college. Now you have the means to do so."

Leah's mind was in turmoil. "I—I can't think that far ahead now."

Her mother patted her hand. "I understand. But please think about it. You know, I never had a decent education, and my life's been . . . well, difficult. Not that an education will make things perfect for you, but it might make things easier." Her mother stood. "Think about it. We can discuss it if you want." Her fingers trailed across Leah's hair and down her cheek. "I miss Neil very much. He was the best thing that ever happened to me. I'm sorry we had so little time together but grateful that we had any at all."

Once her mother had left the room, Leah's mind raced. She had a trust fund. She had money. Suddenly nagging thoughts about her health nibbled into her consciousness and began to erode her awe and pleasure. She wanted to talk to Ethan. She wanted him to help her decide what to do.

Leah hopped off the bed, went down to the basement and knocked on his bedroom door. "Can we talk?" she asked. "I have some big news."

"In a minute," he called.

"I'll wait for you on the front porch."

Outside, the afternoon sun was lowering over the fields. The spring air smelled fresh and clean. She sat in the wooden swing, fidgeting, eager for Ethan to come. She heard the door open and turned just as he stepped out onto the porch. The smile faded from her mouth. Her heart lodged in her throat.

He was dressed Amish.

TWENTY-TWO

"What are you doing?" Leah could hardly get the words out.

"I must go home."

"But this is home!"

"This is *your* home," he said, shaking his head. For the first time she noticed how long his hair had grown. And he now wore it as he had when she'd first met him. "I miss my family, Leah. I have to go back to them."

His words hit her like blows. She wasn't enough for him. Why couldn't she be enough? "But I need you, Ethan. How can you leave me so soon after Neil's death?" It was as if her whole world were disintegrating.

He crouched in front of her and tried to take her hand, but she pulled back. "It has been Neil who has helped me understand where I belong."

Leah listened, unable to accept what Ethan was saying. Neil knew how she felt about Ethan. He wouldn't have urged him to leave. He wouldn't.

"All this time of being around Neil, working for him, talking and listening to him, seeing how hard he fought to live, made me see that a person's life cannot be lived independently of those he loves. Neil wanted you and your mother close to him. He wanted to give you all that he could of himself and of whatever time he had left. Neil was like a father to me in many ways. He reminded me of all the good things that my father stands for." Ethan reached up and raised Leah's chin so that she was forced to look into his eyes. "I am Amish. Just as my father is Amish, and his father before him, and all the fathers before that."

"Eli seems to have adapted." Leah's voice quivered. "He made the decision to break from the Amish."

"Then perhaps I can be the one to bring him back."

"That's dumb! He'll never go back."

Ethan stepped down off the porch and scooped up a handful of soil. He returned and held it out to her. His hands were big, callused, and stained by the heavy, dark soil. "This is my life, Leah. Already Pa has begun to plow the fields. He will plant soon. And Ma will start her garden." His voice was filled with yearning. "I love the land. It is in my soul."

"You belong here, Ethan. With me."

"I cannot stay." He let the soil drop through his fingers. It pattered onto the wooden floor.

"But what about your job with Dr. Prater? And that school he wants to send you to?"

"I will write and tell him I cannot accept."

"It's a way for you to be something else. Somebody else." Tears were pooling in her eyes. She had thought she'd cried them all out over Neil, but this fresh supply came from another area of her heart.

"I must return to my world."

She sprang to her feet. "I've seen your world, Ethan. It's a small, narrow world with no room for change. No room for people to think for themselves or to be different. It's a boring world!" She bounded down the steps and ran out into the field. She ran until she thought her lungs would burst. When she stopped running, she sank to her knees and buried her face in her hands.

Ethan was beside her in seconds. "Leah—"

"Don't touch me!" She twisted away.

"Please."

"I thought you loved me."

He grabbed her shoulders and squeezed until she winced. "I do love you. I've never loved anyone as much as you. Leaving you is like leaving half of myself behind—the half that laughs and loves and will always remember the world of the English. You are right—my

world is small and narrow. And to some, it is even bleak
and backward. But it is my world, Leah." His eyes
burned holes into hers. "Your world is big, and you have
so much of it yet to see."

"I want to see it with you." She started to cry.

He cried too. "Oma is very sick, Leah. My family
needs me. And I need my family. I do not want to be as
Eli. He belongs nowhere."

Belonging. It all came down to belonging. She, of all
people, understood what Ethan meant. She hung her
head and struggled to regain her composure. "When will
you go?"

"There is a bus I can catch to Indy. Another will take
me to Nappanee."

"No." Leah shook her head dully. "I'll drive you
home. I brought you here. I'll take you back."

Leah's mother expressed surprise and regret at Ethan's
announcement. Leah had hoped she would say something to persuade him to stay, but she didn't. She merely
hugged him and told him he'd always have a place to
come to if he ever changed his mind.

Unable to sleep, Leah roused Ethan after midnight
and said, "Let's get it over with."

He asked her to let him drive because it would probably be the last time he ever did so. The trip was long,
but for Leah not nearly long enough. She did not tell him

of the trust fund, mostly because the money would not impress him. He would be happy for her, but it would mean nothing to him.

It was close to five A.M. and morning was already turning the slate sky pink when Ethan stopped at the edge of the Longacre property. He got out of the car slowly. Leah watched him look across the partially plowed fields at the old farmhouse that had been home to his family for more than a hundred years. Flickering lights could be seen through the kitchen window. The household was rising. High up on the second floor, in the window of Ethan's room, a lone lamp glowed. His mother had kept her promise.

A lump of emotion clogged Leah's throat. "You're home," she said.

"Would you like to come in?"

She shook her head. "Not this time."

"What will you do?"

"Drive back."

"The trip is long. You should rest first." He looked concerned.

"I can make it." She started to get back inside the car, but he caught her arm and crushed her against his chest. "Oh, my Leah. I miss you already."

"You'll get over it." She squeezed her eyes shut. Her heart hurt.

He held her at arm's length. "I will never forget you. And I will never love another as I have loved you."

"Your fling is over. You'll be baptized. You'll marry an Amish girl," she said with resignation.

"You were not part of my fling," he said fiercely. "You were part of my life. You will always be in my heart, Leah. Until angels close my eyes."

His face blurred through her tears. "Go," she said. "Go back. Go home."

She watched him as he hopped over the split-rail fence fronting the road. She watched him walk quickly toward the house, toward his family, and out of her life forever.

TWENTY-THREE

The road stretched long in front of Leah. She followed it in a trance, driving by rote, every cell in her body feeling numb. Her world lay in shambles. Neil, the only father she had ever loved, was dead. Ethan was gone, lost to her forever, claimed by his Amish heritage. She had no one. Nothing.

She began to rouse herself from her stupor when her eyelids threatened to close. Realizing that she needed to take a break, she picked up some fast food at a drive-through restaurant window, then got back on the highway and drove to a rest area.

The rest area looked clean, but it was crowded with people. Some had settled on blankets and were having picnics. Kids ran and played. A family tossed a Frisbee to one another. The spring day, scented with new growth and sun-kissed air, only depressed Leah more. How could the world be so happy when she felt so sad?

Leah found a deserted picnic table near the edge of some woods and sat down heavily. She opened the bag, but the smell of the food made her feel queasy. Still, she tried to eat it. She had another three hours to drive.

"Whatcha doing?"

The little girl's voice startled Leah. She turned to see a child of about five looking at her from a nearby pathway.

"Eating lunch," Leah said.

"I ate lunch already."

"That's good." Leah wished the girl would go away. She just wanted to be by herself.

"My mom and me are running away," the little girl said.

Startled by the child's admission, Leah asked, "What are you running away from?"

"Everything. That's our car."

Leah glanced around and saw a battered old car with a trailer hooked to its rear bumper. The back door of the car stood open, and a woman was rummaging inside for something. "Oh, you mean you're moving," Leah said.

"My dolls and my bed and my toys are locked up. We're taking them a long way off. But I'm not scared." She offered Leah a brave smile. "Mom says I'm her big girl. Mom's got a job in . . ." She looked thoughtful. "In someplace. I can't remember."

Leah suppressed a smile. "Where's your dad?"

The child shrugged. "He went away." She looked sad momentarily, then cocked her head. "Do you like french fries? I do."

Leah was about to offer her one when the girl's mother came hurrying over. "Cindy! Cindy, I told you to stay near the car." She stooped by the child and took her by the shoulders. "Stop going off and scaring me. And stop bothering people."

Cindy's lip stuck out and Leah quickly said, "It's all right. She's no bother."

The woman stood. "You can't turn your back for a minute." She looked both apologetic and embarrassed. "I've told her a hundred times not to wander off."

"I was just about to offer her some of my fries. Is it all right?"

The woman looked tired and worn out. "That would be nice of you."

"Here, Cindy." Leah held out the small bag. "Take a bunch."

Eagerly Cindy helped herself. She and her mother thanked Leah; then they hurried to the car. Leah watched them with memories of her own many moves flipping through her thoughts. At the car, Cindy said something to her mother; the mother nodded, and Cindy raced back to Leah. "This is for you," she said. She held out a perfect white feather. "I found it."

Leah took it. "Why, thank you. It's very pretty. It must have come off a beautiful bird."

"It didn't come off a bird. It fell off an angel's wing," Cindy explained patiently. "My mom told me so. It's from our guardian angel. She's with us on the trip, you know."

A lump formed in Leah's throat. "Are you sure you want to give it to me?"

Cindy grinned. "I have two." She darted back to the car and climbed in, and Leah watched until the car and trailer pulled out of sight. Thoughtfully Leah returned to her car. She placed the feather on the seat beside her and stared at it for a long time. Finally she started her car and left the rest area.

As she drove, Leah couldn't get Cindy out of her mind. *So trusting,* Leah thought, *confident that her angel and her mother will always take care of her. Just like my mother has always taken care of me.* The thought took her breath away. True, they had never had a family like Ethan's. But they'd had a family. They *were* a family. Through all the turmoil, moves, marriages and changes, Leah and her mother had always been together. And her mother had fought off every adversary that had threatened to keep them apart.

Leah considered her life. Like the feather beside her,

it could blow away in an instant. What couldn't change was who and what she was, who and what she had become through the adversity of cancer, her father's desertion, Neil's death, Ethan's love. No one could see into the future, but all at once Leah knew she had a future. A gift given to her by Gabriella, Neil, Ethan, her mother and even her grandmother. She could have it, if only she would reach out and take it. Yes, she hurt. Yes, her heart felt battered and bruised. But bruises healed. Hearts mended.

Determination began to replace her depression. And when she turned into the familiar driveway, she wanted to see only one person. She wanted to be held just like a small child. She wanted to cry. Then, in a few days, she wanted to sit down and make some plans. Her mother would help her, Leah was sure.

Leah picked up the feather, jumped out of the car, and hurried to the front door. Throwing it open, she called, "Mom! I'm home."

And in the deepest part of her heart, Leah Lewis-Hall knew it was true.